COPS & ROBBERS

COPS & ROBBERS

A Parker City Mystery

Justin M. Kiska

First published by Level Best Books 2025

Copyright © 2025 by Justin M. Kiska

This novel is entirely a work of fiction. The names, characters and incidents portrayed in it are the work of the author's imagination. Any resemblance to actual persons, living or dead, events or localities is entirely coincidental.

Justin M. Kiska asserts the moral right to be identified as the author of this work.

First edition

ISBN: 978-1-68512-890-6

Cover art by Level Best Designs

This book was professionally typeset on Reedsy.
Find out more at reedsy.com

Praise for Cops & Robbers

"Wow. The older the sin the longer the shadow. Don't miss this deft and gripping tale of 1920s Baltimore and Parker City today. Bootleggers, lowlifes, a nightclub singer and the cream of society. Are any of us really so different? You won't be able to put this book down."— Peter W. J. Hayes, author of the Silver Falchion-nominated Vic Lenoski Mysteries

Chapter One

Baltimore, 1927...

The oppressive summer heat wave that settled over the Mid-Atlantic had nearly brought the entire city to a standstill. No one could remember anything like it in recent history. With scorching days and uncomfortable nights, everyone was miserable. The desire of most Baltimore residents was to avoid going out into the sweltering temperatures during the day, and to try to complete their daily errands in the evening hours when the sun was not so unforgiving. Even then, when they were forced to venture out, it felt as if they were walking through wet rags the moment they stepped through the front door. A person would find themselves completely covered in a slick layer of sweat in the time it took to walk from their building to the corner grocer. And that was in the outer residential neighborhoods of the city.

As one got closer to downtown and the harbor, the office buildings trap and concentrate the heat on the street below. One might expect that the shadow cast by the towering Baltimore Trust Company Building—soon to be the tallest skyscraper in the city at thirty-four stories when construction was completed in the next year—would provide some shelter from the blazing sun. But irony had it that Light Street in the shade remained insufferable.

Making matters worse for the denizens of Baltimore, adding to their reluctance to step outdoors, were the flash thunderstorms that would tear through the city without warning. One minute, the sun would be high overhead, unbearable, baking the pavement at your feet, only to be blacked out in a moment's notice by a thick storm cloud materializing from nowhere, releasing a deluge upon everything beneath it. And if the hope was that the sudden downpour would help to cool things off, one would be sadly disappointed. The rain only added to the merciless humidity already saturating the air.

While the summer was shaping up to be simply dreadful for most, there were a few who were enjoying the blistering days. Those were mostly the children, home from school on summer break, happy to spend hours running through the stream of water spraying into the street from a fire hydrant someone had opened for them. The sounds of the children shouting and laughing filled the otherwise quiet residential streets throughout the many neighborhoods that made up the usually bustling city.

Anyone lucky enough to have an electric fan whirling away at home was able to find a brief respite from the uncomfortable conditions. Even the smallest of breezes could provide a moment of relief. A fact not lost on appliance store salesmen who'd happily sold out of their stock of Westinghouse, General Electric, and Diehl fans in a matter of days. The city's suffering had helped to turn a profit for some. It was basic supply and demand. The building block of the capitalist system at work in Maryland's largest city.

A home with a single fan in it was considered fortunate. But in the fashionable Guilford area, it was not uncommon to find a fan in every room! It was in these stately homes on the northern side of the city where many of Baltimore's most well-to-do found themselves seeking shelter from the brutal heat wave.

The neighborhood itself was relatively new compared to other parts of the city, many of the houses had only been built in the last several years. Ten at the very most. It was an elite suburban oasis on the edge of a growing metropolis. Where designs by some of the city's most notable architects were abundant—Edward Palmer, John Russell Pope, and Laurence Hall among them. Those who could afford something by one of the esteemed designers had no qualms about putting their wealth on display. Whether the money was spent on the lavish facades or to install the latest in household amenities, no expense was spared.

It was a beautiful white stone Colonial on St. Paul Street in the heart of the Guilford area where John J. and Flora Shipley decided to settle only the year before. Sitting above the street, behind a wrought-iron crowned stone fence, a pair of arched stairways led up to the front door, which was covered by a glistening marble portico. From there, guests to the Shipleys' magnificent residence were welcomed into a rich hallway featuring a grand staircase reaching the floors above. On display throughout the entry was the couple's lavish collection of classical artwork. Shipley, a prominent attorney at one of the city's leading law firms, never batted an eye when his beloved wife would find a piece she wanted to take home and hang on their walls. It was safe to say Flora Shipley nee Dorsey wanted for nothing. Her wish was her husband's command. With such a successful, handsome, and devoted husband, Flora was the envy of her friends.

After twenty years of marriage, John J. and Flora couldn't be happier. At only forty-five, he was a partner in a thriving law practice and was making a name for himself in all the right circles. At the same time, she—a handful of years his junior—sat on numerous boards and volunteered her time with various charitable committees around town—all of which were entirely socially acceptable, of course. Always invited to the best parties, they belonged to the most exclusive clubs, ate at the finest restaurants, and made regular appearances at all the proper social functions. One of the couple's favorite outings was attending performances at the Lyric Opera House, where they were proud benefactors.

So far, the morning had been like every other. With a court date that could not be missed, John J. Shipley, Esq. left the house on St. Paul Street at his usual time after a hearty breakfast in the company of his wife. With a crisply pressed suit and his straw boater hat resting at a jaunty angle upon his Brilliantine-slicked hair, he was ready to take on the day and his opponent in court. Departing with an extra spring in his step, he had a strategy that would allow him to bring the case to a quick conclusion that afternoon. A winning strategy that would certainly please his client…and his partners at the firm.

Flora stood in the rose-colored sitting room at the front of the house, watching through the sheer curtains on the window as her husband motored down the road in their shiny black car. Most of their neighbors also had a motorcar. It was not an uncommon sight in the Guilford neighborhood. But theirs was the latest model Ford had manufactured that year. A smile on her lips, as the car drove out of sight, she turned and practically floated across the polished inlaid wooden floors, through the house toward the library where she had a number of letters she was intending to write that morning. There were no committee meetings, luncheons, or card parties on her social schedule for the day, so she intended to catch up on her correspondence. Flora loved writing and sending letters. Or even simple notes to friends living just down the street. It was a tendency she'd inherited from her mother, who would spend countless hours crafting letters to friends and family members.

"Can I get you a cup of tea, Mrs. Shipley?" Martha, the couple's housemaid, asked as the women passed each other in the hallway. A lovely, matronly figure who'd been with the couple for the last ten years, Martha doted on her mistress.

"That would be quite nice. Thank you, Martha. I shall be writing letters this morning," Flora answered, her airy voice drifting along behind her as she continued toward the heavy double doors to the library, next to which hung a gilded mirror she'd purchased at a shop in Paris during the couple's visit three years ago. The trip had been a smashing good time, and whenever she looked in the mirror, fond memories came rushing back.

Briefly stopping to tuck an errant blonde curl back into place behind her ear, she was otherwise pleased with the image that looked back at her. She was wearing her favorite blue day dress along with the string of pearls that she inherited from her grandmother. Even with the slight hint of lines she'd begun noticing at the corners of her eyes, she still presented an extremely youthful appearance. In the right light, one might even say, "girlish." Not that Flora was vain. At least anymore than any of her circle of friends. But she saw nothing wrong with trying to hold on to one's youth for as long as possible. John certainly was. There wasn't a single gray hair on his head.

Taking a seat behind her husband's large mahogany desk, she took a piece of stationary from the top drawer and, with a flourish, addressed the first piece of correspondence—a letter to her sister in Cleveland. It had been three weeks since she'd received a letter from Abigail, and she was feeling terribly negligent for not responding sooner. The two hadn't seen each other in close to five years, and there was hope of a family reunion in the near future. Flora'd hardly begun putting down her thoughts on the matter when Martha appeared at the door with her tea and a slice of pound cake.

"Oh, Martha! You spoil me so. You know how much I love your lemon cake."

"That's why I make sure there's always a fresh one in the kitchen, Mrs. Shipley." The housekeeper smiled. Her motherly presence always put Flora at such great ease. "I have a long list of chores to take care of today, Mrs. Shipley. But if you need anything, you just need to call me. And I'm preparing Mr. Shipley's favorite for dinner this evening. Orange roasted duck with Duchess potatoes on the side and a butterscotch cake for dessert. It sounds as though there will be something to celebrate if court goes the way he anticipates today. He was very excited at breakfast."

"That he was. And that dinner sounds delicious. What would we do without you, Martha?"

With an appreciative nod of her head and a blush on her cheeks, Martha contentedly went back to her work, leaving her mistress to turn her own attention back to her letterwriting. Before she knew it, nearly two hours disappeared. It wasn't until Flora heard the chime of the doorbell that she looked up at the grandfather clock in the corner and saw the time. She could hear Martha's shoes clacking along the hallway as she made her way to answer the door, though for the life of her, Flora couldn't think who would be dropping by at this time. She wasn't expecting anyone. Perhaps they were receiving a delivery. Maybe a surprise John had purchased for her. Deciding now was as good a time as any to take a break and stretch her legs. Flora stepped out of the library only to find herself going a second round with the wayward curl. She really would need to speak to her hairdresser about it. Maybe she'd even be daring enough to try a bob haircut. So many women were wearing their hair in that style these days. She just didn't know if she'd have the courage.

Having once again dealt with the unruly lock of hair, Flora was just turning the corner to see two men in suits standing at the front door. They were the oddest pairing. One was large and broad with a round, fleshy face above a neat little bowtie. The vest of his brown suit strained at the buttons due to his robust frame; his hat pulled down low, casting a shadow on his face. The other man was much smaller—almost a head shorter than his companion—and wiry thin. Flora's initial thought at seeing the man with his sharp, narrow features was that he could use a sandwich at the very least. They certainly didn't look like any door-to-door salesmen she'd ever seen before. Neither of them was carrying a sample case or any sort of product.

Speaking in a hushed voice, she wasn't able to hear what the shorter man was saying to Martha, but she suddenly saw her housekeeper try to take a step back. Before she could, the bigger man reached out his long arm and grabbed her, forcefully shoving a handkerchief into her face. The two men quickly pushed their way into the house. Flora looked on in horror as Martha fell unconscious, sagging in the arms of the tall man in the brown suit like a sack of potatoes, the handkerchief still covering her face.

Flora heard a shrill cry echo from somewhere in the house, only to realize the sound had sprung from her own lips before she'd covered them with a perfectly manicured hand. The intruders at the door also heard the cry, registering there was someone else in the hallway. The skinny man's black, beady eyes immediately focused on Flora. In a flash, he ankled his way towards her before she could will her legs to move. A feeling of sheer terror coursed through her body, freezing her in place.

"Come here, pretty lady," was the last thing Flora heard before everything went black.

Chapter Two

1985…

Tommy Mason sat in his beat-up, but much-loved, Bronco on the side of the road. His hands rested on the steering wheel as his eyes focused on the rearview mirror. Behind him, an unmarked police car with a red bubble light on its roof pulled up and parked. This certainly wasn't how Tommy was expecting to start the day, being pulled over on his way to work. What he'd been pulled over for, he had no idea. He drove this stretch of road every day. He knew the speed limit. There were no stop signs or red lights to run. The Bronco was just in the shop, so he knew there were no lights out or any sort of violations that a cop would think it necessary to pull him over for. And his license plate tags were up-to-date. He was going to have some questions for whoever this patrol officer was.

Keeping his eyes on the rearview mirror, he watched as the door to the police car swung open, and a square, rather unkept-looking officer stepped out. Tommy raised an eyebrow as he watched him approach the Bronco. The officer was wearing a pair of dark Aviator sunglasses and a blue windbreaker with a badge pinned to his chest. He looked as though he hadn't shaved in a couple of days and could use a comb to run through his hair. As he sauntered up to Tommy's window, he placed a traditional eight-point police hat on his head to complete the official appearance.

"Huh…" Tommy grunted, watching the cop giving the Bronco a thorough, yet overly exaggerated examination. "This is going to be fun."

When he reached the driver's side of the truck, Tommy rolled down the window and gave the officer his trademark thousand-watt smile. The same smile that had gotten him out of so many jams in the past. Incidentally, it had also been the cause of a few problems as well. But he preferred to think of the good his smile had done. And might do for him again.

"Good morning, officer. What seems to be the problem?" He tried to sound as cheery as possible.

Tommy expected some sort of response, but instead found himself staring silently at his own reflection in the officer's sunglasses while the man chewed on an enormous wad of gum.

When he finally spoke, he said, "I'm Officer Smith with the Parker City Police Department. Do you know why I pulled you over this morning?"

"Officer Smith? I can't say that I do. I don't think I was speeding. But I guess I could have been. You see, I'm just traveling through Parker, so I don't know the area all that well," Tommy lied.

"Well, you were speeding back there, sir. Sorry to say. It happens sometimes. But unfortunately, I had to pull you over. It's all about safety. You understand."

"Dang, Officer! I really didn't mean to be speedin.'" Tommy had suddenly taken on an accentuated southern drawl. "I guess it's just such a nice mornin' I wasn't paying much attention. Look how beautiful that sky is. So bright blue. I just love the spring. Don't you?"

"Spring is very nice but—"

"And I was just thinkin' about all the flowers. It's been a bang-up season for the flowers this year. Have you noticed how vibrant the flowers have been? I think that's the best word for them. *Vibrant.*"

"I really haven't—"

"I mean, I'm not much of a flower guy, to be honest with you. But something about them this year just got to me. My girlfriend's always bringing home fresh flowers. I guess I've started paying attention to them."

Trying to take control of the conversation, the officer raised his voice slightly. Tommy could hear a hint of irritation, but Smith was trying to keep himself in check. Tommy admired that. "Sir. If I could please see your license and registration card."

"Officer…Smith? Was it? I really am sorry about this. Was I really goin' that fast that you need to give me a ticket? I didn't feel like I was goin' too fast. Not that this old bucket of bolts can even get its giddy-up on to start with. I mean, maybe you could just give me a warning. And I promise the next time I come through Parker City, I'll drive real slow."

"I need to see your license and registration, sir."

Tommy leaned over and opened the glove box, rifled around looking for the Bronco's registration for a moment, then popped back up and said, "Really, I'm very sorry. I must have been daydreamin.' You see, I'm plannin' on askin' my girlfriend to marry me. I'm on my way home. I was in Baltimore for a job last night. And tonight I'm taking Suzanne out…Suzanne's my girlfriend…I'm taking Suzanne out to dinner to pop the question. She's gonna be so surprised. She didn't think I was ever gonna ask her. But I am. I asked for her father's blessing and everything. It's gonna be perfect."

"Uh-huh. Well, it sounds like you're a man in love." The officer's stone-cold demeanor began to melt. A smile slowly spread across his lips. "Maybe there is something we could do."

"That would be so great. I would really appreciate it. Because I really have to be going. But not too fast!" Tommy forced a laugh. He knew he must sound completely ridiculous.

"Let me think here. If I write you up and turn in the speeding ticket as is, it could be a few hundred dollars in fines. Plus, you'll have to show up in traffic court. Nobody likes that. The judge might even say you have to go back to driving school."

"You're kiddin'?" Tommy's eyes went wide, dutifully playing his part.

"Let's see. What can I do?" Smith made a show of scratching his head while he looked off at some point in the distance. "What say you just give me fifty dollars to take care of the warning notice fee right here, and we'll be square. I'll be able to let you get on your way, and I'll fill out all the paperwork later."

"A warning notice fee," Tommy repeated. "Well, fifty sounds better than three hundred any day."

"Hey, not all policemen are hardasses. And you're right. It's a nice day. You caught me in a good mood," Smith said, a smirk curling the side of his lip. "So, fifty dollars, and it's all taken care of."

"Okay. I just want to make sure I got this. I just have to pay you fifty dollars for the warning notice fee, and we'll be all good? No ticket? No traffic court?"

"That's right."

"But you still need my license and registration so you can get my name for the paperwork. Right?" Tommy asked, reaching into his back pocket.

"Um. Yeah. Right. I need your name and address for the warning."

Tommy handed over a black leather wallet and smiled. He watched intently as Officer Smith opened it. He could only imagine what Smith's eyes looked like behind the sunglasses.

"Wha...what's this?" Smith asked.

"You see, *that* is a *real* Parker City Police Department badge," Tommy said, leveling his gaze. "And you can see by my ID card that my name is *Detective* Thomas Mason. I know everyone in the PCPD. Who the hell are you?"

Before Smith could answer, Tommy raised his service revolver from beneath the edge of the window. The color drained from the imposter's face. Tommy knew exactly what was about to happen, so he was fully prepared. As the fake cop dropped the badge wallet, Tommy flung open the driver's side door, hitting Smith square in the hip. Losing his balance, Smith stumbled and fell to his knees. Tommy swung the door again, this time hitting him full-on in his side, sending him sprawling across the pavement. Before he could even think about getting up, still dazed from the unexpected blows, Tommy was standing over him with his foot firmly in the middle of his back.

"You, *dipshit*, are under arrest for impersonating a police office and ruining my good mood."

Chapter Three

Detective Sergeant Ben Winters was sitting at his desk in the Detective Squad's small office at the station, reviewing the final report on the Martin case he and Tommy wrapped up a couple of weeks earlier. It was one of the strangest cases the two detectives had seen. The frozen body of a young woman had been found dumped in a field on the outskirts of town. Frozen, meaning solid as a block of ice. No one knew what to make of it, and it ended up causing quite a stir when it was discovered who the girl was. Needless to say, it drew a decent amount of attention from the press, which neither Ben nor Tommy were all that happy about. Though they weren't exactly strangers to the media spotlight.

In the short four years they'd been detectives with the Parker City Police Department, they'd already handled several cases the likes of which most police detectives would never see throughout the course of their entire careers. Parker City was no longer the sleepy little city it used to be. Times were changing and Ben and Tommy were seeing it firsthand. As the city's economy was beginning to turn around and the population was slowly starting to increase with the new residential developments popping up, it was only natural that the department would be getting more calls.

As the supervising officer of the squad—which consisted of only himself and his partner—a great deal of Ben's time was taken up doing paperwork. Not that Parker was a criminal haven or anything of the sort, but there was enough lawbreaking to keep them busy. And with each incident came a file and a number of reports to go with it. If only people realized how glamorous being a detective really was, Ben thought sarcastically as he put a copy of his report in an envelope that would be sent off to the Parker County State's Attorney's Office that afternoon. Most people just knew what they saw on television and in the movies, which was a very different take on the law enforcement profession in almost every instance. Frequently, there was a lot more action on screen than there was in real life. The first time he'd seen an episode of *Miami Vice*, he couldn't stop laughing.

Laying the envelope aside, Ben reached for his Baltimore Colts mug only to find it empty. Even though the team had left the city in the dead of night the previous year, crushing so many fans, he couldn't bring himself to get rid of the coffee cup. He had too many fond memories of attending games with his father over the years. Deep down, he knew he'd always be a fan of the team. But he was hoping, in the meantime, a new NFL team would find its way to Baltimore in the near future because there was no way he would ever root for the Redskins. That would undoubtedly give his father an aneurysm.

Before diving into the overnight incident reports, Ben needed to get a fresh cup of coffee. It would already be his third of the day, the second since getting to the station. Always one of the first to arrive in the morning, it was usually a toss-up as to whether he or Chief Brent would be the one to start the first pot of coffee in the second-floor breakroom. Ben liked getting into the office early. He enjoyed the quiet. It helped him prepare for the day because once the day shift started clocking in, there was a constant buzz of activity. And Ben never knew when he and Tommy might have to roll out for a call. So, he took whatever extra time that he could in the mornings to get himself and the squad—again, albeit only the two of them—organized.

After refilling his cup and returning to his desk, Ben began reading through the printout of the overnight incidents that had been logged. At first glance, it didn't look as though anything was going to end up on his desk. There were a couple of DUIs, a handful of speeding tickets, and a call for a possible prowler. It had been a quiet spring night. Maybe all the real criminals had been enjoying the lovely evening, Ben thought to himself.

Looking at his watch, Ben was beginning to wonder where his partner was. Tommy rarely came in early, unless they were working on a serious case, but he wasn't usually late. Maybe he stopped for donuts, Ben secretly hoped. Then quickly dismissed the idea. There wasn't a donut shop in the city that would have made him this late. Tapping his fingers on the telephone, Ben was about to call down to Dispatch and have them radio Tommy to see where he was when he heard his partner's unmistakable voice in the hall.

Like a child racing down the stairs on Christmas morning, excited to start unwrapping presents, Tommy bounded into the office and dropped into his chair, throwing his feet up on his desk. The look on his face told Ben he was in for a story. And Tommy's stories could be real doozies.

The two men knew each other so well. They'd grown up together, gone to school together, joined the force together, and had been promoted to detective together. They were closer than best friends, closer than brothers sometimes. Yet, they were different in so many ways. But those differences in their personalities only strengthened them as a team.

When they were tasked with starting the department's new Detective Squad several years earlier, the odds were stacked against them. But they hadn't let their age or short time in uniform deter them. In fact, it was because of their innovative thinking and not being a part of the Good Ole Boys Club that did things the same way they'd always been done that made them so effective. Even if some of their cases hadn't been the kind that made headlines, they would have still been credited with helping set the PCPD on a path to becoming a modern law enforcement agency.

"Where have you been this morning," Ben asked, leaning back in his chair and crossing his arms.

"If you must know. I wasn't even on the clock yet this morning, and I made a bust."

Ben's brow furrowed as he leaned forward, now taking a serious interest in what his partner had to say. He was just expecting to hear another of Tommy's stories about a wild night he'd spent in the company of a female friend. Tommy was a ladies' man who didn't mind kissing and telling. He enjoyed the telling part almost as much as the kissing. Ben only wished some of the tales he'd been told were embellished. But knowing Tommy for so long, he knew they weren't. Which is why Ben's fiancée, Natalie, instructed him that his only job the day of their upcoming wedding was to keep Tommy from sleeping with any of her bridesmaids.

"Excuse me?" Ben said.

"That's right. You heard me." Tommy smiled. "I've been downstairs in Booking getting a dumbass squared away."

Ben sighed. "You're going to make me ask. Aren't you?"

"You better believe I am."

"Alright. What happened?"

"Well, it all started when I was three and my mother—"

"I hate you so much sometimes."

Tommy laughed. "Okay. Okay. I'm just kidding. I thought you could use a laugh after the Orioles' loss last night."

"You're just going to keep poking the bear, aren't you?! You know, technically, I could have you busted down to parking patrol. I'm your commanding officer, might I remind you."

Tommy just looked at Ben from across their desks and shook his head. "You'd never do that because then your days would be so boring without me. And…because I'd have your car towed."

Ben put his head in his hands, and, in defeat, said, "Just tell me what happened this morning."

"I'm driving in on Antietam, and I'm just passing that new shipping warehouse. You know, the big green metal building. All of a sudden, I see a red light flashing in my rearview mirror. When I look back, I see an unmarked car with a bubble light. Well, it was an older Chevy, so I knew it wasn't any of our guys pulling me over. Plus, I know for a fact I wasn't speeding because I had just been thinking about how easy it would be to open up on that long stretch, but I looked down, and I was only going forty-seven."

"Two miles over the speed limit," Ben pointed out.

"Shut up. Anyway, it was an old Chevy, so I thought maybe it was a State Trooper. So, I pulled over and watched this guy get out of the car. The minute I saw him, I knew it was no Maryland State Trooper getting out of that car. He had dark blue pants on like our guys' uniforms and a cheap windbreaker with a badge. If you didn't know any better, sure, he could have passed for a Parker City officer. But being that I *know* everyone that works in this building—and that no one puts a badge on a windbreaker that looks like it came from a gas station—when he introduced himself to me as Officer Smith with the PCPD, I knew he was a fake. He, of course, had no idea who I was. Which I found a little insulting considering I have been in the paper a time or two, but what are you gonna do? So, after telling me that instead of writing me up a ticket that could cost me a few hundred dollars, I could just pay him the warning notice fee right there and—"

"Warning notice fee?"

"Yeah. If I just paid the fifty-dollar fee right there, he'd take care of the rest, and I could be on my way. When I handed the jackass my wallet, and he saw my badge, he almost crapped himself. Then he tried to run, but…well…I nailed him.

"When I opened up his car," Tommy continued, "he had a stack of cash sitting on the passenger seat. He'd been pulling the fake cop stunt all morning."

"Unbelievable," Ben said, still resting his head in his hands. "I have to ask. When you searched his vehicle, did you—"

"Don't worry. I did it by the book. After I cuffed the guy…*and* read him his rights, thank you very much, I even called for a squad car to come pick him up and for a tow for his fakemobile. I wanted to make sure I did everything right so you'd be proud of me, *Dad*."

Ben sighed. Then laughed. If this was the most exciting thing that happened today, he would be just fine with that.

Chapter Four

By the fifteenth time Ben heard the story, it felt as though it now ended with Tommy taking down the fake cop with a series of karate moves after a prolonged fistfight in the middle of the street while dodging oncoming traffic. Not that that was how Tommy was *actually* telling it, but it's what Ben was hearing in his head. The story of Tommy's morning escapade spread like wildfire through the building, giving everyone something to talk about. The fact that a guy impersonating a police officer had the misfortune to pull over an actual police detective—one who had become known for his occasional antics—was giving everyone working at the PCPD a good laugh, which is why they all felt the need to stop by the office to hear the story firsthand. Tommy was a good cop. But he was an even better storyteller.

Even those whose regular duties never required them to set foot on the second floor found a reason to pop into the Detective Squad's office for a moment. Naturally, Tommy was taking it all in stride, thoroughly enjoying the attention. He'd much rather have a day where everyone could spend their time sitting around telling stories and laughing than one where some terrible crime had been committed and they were all needed out on the street working. A boring day for Ben and Tommy was always going to be a good day because it meant no serious crime was being perpetrated.

By three o'clock in the afternoon when Darlene and LuAnn, two of the department's dispatchers, walked out of the office giggling at Tommy's brazen masculine overtures toward them—ironic considering he had been dating Shirley, the third Musketeer from Dispatch at one time—Ben thought everyone in the PCPD must have now been satisfied.

Ben was always amused by Tommy's superpower of being so at ease as the center of attention. He'd always been like that. Ever since the two were kids. Tommy was gregarious and, quite often, outspoken. Never afraid to say what was on his mind, no matter how much trouble he knew he could get into. It was also his defiant, "bad boy" image that the girls always went for. The secret that Ben knew was that Tommy wasn't all that much of a "bad boy." He was a genuinely caring guy with a showman exterior. Ben, on the other hand, was always the more reserved and thoughtful of the two. His actions were far more deliberate.

Together, over the years, the two reined each other in from the extremes. As they'd settled into their roles in the PCPD, Ben was more willing to take some time off and allow himself to relax, while Tommy, on occasion, thought about procedure before acting. As a team, their differences in seeing the world provided a cover for the other's blind spots.

"You do realize," Ben said when the two were finally alone again, "since I wasn't with you this morning when you made the arrest, *you* are going to have to do all the paperwork."

If there was one thing Tommy hated more than anything else, it was doing paperwork. No, that wasn't entirely true. The thing Tommy hated the most was doing paperwork and filling out reports using the computer that Ben insisted would make their lives easier. He didn't see the need for the giant machine sitting on his desk or how it was going to help them solve crime. But he recognized that Ben always knew what he was talking about.

Staring at the IBM monitor, Tommy raised an eyebrow. "I don't suppose—"

"Nope. I wasn't there. I can't do it for you." Ben took a page from Tommy's book and gave him a big smile to let him know there would be no further discussion.

Before Tommy was able to respond with a witty retort, a knock at the open door drew both detectives' attention. Standing there, filling the doorframe, was Chief Nicholas Brent. A former Navy man, the chief was an imposing figure with a barrel chest and arms the size of tree trunks. Brent was frequently found in the station's gym in the basement in the evenings, working out to help blow off steam from the trials and tribulations of the day. In his uniform, Brent easily commanded every room into which he entered. He was a man-made to wear a chief's uniform, not just in presence but personality. There wasn't a single member of the PCPD that did not respect the chief. And in turn, Nick Brent would do anything to take care of his people.

Leaning against the door jam and crossing his arms after getting their attention, Brent sighed. "Why is it that when I heard someone posing as a police officer was arrested because he pulled over an actual off-duty officer, I didn't even need anyone to tell me *you* were the off-duty officer?"

"Chief," Tommy said, turning on his Cheshire Cat-like smile. "I don't go out looking for these things to happen. They just do. I was minding my own business. On my way into the office…early, I might add," he paused to throw a look at Ben, "when this jack wagon pulls me over and tries to take me for fifty bucks."

"And it was *him* who asked for the money? Not you offering it to him?" the chief asked, his gaze firm.

"Chief!" Tommy mockingly clutched his chest in shock. "I can't believe you would even suggest that I tried to entrap the scumbag like that. Besides, he was using a bubble light to pull people over; he was dressed…well, sort of…dressed like a cop, *and* identified himself as such, which was breaking the law in the first place. The trying to get money out of me was a whole separate charge."

"And all of this," Ben jumped in, "will be detailed in the report Tommy is working on…right now…and will file before he leaves tonight."

Tommy slowly turned to look at his partner. "Right."

"Good. I'll look forward to reading that," Brent said, running a finger along his ginger mustache. He knew as well as anyone how much Tommy hated filling out reports, so was more than happy to give him a ribbing with Ben's help. Then, seeing the day's newspaper lying on the corner of Ben's desk, he changed the subject and asked, "Ben, did you read the article about the string of robberies in Wakeville?"

Picking up the copy of the *Herald-Dispatch*, Ben tossed it over to Tommy's desk for him to see it.

"Do you think it's anything we need to look out for?" the chief asked.

Wakeville was one of Parker County's dozen municipalities. The one closest to Parker City, in fact. So close that they almost shared a town boundary on Parker City's northern side. It was only natural to think whenever the robbers felt they'd overstayed their welcome in Wakeville they could hop over the town line and start causing problems in Parker City.

"I've read the bulletins from the Sheriff's Department," Ben said, "and they think it might just be a gang of kids, which leads them to think they're staying pretty close to home. Hopefully, that means they won't try anything here."

"I've seen the same bulletins, and I'm not so convinced we're talking about a group of kids," Brent offered. "Just to be safe, I'm going to have some units do additional runs through the Taverndale and Harper's Mill neighborhoods up there."

"But if these punks do come our way," Tommy interjected after quickly reading the article on the front page of the paper, "Ben and I will be ready for them, Chief. You can count on us." He punctuated the promise by jumping to his feet and saluting.

Rolling his eyes, Brent sighed and headed for his office down the hall without saying another word.

Chapter Five

Baltimore, 1927…

Flora Shipley was inconsolable as she watched the police officer replace the white sheet over Martha's face. Her lifeless body lay in the center of the hallway, the focus of the small group of men gathered around it. Flora had been introduced to all of them as they arrived but she couldn't remember any of their names. Everything was such a blur. There were more men throughout the house. She didn't know how many. She'd lost count. She felt as though she'd been drifting in and out since…since she'd come to staring up into the face of her next-door neighbor. She, too, had been lying on the floor in the hallway until Mrs. Clancy helped her to her feet.

She explained to Flora she'd come over to ask about a recipe they'd been talking about at bridge club when she saw the front door was open. At first, she thought because of the heat, it was just a way to try and keep the air moving and cool the house down a bit. But as she reached the top of the stairs, she saw Martha and Flora lying there in the hall.

After getting Flora into a chair, Mrs. Clancy quickly rang for the police. After the first patrol car arrived and the officers saw the state of things, a swarm of additional men quickly descended upon the St. Paul Street home. With each new arrival, Flora was asked to repeat her story. Having to relive the ordeal over and over again was sending her into a nervous panic. Her breathing was heavy and uneven, making her feel as though she would faint at any moment. The noise created by all the men talking over one another and asking her questions was thundering in her head like a drum.

The first moment of relief she felt was when she saw her husband burst through the front door and rush to her side. After a few words in her ear—words she couldn't recall—he began barking orders at the police officers filling his house. Flora felt better knowing her husband was taking control. She always felt better when John was around. But even though the policemen seemed to be listening to him, she still didn't really understand what was happening around here. Everything was so hazy. Her eyes were sore, and her throat hurt, on top of which she was sporting a throbbing headache. She desperately wanted to ask someone for a cigarette, but suddenly, no one was paying any attention to her. She'd suddenly become the last thing on anybody's mind.

Flora watched as two men from the city morgue and a uniformed policeman worked to place Martha's body onto a stretcher. She held on to John J., nearly crushing his forearm, as the men in their long white coats maneuvered the litter through the front door and down the curved stairs to the waiting coroner's truck.

Outside, a group of neighbors gathered to watch the activity. No one was quite sure what was happening at the Shipley's, but the assemblage of police cars lining the street told them something serious had happened in their otherwise peaceful neighborhood. Several patrolmen, sweating through their uniforms in the harsh afternoon heat, organized the crowd across the street, trying to keep them at a distance. A couple of the more inquisitive ladies from down the street did their best to talk their way past the policemen, insisting that Flora would most certainly need them, but they were corralled along with the rest. Forced to observe the comings and goings with their insatiable curiosity unsatisfied.

With all the uproar, someone also tipped off the press, and a handful of newsmen had made their way to St. Paul Street to try to get the scoop on what necessitated such a response from the Baltimore police force. The reporters knew if a crime had been committed in the wealthier part of town, the headlines it would produce would drive circulation sky-high. But at the moment, they, like all the residents of the Guilford area, were being kept at bay without any information being passed to them, making for a frustrated gang of newspapermen.

Leading Flora down the hall away from the commotion in the entryway, John J. ushered Flora into the library where she'd spent the morning writing letters. Taking a seat in one of the large leather chairs next to the fireplace, she watched as two men followed them into the library. One of them was wearing a police uniform, and the other a suit. John J. closed the doors to the library, then moved the chair on the other side of the fireplace closer to hers so he could sit and hold her hand.

Once everyone was settled, the man in the suit spoke up.

"Mrs. Shipley, my name is Lieutenant Cranshaw. I'm a detective with the Baltimore Police Department. This is my boss, Captain Lawson. We're both terribly sorry about what happened to you today. And my condolences on the death of your maid."

The detective's voice was smooth and comforting even though the words cut Flora like a knife. She couldn't believe that Martha was dead. It all seemed to be a nightmare from which she couldn't escape. She felt completely numb. The thought of waking up the next morning and Martha not greeting her in the kitchen when she came down for breakfast broke her heart.

Having become lost in her sorrow, it wasn't until John squeezed her hand that she realized she'd been staring at the detective without saying a word. To the men, she appeared to be in something of a trance. She didn't know how long she'd been sitting in that state, but obviously, her pause was noticeable. Blinking several times and forcing back a new flood of tears, Flora tried to smile in appreciation of Cranshaw's sympathy.

The detective appeared to be slightly older than John. At least, she thought he was because of the gray streaks in his hair. He was also handsome, like John, but in a different way. Her husband was dapper and sophisticated. Detective Cranshaw was a little rough around the edges. His broad shoulders and slightly crooked nose made Flora wonder if he might have been a boxer at some point in his life. The imperfection of his strong, square face only added to his rugged appeal. And he certainly looked like he still worked on his physical fitness and could lay out a robber with a swift blow.

Flora realized that Cranshaw was speaking to her again.

"—you've been asked before, but I am hoping you can tell me again exactly what happened today."

"It will be alright, darling. Just tell the detective everything you remember." John squeezed her hand again, giving her the courage to tell her story one more time.

"Um, yes. Of course." Her throat felt raw; her voice was barely above a whisper. "After John left for court this morning, I came in here to the library. There were several letters I'd been meaning to write. One of them was to my sister in Ohio. The others were to friends around town. I'd been putting off writing for far too long. I completely lost track of time. I didn't realize how long I'd been in here until I heard the door. Someone rang the bell."

"Do you remember what time that was?" Cranshaw asked, his pen poised over the pad on which he'd been scribbling notes.

"I do. When I heard the bell, I looked up at the clock." She pointed to the grandfather clock in the corner of the room. "It was just past eleven o'clock. Like I said. I'd lost track of time."

"Up until then, what had your maid been doing?"

"Her daily chores around the house."

"When you heard the doorbell, what did you do then?"

"I walked into the hallway. I couldn't think who might be dropping by. There's always the chance one of the ladies on the street might pop in. But with this heat... I wasn't expecting anyone." Flora shrugged, giving the detective a weak smile.

"What did you see when you walked into the hall?" Cranshaw's dark eyes were focused on Flora. He was carefully listening to every word she said, causing her to feel all balled up inside. She was beginning to worry she was going to say something wrong and didn't want to sound like some Dumb Dora.

With a quiver in her voice, Flora said, "Martha was standing at the door talking to two men. And then—"

Captain Lawson spoke for the first time, brusquely cutting her off by asking, "Do you remember what they looked like? Think hard about this. It's very important."

Cranshaw visibly bristled at the gruffness of his boss's interruption. Even John J. stiffened slightly at the unexpected interruption. The police captain didn't take any notice. Flora felt even more unsure of herself now that it was clear Lawson was so interested in the specifics of the men's appearance. Her memory was fuzzy at best. After coming to, she'd been in such a daze, having a difficult time distinguishing between reality and the images her mind was creating. If Martha were around, she would have brought her a cup of tea to help settle her nerves. The thought of Martha lying lifeless on the floor of the hallway brought tears to her eyes again. Placing her hand over her mouth, John handed her his handkerchief to catch the tears streaming down her cheeks.

Seeing the state she was in, Detective Cranshaw turned to her husband and suggested, "Maybe a brandy to help her nerves?"

"Good thinking, Lieutenant," the attorney said, jumping to his feet and moving swiftly over to the sideboard near his desk.

Lawson sat, anxiously tapping his fingers on his knees, as Flora took a sip of the dark amber liquid from the intricately etched crystal tumbler. He did not usually make appearances at crime scenes, but due to the nature of the incident, he'd been directed by Police Commissioner Gaither himself to accompany Lieutenant Cranshaw. The Shipleys' stature in the community, not to mention John J.'s friendship with Mayor Broening, demanded special attention. For his part, Cranshaw wished the captain had remained back at the precinct and allowed him to handle matters. The only thing that could hinder him any further would be if the commissioner himself walked through the door.

Cranshaw liked to conduct his investigations in a specific manner, and having his superior there, breathing down his neck, was unsettling for him. When he'd arrived at the Shipleys' home on St. Paul Street, he'd been unhappy to find so many patrol officers swarming the scene. Lawson must have sent every available man and then some when the call came in. The detective needed to take firm control of the situation and started handing out assignments to bring order to the ruckus. Just when he thought he'd taken everything in hand, Captain Lawson marched through the front door and stirred up the beehive once again.

Flora felt the warmth of the brandy easing its way through her after a few tentative sips. She did not drink very often, so on the occasions she did, the alcohol's effect was precipitous. For the first time, she was thankful for this. Her nerves were already beginning to untie themselves, allowing her to feel like she could breathe again.

"Now, Mrs. Shipley, you were saying," Cranshaw said in his calm, even tone, "when you walked into the hallway, you saw two men standing outside the door talking to your maid."

"Martha."

"Yes. Talking to Martha. Did you hear anything they said?"

"No. I couldn't hear anything. But all of a sudden, one of the men grabbed Martha. He put a handkerchief over her face. I guess to keep her from screaming…"

"Actually, Mrs. Shipley, the handkerchief was doused with chloroform. We found it next to Martha when we arrived. Chloroform is an anesthetic…a powerful sedative. When inhaled, it causes one to pass out. And in some instances, it can be fatal."

"Is that what happened to Martha? The reason she…"

Cranshaw's eyes were very compassionate as he weighed how much he thought he should tell Flora. He didn't want to place any more strain on her nervous system, but he believed in being honest with the victims and witnesses he spoke with.

After a moment, he finally said, "The coroner will make the final determination. But it could be that she died due to the chloroform. It is possible too much got into her system. We've seen chloroform poisoning before. But there is also the chance that the situation proved too stressful for Martha, and she suffered a heart attack. I'm not a doctor, but I would guess it will be one of those two causes.

"Everything you tell us about what you remember will help us find the men who did this. It doesn't matter how small the detail." Casting a quick glance at Captain Lawson, then turning back to Flora, the lieutenant asked, "Do you remember what the two men looked like?"

Chapter Six

Shortly after Flora's interview with Lieutenant Cranshaw, she was helped upstairs to her room by John J. and the family's doctor, who finally arrived after having been hastily sent for. Settling Flora into bed surrounded by goose-down pillows, the doctor gave her a mild sedative to help her sleep. For a moment, as she drifted off, able to forget about the horrors of the day, John J. watched her. A terrible pain filled his chest. He was, without question, upset about Martha's death. Not as much as Flora, of course, but he and their maid didn't have the same relationship. What terrified him the most was the thought of what would have happened if Flora had also met the same fate. He didn't know if he would be able to go on without her. Nor would he have any desire to, he admitted to himself.

The thought of losing Flora caused a lump to form in his throat. And to his surprise, he found himself fighting back tears. He couldn't recall the last time he'd cried. He told himself he was made of sterner stuff and needed to pull himself together before returning downstairs to speak with the lieutenant who was waiting for him.

Splashing some cold water on his face and leaving his suit jacket hanging on the valet stand next to the bed, John J. descended the stairs in his shirtsleeves to find Lieutenant Cranshaw and Captain Lawson in the middle of a hushed conversation. The captain was wiping the sweat from his forehead with a handkerchief as he saw the lawyer coming toward them.

"Captain!" Shipley's voice boomed off the walls, his frustration finally boiling over. The cool, calm demeanor he'd exhibited while they'd all been speaking with his wife was completely shed. Taking its place was the ruthless courtroom attorney John J. Shipley was known to be. "I demand to know what exactly is going on here! I'm not some rube off the street. Why do I have the feeling there's something you aren't saying?"

Before Lawson could answer, Cranshaw, who'd been using his fedora as a fan just a moment before, laid the hat on the side table next to the stairs and turned to Shipley, asking, "Sir, since you've arrived home, have you had a chance to look around to see if anything is missing?"

With a look of indignation, John J. sharply responded, "I have been tending to my wife, *Lieutenant.*"

"I understand. I do, sir. But would you mind taking a quick look around and telling us if anything has been taken? Anything of value."

"Taken? What are you saying, man?"

"What happened here today, Mr. Shipley," Captain Lawson began, stumbling over his words, "seems to fit with several other incidents over the last few weeks. Two men show up at the front door and force their way into the house. They use chloroform to knock out whoever answers the door and anyone else in the house. Then, they grab whatever valuables they can and run."

"This has happened before?!" the lawyer exploded.

"Until today, no one has died," Lawson offered, thinking, for some unknown reason, that would assuage him.

"I haven't read anything about these robberies. Why haven't they been reported on in the papers? Why haven't the police warned anyone? You've known this is happening but not done anything about it? I will have a word with Commissioner Gaither about this. I'll go directly to the mayor!"

Cranshaw now put himself in the line of fire, saying, "It's true, Mr. Shipley. We have been keeping these robberies under wraps. The commissioner didn't want to needlessly worry anyone. The entire city could end up in a panic if the matter isn't handled correctly. Which is why I have been assigned the investigation."

Shipley's fists were tightly clenched, held firmly at his side. He couldn't believe what he was hearing. He was, by nature, not a violet fellow. But he was fighting back the urge to take a swing at the detective.

The lieutenant looked through his notebook and said, "I've gone back and reinterviewed all of the victims, and everyone gives the same description of the men as your wife. We have an idea of who we're looking for now. And if I'm able to find some connection between all of the houses that were robbed, that could lead us to who's behind all of this."

"Lieutenant Cranshaw is one of my best detectives, Mr. Shipley. If there's anyone who can get to the bottom of things, he can," Lawson said, knowing full well the mayor and police commissioner were expecting results. Even more than John J. Shipley.

Chapter Seven

Cranshaw sat at his desk in the station house on Keswick Road, only a mile from the Shipleys' as the crow flies. The office was dark except for the single desk lamp that he'd turned on as the sun began to set a couple of hours earlier. Its dim glow, combined with the streetlamp's outside, cast strange shadowy tendrils along the gray plaster walls. As cars trundled along the street, the lights and reflections made it look like a parade of ghostly apparitions were marching through the small office.

Even though the temperature outside was still warm, with the sun having retreated below the horizon, the air had cooled significantly. This at least allowed Cranshaw to open the window and let in some fresh air, humid as it was. But he wasn't going to complain. The warm evening breeze helped to clear out the lingering smell of stale cigarette smoke and sweat. Over the last week or so, during the day, the office was as warm as an oven. Making it the last place he wanted to spend his time. He'd been happy to be out on the streets working. But this evening, he needed to focus on the string of robberies that was plaguing Baltimore's north side.

An ashtray full of cigarette butts sat next to the four police reports spread out in front of him on the well-worn blotter. As he carefully reread each one, he absentmindedly ran his thumb along the deep gouge in the otherwise smooth surface of the desk.

Nearly everyone else who worked in this section of the building had gone home hours ago, their days ending at a decent time. Knowing he needed to find some connection between the robberies, Cranshaw had bought a sandwich and a coffee from a diner around the corner from the station and hunkered down at his desk to reexamine all the reports that had been written up about the four incidents over the last three weeks.

After reviewing each one, as well as his own notes from his interviews with the homeowners, Cranshaw wrote out a full list of the items that had been stolen. The amount taken added up to a small fortune. Silver cigarette boxes, crystal vases, jewelry; all items easily sold by a fence and hard to identify. He found that of particular note. If they'd stolen any of the paintings and statues that filled the houses they'd hit, those pieces would be easily recognizable. It meant the thieves thought the crimes through. They were only after certain *types* of items. They weren't just a smash-and-grab lot, Cranshaw began to understand.

He hated that he was coming into the investigation weeks behind, but the first two robberies hadn't been connected right away. Different patrolmen had been sent to get reports and both had taken their time filing the paperwork. It wasn't until the third robbery, only the week before, that the officer from the first crime scene went to his sergeant and pointed out the similarities to the call he'd responded to. Once the second robbery was compared to the others, everyone in the precinct realized they had a gang on their hands targeting upper-class homes on the north side of the city. Captain Lawson was the one with the unfortunate duty of passing the news up the chain of command. Which, in turn, sent the message straight back down that Lawson needed to get the situation under control.

The next morning, the captain called Cranshaw into his office and turned the entire case over to him. As the district's lead detective, it made sense that he would be put in charge of the investigation. But there seemed to be another, unspoken, reason behind Lawson's assignment. Cranshaw was now also going to be the fall guy if the ring of thieves wasn't caught in short order. The mayor and police commissioner wanted someone who could be held responsible if there was a failure to apprehend the miscreants.

A map of Baltimore's Northern Police District was tacked to the wall next to Cranshaw's desk. With a pin placed at the location of each robbery, he saw straight away that they had all taken place in or around the Guilford neighborhood. That wasn't a surprise, as that was one of the wealthiest areas in the city. Doctors, lawyers, bankers, businessmen all lived in the big expensive houses. For a gang of crooks, they were all prime targets. Up until now though, there hadn't been much crime in that particular area to speak of. Cranshaw could only assume it was because the criminal element in the city knew better than to make enemies with some of the city's most powerful and influential residents. Even if they were ripe pickings, as far as the lieutenant was concerned. Just in the last few days, he'd seen how Baltimore's elite put their wealth on display for all to see. He could only surmise that they thought they were untouchable.

That was a notion that would be shattered when they woke up and read the headlines in the papers tomorrow morning. With such a buzz of activity at the Shipleys', there was no way to avoid speaking to the gaggle of reporters who'd shown up, pencils poised to record any tidbit of information anyone was willing to share with them. A couple of the guys were already snooping around about the recent robberies. But no one in the department was talking—by direct order of the police commissioner. Now, the reporters had their story. Judging by the questions with which they were peppered as he and Captain Lawson stood on the steps of the Shipleys' home, Cranshaw knew it was going to be sensational, bordering on scandalous.

No doubt, when the mayor read the newspapers in the morning, he was going to be spitting mad. If Baltimore's most privileged were being "attacked" and robbed in their own homes, the idea of it being a city of law and order would be seen as a myth. His promise of making the voters feel safe would be right out the window. And if he didn't make some headway on the case, the lieutenant was all too aware of who would be to blame.

Chapter Eight

Cranshaw realized he'd done as much as he could for the night when all of the typing on the police reports began blurring together before his weary eyes, and he discovered he had no more cigarettes. Turning off the lamp on his desk and locking the door behind him, he bid goodnight to a pair of young patrolmen he passed on his way out of the building. He could still remember when he was their age, having just joined the force and been assigned the night shift. Stepping outside onto the empty street in front of the station, he wished for them a quiet night ahead.

He loosened his collar as he walked down the street, though the gesture was pointless. The night was still, yet the heat clung to him, pressing in from all sides. It was nearly midnight, and the temperature-though better than it was when the sun's rays were out in full force- showed no mercy. A trickle of sweat ran down his spine, sticking his shirt to his back. Cranshaw would have given anything for a cool, refreshing breeze, something to break the stagnant air. The night air was thick and humid.

Passing the dim streetlamps on his path home, he would occasionally pause to wipe the sweat from his brow, all the while his mind drifting from one thought to the next. There was something peaceful about Baltimore in the wee hours of the morning. Yet, he couldn't help thinking how the city had changed so much since his boyhood. Back then, he remembered Baltimore's summers being filled with laughter, with children chasing each other down the streets and women sitting on stoops, fanning themselves and sharing stories. It was a different kind of heat back then—hard and relentless, yes, but somehow bearable. Now, it felt suffocating, oppressive. The city had turned hard over the years, and summer brought out the worst in it. Maybe it always had; he was just too young to realize it back then.

No, there was no denying that the changes weren't just in his head. Baltimore itself seemed darker, and, in some places, more sinister. Prohibition had ripped through the city like a fever, bringing with it speakeasies and illegal gambling dens. The Belvedere Room was just one of the many places that had sprung up in the shadows, thriving on secrecy and vice. It was a dangerous place masquerading as respectable, a polished front for the corruption and violence that was beginning to ooze beneath the surface of the city. Places like that didn't just happen-they grew from a wanton desire.

At the corner of 34th Street and Hickory Avenue, as he passed beneath it, the streetlight flickered. He remembered how, as a boy, he used to think that these gaslights were little watchmen keeping the neighborhood safe. Now, as a police lieutenant, he knew better.

Walking down Hickory Avenue, he found himself in one of the last places in the city that truly still bore traces of the life he remembered. The cobblestones were uneven under his feet, but he welcomed their familiarity. He had walked this very street as a boy, passing by corner stores selling penny candy and fresh bread, his mother's hand firmly around his wrist as they went to Sunday services.

Cranshaw thought of the men he'd grown up with, boys he'd fought and laughed with. Some of them had left the city, chasing dreams elsewhere. Others had stayed, making a good life for themselves. Some were lost to the Great War. And others were now buried in the very organizations responsible for the crime threatening the city.

As the modest home he shared with his wife and two boys came into view, a breeze picked up, bringing with it the faint, acrid smell of coal smoke from the nearby factories. He shook his head, thinking of his father, who had worked long hours in one of those very factories. Cranshaw could still see his father's rough hands, stained from years of labor, hands that had built this city as much as anyone.

Cranshaw's mind wandered back to the case files sitting on his desk. It had been some time since he'd worked robberies—at least home robberies. For close to ten years now, when there was a serious case that could potentially become a headache for the higher-ups, he was one of the detectives put in charge of the investigation. His track record for getting results earned him a solid reputation within the department. Hoping after a few hours of sleep and a hearty breakfast, fresh eyes might allow him to see something in the reports he'd missed. Something that could connect the victims or give him an idea of who might be perpetrating such daring daylight robberies.

Arriving at the steps to his house, Cranshaw let out a long breath, feeling the weight of the day settle onto his shoulders. The last thought that ran through his head before going inside was that Baltimore was his city. For better or worse, he'd continue to do whatever he could to keep the city he remembered from his youth from completely slipping away.

Chapter Nine

1985...

As the clock hanging on the wall showed exactly five-thirty, Tommy said, "All…," then paused. He tapped a couple more keys on the keyboard and said, "Finished."

He hated using the computer. Not just because he was terrible at typing-he never used anything more than his index fingers to stab at the keys-he simply didn't see the need for the machine. He was yet to see how it was going to make his job any easier, as Ben was constantly telling him. But Ben was always keeping up with the latest technology. He loved his gadgets and gizmos. So, Tommy was willing to trust his friend. He'd never led him astray before. Just because he was willing to give Ben the benefit of the doubt, however, didn't mean he needed to like it. Or refrain from complaining. Which he did. Quite frequently. And quite loudly.

"I finished filling out my report on the arrest this morning," Tommy said, looking over the monitor at his partner. A triumphant expression plastered on his face.

"That wasn't so bad. Was it?" Ben asked, not even trying to hide his patronizing tone. Or looking up from the paper he was reading.

"I don't know. I feel like my fingers are cramping up and—"

"They're not," Ben quickly shot back.

"I'm going to need them tonight. I have another date with Christine."

Ben rolled his eyes. He didn't need to hear about whatever sexual escapades his friend was planning for the evening. But he had to admit, Tommy sounded like he really liked Christine. Though, to be fair, he always sounded like he *really* liked whatever woman he was spending his time with. And there'd been many women over the years. Many, many women. Tommy's rugged good looks drew women to him. Which was no surprise considering he bore a striking resemblance to the dashing star of *Magnum P.I.*, Tom Selleck, right down to the mustache. Tommy was the guy every woman wanted to date. For his part, Ben was the guy every woman wanted to take home to meet her mother. The only TV character he'd ever been compared to was Ron Howard's Richie Cunningham on *Happy Days*. And it wasn't in a flattering way.

"I'm going to print this report and personally walk it down the hall to the chief myself. Then, I am going to continue downstairs and out the door and meet Christine at Casa Tamale. After that, we're going to go back to my—"

Ben held up his hand. "I'm sure you two will have a good time, whatever it is you will be doing. You can tell me all about it tomorrow," he said, shaking his head.

"What will you and the lovely Natalie be doing tonight?" Tommy asked as he stood up and pulled on his corduroy sport coat.

"Nat is doing some wedding planning with a couple of the girls tonight and I have been requested to make an appearance at a reception over at the Harlequin. The mayor and members of the City Council will be there, and the chief wants me to help talk up his reorganization plan."

"What's this? Benjamin Winters politicking? I never thought I would see the day. How the mighty have fallen," Tommy said, raising his eyes to the ceiling, shaking his fists at the unseen universal forces.

"I *am not* politicking. I'm going to be there to answer any questions anyone might ask about why Chief Brent's plan is going to be good for the department and the city."

It was Tommy's turn to roll his eyes. They both knew the truth. Because of the cases that had landed the two young detectives in the spotlight, Ben had a little bit of star power behind him. So did Tommy, for that matter, but the chief knew Tommy was *not* the guy he wanted talking to the City

Council. As much as Ben hated playing politics, he was good at it. Of the two detectives in the department, he was the diplomat and the perfect candidate to serve as the face of Chief Brent's plan to reorganize the Parker City police to turn the force into a modern, forward-looking law enforcement agency that would seamlessly integrate with the mayor's plan to revitalize the city. Just thinking about all those words and catchphrases put Tommy to sleep, so it was best for Ben to do the talking.

After thinking for a minute, Tommy tilted his head and asked, "Is there gonna be an open bar?"

Chapter Ten

In 1978 a flood devastated Parker's downtown, the very heart of the city. The once thriving commercial corridor had already fallen on hard times due to the decade's economic downturn. But the flood waters that raged through the city after the Tasker River overflowed pushed what businesses remained out of existence. Downtown, the once vibrant destination for Parkertons looking to shop and dine, had been turned into a ghost town. Even the Center Square, made up of four grand, pre-Civil War buildings with their once gleaming marble and stone facades, sat boarded up and abandoned following the disaster.

Not far down the street from Parker's Center Square sat the Harlequin Theatre. At one time, the former Vaudeville house-turned-movie palace was the crown jewel of Downtown. Built at the turn of the century by one of the city's richest residents and a descendant of not one but *two* of Parker's five founding families, the theater had been the hub of art and culture in the city. Some of the greatest performers on the Vaudeville circuit, including W.C. Fields, Al Jolson, and Jimmy Durante, had all tread the boards at Parker City's venerable showplace.

As with so many of the majestic Vaudeville houses, though, the Harlequin saw audiences dwindle during the Depression and was eventually converted into a "movie palace," giving theater-goers a chance to escape their everyday lives by watching Hollywood's latest comedies and dramas come to life on the enormous silver screen for less than a quarter. The rise in television became the theater's next threat, followed by the opening of the new mega-movieplex just outside of town. As if times weren't already difficult for the

Harlequin, the Great Flood of '78 caused so much damage, there had been serious talk about the building simply being torn down.

But the city's young, energetic mayor, Charlie Oland, refused to hear of it. He set out on a plan to not only restore Downtown to its former glory, but to make the Harlequin the centerpiece of the revitalization. It was taking time, but after nearly seven years, restoration work on the theater began in earnest at the beginning of the year. No one expected the project to be completed quickly, but the reception that evening was to show off the work that had been done in the lobby. The countless hours spent clearing out the rotted wood and decaying waste left behind from the flood; cleaning and polishing the original marble flooring that greeted guests as they walked through the newly installed brass-plated doors; and replacing the badly dated turquoise wallpaper-what little had survived from a renovation decades before-was stripped down and replaced with an elegant cream and gold wall covering, much more suited to a modern sense of style.

Even though the lobby had been completely refreshed and brought back to life for the present day, it still presented a striking, classic image, Ben thought as he stepped through the doors and surveyed the crowd. A lively energy filled the large space as the guests mingled, discussing everything from upcoming events to last night's sports scores beneath shimmering crystal chandeliers. Seeing the opulence of it all before him, Ben would never know that beyond the giant doors at the end of the long lobby remained a dilapidated, debris-filled auditorium that, during the height of the flood in '78, was submerged three feet beneath the water.

Ben recognized many of the faces in the crowd, nodding hello to several. They were Parker's movers and shakers, all there to help raise funds to continue cleaning up the theater in anticipation of a grand reopening at a date yet to be determined. No doubt, that occasion would be based, in part, on how much money was raised this evening. Ben couldn't even venture a guess at the amount of money it would take to restore the historic theater to its former glory. He'd only ever seen photographs of the Harlequin during its heyday, with the grandeur of the showplace evident even in the black and white pictures.

As Ben was admiring some of the large posters that had been put on display featuring former stars who'd graced the stage of the theater, he heard a voice behind him call out, "Detective Sergeant Ben Winters. So good of you to join us for such an important event."

Turning, he found himself looking into the bright eyes of Charlie Oland, Parker City's enthusiastic and much-loved mayor. If ever there was a politician straight out of central casting, Ben thought, it was Oland. With his chiseled chin and perfectly coiffed immovable hair, he possessed the ability to make anyone with whom he was speaking feel as if they were the only person in the world. It was a gift for a man in his position. And though Ben was usually a little weary of public figures and their true motives, Oland seemed genuine. Ben actually liked the guy. Over the last several years, whenever they'd interacted with one another, he always walked away feeling as if he knew exactly where the mayor stood and, in return, he'd listened to Ben and taken what he'd said seriously.

More importantly, Oland proved himself to be trustworthy because he always did what he said he was going to. So, when he informed Chief Brent he was going to do everything in his power to help institute the reorganization plan for the PCPD, both the chief and Ben took him at his word. They knew, however, it wasn't entirely up to the mayor. If it were, there'd be no question that Brent could begin implementing his changes. It was the City Council that needed to be brought on board because there was a significant price tag that went along with the plan, and they would need to find the money in the budget to make it happen. And money was always an issue. Especially when Parker City was finally beginning to see a turnaround in its economic fortunes.

Shaking the mayor's outstretched hand, Ben couldn't help but notice the glint from his diamond-studded cufflinks.

"A gift from my wife," Oland said, observing Ben's gaze.

"Very nice."

"Are you a fan of the theater, Sergeant?" the mayor asked as he waved at someone over Ben's shoulder. "I'm always interested in finding out what people's interests and hobbies are."

"My fiancée is more of a theater fan, but I've been to a few shows that I've enjoyed. I certainly think the restoration of the Harlequin is a good cause, though. I'm actually here as a guest of Chief Brent this evening."

"No better time to talk to Councilmen Higgins and Wynn than after they've had a few glasses of champagne," Oland said with a wink and a sly smile.

"I don't think I would put it exactly like that, sir."

"I would!" The mayor laughed. "Oh, and here's the chief now."

The crowd parted like the Red Sea as Nick Brent entered and made his way toward the men, shaking hands with some of the guests as he passed.

"Good evening, Mr. Mayor. Detective."

"Great to see you, Chief. Detective Winters and I were just saying how we all need to have a chat with Dean and Andy over there."

Brent saw the council members talking with the head of the Chamber of Commerce near the bar. "Maybe we should wait until they've had a chance to get a couple more drinks in them."

With a grin, Oland turned to Ben and said, "See? I told you. The chief knows what he's doing."

Ben found it somewhat fascinating that even though the gathering was to benefit the Harlequin, there was clearly a strategy in place to lobby for the chief's reorganization plan at some point during the evening. He wondered if that's how it always worked. Attend a function for one cause but negotiate deals and agreements for something else entirely at the same time. There was too much strategy and gamesmanship involved for him.

While the three continued talking, several people stopped by their little group to say a few words. Oland always made it a point to introduce Ben and the chief, even though Brent's uniform made it perfectly clear who he was. It was a small gesture that Ben found very telling of the type of person Charlie Oland was. To him, everyone was someone and deserved recognition.

Ben was a little surprised the mayor was spending so much time with him and Brent. He would have expected him to be working the room and glad-handing all the guests. At one point, as an elderly woman with a head full of strikingly white hair passed by, Oland interrupted them to attract her attention. When she joined them, Ben got the impression she may just have been the most sophisticated person in the room. There was something about the way she carried herself that set her apart from everyone else. Her perfectly applied makeup made it difficult for Ben to guess her age. And she wore a deep purple, tailored dress suit that reminded Ben of a costume Alexis Carrington might wear on *Dynasty*. But it was the glistening emerald and ruby-encrusted brooch that caught his eye. Between that and the mayor's cufflinks—if the stones were all genuine, he thought the two pieces might cost an entire year's salary.

"Chief Brent, Detective Winters, I would like to introduce Clara Daschle. She is the chairwoman of the Harlequin Restoration Committee. Clara, this is Nicolas Brent and the police department's chief detective, Ben Winters."

"How do you do, gentlemen?" she asked, her voice smooth as silk. "Thank you for joining us tonight. Are you fans of the performing arts?"

"I do try and take in an opera whenever I can," Brent offered. "Anything by Monteverdi or Rossini especially."

Ben looked at the chief in complete surprise. They'd been working together for over five years, and he had no idea the man liked opera. Not that it ever came up. But it was just so unexpected.

Seeing Ben's reaction, the chief said, "I'm not just a baseball fan."

With a wicked twinkle in her eye, Clara Daschle pointed out, "Maybe our city's chief detective isn't as great a detective as we think."

"I'm wondering that myself," Ben agreed with a smile.

"Once the Harlequin is reopened, maybe we'll be able to bring in some opera productions for you, Nicolas," she suggested. "I have some friends who may be able to help with that. Maybe there could even be a small part for you."

Ben had never seen Brent blush before. "Well, Mrs. Daschle, I might enjoy singing in the shower every now and then, but I don't think anyone would want to hear me do it on the stage. My wife would be the first to tell you that I can't sing."

"I've known many people who never let that stop them," she said with a laugh.

"Mr. Mayor, Chief Brent, can I get a photograph?"

Everyone turned to see a photographer standing there with a press tag clipped to the breast pocket of his jacket. He began snapping pictures even before the group managed to fully arrange themselves. Once they had, and the photog was satisfied he'd gotten a couple dozen good shots, he jotted down their names in a little notebook and disappeared into the crowd.

"Well, it's been a pleasure meeting you, gentlemen, but I really must mingle," Clara said with a slight nod of her head. Like that, she glided away toward the next group of guests.

As Ben walked toward the bar to order a soda, several framed photos on display drew his attention. Looking closely at one of them, he thought the woman in the center of the shot, standing behind a microphone, looked very much like a young Clara Daschle. Looking across the sea of people in the lobby, he spotted her standing in the middle of a group, telling a story with animated, yet elegant hand gestures. Looking back at the photo, then to Daschle once again, he was fairly certain she was the woman in the picture.

Could she have been a performer at the Harlequin when she was younger, Ben wondered. It could be a significant reason she was the one spearheading the campaign to reopen the theatre. She had a personal connection to it. As he cast one more look in her direction, their eyes met. Ben thought in that instant she must have read his mind from the other side of the room because she winked and nodded her head ever so slightly. Ben couldn't help but smile.

Meeting the graceful Clara Daschle was the highlight of Ben's evening. For the remainder of the night, he and the chief spent their time listening to one person after another extoll their theories on community policing and what the department should be doing. That was in addition to hearing why Councilmen Higgins and Wynn were still on the fence about making any changes to the PCPD anytime soon. They didn't want to move too quickly on a plan that could "upend the department's operations." Which, ironically, was the exact thing the chief wanted to do. After nearly two hours of smiling and nodding, Ben's mind was completely numb. Which is why, while driving home, he promised himself to avoid any such future functions at all costs.

45

Chapter Eleven

Ben arrived home to find Natalie sitting on the sofa in the living room with her wedding notebook open in front of her. He wasn't entirely certain what planning she was still doing for the wedding, considering he thought all of the details had been finalized weeks ago. The wedding itself was less than two months away, and Ben had been counting down the days. Not that much was going to change after the big day, though, considering he and Nat had been living together for a couple of years now. But everything would be official.

The couple first met several years earlier when Ben was working the Spring Strangler case. A history teacher at Tasker High School, two of Nat's students were victims of the killer, and when Ben and Tommy showed up to ask some questions, even under the tragic circumstances, there was a spark that Tommy was all too happy to point out. After the case was closed and their paths crossed a few more times by chance, Ben took the universe's hint and asked her out. The rest, as Tommy says, was *history*—a reference to the subject Natalie taught. Tommy thought he was being clever. Ben thought he was being a pain in the ass. Either way, Tommy was thrilled to see his best friend so happy. And important to Ben, Tommy and Natalie really got along. To be fair, she probably rolled her eyes at some of Tommy's comments as much as Ben did, but that just showed how perfect the two were for each other.

Walking up behind the sofa and putting his arms around her, Ben saw she was updating the guest list with the latest RSVPs. "Has your mother decided if she's coming or not?" he asked, kissing her on the top of the head.

"I told her, if she doesn't send in her official response card, there will *not* be a seat for her at the reception."

"Yeah. I'd love to see someone try and keep your mother away." Ben laughed at the thought of Tommy trying to barricade the doors of the reception hall from Rose, his soon-to-be mother-in-law. Heaven help him. His money would be on Rose in that match-up. Hell, Tommy'd met Nat's mother. He'd probably put *his* money on her, too!

All kidding aside, Ben really liked Nat's parents. They reminded him a lot of his own. Thankfully, all four of them got along well. Ben realized how lucky he was that all the people closest to him meshed. He heard horror stories and jokes about in-laws all the time, but was yet to have any of his own terrible experiences.

Loosening his tie, he sat down on the couch next to Nat. He picked up the wedding notebook and started flipping through the pages. There were more notes and details in it than in one of his case files. And that was saying something, considering how meticulous and thorough he was.

He and Nat spent the next hour sitting on the sofa watching television and catching up on each other's days. As always, she asked what kind of trouble Tommy had gotten himself into. When Ben told her the story about his partner's run-in with the fake Parker City Police officer that morning, she couldn't do anything but laugh and ask if the imposter made it out alive. Or worse, needed therapy after trying to pull one over on Tommy, who himself could be a pretty slick con man when he needed to be.

When she asked about the night's reception at the Harlequin, he admitted it paled in comparison to Tommy's morning. Once he told her about the plans for the theater and meeting Clara Daschle, Natalie said she'd be interested in volunteering to help with the project just as soon as the wedding was behind them.

After the late news and watching Johnny Carson's opening monologue on *The Tonight Show*, they decided it was time for bed. Ben had an early meeting with the chief and Captain Nelson, the department's Operations Commander and Brent's number two, to go over the most recent crime stats before the two top officers sat down with a reporter from the *Herald-*

Dispatch to do an in-depth piece on the PCPD. While Chief Brent always kept a watchful eye on the department's stats, Captain Nelson was a numbers guy. He could take a set of data points and analyze them seven ways from Sunday. It wasn't just that he thought it helped the department to take a deep-dive into the numbers and look for trends, he enjoyed it. Though Ben thought there were times basing certain decisions on the numbers wasn't always the best practice, he understood where Nelson was coming from. The captain used statistics and numbers to support his conclusions, like Ben used evidence to solve a case.

Neither of the men was looking forward to sitting for the interview, Ben knew, but it was all part of a bigger plan to help build support for the chief's reorganization. Once again, Ben was glad he wasn't the one spearheading this new effort. He'd help wherever and whenever he was needed, but then happily disappear back into his office and wait for his next rollout. He was much happier doing the work of a detective and was more than willing to leave the running of the department, and its PR, to the top brass.

Chapter Twelve

The next morning, Ben awoke to a gray sky over the city. It wasn't even that there were dark clouds overhead. It was just a solid gray sky. Even the trees and flowers, which were in full bloom and yesterday looked so alive and vibrant with color, took on a darker, bland hue. Ben was looking out the bedroom window when Natalie appeared behind him with a copy of the morning's *Herald-Dispatch*.

"It looks like someone made the front page," she said with a grin, opening the paper for him to see.

She was right. There he was in a photograph on the front page, standing next to Chief Brent, Mayor Oland, and Clara Daschle. It appeared alongside a spread of photos taken at the Harlequin reception the night before. It was the largest of the pictures, right in the center, directly under the banner headline. Not that it mattered to him, but he knew Tommy would have a smart-ass remark to make when he got to the office.

"Looking pretty handsome, Detective Sergeant," Nat said with a devilish grin. "It's a half-day at school today. I don't have to be in until later. Unless you've got a serial killer you're looking for, I think we should go back to bed for a while."

As he felt his cheeks flush, Ben looked at his watch and did some quick calculations.

"I know. You have a meeting to get to. But I'll make sure you're there on time," she said, seeing the look of concern on his face and reading his mind. Then, grabbing his tie, she pulled him to the bed with no objection.

Chapter Thirteen

"I thought for sure you would have stopped in here before you met with Brent this morning," Tommy said, looking over the top of the newspaper as Ben walked into the Detective Squad's office after his meeting.

"I was running a little late this morning. I went straight into the chief's when I got here. Why were you here so early?" Ben took off his suit jacket and hung it on the back of his chair.

"I didn't…wait a minute." Tommy folded the paper and laid it on his desk. "You don't run late. Is everything alright?"

"Yeah. Everything's fine. I just got a slow start this morning." Ben sat down at his desk and started sorting through a stack of folders. "Chief Brent thinks he's going to be able to—"

"No." Tommy stopped him abruptly. "No. I'm not buying it. *You* don't get a late start. *I'm* the one who gets a late start. And that's usually because I'm…. Oh! I see. I get it. You got *a late start*," he said, wiggling his eyebrows. A giant grin spread across his face, making him look like a pubescent teenager who just found his father's stack of *Playboy* magazines.

Ben held up his index finger and warned his partner, "Not a single word, you jackass."

"I know why you were late this morning," Tommy taunted.

Raising an eyebrow, Ben said, "I know I have threatened to bust you back down to traffic duty before, but this time…I mean it."

Putting his hand on his chest in mock bewilderment, Tommy said, "I would have assumed someone who spent the morning the way you did would be in a better mood."

Ben picked up a pen and threw it at him. Tommy reacted quickly enough, using the newspaper on his desk to bat it away.

"Oh, yeah. And then there's this," he said, pointing at the picture on the front page. "I thought the great Detective Ben Winters didn't do politics. You're looking pretty chummy with the mayor here."

"Believe me," Ben said, finding the folder he'd been looking for, "it wasn't my scene. I had a drink. I had a couple of hors' d'oeuvres, talked to a few people, and I got out of there. There was no shortage of people who, once they found out who I was, were willing to share their thoughts on how the PCPD should be fighting crime."

"Better you than me," Tommy said, tossing the paper in the wastebasket next to his desk. "I'm gonna run down the hall and grab a cup of coffee. You want one?"

"Yes, please."

As Tommy bounced out of the office and headed for the break room down the hallway, Ben scanned through the pages of the file in front of him. He needed to follow up with Captain Nelson about one of the topics from their meeting. He just needed to find the bits of information the captain was asking about. When he found the numbers he was after, he jotted them down on a piece of notepaper and was just about to take them to Captain Nelson when his telephone rang.

"Detective Winters," he answered.

"Hi, sweetie. It's Shirley." She was one of the department's dispatchers, as well as one of Tommy's former casual on-again, off-again relationships. Ben would have known exactly who it was even if she hadn't said.

"Morning, Shirley. How are you doing?"

"I'm good, sugar. It hasn't been too busy down here. Don't go gettin' me wrong. That's a good thing. But…we just got a call."

"What do you have?" Ben asked.

"B&E, possible robbery. Four-seventy-two Richmond Street."

"Richmond Street," Ben repeated, thinking for a moment. "Is that up in—"

"Harper's Mill," Shirley answered. "You got it, sugar."

"Who made the call?"

"Homeowner. I have Thompson on his way. He was on patrol up there, but I thought I should give you the heads up, considering what's been going on in Wakeville. If they jumped the line into Parker City…"

Ben sighed. "Yeah. Alright, Tommy and I'll head out."

"Roger that, cupcake."

Thoughtfully, Ben returned the receiver to its place, disconnecting from Shirley. If this break-in was related to the recent incidents in Wakeville, it could be a problem. It meant whoever was behind the robberies was getting bolder, expanding their horizons. They'd also moved on from hitting relatively middle-class homes in a sparsely populated town to one of the wealthiest neighborhoods in a city with its own police force.

"Well, dammit," Ben said as Tommy walked back into the office carrying two steaming mugs of coffee.

Looking at his partner and registering his troubled expression, Tommy cocked his head and said, "I don't know what it is, but I already know I don't like it."

Chapter Fourteen

1927…

As Lieutenant Cranshaw feared, every single morning paper hit the newsstands with blaring headlines about a burglary crew turned murderers on the loose in Baltimore's north side. Despite the coroner's pending report on the Shipleys' deceased housemaid, the press had already convicted the burglars in the court of public opinion.

As newspapers across the city were unfolded and read at breakfast tables and on the buses and trolleys to work, residents found themselves split in their reaction to the news. In the more well-to-do neighborhoods, especially in the affluent enclave of Guilford—the epicenter of the newly divulged crime wave—people were in a full-blown panic. Fearful they could be next on the burglar's list. At the same time, the average Joe on the street didn't see much to worry about, so went about the day not thinking much more about the story he'd read in the paper. It was a city divided.

To see the crowded sidewalks along Howard Street and Lexington, with men and women making their way through the summer heat to their morning destinations, it was clear the vast majority of the city was going about its business as usual. The street cars making their way from one side of the city to the other were just as crowded as the previous morning-not that any of those who might be considered targets of the robbery crew used the trolley line on a regular basis. But the line of cars rattling down the street hadn't either. Even with this dark cloud looming over Baltimore, the city kept moving.

Where there was a sign of concern was in the high-end department stores like Hutzler Brothers. A magnificent five-story building with an ornately decorated façade of gray Nova Scotia stone located on Howard Street claimed one could spend an entire day in the store. Shoppers could lunch in one of the two restaurants while shopping then get a haircut in the Circle Room Beauty Salon or a shoeshine at the Shoe Fixery. But on that morning, the grand shopping palace was nearly deserted as its more well-to-do clientele were so fearful of leaving the safety and security of their lavish homes. Even though, ironically, it was those very homes that were attracting the burglars.

Several blocks north of Hutzler's, one man was particularly displeased with the day's news: Bob Franklin. Known by many simply as Big Bob, he was the undisputed boss of Baltimore's underworld. With a finger in every illegal pie, from gambling to prostitution to bootlegging, there was not a single criminal act that took place in any part of the city that he himself wasn't aware of or hadn't personally given his stamp of approval. Anyone who came into *his* town and tried to go into "business"—of the illicit nature—without his consent, soon discovered they'd made an egregious error. Which is why the headline in *The Baltimore Sun* was so disturbing to him.

Big Bob Franklin was a rather unusual figure in the criminal community. Unlike other gangland bosses around the country, he hadn't come up on the streets, fighting his way to the top. He was a Harvard-educated man from a respectable family. He'd been a practicing attorney, who, through twists and turns of fate, represented the interests of some of Baltimore's more unsavory characters until he realized he could put these criminal ventures together himself to create his own organization that rivaled those in Chicago and New York.

Running his own clients out of business was just the first step in his rise to power. He started using the profits from his newly acquired enterprises to buy off anyone and everyone who could pose a threat to him. Those who refused to play ball and look the other way when Big Bob needed them to would occasionally find themselves floating in Baltimore Harbor or worse. With a firm grip on every illegal activity in Baltimore, Big Bob ran his operation with precision, unafraid to eliminate competition. But now, the headlines threatened his carefully cultivated empire. The recent daring burglaries, unknown to the public, were a direct challenge to his authority, and he was not one to tolerate such insolence. Even if they were just home robberies, they were unsanctioned and could not be allowed to continue.

Over the last decade or so, he'd had free rein to build his organization and line his pockets with very little standing in his way. Unfortunately for him, the police commissioner was beginning to take a keen interest in the "extracurricular activities" of members of the police force and was bringing in new detectives with whom Franklin didn't have a "relationship." Which meant he was feeling more heat than he'd felt in a long time, putting his ventures at risk. As if worrying about the authorities taking a new look at him and his businesses wasn't bad enough, now he had a gang openly challenging his authority! He was under attack from both sides.

"I wanna know who these mugs are who think they can come into my town and stir up this kind of trouble!" Big Bob slammed the newspaper down on his desk with such force it shook the room. His gravelly baritone was filled with white-hot rage. His usually calm, calculated demeanor was replaced with a fury very few of his underlings ever witnessed.

"Nobody challenges me. *Nobody*! I run this town, and penny-ante shit like this will not be tolerated."

Even though the first robberies hadn't been reported by the press, Bob Franklin still knew about them. Word spread quickly in his world. And when the word was that Big Bob was being made to look the fool, it spread damn fast. Which meant he needed to move even faster to put a stop to it. He couldn't look like he was weak in any way. He'd run the city with an iron fist for too long to allow this. Even though the transgression perpetrated against *him* was a simple set of robberies he hadn't condoned, it still sent a message that he wasn't fully in control any longer, and there could be space for someone else to step forward and challenge the crime boss.

Gritting his teeth, he ran a hand through his ever-thinning hair. When he was young, he'd had a thick mane of black hair. At sixty, what gray hair remained was scarcely enough to comb over his scalp. The rapidly retreating hairline only made the wrinkles that perpetually creased his forehead more noticeable.

Flush with anger, his dark eyes fixed upon the tall man across from him. On the other side of the desk, leaning against the wall next to the door with his arms crossed over his broad chest and a cigarette dangling from his lips, was Big Bob's enforcer, Gustov Schultz. The man he turned to when there was a "problem" needing to be solved.

"Is there any word on who's behind this?" he barked, stabbing his middle finger at the newspaper.

"Nein," the German said without moving a muscle. "No vun is villing to admit to knowing anyzing."

The answer, while expected, only served to ratchet up his anger. Following news of the first robbery reaching him, he'd ordered his trusted lieutenant to do whatever it took to find out who was playing such a dangerous game. Schultz, a man who usually got results, had hit a brick wall with his inquiries. Well, several of the lowlifes he'd questioned were actually the ones who hit the brick wall. Even as the crew continued to pull off such audacious break-ins in broad daylight, the former infantry officer from Munich knew it was only a matter of time before he was able to identify the men causing his boss such distress. When he did, Big Bob had given him a free hand in teaching them a lesson. If he felt these men were of the unteachable variety, then he was instructed to resolve the issue in a more permanent manner, as he'd done so many times before at the behest of his employer.

Hefting himself to his feet, Big Bob Franklin took a smoldering cigar from the crystal ashtray on his desk and jammed it between his teeth. With puffs of thick blue smoke trailing behind him, he paced the floor, looking like a massive steam locomotive…if a steam engine wore an expensive pinstriped suit and a white carnation in his lapel.

"What about the police? What do they know?"

Schultz scoffed. "Nussing. Zair useless. You've zaid zo yourzelf."

"But now that it's on the front page they're going to have to look into it. That pain-in-the-ass police commissioner must be apoplectic. He won't let this tarnish his reputation."

The German's forehead wrinkled. "Ap-o-plec-"

"Enraged. Furious," Bob explained off-handedly. He admired that Schulz was doing his damnedest to learn the language now that he was in America. But he wasn't in the mood to play teacher today.

"Ah. Like you," the German said, nodding his head up and down.

Big Bob Franklin slowly turned to look at him. "I'm more than *apoplectic*. Someone is out there upsetting the natural order of things. The order *I* have worked so carefully to instill in this town."

"Und, you are not getting your cut," Schultz pointed out distractedly, holding his cigarette in front of him, watching the smoke lazily drift toward the ceiling.

"*Und* I'm not getting my cut!" Franklin agreed, his voice thundering off the dark wood-paneled walls of his office.

Chapter Fifteen

After reassurances from Schultz that he would indeed be able to find the illusive crew and bring an end to their string of brazen robberies, Big Bob Franklin took a few minutes to compose himself before leaving his office and heading downstairs for the evening. After throwing back two snifters of the finest Scotch from across the Atlantic—having travelled a circuitous route to reach his lips due to the 18th Amendment, which introduced Prohibition to the United States—he was feeling more like his usual calm, collected self. He trusted that Schultz would not let him down, allowing him to focus on other aspects of his business. That's what he paid the German for, after all.

Standing in front of the large window behind his desk, looking down on East Chase Street below, Big Bob observed a nondescript truck turn into the alley beside the building. Following behind it was a long black sedan. Glancing at his pocket watch, he was pleased to see that the delivery was right on time. It was the week's shipment of whiskey. The crates on the truck, which had made the journey south from Canada over the border and continued on a secret path to the stockyard in Pennsylvania where his men had picked them up, would be unloaded and taken down to the cellar under the building. There, the bottles of booze would be unpacked and stored, ready to be uncorked and served at the Platinum Peacock, the crown jewel of Bob Franklin's empire.

The Peacock, as it was simply known, was one of the most popular entertainment spots in the city: a supper club where guests arrived for cocktails and casual conversation before dinner and the floor show began.

Once the show was concluded, the band played on so guests could dance well into the early hours of the next day if they desired. In Baltimore's high society, it was on the list of places to be seen at least once a week, if not more. It was also one of the best places to go in the city if you didn't care much for Prohibition. At the Peacock, one could enjoy a cocktail without fear of getting caught up in a raid by authorities out to enforce the wildly unpopular ban on alcohol. A ban anyone in law enforcement would admit had proved to do very little to stem the flow of liquor and its effects on the country. In fact, it wasn't uncommon to see a judge or city councilman sitting at a table lined with glasses of spirits. Big Bob welcomed everyone to his establishment.

Followed by Gustov Schulz, the boss descended the stairs to the lobby of the club where there was already a long line of patrons waiting to be seated. The Peacock was always jumping and rarely was there an empty table. But in the last few days, as the temperature rose, so did people's desire to spend the evening at the club. The reason for this was because Bob Franklin, in his infinite wisdom, had had mechanical air coolers installed. The same type of system as the ones that could be found in large theaters and movie houses. Not only could the denizens of Baltimore enjoy an evening of entertainment, fine dining, and the best bootleg and smuggled alcohol available, they could do it in a sanctuary from the blazing heatwave outside.

Tucked away in the heart of Baltimore's Mount Vernon neighborhood, the Platinum Peacock sat behind a nondescript door, around the corner from the entrance to an unassuming brick building that was constructed shortly after the smoke from the Civil War cleared. The only indication as to what sat behind the heavy steel door was a small carving depicting the club's namesake bird etched into the center panel.

Inside, money was of no concern when it came to making the Platinum Peacock the fanciest speakeasy in the city, lavishly decorated with plush velvet curtains, ornate chandeliers dripping with twinkling crystals, and mahogany paneling accompanying the original brick foundation of the building. The dim lighting cast a soft glow over the entire room, creating an atmosphere of secrecy and allure. The air was thick with the sweet scent of tobacco smoke and perfume, along with the faint hint of spirits being poured at the bar.

The bar itself was a work of art, crafted from polished oak and adorned with intricate carvings. Behind it, rows of gleaming liquor bottles stood like sentinels, offering a tantalizing array of illicit drinks. The bartenders, dressed in sharp suits, mix cocktails with skill and flair, their movements as smooth as the jazz music being played by the band sitting on the stage.

Seated at polished tables in large leather chairs, the club's clientele, a mix of the town's elite, as well as curious thrill-seekers, found themselves surrounded by a relaxed, carefree atmosphere as they sipped their forbidden beverages and enjoyed the company of their fellow revelers. The Peacock was *the* place in Baltimore where secrets were shared, deals were made, and memories created.

Shaking hands with several of the club's regulars, Big Bob made his way to the front of the line of those still waiting to enter. The maître d,' with his slicked-back hair and perfectly tailored tuxedo, stood behind the podium directing the lovely hostesses as to where guests were to be seated. When he saw his boss approaching, he dutifully stepped forward to personally accompany Big Bob to his usual table on the main floor directly in front of the stage.

There was more handshaking and back-slapping as the club's owner weaved his way through the rows of tables. A true cross-section of Baltimore could be found at the Peacock on any given night. Some of Big Bob's guests were there for the entertainment, while others, the food. But the majority were there for the fine booze the city's criminal kingpin was making available. And the liquor was already flowing freely when Big Bob took his seat like a king on his thrown. Surveying the room, he couldn't help but smile to himself. The buoyant atmosphere made it feel like this was the biggest party in town. In a sense, it was. When it all boiled down to it, though, as far as Bob Franklin was truly concerned, he was looking out at a sea of dollar signs.

Chapter Sixteen

As Big Bob Franklin settled into his seat, cigar in one hand and a glass of Scotch in the other, the evening unfolded with its usual elegance and fervor. The band played on, filling the air with melodies that mingled with the clinking of glasses and the hum of lively conversations. Gustov Schultz, sitting next to his boss, kept an eye out for anything that could disrupt the festivities.

Despite the air of celebration, a shadow lingered in the corner of Big Bob's mind. The recent string of robberies was extremely unsettling. He knew that Schultz was capable, but the crew they were up against seemed to always be one step ahead. Bob couldn't shake the feeling that there was more to this than met the eye.

Lost in thought, Bob didn't see the man approach his table until he slid into the seat across from him. The familiar face of Joe Dixon greeted him with a thin smile under his even thinner pencil mustache. Dixon was a regular at the Platinum Peacock, though his visits were purely for pleasure, not of a professional nature. Good for Bob Franklin, considering he was Baltimore Police Captain Joseph Dixon of the city's Western District.

"Evening, Bob," Dixon said. "Mind if I join you?"

"Of course, Joe. Always a pleasure," Bob replied.

As Dixon settled in, Bob couldn't help but feel a twinge of unease. Dixon was known for his sharp wit and keen observation skills, which is how he'd risen in the ranks so quickly, making him the department's youngest precinct captain. Unlike other younger members of the force, however, Dixon did not possess the same idealistic convictions. When Big Bob sent a representative to meet with him a couple years earlier, he was all too happy to accept the envelope stuffed with cash, sweeping it into his desk drawer without saying a word.

"So, Bob, heard about these robberies?" Dixon asked casually, taking a sip of his drink.

Bob nodded, his expression guarded. "Yes, unfortunate business."

"Any idea who's behind them?"

Cutting his eyes quickly toward Schultz, then back to the captain, he said, "Not yet. But I have full confidence we'll be able to learn that information in short order."

Dixon raised an eyebrow. "Of course. Gustov is on it, eh? You're a capable fella, my friend, but these mooks seem to be quite cunning. And you might be running out of time to catch them."

"How's that?" Bob asked, his eyes narrowing.

"Word is, Cranshaw's been put on the case."

Big Bob was well acquainted with the esteemed Lieutenant Cranshaw. Unflappable and rigidly principled, Cranshaw seemed to have made it a personal mission in life to be a constant thorn in his side and an increasing impediment to his organization. Unlike Joe Dixon, the detective had not taken to Bob's gracious overtures. After a thick envelope of greenbacks appeared on the detective's desk one morning, he had a messenger return it to the crime boss's extravagant apartment at the top of the Belvedere Hotel. When Bob opened the envelope, all the money he'd generously offered poured out, torn into hundreds of little pieces.

The thought of the righteous detective getting to the thieves before he did didn't sit well with Big Bob. But if Schultz found the news of his new competition troubling, he wasn't showing it. The German was just sitting there with a cigarette, tapping his fingers to the beat of the music the band was playing.

"Have you considered," Dixon began to ask, "that there might be more to these robberies?"

Bob paused, weighing his words carefully, trying to keep his growing frustration under control. "What do you mean by that, Joe?"

"I mean, Bob, these robberies may have a pattern to them. At least, this is what I've started hearing. They may not be random acts. Someone could be orchestrating the whole thing, someone with a plan," Dixon explained.

Bob felt his cheeks flush. Could it be possible? Was there a mastermind behind these crimes, pulling the strings from the shadows? He had to admit, it made sense. The precision and coordination of the robberies hinted at a higher intelligence at work. Someone with the steel to go up against the most powerful man in the city and not seem to be too concerned about it.

"Joe, I appreciate your insight. If what you say is true, then we may be dealing with a much bigger threat than we anticipated," Bob said, his voice low.

Dixon nodded, his gaze intense. "Exactly. I'll keep my ears to the ground, see what else I can dig up."

Bob clasped the captain's hand firmly. "Thank you, Joe. Your help is invaluable."

With a renewed sense of determination, Bob turned his attention back to the evening's revelry and prepared to watch the night's floor show. He was hoping for a few minutes when he would be able to forget about the storm that was building steam around him. And he always loved watching Clara's act. Her voice entranced him like none of the other showgirls' ever had. Part of the reason people came to the Peacock-other than the booze-was to see her perform. She was one of the best headliners who'd ever been featured at the Peacock. He saw her as one of his finest investments. Certainly one of his most attractive.

As if he was able to tell that his employer was ready to be carried away by the dulcet tones of the club's headliner, the band leader tapped his baton on the music stand, preparing the musicians for the next number. After counting them in, the drums began to roll as the lights dimmed. A growing anticipation quickly spread, culminating as a sultry figure glided from the shadows onto the stage. The woman's silhouette, illuminated from behind by the hazy purple glow of the stage lights, revealed a tall, curvaceous form draped in a shimmering gown. The band began to play as a spotlight sparked to life, revealing Clara Mowry. Her hair, a cascade of thick, black curls, framed a face cloaked in mystery. She took the microphone, her voice a velvet whisper that silenced the room. The band played softly behind her, a subtle rhythm that matched the beating of every heart in the audience. As she began to sing, her eyes seemed to pierce through the smoky haze, drawing each listener into her spell.

Chapter Seventeen

The entire club was captivated by Clara's performance. Her voice was a hypnotic melody that drifted through the room with each song. As she sang, her sparkling, violet eyes would scan the crowd, lingering on each face. Her simple gaze could effortlessly make a man blush, instantly raising his blood pressure. She very much enjoyed teasing the audience. Taking them right to the very edge with her seductive voice, only to leave them yearning for more. Clara was a master of her art, and she knew it.

Concluding her set, as she did each evening, with her rendition of Ben Bernie's "Sleepy Time Gal," Clara Mowry left the audience on their feet. She could still hear the applause as she made her way back to her dressing room, where she'd change out of one gown into another before returning to the dining room for a drink, and possibly some dancing if she found someone who took her fancy. For the most part, the club was filled with regulars tonight. But there'd been a couple of new faces she'd noticed. Faces that went along with fellas she'd like to learn a little more about.

The backstage area at the Peacock was a claustrophobic affair. There were just a few dressing rooms along a cramped hallway behind the stage and down the stairs. As the featured performer, Clara was lucky to have her own private room. The other two were crammed with the showgirls who would perform later in the evening or sometimes be brought on as backup singers for Clara. Each one of whom thought they had what it took to replace Clara, so she found herself weary of most of the girls. She tried to be as friendly as possible, but when most of them looked at her with daggers in their eyes, she preferred to keep to herself or spend time out with the swanky clientele.

A couple of the girls in their flapper dresses—the only two she really got along with—passed Clara on the narrow stairs. One asking, "Is it a good crowd out there tonight?"

"The juice joint's jumpin,'" Clara responded with a grin.

The other girl suddenly stopped at the top of the stairs and turned around, calling back to Clara. "I almost forgot. You've got company in your dressing room. They came in the back while you were on stage."

"Thanks, Lucy," Clara said.

Pushing past towers of crates lining the hall, Clara noticed one was filled with bottles of champagne. A pleasant surprise, she thought to herself. Knowing this wasn't where the hooch was normally stored, she felt no qualms about grabbing a bottle. She knew that Big Bob wouldn't mind. With her newfound bubbly in hand, Clara threw open the door to her dressing room and waltzed in like the star she was. A dramatic entrance indeed.

"Hello, boys." She already knew who to expect waiting for her.

Once or twice a week, the Alphabet Boys would stop by to see her. That's how they were known around the Peacock and other circles throughout the city on account of their names. Roy Abbott, Ernie Bernstein, and Lester "Mo" Conklin-Abbott, Bernstein, Conklin-A.B.C. The three hoods had formed something of a gang. At least, that's what they liked to think of themselves. Bob Franklin and his crew, on the other hand, didn't think too much about the guys. As long as they followed the rules and didn't cross Big Bob, they could call themselves whatever they liked. And on the rare occasion, Big Bob had a job that might require an expendable fall guy or two, he'd call on the Alphabet Boys and throw some work their way.

"Howya doin,' Doll?" Mo Conklin asked, jumping out of the chair at her make-up table and crossing the small dressing room to give Clara a hug. The two'd known each other a long time. And while Bernstein and Abbott both had the hots for the showgirl, Conklin had never once tried making a pass at her, always remaining the perfect gentleman in her presence.

"Just ducky," she answered, sitting down in the small wooden chair Conklin had left for her and throwing her long legs up on the make-up table. Her dress slid down, revealing a good portion of one of her stockinged legs. In the mirror, she could see Ernie eyeing her gams and thought he looked like he might burst. "Got a cigarette for me, Ernie?"

The scrawny little man nearly tripped over his own feet as he pulled a pack of smokes from his jacket pocket and tried to extract one for her. Clara wondered if this was how he was with all dames or just her. She always thought of him as a real pushover. She'd heard he had a temper, especially when things didn't go his way. But around Clara, he seemed to transform into a nervous, bumbling mess. Could there really be a temper in there? She doubted it.

"Sure thing, Clara," Ernie stammered, handing her a cigarette and lighting it for her.

Clara took a long drag, exhaling a puff of smoke towards the plaster ceiling. "So, what brings you boys by tonight? Big Bob got another job for you?" She directed the question pointedly toward Conklin, who was now leaning against the wall with his arms crossed.

"Not exactly," he answered with a sly smile. "Just thought we'd drop by and see if anyone has the skinny on the burglary crew that was in the paper today."

"And to see your second act," Roy Abbott offered. "You always put on a real good show."

Clara smiled, knowing that flattery was just part of the game with these boys. She took another drag of the cigarette as the room fell into silence.

Conklin sidled over and took a seat on the edge of the dressing table, his handsome features now glowing from the burning light bulbs around the mirror. "Have you heard anything? About the robberies?"

"You bet your buttons I have," she said before sending another plume of smoke into the air. "It's all some of the fellas around here can talk about. And from what I hear, Bob's furious, and Schultz is on the warpath."

"That kaiser-loving Kraut," Abbott scoffed from his corner of the room. It would only be Roy Abbott who could possibly get away with a remark like that because as big as Gustov Schultz was, Abbott was bigger. He wasn't the smartest guy on the street, but he had the size that could send a strong message.

Narrowing her eyes, Clara said, "He's already put a few guys through walls trying to find out who these schnooks are."

"So, nobody knows who they are?" Conklin asked, trying to sound as casual as possible.

Clara watched him shoot a look over to Bernstein who'd managed to finally compose himself, now eagerly following the conversation.

"That's right. Nobody knows who these palookas are. And I certainly wouldn't want to be them when Big Bob does find out."

Clara leaned back in her chair, taking a long drag of her cigarette as she watched the Alphabet Boys closely. She could tell that they were interested in more than just the gossip.

"Why the sudden interest in the burglaries, boys?" Clara asked, blowing a smoke ring in Abbott's direction. "You thinking of going into the detective business or something?"

Ernie Bernstein chuckled nervously, shifting his weight from side to side. "Nah, nothing like that, Clara. Just curious, is all."

Clara raised an eyebrow, not buying it for a second. These boys were up to something.

"Maybe if we figure out who these guys are," Abbott began, "Big Bob will offer a reward."

"Yeah. Show his gratitude. Like that," Bernstein added.

"Well, if you're looking for information, you've come to the wrong place," Clara said, stubbing out her cigarette in the ashtray on the table. "I may hear things around here, but I don't go spreading rumors. Not that there's any rumors to be spread. No one knows anything. And if they do, they aren't talking to the likes of me."

Mo Conklin stood, his expression serious. "We just thought that, maybe, you might have heard something that could help us out. That's all."

Clara studied the three men and smiled. "I promise, if I hear anything, I'll let you know."

With a wink and a smile, Conklin said, "That's all we can ask, Doll."

69

Chapter Eighteen

The Alphabet Boys said goodbye to Clara and left the dressing room, winding their way through the narrow corridors usually reserved for the staff of the Platinum Peacock. None of the men spoke, Bernstein and Abbott obediently following Mo Conklin as he led them out to the main dining room. Earlier, Conklin arranged for a table for them to see the second show. With the crowd, however, all that could be spared for three relative nobodies was a small table in the back corner of the dining room. That was fine with the boys. They were there to have a couple drinks and hear Clara sing. It didn't matter if they weren't seated down front, they were still in the room with all the glitz and glamor.

Scanning the crowd, Conklin saw Bob Franklin seated at his usual table at the front of the stage. A couple of dames were seated on either side of the big man. But even from this distance, Conklin could tell Big Bob wasn't paying much attention to his hotsy-totsy companions. He looked distracted. He didn't appear to be enjoying himself or the jovial atmosphere surrounding him. Normally, the club owner would be circulating around the room, greeting the diners and basking in their adoration. Tonight, he looked sullen and absorbed by his inner thoughts.

Conklin smiled. He knew the robberies must be getting to him. He couldn't think of the last time anyone dared to challenge the boss's authority in such a public way. Bob Franklin was not the type of person anyone wanted to cross. On purpose or by accident. So, to see a gang he had no control over operating right under his nose was devastating for his reputation.

Word on the street was that no one knew who the crew was. Whether they were locals taking their lives in their own hands, or new to town and didn't know they were taking their lives in their own hands, it was hard to believe there was anyone capable of pulling off such daring burglaries who didn't know Big Bob Franklin ran Baltimore.

Conklin's smile grew even wider as he thought about it.

"What ya smilin' at, Mo?" Abbott asked, putting his glass down after taking a slug of his whiskey.

"Just thinking, Roy. That's all. Look at all the stones in this place. That woman's necklace alone must be worth a couple grand."

"You want me to go get a closer look?" Bernstein asked, starting to push himself to his feet.

Conklin put a firm hand on his friend's arm and eased him back into his seat. "No, Ernie. You know how it works. Cam picks the marks. And after I talk to Cam tonight, then we'll know who's next. Just be patient, boys."

"Is Cam here?" Abbott asked, looking around at the swanky assemblage.

"Uh-huh," Conklin confirmed. He drained his glass and signaled the waiter to bring another.

"I still don't understand why Roy and I can't meet Cam."

"Safety," Mo said without missing a beat. "I'm the only connection to Cam, which means I'm also the only connection to you two goons. If anything ever goes wrong, I'm the only one who can put the pieces together so you're all protected."

For the briefest moment, Bernstein thought that also meant Mo was the only one who could finger *all of them* if he got pinched by the cops. But he quickly dismissed the idea. There was no one he trusted more than Conklin. His friend would never rat them out. Not a chance. The only person he trusted more than Conklin was Roy Abbott.

He and Roy grew up together in one of the not-so-nice neighborhoods of Baltimore. The Abbotts lived in the apartment across the hall from the Bernsteins and their mothers had gotten to be friends. Neither family had much money, but they survived. The experience was the same for so many families in the city. The fathers would be up and out early, heading off to a long day of work. The mothers would take care of the household chores while the kids went to school. Not that education was all that important a part of the boys' early lives.

The most valuable lessons they learned came from the streets. But as a small Jewish kid from a poor family, Ernie Bernstein was a constant target for the bigger boys. He was always being picked on and had no way to defend himself other than his wits. Unfortunately, his wits were no match for the other kids' fists. Roy, however, had always been big for his age, and that alone gained him some deference from the other kids. That and not being afraid to throw a punch that could knock the unlucky recipient on his ass. Since the families were friends, Abbott became Bernstein's protector. And once the bullies knew that little Ernie was not to be messed with, a long-lasting bond formed.

With the path that they were on, it would have been inevitable for them to end up as menial laborers, part of the city's forgotten working class, just like their fathers. But then, one night, while the two were drinking in one of the many out-of-the-way gin mills that had popped up since the government decided alcohol was the root of all evil, they'd had the good fortune to cross paths with Lester "Mo" Conklin who was sitting at the other end of the bar acting like he owned the joint. By the end of the evening, the three had thrown back so much bootleg hooch they could barely stand.

They were in such a poor state that a pair of cops who'd stopped for a cup of coffee at a twenty-four-hour greasy spoon saw them stumbling down the street and were getting ready to run them all in. Until Conklin, just as soused as his new friends, made up the most fantastic story and convinced the police to let them go on their way. That's when Roy and Ernie realized Mo had a silver tongue. He performed the most amazing verbal song and dance either of the hoods had ever seen.

With Abbott's muscle, Bernstein's brains, and Conklin's charismatic charm, the three thought they might be able to work together to better their collective situation. As word of the Alphabet Boys' services spread among Big Bob's underlings, they started picking up some of the jobs no one else was interested in. Running numbers, collecting outstanding debts, the kind of thing that could get a fella's hands dirty. They were still the low men on the totem pole, but they'd gotten their foot in the door to Franklin's operation, and it was all part of a plan.

"Ya think we may want to lay low for a few days?" Bernstein asked, lighting a fresh cigarette. "I mean, with the story in the paper and all."

"I know what you mean," Conklin answered, giving him a look that said to lower his voice. "I'll see what Cam says, and then…then we'll decide what to do. But tomorrow morning, I'm going to take the goods over to Rafferty and unload them. That'll give us some cabbage to play with for a while."

Bernstein was fidgeting with his lighter. "If we're gonna have the fuzz on us now, Mo—"

"Would you keep your voice down, you schnook?"

Putting his lighter back in his pocket, he leaned in and lowered his voice. "Sorry, Mo."

Conklin was about to say something when a shadow spilled across the table. The light from the chandeliers was completely eclipsed by the hulking form of Gustov Schultz standing in front of them. A sour expression played across the German's face as he warily eyed the Alphabet Boys.

"Und vut are you boyz doing here? I don't believe za boss has any verk for you tonight."

"Relax, Schultzy," Conklin said with a smile. "Tonight, we're just paying customers here for the late show. That's all."

Not paying much attention to what Conklin was saying, the big man's iron-cold gaze settled on Ernie Bernstein, who quickly began nervously shifting from side to side in his seat. He was about to say something when one of the girls who'd been sitting with Big Bob appeared at his side and whispered that Franklin was looking for him. Throwing one last look around the table, Schultz grunted, then turned and walked away. Big Bob's girl was right behind him. Conklin admired her curves as he watched her sashay back to her table.

"You might not wanna let Clara catch you looking at another dame like that," Abbott said. He was grinning like a schoolboy.

"Enough of that. You know Clara and I have known each other a long time. It's not like that."

"But I bet it could be," he continued, baiting his friend.

"Knock it off, Roy."

"Yeah. Knock it off, Roy. You heard him," Bernstein said.

Abbott put his hands up in surrender. "Okay. Okay. I was just goofing with ya."

"No. It's alright," Conklin admitted. "I just didn't like the way that Kraut was looking at us, is all."

"You don't think he's on to us, do you?" Bernstein asked, starting to get worked up again.

"Nah. You heard what Clara said," Conklin reminded him, trying to sound confident. "They don't know who's pulling the jobs. We just need to be careful."

At that moment, from across the dining room, Schultz looked back at the Alphabet Boys' table, his eyes locking on Conklin's. They stared at each other for what felt like an eternity before the corner of the German's mouth curled into a smirk, and he finally looked away. That's when Mo realized he'd been holding his breath. Letting it out slowly, he reached into his pocket for his pack of cigarettes, suddenly desperate for a smoke.

CHAPTER Nineteen

1985...

Ben pulled the unmarked Crown Vic to the curb along Richmond Street in the upscale neighborhood of Harper's Mill. Tudor-style mini-mansions, as Ben thought of them, lined the street. More than a century newer than the grand manor homes that lined Jefferson Park, this was a development still under construction. Richmond and the two streets on either side of it were just the first phase in the plan. A plan that would culminate with one hundred, three thousand plus square foot homes on the northern edge of Parker City.

As the downtown was still struggling to pull itself out of the desolate situation it had found itself in for so many years, the outer regions of the city were quickly growing. And a neighborhood like Harper's Mill brought money into the city.

"Nice neighborhood," Ben observed, looking over the lush green lawns and brightly colored flower beds.

"Except for all the construction equipment," Tommy pointed out.

"But they're still building."

"Yeah, but if I were driving home to one of these houses, I'd hate to have to go through all the dirt and building materials piled up along the road. Here's something I'm curious about, though. Look at that grass. It's perfect. When have you been in any development under construction of any kind and seen grass like that? I tell you, these rich people know what they're doing. I really need to find a rich woman to—"

"Marry?"

"Adopt me!"

Ben laughed. Taking out his notebook, he double-checked the address of the B&E. Not that there was any question as to which of the houses on the street they were heading for. All they needed to do was look for the house with the PCPD squad car parked in the driveway.

Pulling his sports coat on as the two detectives started up the walkway to the front door, Tommy clarified, "The concern here is that whoever's been pulling the burglaries over in Wakeville has decided to move south into Parker City. I guess it would be a natural progression to move on to bigger places in a wealthier neighborhood. But the actual distance between here and Wakeville is still a few miles. Sort of takes them out of their comfort zone, doesn't it?"

"It's possible this break-in has nothing to do with what's going on in Wakeville," Ben said. "I agree with you. If it's just a bunch of local kids, I doubt they are going to leave their hometown. That's what the Sheriff's Department thinks, at any rate. But…you never know. Which is why we're here."

"Who'd they say got the call?" Tommy asked, ringing the doorbell.

"Thompson."

"Thank God it isn't LuCoco. I've actually gone a whole week without seeing his fat—"

"Hello." Ben cut his partner off as the front door swung open. A man Ben guessed to be in his late fifties or early sixties stood in the doorway. "I'm Detective Winters. This is my partner, Detective Mason. We received a call about a possible break-in."

"Yes. Come in. Please," the man said, stepping aside for the detectives to enter the foyer. "We're through here."

He led Ben and Tommy through the entry and down a short hallway. Taking in what they could before they started asking questions, Ben and Tommy found the home to be subtly decorated with a cream and tan toned wallpaper and some landscapes hanging on the walls, no bright colors or abstract artwork. At the end of the hall was a large kitchen with windows looking out on the backyard. All of the appliances were new and state of the art, including, Ben noted, the expensive microwave oven sitting on the counter. Off the kitchen, they stepped into the dining room where they found Officer Neil Thompson speaking with a woman Ben assumed to be the wife of the man who answered the door.

"Sergeant," Thompson said, standing as Ben walked into the room. "Detective." He nodded to Tommy.

Ben quickly returned Thompson's greeting, then introduced himself and Tommy again.

"This is Millie and James Hubbard," Thompson noted.

"You can call me Jim," the man said, extending his hand to Ben.

"Jim Hubbard," Tommy repeated. "As in Jim Hubbard Autos?"

The recognition caused the man to beam with pride. "One and the same. At Hubbard Autos, we have the best cars in town, so come on down."

Ben thought the name sounded familiar but couldn't place it at first. Now, he recognized the man from the billboard…and the annoying, rhyming tagline. It must have done the trick, though. Hubbard Autos was the largest car dealership in Parker and its namesake was something of a local celebrity because he appeared in all the company's advertisements.

"Are either of you boys in the market for a car?" the salesman asked with an eagerness in his voice.

"Jim!" his wife scalded. "They are the police! We've been robbed. Can you stop selling long enough to let them do their jobs?"

"Sorry." Hubbard gave Ben and Tommy a sheepish look. "Force of habit."

"Understandable," Ben said, for no other reason than he couldn't think of a better way to respond. "As I said, we're here because you reported a break-in."

"Yes," Millie Hubbard said, taking control of the conversation, at the same time giving her husband a stern look. "Jim and I were away yesterday."

"My sister's birthday," Jim interjected.

"When we got home, we found the back door open, one of the panes of glass was smashed."

"We didn't touch anything," her husband quickly added. "Called you lot right away, and they sent this nice young man right over."

"Have you found that anything's been taken?" Ben asked.

"Yes," Jim said, "the safe in my study."

"They broke into your safe?" Ben said, jotting some notes in his notebook.

"No. They stole the whole safe."

There was a momentary pause as Ben looked to his partner, who simply shrugged and shook his head.

"Okay. Other than the…safe, was anything else taken?"

"Not that we can tell at this point," Millie answered, folding her arms over her chest. "We haven't had a chance to look through everything, but I can tell you all of my jewelry is still upstairs. They didn't take any of that. I looked in my jewelry box right away. I have some family heirlooms in there."

"They didn't touch my dealership awards either," Jim Hubbard added, only to receive another glare from his wife. "What? They're valuable."

"And all of your electronics are still here?" Tommy asked, quickly changing the subject before they had a murder on their hands as well as a B&E. After reading the reports from the Sheriff's Department Ben had given him, he knew those were the items that the Wakeville robbers seemed to be most interested in.

"We have three televisions. Each one with a video recorder," Jim Hubbard said proudly. "They weren't touched."

Ben made another note.

"Would you show us your study where you kept the safe, please?"

"This way, detectives," Jim said, leading them out of the dining room, back through the kitchen and foyer, and along another short hallway.

The study was a comfortable yet elegantly decorated room with a desk, credenza, a couple of bookcases, and one of the house's three televisions set up in the corner.

"That's a twenty-seven inch right there," Hubbard acknowledged proudly, seeing Ben examining the television set.

"Must have cost a pretty penny," Tommy said.

"Worth *every penny*, Detective." Then, turning back to Ben, he said, "I don't bring much work home with me these days, but when I do, this is where I do it. The safe was over here in this little closet."

Opening the door, Ben observed a standard closet, except there were two file cabinets with an empty space between them. From the indentation on the carpet, it was clear that was where the safe once sat. It wasn't a large safe, which explained how it was the burglars could actually steal it. When Hubbard said the safe was stolen, all Ben could imagine was a giant safe being ripped right out of the wall like in a cartoon. Even so, a safe a few feet square wasn't all that light or easy to move.

"What was it you kept in the safe, Mr. Hubbard?" Ben asked as he knelt down to look at the void between the filing cabinets.

"Some personal papers. Insurance documents. Our wills."

"And cash," Millie said from the doorway. "Jim liked to keep cash around so we didn't have to use the credit card."

"I guess I'm just old-fashioned that way."

"How much money did you keep on hand?" Tommy asked.

"About ten thousand dollars."

Tommy involuntarily let out a little whistle.

"Did many people know you kept that kind of money in the house?" Ben asked, standing up and looking around the room to see if anything else looked as if it had been disturbed.

"Our kids. Some of the guys at the dealership, probably." Jim shrugged.

"The way Jim flashes money around, people probably just figured we kept money in the house." Millie's words were pointed. Both Ben and Tommy felt this might have been the subject of some heated discussions between the two.

Thinking for a moment, Ben turned to Tommy and said, "Alright, why don't you take a look around in here? See if anything stands out, then give CSU a call and get them over here to do their thing. If we get lucky, we'll find some fingerprints that don't belong. We're going to want to make sure the Sheriff's Department gets copies of everything. We'll see if this may have anything to do with what's been happening in Wakeville.

"While you're doing that," Ben continued, "Officer Thompson and I will take a look at the back door. I'd like to see how they got in."

"Your wish is my command," Tommy said, already beginning a cursory examination of the study.

Chapter Twenty

Neil Thompson was just a few years younger than Ben and Tommy, and he'd already proven himself to be one of the best officers the Parker City Police Department had on patrol. He was smart, intuitive, and willing to learn. He wasn't part of the department's old guard. He wasn't afraid to adapt and adopt new policing techniques. Officer Thompson, and the other younger officers like him, were going to be the ones to help Ben and Chief Brent modernize the entire force. And, if plans were approved and Ben was able to expand the Detective Squad, Thompson was at the top of his list to join the team.

"What do you think?" Ben asked Thompson as they examined the backdoor to the house, the probable entry point for the robbers. Judging by the broken glass.

"I looked around and didn't see anywhere else they could have gotten in. All the other doors and windows are intact. So, this has to be the spot. They smashed the glass, reached in, and flipped the lock. Then walked right in," Thompson speculated.

"As for the burglary itself?"

Thompson paused for a moment, thinking through what he'd been able to observe since arriving, then said, "Well, the Hubbards seem genuinely upset. Though he seems to be handling it better. Especially for just losing ten thousand dollars. But who steals a whole safe?"

"That is new. Never seen that before," Ben agreed.

"I don't think they're trying to pull anything," Thompson continued. "But I am a little confused about the broken glass."

"What about it?" Ben looked at the shards scattered on the ground.

"Well, there's pieces inside and outside. If someone was standing outside and broke the glass so they could reach in and unlock the door," he said, demonstrating, "the glass should all be on the inside."

"Ah," Ben said, now understanding what he was getting at. "Popular misconception. When a pane of glass is broken, it can go in *any* direction. It doesn't all just go one way. When they try and prove someone broke a glass from the inside to make it look like a break-in, like on TV, that isn't entirely accurate. A little bit of dramatic license."

"You mean everything on TV isn't true?" Thompson asked with a smile.

Ben laughed. "Alright, smart-ass. Don't start taking after Tommy. But it was still a good observation."

"It's interesting that they only took the safe, though. They could have taken anything, but they took the heaviest, most difficult item. That just doesn't make sense. How would they know that there was actually anything of value in it? It could have just been papers. What? They just happened to get lucky? I don't buy that." Thompson was looking around the little patio area where they were standing to see if there was anything else of note.

"Good point," Ben said. "Okay, here's what we're going to do. We're going to talk to the Hubbards again. Separately. We'll start at the beginning. Ask them all the same questions, plus any more we've come up with. See if they tell us the same things they did the first time. And see what each of them says was kept in the safe and who knew it was there. My gut says this was a real break-in, but because only the safe was taken, I think the robbers might have known what they were looking for."

"Plus," Thompson added, "to steal a safe, you have to *know* you're going to be able to get into it. Either they somehow know the combination, or they're safecrackers."

"So…did one of the Hubbards say something to someone about the safe and what they kept in it?" Ben raised his eyebrows and shrugged.

"Do you think this has anything to do with the Wakeville burglaries?"

Ben exhaled and looked back down at the broken glass at his feet. Thinking through everything he'd read in the bulletins from the sheriff and comparing it with what he'd already seen at the Hubbards' house, he was inclined to think this was an "isolated incident" not connected to the other robberies. But he certainly wasn't willing to rule anything out just yet.

"We're going to keep our minds open about that," he finally answered. "But at first glance, the MOs don't line up. We need to see what CSU says."

The Crime Scene Unit's findings would be key. If they found a print from someone who shouldn't have been in the Hubbards' house, then there was a chance the investigation could get wrapped up fairly quickly. If they didn't find anything useful that pointed the detectives in the right direction, then they'd have to regroup and find a new way of solving the case. Short of an outright confession-which in itself could be fake and/or misleading-forensic evidence was the key to solving any case.

Would CSU find anything to tie this robbery to the ones in Wakeville? Ben's gut was telling him they wouldn't. But he couldn't be sure. Making an assumption like that would close off possible avenues of inquiry. Right now, as they were just beginning the investigation, all possibilities needed to remain on the table.

Ben was getting ready to head back into the house when an electronic beeping began sounding. He and Thompson looked around to see where it was coming from. Then Ben remembered and reached into his jacket pocket and pulled out a new pager that he'd forgotten all about.

"I got this last week," he said, holding it up to look at the number on the little digital screen. "Captain Nelson figured with this, if I wasn't near a radio, Dispatch could still get in contact with me."

"Doesn't that mean you're on call twenty-four-seven now?"

Ben chuckled. "I always was. Now, it's just easier for them to find me. I'm going to go ask if I can borrow their phone and make a call."

"You can use the one here in the kitchen, Detective." Millie Hubbard was standing just inside the doorway.

"Thank you," Ben said as she pointed toward the telephone hanging on the wall next to the refrigerator.

Punching in the numbers from the pager, he recognized it as one of the lines into the Dispatch office. Waiting for someone to answer, Ben watched as Millie began brewing a pot of coffee. The minute the smell of the hot, fresh caffeine filled the air, Ben knew he needed a pick-me-up. He hadn't had any coffee since before Natalie…distracted him that morning.

"Parker City Police Dispatch, how may I assist you?" Her southern accent was heavy today.

"Shirley, it's Ben. You paged me. What's up?"

"You aren't gonna believe this, sugar. I've got another B&E call for you."

"Are you serious?"

"As a heart attack, honey. There's a difference with this one, though."

"What would that be?" Ben asked, preparing himself.

"It comes with a body."

Chapter Twenty-One

As Ben scribbled the address of the second break-in down in his notebook, he realized it was only one street away. The second call had also come from the Harper's Mill neighborhood. And apparently, this time, the robbers had left behind a dead body. Ben felt a knot begin to form in the pit of his stomach. He was already unhappy with the possibility Wakeville's troubles had boiled over into his jurisdiction. But now, if these were the same robbers and they'd not only expanded their territory but turned violent, it was a whole new ballgame.

Ben quickly reminded himself he couldn't allow himself to jump to any conclusions. He and Tommy needed to examine each incident separately until there was evidence to connect them. And in order of importance, a dead body trumped a B&E any day.

Turning to Officer Thompson, he relayed his conversation with Shirley. He kept his voice low because after starting the coffee, Millie had wandered into a different room and he didn't want her returning and overhearing their conversation. As he spoke, the young patrolman remained silent, nodding his head. He could read Ben's mind and knew exactly what he was thinking and the concerns he had.

"Tommy's going to come with me," Ben said, "so I want you to take over here. Do exactly what we were just talking about outside. Are you alright with that?"

"Yes, sir."

"If you want help, I can have someone sent out."

"I think I have it covered. But if I need help, I'll make the call."

Ben left the kitchen feeling confident in leaving Thompson to handle the scene. He needed to find Tommy, which he did, in the foyer speaking with the Hubbards. Giving Tommy a silent nod to step outside, Ben turned to the homeowners and said, "We've just had another call that may relate to your break-in. Detective Mason and I are going to investigate that, and Officer Thompson will be staying here to speak with you further and work with the Crime Scene Unit.

"Detective Mason or I will check in with you again once we've been able to review everything. In the meantime, if you have any questions, you can call the PCPD and ask to speak with either of us.

"Officer Thompson will take it from here," Ben said, gesturing to the patrolman standing behind the Hubbards.

"Mr. Hubbard, Mrs. Hubbard, if I could get you to join me in the kitchen until CSU arrives," Thompson said with a smile.

"Thanks, Neil," Ben said as he followed Tommy out the front door.

As they were climbing into the car, Tommy ran a finger over his mustache. Ben knew that meant his friend was thinking.

"What's on your mind?"

Tommy shrugged. "I'm just waiting to hear exactly how our day is about to get worse." Then he pulled a pack of cigarettes out of his pocket. He figured he might as well get a smoke in while he could. As was his custom, he offered one to Ben, who, as was his custom, declined, having never smoked a day in his life. Tommy just figured one day he'd give in.

Easing the Crown Vic away from the curb, Ben explained the situation. "There's been another B&E."

"Where?"

"One street over."

"Crap," Tommy said between puffs.

"It gets worse."

"Of course it does. What did they take?"

Giving his partner a sideways glance as he made the turn onto Annapolis Way, Ben said, "Well…. It isn't necessarily what they took. It's more what they left behind."

"Do I even want to know what that means?"

"There's a dead body."

"I guess it could be worse."

"How's that?" Ben asked.

"There could be—" Tommy began.

"—two dead bodies," they finished in unison.

Chapter Twenty-Two

The house at 1120 Annapolis Way, being a part of the same upscale neighborhood built by the same builder, looked very similar to the Hubbards.' It was a mini-mansion sitting on a residential street alongside other mini-mansions. On what had turned into a beautiful spring day, with a bright blue sky overhead and a gentle breeze rustling through the trees, the view Ben saw through the windshield could easily have graced the cover of a real estate brochure. That is, if the two Parker City Police cruisers weren't sitting in front of the house.

"I guess this is the place," Tommy said, tossing his cigarette butt into the street as he stepped out of the car. "Did Shirley say who caught the call?"

"No. She didn't. But if it's LuCoco, you need to play nice. I hear he might finally be ready to put in his papers."

"Buck might retire? He might actually pull the pin? The hell you say."

"Just a rumor I heard," Ben replied as the two detectives reached the front door.

"Well, it's long overdue, if you ask me. He should have been put out to pasture years ago."

Tommy's dislike of Buck LuCoco was well known throughout the department. Not that Ben was any fonder of him, he was just much less vocal about his issues with the veteran patrol officer. LuCoco was one of the last of the good ole boys. A relic of the days when "throwing the book" at a person meant *literally* hitting them with a telephone book to get them to talk.

Through the decorative etched glass window that filled the center of the oversized door, they could only see the back of a uniformed officer standing in the entryway. Ben gave a couple quick knocks and watched as the officer turned and opened the door. As his large frame filled the window, Ben already knew who would be standing on the other side of the door when it opened.

"Karma's a bitch," Tommy said when he saw Officer LuCoco standing there, his shirt buttons at the point of becoming deadly projectiles they were straining so much against his large stomach.

"How's that?" LuCoco asked.

"Sorry. It's nothing," Tommy sighed. "Ben and I were just talking about…. It doesn't matter."

"Whatever. It's good you're here now because we got a dead body inside," LuCoco announced matter-of-factly.

"That's what we were told," Ben said, steering the conversation back on track.

"And once again, there's a dead body, and you're here," Tommy pointed out.

It had become somewhat coincidental that whenever a body turned up in Parker City over the last several years, Buck LuCoco was the patrol officer first on the scene. At one point, Tommy—only half jokingly—suggested they should open an investigation into him. To which Ben pointed out that there were usually only about fifteen officers on patrol at any one time in the city, so the odds of LuCoco showing up were pretty good. Especially considering he was a senior patrolman.

"Lucky me," LuCoco said, wiping his sweaty brow with a wrinkled handkerchief. "I wasn't even supposed to be on duty today, but I switched with Dickerson. He's gonna owe me for this. No good deed goes unpunished, I tell ya."

"Why don't you just tell us what you've got," Ben said, poised to get on with it.

"I'm just the backup on this one," LuCoco admitted. "Spurrier caught the call and was first on the scene. He's down the hall there with the housekeeper." He motioned with his chin. "I figure this place is gonna be crawling with people pretty soon, so I'm starting the log. You're officially the third and fourth entries to the scene."

Tommy gave Ben a quick glance. It was fleeting, but Ben read it perfectly. They were both surprised that LuCoco had taken the initiative and done something helpful without being instructed to.

"I also put in a call for CSU," LuCoco added as Ben and Tommy were leaving the foyer to find Officer Spurrier. Both detectives stopped in their tracks.

"It sounds like you've got everything under control," Ben said, hoping he didn't sound as stunned as he felt. He was the first to give everyone the benefit of the doubt, but over the years, he'd come to expect very little from LuCoco. This was all very disconcerting.

When they were out of earshot, Tommy said, "So, what? Now that he's retiring, he decides to be a useful member of the department? Unbelievable."

"Let's not look a gift horse in the mouth," Ben suggested as they stepped into the kitchen, where they found Officer Brian Spurrier sitting at a small dinette table along with a middle-aged woman sobbing into a bright pink handkerchief.

"Detectives," Spurrier said when he saw them. Getting to his feet, he walked over to Ben and quietly said, "This is Liliana Rey. She was the victim's housekeeper. Comes in two or three times a week to clean. She found the body when she got here today."

"Did you have a chance to look around?"

"Just real quick. The body's in the living room. There's a set of doors out to the back patio in there. The glass is smashed on one of them. Looks like that's how they got in."

Ben looked to Tommy, who acknowledged with a nod that it sounded similar to what happened at the Hubbards.' But in that instance, they were thinking the robbers broke in specifically to steal the safe. If the same people were behind this one as well, what were they after here? And was it worth killing for?

"Did you examine the body?" Ben asked.

"Only visually. I didn't touch anything. With the position of the body, I could only see part of her face. It looks like there could be bruising."

"Any blood?" Tommy asked.

"None that I can see. But there is a statue or something on the floor next to her. She could have been hit with it."

Ben turned to his partner. "Why don't you try to calm Liliana down and see what you can get from her? I'll take a look at the living room."

"You always get the easy jobs," Tommy protested.

Ben raised an eyebrow and shook his head.

As he followed Spurrier into the living room, he asked if he'd gotten an ID on the victim yet, to which the officer responded, "I was barely able to get the housekeeper's, and how she was connected to the victim, she was so out of it. When I asked who it was she worked for, she just started crying hysterically. I'm guessing they were close."

"Okay. Then we still need an ID," Ben said, stepping into the living room, not seeing the body as it obscured the sofa.

But he did see the doors Spurrier suggested to be the robbers/possible killers' entry point. It was a large set of French doors that let in all the afternoon sun. While he would have usually examined the body first, something about them caught his attention. The majority of the broken pieces of glass appeared to be on the outside, lying scattered on the patio. He thought it interesting, considering the conversation he'd just had with Neil Thompson regarding the directionality of broken glass. While there were pieces lying inside on the hardwood floors, there were a lot more on the outside of the door. Ben wasn't entirely certain why, but that bothered him. He made a mental note to check with the forensic guys about that. He wanted to make sure what he'd said about glass going both ways was accurate. If not, well…that could put things in a different light.

Turning, he saw Spurrier kneeling on the other side of the sofa, just his head visible above the white, overstuffed cushions. Ben walked around to join him, then froze.

"Like I said," Spurrier began, "we don't have an ID yet. I haven't had a chance to look around for a purse or wallet or anything. I was waiting for you to get here."

Ben closed his eyes and pinched the bridge of his nose, a numb sensation running through his body. "I actually know who she is," he said.

At his feet, Clara Daschle wore the same purple, *Dynasty*-esque dress she was wearing the night before at the Harlequin reception when he'd met her.

Chapter Twenty-Three

1927…

Lester "Mo" Conklin lit a cigarette as he stepped into the dimly lit alley behind the Platinum Peacock. He figured that after the run-in with Gustov Schultz, Big Bob's Bavarian muscle, inside the club earlier in the evening, it was best to sneak out the back after meeting up with Cam to discuss the Alphabet Boys' next move. Standing there with the wisps of smoke disappearing into the damp night air, Conklin was confident no one knew he, along with Roy Abbott and Ernie Bernstein, were the guys pulling the jobs up in Guilford. How could they? To everyone who mattered in the seedy Baltimore underworld, the Alphabet Boys were just low men on the totem pole in Big Bob's organization. No one thought they would have the brains or the nerve to go up against the powerful crime boss. It was a reputation Conklin had been working hard to cultivate over the last few weeks. He wanted him and his boys to be seen as just another bunch of gofers for Bob Franklin. Happy to pick up whatever scraps of work were thrown their way.

There was no question they'd been given some crap work. Mo was certain Schultz was the one keeping his thumb on them. For what reason, he didn't know. If the German simply didn't like how charming and charismatic he could be, he couldn't help that. The Krout was a cold fish as far as he was concerned. Big and brooding. Conklin figured oil and water just didn't mix. But he thought there could be something else to it. Not that he'd bring it up, but he wondered if it had something to do with Ernie being a part of the gang. He'd heard stories about some of the things happening over in Germany, with a certain part of the population turning a dubious eye on their Jewish neighbors. Conklin had no idea if Schultz was a follower of that new Hitler fellow who was causing such a fuss. But whenever Schultz and Bernstein were in a room together, he could definitely feel the tension.

An even more convincing reason he was confident that no one knew they were the culprits was that they were still breathing. If Schultz even suspected they were the guys he was looking for, they would have been yanked off the street and taken to one of the numerous locations where the big guy liked to have "discussions" with people who were causing problems. So far, they still possessed all their fingers and hadn't been beaten to bloody pulps. All very good signs as far as Mo was concerned.

Taking a moment to let the much-needed nicotine work its way into his system, he wondered if the air was actually beginning to cool or if it was just his imagination. The heat never really bothered him, but even he was willing to admit the recent heatwave was brutal. But he also knew it provided some cover for the robberies. Like everyone else in the city, the heat was slowing the cops down.

After the last robbery, he'd watched from across the street as the city's police lumbered around, spending more time mopping their brows and hunting for some shade than investigating the scene. That was, until that police detective showed up and made everyone hop-to. According to the article Conklin read in the paper that morning, it was a Lieutenant Cranshaw who was now in charge of finding out who was behind the trouble in north Baltimore.

Up until the robbery the day before, no one had gotten hurt. Sure, the chloroform may have left their victims with a headache and a dry mouth, but the maid at the house on St. Paul was the first person to die. That hadn't been part of the plan. They were strictly an in-and-out crew. Push their way in, knock out anyone who was there, grab the most valuable items that were the easiest to get their hands on, and then be out the door in just a few minutes. Simple. The first three jobs went like clockwork. Even the last robbery appeared to go according to plan. It wasn't until he watched the coroner's men carry the body out of the house covered in a white sheet that Conklin knew anyone was dead. He'd read the details, like the rest of Baltimore, in the paper.

But the old lady's death was an accident, and there wasn't anything he could do about it. Nor was he going to allow it to interfere with future plans. Though, he did have to acknowledge it drew unwanted attention and was going to put potential future targets on guard.

Both Bernstein and Abbott suggested laying low for a little while when they learned of the death that morning. They were afraid it would spur the police to pour all the resources they had available into tracking them down. But Conklin wasn't concerned. Even with the police taking a closer look at the robberies, he knew they'd still be falling all over themselves.

No, he was certain, if there was anyone they needed to be concerned about, it was Gustov Schultz. He didn't have to play by the same rules the police did. So, if he discovered it was the Alphabet Boys behind the robberies, they were as good as dead. Schultz would make sure anyone challenging Big Bob was taught a lesson. One that would also serve as a warning to anyone else thick enough to try and undermine Bob Franklin on his own turf.

Conklin shuddered to think what Schultz might do to them. He'd only heard stories of what the guy did to people who crossed him or Big Bob. The lucky ones were found floating in the Chesapeake Bay with a bullet in the back of their head. The rest...wished they'd gotten off so easy.

The clatter of trashcans suddenly drew his attention toward the rear of the alley. It was far too dark back there between the buildings to tell if there was someone in the alley with him, but something had made the noise. Surprising himself at how jumpy he was feeling, Conklin let out a sigh of relief when a tabby cat sauntered out of the shadows, not even bothering to look in his direction as it padded its way by.

"Stupid cat," he muttered, flicking the butt of his cigarette at its mangy behind. Too much force behind it, the spent cig arched over the feline, landing directly in its path. Mo would have sworn to anyone who would listen that the animal stopped, turned its head toward him, and gave him a dirty look before continuing on its way.

"I like dogs better anyway," he announced to the empty alleyway, feeling a bit foolish. Then, lighting another cigarette, he started for home, where he'd meet back up with Ernie and Roy so they could discuss what was next for the Alphabet Boys.

Chapter Twenty-Four

Although he could have easily walked from the Platinum Peacock to the apartment house where he shared a pair of rooms with Ernie and Roy, the oppressive heat would have been too much to bear, even at the late hour. He'd been sadly mistaken when he thought the heatwave might be relenting. The minute he stepped from the alley, he realized just how wrong he'd been. Instead of turning himself into a sweaty mess from an uncomfortable trek home, he hailed a cab and let the night air—warm as it was—play across his face as he watched the city whiz by through the open window.

Baltimore was nothing like the little backwater town he'd grown up in. Mo'd hated it there. He didn't have a terrible childhood, but he knew there was so much more out there. That's why he struck out for the big city the minute he was able. Not that he'd had any idea what he was going to do once he arrived. He just knew there would be much more excitement and opportunities around every corner.

When he'd first arrived, he spent days walking the streets admiring the buildings. He'd never seen anything like them. Stretching into the sky ten and eleven stories high. It was amazing. Not to mention the restaurants and stores that lined all of the city's main boulevards. The first time he stepped foot in a department store, Mo thought he'd died and gone to heaven. He was used to little mom-and-pop run shops, not the massive emporiums with every type of merchandise you could imagine at one's fingertips. Of course, he didn't have the green to actually buy anything.

There was also an endless supply of entertainment in the city. With his quick wit and charm, he'd usually talk his way into one of the theaters where he could watch whatever show was appearing. There were close to a dozen theaters to choose from depending on if he wanted to see a live Vaudeville show or a moving picture. If he couldn't decide, he went to the Hippodrome, the only theater in town that operated as a movie house *and* performance venue.

Mo quickly fell in love with Baltimore and vowed never to leave. But to do that, he needed to find a way to become a part of the hustle and bustle. He needed a plan. Luckily, that's something Mo Conklin was good at. Figuring out a way to survive.

At some point on the ride home, he must have begun to doze off because before he knew it, the cab pulled up in front of his building. Paying his fare and sending the cabbie off into the night with an unexpectedly generous tip, he jogged up the cracked cement steps to the door of the Tacoma Grand Hotel. Conklin couldn't help but note how unfitting the grandiose name was for the rundown building. If the owners were hoping to mask its dilapidated state with an air of sophistication, one glance at the crumbling brown bricks and decaying wooden window frames was enough to dispel any illusion of luxury.

Unlocking the front door required a delicate touch, a skill Ernie and Roy sorely lacked. Conklin said it took finesse, like wooing a fine woman—joking that it was a talent neither of his friends possessed. Usually, residents would need to fidget with the key when it was in the lock to get it in just the right position to release the locking mechanism. The troublesome entrance was just one of many issues plaguing the apartment house.

Climbing the rickety stairs to the third floor, each step creaked and moaned under the weight of his feet. He was afraid that one day, he was going to end up putting his foot right through one of the aging boards and falling to the checkered lobby floor below. Pausing momentarily to look over the railing, it was a thought he didn't relish. But if the stairs could hold Roy Abbott's large, hulking form, he should be fine. That didn't stop him from picking up his pace and taking the last few steps two at a time just to be safe. He saw no reason to tempt fate.

Conklin was stripping his suit jacket off as he walked down the hallway toward apartment 309. The gold and burgundy wallpaper that at one time must have been new and inviting was now badly faded and peeling at nearly every seam. In some places, the graying plaster walls behind the covering were completely exposed. And at the end of the hall sat apartment number 309. But to stand in front of the battered wooden door, one might believe they were about to enter apartment 306 because the tarnished bronze 9 had lost a nail and dangled upside down.

After spending the evening in the glamorous Platinum Peacock, where everything sparkled, exuding lavishness and excess, the Tacoma was a reminder of the stark contrasts that existed in Baltimore. Even within one's own life.

Stepping into the small main room of the apartment, Conklin found Bernstein and Abbott reclining on the threadbare sofa in their undershirts and trousers, fanning themselves with their fedoras. Even with the window opened, it didn't seem to matter. There was no movement in the air. The humidity, mixed with the lingering cigarette smoke, created a haze that filled the room.

Hanging his own hat on a hook next to the door, Conklin observed his pathetic-looking friends and decided that the next house they hit, they were going to make sure to take any electric fans they found. And according to Cam, their next target was very promising.

The two had worked out the perfect system. Cam did the scouting, working inside the Peacock allowed for the perfect opportunity to meet the club's moneyed patrons and find out where they lived. Through casual conversation, Cam was always able to learn exactly how wealthy someone was, because more often than not-especially in a setting like the Peacock-they were looking for a way to show off. Running one's mouth was a sure-fire way to end up on Cam's list. From there, Cam would pass along whatever had been learned to Mo. He'd then send Ernie to have a look at the house and observe for a day or two so they could figure out the best time to appear on the doorstep and "invite themselves inside." Two of them would then go in and grab what they could, including any specific items

Cam learned about, while the third man waited outside in a forgettable Ford sedan that looked like a hundred others in the city that they'd bought on the cheap for the sole purpose of being the getaway car. A few days after the robbery, Conklin would take the goods to their fence, collect the money, and deliver it to Cam at the Platinum Peacock to be divvied up amongst the crew. Then, the process would start all over again.

So far, the scheme was working perfectly. They'd made enough scratch in the last few weeks to keep them all sitting pretty for a little while. But none of them were ready to call it quits. They all knew the heat was on, but that wasn't going to stop them. Cam had already identified a long list of potential targets. That was the one thing it didn't appear anyone had been able to put together yet. That all of the robbery victims were patrons of the Platinum Peacock. Whether that was because no one thought to ask or those who'd been robbed feared what might happen to them if they admitted to frequenting the popular speakeasy, no one on the crew could say.

Nor did they care.

"What are you bums doing?" Conklin threw his jacket on the back of an armchair, then walked over to the window to see if he could open it any further.

"It's up as high as it can go," Abbott groused.

"I thought you two would be asleep by now," Conklin said, leaning on the wall next to the window.

"We wanted to hear what Cam had to say?" Bernstein said, eagerly sitting forward on the sofa. "Do we have a new address?"

The corner of Mo Conklin's lip curled upward. "That we do, boys. And Cam thinks this might be the biggest score yet."

Chapter Twenty-Five

Bob Franklin sat behind his desk with a smoldering cigar clenched between his teeth as he listened to his bookkeeper explain the week's figures. By all accounts, business was booming. Residents of Baltimore were actively looking for ways to break the law. Every time they did, Big Bob made money. The brothels were raking in the dough while his gambling dens were seeing more and more people willing to take a chance with their hard-earned wages. Even his legitimate establishments like the bakery near the courthouse and the warehouse by the docks—which did, at times, find itself housing illegal spirits-were seeing record profits.

Even the news of his growing wealth, however, could not distract Big Bob from thinking about the robberies. All those around him knew he'd become obsessed with finding out who was pulling the jobs and making him look so impotent. One of his lieutenants even dared suggest Franklin might be concerned a bigger outfit from Philly or Jersey might try muscling in if he couldn't get his territory under control. That same individual, after taking a ride with Gustov Schultz to check on some of Franklin's properties, hadn't been seen since.

"Of course, the Peacock is doing bang-up business," Albert Carson, Big Bob's accountant, said, looking at the large ledger in front of him, running a finger down the income column.

"I've seen you there every night this week," Franklin said, tapping his cigar against the side of the ashtray on his desk. "You used to only come in once a week, maybe."

"Oh," the small, bespeckled man said as he nervously brushed the bushy mustache under his nose. "My wife is out of town visiting her sister. So, I thought I would take advantage of her absence."

"That right, Albert?" Big Bob asked, his eyes narrowing for a moment. He watched a bead of sweat run down the number man's cheek. "Well, I'm glad you're enjoying yourself. You're a hard worker. You deserve to have a little fun."

"I especially like watching Miss Mowry perform," the man admitted as his entire face turned bright pink.

"Albert, Albert, Albert. You scoundrel." Franklin smirked.

"It's just a little harmless fun," Carson offered with a weak smile.

"Sure it is," Big Bob agreed with a grin that seemed to put the anxious little man at ease.

Then, as Franklin made a show of looking at his pocket watch, Albert Carson took it as a signal that it was time to leave. He began gathering up the ledgers he'd carried into the office, making sure not to leave anything behind.

"I'll see you next week," Big Bob said as the accountant precariously balanced the stack of ledgers on his way out the door. "Unless I see you at the Peacock before then."

After Carson closed the door behind him, silence filled the office. Stubbing the remains of his cigar out, Bob Franklin stood and began pacing behind his desk. It was as much to stretch his legs as it was to alleviate the growing sense of frustration he felt coursing through him. The headline in the day's edition of *The Baltimore Sun* lying on his desk, staring at him, wasn't helping matters. It had been three days since the last robbery in Guilford, and the police still had no leads. Grabbing the paper in a fit of anger, he flung it across the room just as Gustov Schultz marched into the office, followed by Clayton Munsey, the Platinum Peacock's maître d'.

Both Schultz and Munsey paused as they watched the pages of the newspaper flutter to the ground in front of them. Having never seen his boss in such a state, Munsey's eyes widened in surprise. His regular interactions with Bob Franklin were downstairs in the club when he was in a much more jovial mood. He'd heard him raise his voice once or twice, but he'd never seen him throw things before. The Peacock's host was lucky enough to have never been on the receiving end of Big Bob's temper.

Schultz, on the other hand, was very familiar with Franklin's flare-ups, so didn't think much of it and walked right over the papers. Stepping up to the boss's desk, he laid a sheet of paper down and pointed to the four names he'd written.

"What's this?" Big Bob asked, picking up the paper, trying to decipher the jumbled letters. Schultz picked up speaking the language pretty quickly, but writing in it was proving to be another story.

"I talked to Dixon," the German answered. "Zees are za names of the people who ver robbed."

"Yeah. So?" Franklin tossed the paper back onto the desk.

"All of zem have been to zee Peacock recently."

Big Bob snatched the paper up again and looked closely at the names. "Really? Is this true, Clayton?"

Schultz snapped his thick, meaty fingers in Munsey's direction and waited for the maître d' to hand him a large leather-bound reservation book.

"It appears to be the case, Mr. Franklin. But it certainly could just be a coincidence. Most of Baltimore's most affluent residents come to the Peacock," Munsey acknowledged as he pointed out the entries in the reservation book.

Big Bob's eyes blazed as he turned the new information over in his head. Not only was there a gang of hoods out there making him look bad, but they were doing it by robbing his guests! Was there a chance Munsey was right and it was simply a coincidence? All the wealthiest people *did* come to the Platinum Peacock. They were bound to be the ones most vulnerable when picking targets. They had everything people wanted, after all. But were they being specifically picked out because they'd been at the club? Franklin was fuming as he took the book and flipped through the pages, looking at all the names of potential victims.

Practically throwing the book back at Schultz, he instructed him to talk to everyone working in the club. "I want to know if anyone knows *anything*. If they've heard *anything*. If they've seen *anything*," he growled. "I don't care what you need to do. Find out who's behind this and if they're using my club!"

Chapter Twenty-Six

1985...

Lacking its own dedicated forensics team was a perennial headache for the Parker City Police Department. Like most of the jurisdictions in Maryland, it too relied on the State Police for technical services. Lucky for Parker City, the State's Crime Scene Unit that covered the western region was based out of the Parker County State Police Barracks, which usually allowed them to respond in a relatively timely fashion. But when there was an active day full of calls, with resources being limited and shared, it could take time before CSU arrived at a particular crime scene.

As the department's chief detective, Ben had full operational control over the way in which investigations were handled. That being the case, he'd called in and lowered the priority level for the Hubbard residence and diverted the CSU team to Clara Daschle's instead. It was a simple matter of priorities. Especially when the victim was a friend of the mayor's, which was likely to draw a great deal of attention.

Due to a spate of recent robberies, though, when Ben spoke with the head of the regional Crime Scene Unit, Lieutenant Clover agreed to send at least one forensic tech to the crime scene at the Hubbards to get the ball rolling. Ben had formed a good working relationship with Clover over the years. He knew the CSU chief was meticulous, as was his team. If there was evidence at either scene, they'd find it.

In addition to CSU, when there was a body involved and the cause of death was unclear, the Medical Examiner's Office needed to be brought in. It was like a choreographed dance at the crime scene as everyone tended to their assigned duties. All under Ben's direction.

By the time Chief Brent arrived, Clara Daschle's home was a hive of activity. While Ben coordinated with the assistant medical examiner, and his technicians and the crime scene investigators, and the officers now securing the property, Tommy led a crew of patrolmen room-by-room through the house, looking for anything out of the ordinary.

"It's possible," Tommy suggested to Ben and the chief, "that she interrupted the robbers before they were able to take anything. This house looks like it could be in a magazine. Every room is immaculate. We can't tell if anything's missing. I even went through her jewelry boxes. *Plural.* The woman had a lot of jewelry. And it all looks expensive. There was only one open space with a bunch of old pins.

"I remember her wearing a brooch last night," Ben said, thinking back to the previous evening. "It was covered in gems. If they were real, it was definitely expensive."

"That's right," the chief agreed. "It was pretty flashy. I do remember it now that you bring it up."

The three were gathered in the kitchen where Ben and Tommy were bringing the chief on what little they knew so far. Brent did not personally appear at every call the PCPD received. He trusted his men and knew they were able to handle whatever was thrown at them. But when there was an incident that was going to attract attention and create headlines, he liked to see things firsthand. Especially in this instance. Having just met Clara Daschle the previous evening, he, like Ben, felt slightly shell-shocked. But he also knew that because of her ties to the mayor and her work on the board renovating the Harlequin, there was going to be pressure to find out exactly what happened to her and find whoever did it as quickly as possible.

With the body having not yet been moved, Ben couldn't see if she was still wearing the brooch. In the old days, police would simply roll the body over and start going through the pockets to try and find any identification or "clues" that might lead to the killer. Nowadays, both the ME and the forensic team followed a specific protocol when handling the body. Which meant the police were to keep their hands off.

Walking back to the living room, Ben was just in time to see the two ME technicians carefully rolling Clara Daschle's body onto its back as the assistant medical examiner supervised. Stepping closer, Ben immediately saw that there was a tear in her dress where the jewel-encrusted brooch had been. The material was shredded as if someone ripped the piece off her.

"Have you been able to determine a cause of death?" Ben asked the assistant ME, who was feverishly writing notes on a clipboard.

Looking up from his paperwork and rubbing his eyes with the back of his gloved hand, he said, "My initial thought…blunt force trauma. There's several…well, what appear to be several, blows to the head. I can only guess it was with that bronze statuette." He pointed to an evidence bag one of his techs was now holding. Inside was the statue they found lying next to the body when they arrived. "Obviously, this is all preliminary, but one plus one equals two. There's no gunshot wound visible; no stab wound either. I see no signs of strangulation. But what I *can* see is that she was hit in the head, and there's an object perfect for hitting someone in the head next to her. I know some of my colleagues wouldn't feel comfortable making the jump, but…what can I say? I like living on the edge. I'm putting my money on blunt force trauma."

Ben never heard an ME talk so candidly. It was true. They all usually wanted to wait for the official autopsy and never wanted to theorize for fear of being wrong. They always hedged their bets, if they theorized at all. This guy just called it like he saw it.

"Of course," the ME continued, "I guess she could have died from a heart attack, then knocked the statue over as she was falling, and it hit her on the head…then bounced and did it again a couple more times."

"Uh…. Is there any chance that's what actually happened?" Ben asked, an obvious note of hesitation in his voice.

The assistant medical examiner looked at him and tilted his head. "No. I just thought I would throw it out there."

"Okay then. What about time of death? Any idea?"

"Judging by the state of the body…liver temp…et cetera…for the moment, I can only say she's been dead for over twelve hours. I'm fairly confident I'll be able to narrow that window for you. But don't expect me to be able to say she died at exactly twelve-forty-two and thirty-three seconds last night or anything like that. I'm good, but not a miracle worker."

Ben bit his lower lip to keep from smiling. He'd never been happier that his partner was in a different room. If this guy and Tommy got talking, he was afraid they'd come up with some hair-brained theory as to what happened that would probably involve aliens or some sort of conspiracy. Tommy loved throwing out crazy ideas at crime scenes. Over the years, they'd learned most of the staff at the Medical Examiner's Office didn't enjoy Tommy's humor. Ben was afraid this guy would. And might even encourage him.

Clara Daschle had been dead for more than twelve hours. Looking at his watch, Ben noted the time at just after one in the afternoon. So, she died sometime before midnight. And he'd seen her alive and well when he left the reception around nine o'clock. That narrowed down the window. Sometime between nine and midnight, Clara Daschle returned to her home and was bludgeoned to death with a decorative statue.

Ben hoped they would be able to find some fingerprints on the statue. So far, it was the only piece of evidence collected for further examination. Until a CSU tech walked up to Ben with an evidence bag containing a small object.

"Detective, we found this under the body. We'll take it back to the lab with us, but I thought you might want to get a look at it first."

Handing over the plastic bag, Ben's heart stopped. Just as memorable as Clara Daschle's brooch were the diamond cufflinks he'd seen Mayor Charlie Oland wearing at the Harlequin. One of which he was now holding.

Chapter Twenty-Seven

"Well...there's no way this is good," Tommy said after Ben explained what was in the evidence bag.

The detectives, along with the chief, had moved into a formal sitting room in the front of the house off the foyer so they could speak privately. Ben wanted to keep the fact he could identify the owner of the cufflink to only the three of them for the time being.

"You're sure this belongs to the mayor?" Tommy asked. "It doesn't just *resemble* the ones he was wearing last night?"

"It's pretty distinctive, don't you think?" Ben pointed out.

"That's one of the cufflinks Mayor Oland was wearing. No doubt," Chief Brent confirmed, looking over Tommy's shoulder, a pained expression on his face. He was still wearing his signature Aviator sunglasses, but Ben could tell he wasn't happy.

It was bad enough finding the mayor's cufflink at the crime scene—if it had been on the floor under the sofa or behind a pillow, it could be easily explained away. Mayor Oland, being the nice guy he was, might have offered to give Clara Daschle a lift home after the reception. He could have walked her to the door, she asked if he wanted to come in for a cup of coffee and while he was inside, the cufflink came undone and fell off. He just didn't notice it before he left. Things happen. It was possible and an easy explanation.

But in this case, the offending object was found *under* the victim. And with no signs that the body had been moved—the assumption being she was struck with the statue and fell where she was standing—they could theorize

Clara Daschle grabbed the cufflink and pulled it off while struggling with her attacker. In many cases, if an item that didn't belong to the victim was found on or under them, it usually pointed to their killer.

No one said it, but it's what all three men were thinking.

"Okay. Alright. It's possible the mayor lost his cufflink and left, and then the victim happened to land on it after she was attacked. A coincidence," Tommy suggested.

"I didn't think you two believed in coincidence," the chief commented, taking the evidence bag from Tommy and giving its contents a more thorough examination.

"We don't," Tommy conceded.

"And we don't want to jump to any conclusions," Ben pointed out. "There could be a perfectly reasonable and innocent explanation for why the mayor's cufflink ended up here at the crime scene. I don't think any of us want to make any accusations without having all the facts. Which means we need to hear what he has to say. We're going to have to talk to him." Ben looked to the chief, waiting for his reaction.

"Of course," Brent agreed. He wasn't one of those police chiefs who would give the mayor a free pass just because of the office he held. If the evidence pointed in Charlie Oland's direction, he'd need to be questioned. At the same time, though, Brent understood the ramifications of going after a mayor. Even if it was just to ask some questions. He didn't want word leaking out that Oland *could* be a potential suspect. That could cause a feeding frenzy in the press. Especially in a small city like Parker. Simply finding his cufflink at a crime scene did not a murderer make.

"When you do talk to him," Brent began, "you'll have to be discreet. He doesn't get any special treatment, understand? But there's also no reason to rock the boat unnecessarily. If he cooperates fully, then there shouldn't be a problem. We don't need to go shouting the fact we're questioning him from the rooftops or anything like that. And absolutely no talking to any reporters."

"Naturally," Tommy said. "But what if he won't cooperate and doesn't want to talk?"

Brent let out a long sigh thinking about the trouble that would cause. "Let's hope that isn't the case. If it is, though, then you follow procedure to the letter. I'll back you whatever you do. As long as you do it the right way."

"When have we ever not done something the right way?" Tommy asked with a grin that would have made the Big Bad Wolf proud.

Chapter Twenty-Eight

After discussing their strategy for moving forward, Chief Brent left the scene and the investigation in his detectives' capable hands, saying he was heading back to the station to find out what the mayor's schedule for the day looked like. The group agreed it would be best not to just show up at his office at City Hall and surprise him. At the same time though, they didn't want to tip him off in case he did end up being a person of interest. So, a call from the chief of police asking about the mayor's schedule, especially considering the amount of time they'd been spending working together on the plan to reorganize the PCPD, would not send up any red flags. It sounded to all of them like a good way to approach the situation of finding time to meet with Charlie Oland.

Brent was just pulling away as the assistant medical examiner and his two technicians were removing Clara Daschle's body from the house and loading it into the van for the trip to Baltimore, where it would undergo a full postmortem. After speaking with them, Ben did not expect to learn anything new from the autopsy itself. They all agreed the most likely cause of death was blunt force trauma to the head. So, unless something came back that was a complete surprise, coming up with a more accurate time of death was all Ben hoped to get from the ME.

Ben then asked Tommy to keep an eye on the CSU team as they wrapped up their work so he could take a walk through the house for himself. That way, when they got back to the station, they'd both have their own set of notes and impressions from the scene that they could compare. Ben and Tommy frequently saw the same thing in two different ways. Not that either was right and the other was wrong, they simply came at things with two different perspectives making their overall, combined observations so much stronger. Together they were able to see the "full picture."

Walking through Clara Daschle's bedroom, Ben was taken with the old-school elegance in her decorating style. Even in the few minutes he'd spoken with her at the reception, he knew she was a woman with class and style. It went beyond her clothing. It was the way she presented herself and spoke. She was obviously a worldly woman who had experienced everything life had to offer. Judging by what Ben saw throughout the house, she was also a woman of means. They were going to need to do a full background check on her to learn everything they could about her life.

Along the short hallway leading to the master bathroom, Ben stopped to examine a set of photos hanging on the wall. One of which looked very similar to the picture he'd seen at the theater the night before. It was a black and white photograph of a young Clara Daschle on stage in a sparkling evening gown behind an old-fashioned microphone like he'd seen in the movies. She was a beautiful woman, Ben noted, and she'd clearly been a performer at some point in her life. Which explained why she was involved in the renovations of the Harlequin. A classic theater like that must have held a special place in her heart.

As Ben cast his eyes over the bedroom one more time, it looked like everything was exactly where it was supposed to be. The bed, covered in pillows, was made, none of the dresser drawers were pulled out, all of the pictures on the wall hung perfectly straight, and there was nothing thrown on the floor. Walking over and opening one of the antique jewelry boxes on her dresser, Ben saw it was filled with various pieces. Diamonds, rubies, sapphires, were all accounted for. If they were genuine—and Ben had no reason to believe they weren't-they would be worth a fortune. And they hadn't been touched.

The four other bedrooms on the second floor of the house were as pristine as the master. If someone had gone through them, either they didn't touch anything, or they were experts at covering their tracks. So far, it was one of the cleanest break-ins Ben had ever seen. Which got him thinking.

The only thing they could determine that was taken—other than Clara Daschle's life—was the jeweled brooch she'd been wearing. Did that mean she arrived home last evening just as the robber, or robbers, were breaking in and interrupted them? That would explain why nothing except the brooch was missing. After she was killed, whoever broke in decided to flee rather than stick around any longer. Plus, they'd already scored at the Hubbards' house, having gotten away with their safe. Assuming the break-ins were perpetrated by the same person, or persons.

Ben had an uneasy feeling as he descended the curved staircase, where he joined his partner in the foyer. In all the reports, he'd never read that the robbers in Wakeville hit two houses in one night. If these were the same suspects, why'd that change?

Together, Ben and Tommy watched the Crime Scene Unit carry their equipment out to the van with the emblem of the Maryland State Troopers on the side. As CSU drove away, Buck LuCoco recorded their departure time on the crime scene log. Outside in the driveway, Officer Brian Spurrier was standing, talking with the two other patrolmen who'd helped secure and search the house.

"We need to lock up here," Ben said to Tommy. "The housekeeper gave you the key?"

"Right here," he said, the key dangling from the silver keychain hanging on his finger.

"Did the backdoor get boarded up?" Ben was trying to mentally check things off his list.

"Yeah. All taken care of."

Taking the key from Tommy, Ben said, "Alright. Then we can shut things down here, send the guys on their way, and head back to the station. We'll need to track down next of kin for notification. Did the housekeeper say anything about who that might be?"

"Nope. She claimed that she and Daschle were close but couldn't really say much more." Tommy shrugged. "She was pretty out of it. Couldn't stop crying. I had someone take her home and figured we could follow up with her after she's had a chance to pull herself together."

"Did you-"

"Make sure someone was with her when they got her home and didn't leave her there by herself to suffer through her grief alone? I gave Bronson specific instructions. Have no fear. I've picked up a few things over the years."

Ben smiled. "Who knows? You might actually make a half-decent detective someday."

"Aw. Gee, *Dad*, do you really think so?" Tommy kicked the ground in an aw-shucks motion that made both of them laugh.

"Are we done here?" LuCoco asked, walking up behind them. "Can I let the guys head out? Spurrier is gonna have to write up his report."

"Since when do you care about paperwork, Buck?" Tommy asked, not even trying to hide the sardonic tone.

"Hey, I have no problem with paperwork...when it's someone else's," LuCoco said, finding himself so humorous he let out a deep, hearty laugh. Then he turned and walked over to the other patrol officers.

"I don't like this new Buck," Tommy said.

"You didn't like the old Buck either," Ben pointed out.

"At least I'm consistent."

Chapter Twenty-Nine

On the way back to the station, it occurred to both Ben and Tommy that it was well past lunchtime. The sound of their stomachs audibly protesting the absence of food only reinforced how famished they were. It wasn't the first time they'd been so wrapped up in work they missed a meal, but feeling they might be working late and not have a chance for dinner either, they thought it best to grab something quick to eat. But since they were just at the beginning of an investigation and didn't want to lose any of the initial momentum, driving through McDonald's for some Big Macs and fries was their least time-consuming option.

Chief Brent walked into the Detective Squad's office just as Ben was taking a bite of his burger. Ben hoped the chief wouldn't immediately start asking questions. Or, if he did, they were long enough to give him a chance to down the bite of Big Mac.

Seeing Ben's dilemma, Brent smiled, saying, "You're alright, Detective. Take your time. Don't choke. We don't want another body on our hands."

Ben nodded appreciatively.

"I spoke with Mayor Oland," Brent continued. "I didn't tell him about Daschle. But I did ask if you and I could stop by his office to brief him on a case that may get some press coverage. I thought it best for just Ben and I to go so we don't draw too much attention," he explained, looking to Tommy, who was contently munching on a handful of salty French fries. "I also don't want to spook him. If we all march into his office, he might be suspicious from the jump. I don't want it to look like we're ganging up on him."

"I completely understand," Tommy said between bites. "With just the two of you, it comes off as more casual. He keeps his guard down. Makes sense. Good thinking."

"He says he can see us at five-fifteen over at his office."

Ben looked at his watch. That would give him and Tommy just enough time to go through their notes and start to put everything together. For their very first case four years ago, Ben had squeezed a blackboard into the small office where they were able to write important notes to help organize the investigation. It was a practice that stuck. Until they had any of the reports from the Medical Examiner's Office or CSU, they'd start filling the board with their own notes and observations from the scene.

Agreeing to meet in the chief's office before walking next door to City Hall, Ben quickly finished their late lunch/early dinner, hoping the speed at which he did would not cause indigestion. His stomach was already in knots. He didn't need to make it any worse.

There was always anxiety when beginning a new case. He hoped that would never go away because if it did, he was afraid it would mean he'd become too desensitized and accustomed to the darker side of society. He never wanted to be one of those police detectives who completely shut off their emotions. It was important to stay focused, neutral, and open to whatever the investigation uncovered. But not to let one's own humanity in, Ben felt, would actually be detrimental in the long run.

As he began writing on the blackboard, Tommy read while finishing his meal.

"I have a question," Tommy declared, crushing the Styrofoam container his burger came in and throwing it in the trashcan. "Our first thought was that the break-in at Clara Daschle's could be connected to the one at the Hubbards' because of its proximity and seemingly identical point of entrance, correct?"

Ben nodded in agreement.

"But then, we found a cufflink *underneath* Daschle's body that we are almost one hundred percent certain belongs to the mayor, correct?"

Ben nodded again, following his partner's train of thought.

"The placement of said cufflink gives us a possible suspect, correct?"

Once again, Ben agreed.

"So, does that mean we think Charlie Oland also broke into the Hubbards' house? And the ones in Wakeville, if they are all related?"

"Technically," Ben began, "that was five questions. But I get it. Yeah. The idea of the mayor running around in his off-hours breaking into houses doesn't sound like a solid theory."

"Ya think?" Tommy asked, wiping his mouth and brushing the crumbs from his mustache. "But we're okay with the fact he might have killed someone?"

"No, we're just leaving open the possibility. Remember, we don't jump to any conclusions, one way or the other. We just need to follow the evidence wherever it points us."

"And right now, that direction is…where exactly?"

Looking at the blackboard and reading what he'd already transferred over from his notebook, Ben couldn't argue with Tommy's questions and where he was going with them. It also disturbed him to think how easy it was for them to accept the mayor as a possible murder suspect. Not that there was a single profile that fit *all* killers, but nothing in his interactions with the energetic public figure would have ever led him to think one day he might be putting his photo up on the board and labeling him a person of interest. It was troubling. But Ben had literally just said they needed to follow the evidence. He believed that. But his gut was telling him there was going to be a very simple and innocent reason why Charlie Oland's cufflink was found at the scene. If not…then he'd cross that bridge when he got to it.

Regardless, they would need to build a profile of Clara Daschle and learn whatever they could about her. Including who her next of kin was and who should be notified of her passing. Ben gave Tommy the task of starting to look into her life and background so they could start to put together a better picture of the woman. Even though the working theory was that she'd interrupted a burglary, Ben still wanted to know who she was. In their brief meeting the evening before, he instantly formed the distinct impression Daschle was a dynamic figure. The way she spoke and the things she said led him to believe she'd lived a fruitful and exciting life.

And in the back of his mind, Ben was concerned that what they had might not be a robbery gone wrong. He couldn't help thinking about the broken glass by the door of the room where Daschle's body was found. Even though a few hours earlier he'd told Neil Thompson that shards of glass could fall inside *and* outside the door when it was broken, he didn't like that almost all of the broken glass was on the patio outside, as if someone inside the house broke the glass to make it *look* like a break-in. It was one of the details he'd written in his notebook that was nagging at him, becoming louder the more he thought about it. If that were the case, and someone was trying to stage the scene to make it look like a break-in, then maybe something in Clara Daschle's life would tell them why someone would want her dead.

Ben wasn't ready to share his concern with Tommy, though. He didn't have anything to support the idea anyway. It was just another possibility that *might* have to be considered. That was all. The first thing he needed to do was find out how the mayor's cufflink ended up at the crime scene.

Chapter Thirty

Parker's City Hall sat just around the corner from the police station and shared a parking lot situated behind both buildings. While the two structures had been designed by the same architect and built in the 1890s, the number of similarities the two shared were dwarfed by their differences. The PCPD headquarters was a two-story, red brick building that could use a new roof and possibly some work on its foundation; City Hall was a magnificent red brick government palace with gleaming white marble columns and hand-carved stonework around its parapet. At the very top, like a crown on the head of a king, a clock tower sat. Inside, visitors stepped into a large lobby with marble floors and rich wood finishes. Those arriving at the headquarters of the Parker City Police entered a narrow vestibule with worn linoleum flooring and institutional-colored walls. The two buildings might have been brothers in some regards, but it was clear which one was the favorite.

Checking in with the matronly clerk sitting behind the reception desk in the lobby, Chief Brent and Ben were pleasantly greeted by Mrs. Cupperman, who, for nearly two decades, was the first person visitors to City Hall encountered. Even if their names hadn't been on the guest log, she wouldn't have thought too much about the police chief stopping in to see the mayor without an appointment. And though both men knew the way to the mayor's office, she still directed them up the grand staircase leading toward the administrative offices of the city's government.

Having obviously been given a heads-up by Mrs. Cupperman downstairs that they were on their way, Oland's personal secretary was standing in the hallway outside the mayor's reception area waiting for them. Unlike Chief Brent's secretary, who'd worked for the previous chief and was a force to be reckoned with, as well as an institution in the PCPD—most people believing she started working for the department sometime in the 1800s-the mayor's right-hand woman was a cheerful, energetic, young thing. Only recently graduated from Hammermill College right there in Parker City, she was looking to get her foot in the political door.

"Chief Brent, Detective Sergeant Winters, so good to see you," she said, firmly shaking each of their hands, then ushing them directly through the outer office area to the mayor's door. "Mayor Oland is all ready for you."

"Right on time," Brent said, looking at his watch.

From behind a broad smile, she answered, "We pride ourselves on keeping on schedule. Can I get either of you something to drink?"

After both graciously declined the offer, they were shown into Charlie Oland's inner sanctum, the very ornate office of the mayor with a marble fireplace along one wall and a glistening crystal chandelier hanging over-head. Standing behind his large mahogany desk, Oland looked as dashing as ever in an impeccably tailored charcoal suit and red tie. It was the end of the workday for most, when people were ready to shed their formal work attire and slip into something more relaxed after a long day. Oland, without a single hair out of place, looked as though he just stepped from the pages of a fashion magazine.

"Have a seat, gentlemen," the mayor said, motioning to the guest chairs in front of the desk. "I understand there's a case you wanted to tell me about. Don't get me wrong, I like you both very much. But when you come to talk business, I become concerned."

On the short walk from the police station to City Hall, Ben and the chief had discussed how to approach the mayor with the news of Clara Daschle's death. As much as they would like to catch him off guard to get his most genuine reaction to their questions, they were aware of the line they would need to walk with regard to his rights. As a suspect, there would be an argument to be made that they should Mirandize him before making any inquiries. But simply by the fact of taking the time and formally reading him those rights, they would lose the element of "surprise," so-to-speak.

"Don't keep me in suspense," Oland said, looking over his desk at the two officers. "Tell me. What's happening?"

"Before we do," Brent began, leaning forward in his seat, "Detective Winters has a question for you."

Lowering himself into the large, green leather chair that those around City Hall referred to as "the king chair," Oland's brow furrowed slightly as he said, "Alright."

"Mr. Mayor, when was the last time you saw Clara Daschle?" Ben asked, getting straight to it.

Oland chuckled. "Last night at the Harlequin. We were all there." Giving Ben a mischievous grin, playfully ribbing the detective, he then asked, "Did someone have a little too much to drink last night and forget?"

Ben smiled in response. "No, sir. I'm just trying to determine what time it was when you last saw Mrs. Daschle."

"We both stayed for the entire reception."

"So, you both left the theater at the same time, then?"

"Yes. I actually offered her a ride home. We were still talking about the renovations." Pausing, laying his hands on the desk and leaning forward, he asked, "Detective, what is this all about?" It was the standard question someone being questioned by the police asked when they didn't already know why they were being questioned by the police.

Ben looked to the chief, then back to Oland. "Sir, I'm sorry to tell you, Clara Daschle was found dead in her home this morning by her housekeeper."

"Oh, my God," the mayor said, bolting out of his chair. "Not Clara. She was in such a good mood last night, and she looked wonderful. Funny, I even remember thinking last night, I hope I'm in such good shape when I'm her age. Do you know what happened? Please tell me she didn't slip and fall or anything like that. I'd feel terrible if I'd taken her home but not have been there when…." His voice trailed off as it looked to Ben that he was imagining the worst possible scenario.

Once again, Ben looked at the chief, both realizing that the mayor was under the impression Daschle had died of natural causes. Or at least he was acting like that's what he thought.

"No, Mr. Mayor," Chief Brent said, his baritone voice sounding even lower. "It is not official yet, but it does appear that Mrs. Daschle was murdered."

That stopped Oland in his tracks. The range of emotions that passed over his face in a matter of seconds was either the best performance Ben had ever seen, or the mayor was truly in shock and grief-stricken.

"I don't understand, Nick. What do you mean murdered? Detective?"

"Yes, sir. She was discovered with blunt force trauma to the head. Initial observations are that she might have walked in on a robbery."

"No. That's impossible. I drove her home, then went inside so we could finish talking. There was no one there. I remember seeing her turn off her alarm system."

"How long were you in Mrs. Daschle's house last evening?" Ben was fighting the urge to pull the notebook from his pocket and begin taking notes. He wanted to keep the conversation going, though.

"Oh, it wasn't that long. Maybe a half an hour." Oland returned to his seat and began tapping his fingers on the desk absentmindedly. "I don't believe this. Someone broke in and killed her. But I was there. If I had just stayed a little while longer, maybe...."

Charlie Oland's usual rich tan complexion had turned to a dull shade of gray as he absorbed the news. Ben's gut was instantly telling him that the mayor's reaction was of true surprise and that he wasn't responsible. Which meant he would no longer need to be treated as a suspect. *Except* there was still the matter of his cufflink.

"Mr. Mayor—"

"Please," he said, cutting Ben off quickly, "call me Charlie. I think under the circumstance, we really don't need to stand on ceremony."

"Alright.... If I can ask you a few more questions? You never know how important the smallest detail could end up being."

"Of course. I'll tell you whatever I can."

"What time did you arrive at Mrs. Daschle's home?"

Oland exhaled as he thought back to the previous evening. "It must have been sometime around ten o'clock. The reception was wrapping up around nine-thirty. We spoke to a few people before leaving and it doesn't take long to get from the theater up to Harper's Mill. Especially at that time on a weeknight."

The urge to take notes finally won out and Ben was now scribbling details down as the mayor spoke. "And you say you were in her house for half an hour?"

"Something like that. She had some of the plans for the restoration she wanted to show me."

"Weren't they on display at the fundraiser last night?" Ben asked, trying not to sound like the question was somehow accusatory.

"Some of the plans were," Oland agreed. "The big fancy posters were designed to try and convince those in attendance last night to open their wallets. The designs she was showing me were more detailed from the architect working on the restoration. These were the sorts of drawings the general public wouldn't care much about."

Charlie Oland was known for being a detail-oriented mayor. No matter the issue being discussed or the project being presented, he always seemed to know every single detail. From the broadest strokes right down to the most minute aspect. His uncanny attention to detail surprised many people who were not aware of exactly how much of a hands-on mayor Oland was.

"And when you left around ten-thirty," Ben continued, "Mrs. Daschle was alive and well?"

"Yes. Absolutely." Oland paused as he turned the questions he'd been asked over in his head. Ben saw it coming just before he asked, "Detective, do you think I did this to Clara?"

"Charlie," Chief Brent said, "Ben's just trying to put together a timeline for last evening. With what you just told us and the ME's initial estimation, it would narrow the time of death to between ten-thirty and about midnight. That helps us immensely." The chief paused before continuing. "However..." The word hung in the air for what seemed like an eternity. "There was something discovered at the crime scene that we do need you to explain."

The mayor sat forward in his chair and tilted his head, his eyes narrowing. "What did you find?"

Brent looked to Ben.

"A cufflink was found under Mrs. Daschle's body," Ben said. "I was able to identify it as one of the cufflinks you were wearing last evening. They were very memorable."

Oland looked confused, obviously thinking through the events of the night before. "I always take my suit jacket off before I get in the car. I lay it in the backseat. When we got to Clara's I know I loosened my tie and rolled up my sleeves. I thought I put my cufflinks in my pocket. I guess one of them fell out."

"You didn't notice one missing when you got home?" Ben asked again, hoping the question didn't sound as critical as it felt.

The mayor paused, casting his mind back. "When I got home," he answered slowly, thinking carefully, "I really wasn't paying much attention. There were a bunch of messages waiting for me that I went though and a few papers I needed to read for this morning. It was so late when I finally went upstairs and got undressed. I just laid my pants on the chair in my bedroom. I wasn't even thinking about emptying my pockets. I figured I would just hang my suit up this morning."

"Did you?"

"Did I what?"

"Hang your suit up this morning?" Ben asked.

"Actually…no. I didn't. I got distracted by a phone call. Never went back into the bedroom. My pants and jacket could still be on the chair. Unless my wife hung them up for me."

"What about your wallet?"

"My wallet? What about it?"

"Do you keep it in your back pocket like most men?"

"Yes. I do."

"Did you take that out of your pants last evening when you got undressed?"

Oland leaned back in his chair and smiled as he thought about the question. "You really are a good detective. Impressive. I see what you're doing. If I took my wallet out of my pocket, why didn't I take the cufflinks out as well."

Ben didn't answer; he just gave a slight nod.

"I have a very simple explanation for that. I always leave my wallet on my desk. When I get home, I go straight into my study, and that is where I leave my briefcase and wallet. It's quite often the last room I'm in before I go to bed, and it's always the last room I'm in before leaving in the morning. I grab my wallet and briefcase and head out to the car. I live by my morning routine. And I've never once misplaced my wallet. Or my car keys, for that matter. They're usually with my wallet."

Everything Oland offered by way of explanation was certainly plausible, Ben thought. And if the mayor had rolled up his sleeves at Clara Daschle's house and put the cufflinks in his pocket, one could have fallen out. If he didn't usually put things in his pocket, he might not remember to empty them. Especially if it was late. It was a convenient justification. But one that made a reasonable deal of sense.

"When you left Clara Daschle's last evening, did you see anything suspicious? Anyone lingering around outside or sitting in a car?"

"I truly wish I had. But Harper's Mill is one of the safest neighborhoods in the city. Everything looked…normal. I didn't see anyone out walking around and didn't pay any attention to any of the cars on the street. If there were any, for that matter. There might have been one or two. Nothing stood out to me or caught my attention."

"Well," the chief said, letting out a sigh, "there was another incident in Harper's Mill that we were already investigating when we got the call about Mrs. Daschle. A break-in."

"Dammit!" The mayor smacked his hand on the top of his desk. "So, this could all be because of what's happening in Wakeville?"

"We're not ready to make that connection just yet. We will be working with the Parker County Sheriff's Department and comparing notes, but for the time being, we don't want to jump to any conclusions. However, Detectives Winters and Mason will be keeping an eye out for anything that could tie all of these break-ins together."

The news of the robbery at the Hubbards' brought with it a complete change in Oland's demeanor. Gone was the eager-to-share-whatever-information-might-help-possible witness to a murder, replaced by a mayor who was now afraid a series of burglaries one town over had spilled across the border into his own city and brought about the death of a friend in the process. Ben knew the mayor now had more to think about, so he was willing to take everything he'd learned and add it to the board back in the office. If there were any follow-up questions, he could circle back with Oland later. For now, he was going to leave the office, having removed Charlie Oland from the list of suspects. The only problem with doing that was that there were no other names on the list, leaving them with no more leads.

Chapter Thirty-One

1927…

Clara Mowry sat at the empty bar of the Platinum Peacock, a glass of whiskey in front of her, watching as the wait staff scurried about setting tables for the evening. She was wrapped in her favorite silk robe with her raven locks flowing loosely down over her shoulders. There were still several hours before she needed to disappear into her dressing room to prepare for that evening's performances, but even as she strolled through the club without being all dolled up, she was the most beautiful woman working in the joint. As she sat on the bar stool with her legs crossed, she took a devilish pleasure in seeing the waiters and busboys try to avoid looking at her exposed leg when her robe would fall open…by accident.

Growing up, her family never had very much in the way of material things, but her father always found a way to put food on the table. He worked two jobs, and her mother helped alter clothing for one of the nicer dress shops in town. Like most of the girls in her neighborhood though, a formal education hadn't been a priority. It wasn't until recently that she learned a group of society women in her hometown had formed a school for girls and began encouraging a standardized program of education. But she was convinced the lessons life had taught her were far more valuable than anything she could have learned in a classroom or from a bunch of books.

As Clara blossomed into a stunningly gorgeous young woman, she realized her beauty would be the key to her success. Her good looks began to open many doors for her. And the attention she was beginning to receive was exhilarating. Then, one day, after singing along to a phonograph record being played as a demonstration in a department store, she discovered her looks weren't her only asset. As her mesmerizing voice intertwined with the tune floating through the air, she experienced the biggest thrill seeing all the shoppers gathered around listening to her, their eyes shimmering with delight. That's when she knew she was meant to perform. So, she found every opportunity to visit the Vaudeville house in town and make friends with anyone whose eye she could attract. It wasn't long before a manager for one of the acts traveling through helped her make her way to Baltimore. But when she arrived in the big city, she split and quickly struck out on her own.

With her brains, talent, and dazzling good looks, she found no difficulty getting a job in one of Bob Franklin's dinner clubs. The manager who'd hired her was a real daisy but always put on a good show of being overly masculine, making passes at all the girls in the show. Some of them would joke that if they ever accepted his overtures, he wouldn't know what to do with them. But Clara understood he had a part to play. And so did she. She'd play along with him without crossing any lines, which quickly made her a favorite. One night when the headliner came down with laryngitis, instead of putting one of the girls with more experience on in her place, Clara got the nod. It was her big break because Big Bob himself happened to be in the audience that evening. After her performance, one of the waiters found Clara backstage and said that the boss wanted to meet her.

Putting her nerves aside, she sashayed over to Bob Franklin's table with her brightest smile and a twinkle in her eyes.

"That was some performance," Franklin said, offering her the seat next to him.

"Thank you," she said demurely, putting on her own show.

"Where'd you come from, doll face?"

"I've been working here at the club for a couple months now."

"And you're already—"

"Lorelei come down with laryngitis. Mr. Gleason asked me to fill in."

Then, lowering her voice and coyly looking at Franklin through her long lashes, she said, "I don't think some of the other girls are too pleased. But I was just doing what I was asked."

"Of course you were," Big Bob agreed. "And you were wonderful."

"Thank you. That means a lot coming from someone like you."

By the look on his face, Clara could tell she'd hooked him. It wasn't even a week later when one of Big Bob's men showed up at her boarding house to escort her to Franklin's office, where he'd asked her to be the new headliner at the Platinum Peacock. She was now living a life many girls dreamed of. But she wasn't finished. She still had plans for the future. She was going to perform on legitimate stages in theaters all across the country one day.

Sitting there at the bar, Clara used one hand to flip through a recent issue of *McCall's*, while in her other, she held a silver, filigreed cigarette holder, at the end of which was her fifth or sixth cig of the day. Her long, elegant fingers slowly moved along the pages of the magazine, tracing the outline of the dresses the women were wearing. How she wished she could have them all. Knowing one day, she might.

As much as she loved performing for the club's guests, experiencing the rush of adrenaline as she stepped out onto the stage, she found the quiet moments before the doors opened when she could lose herself in a magazine or a good book precious to her. She'd been tickled to see one of her favorite authors, Kathleen Norris, had a story in that issue of *McCall's*. Her dilemma was whether to begin reading it now or wait and save it for after the show when she would need something to help bring her down after the buzz of performing. She always found herself needing something to help calm her after a night on stage. Even having a few drinks afterward only seemed to keep the excitement going as she would partake in the festive atmosphere well into the early hours of the morning.

Opting to save the story for when she got home—she was planning on leaving directly after the show tonight—it gave her something to look forward to. As she stubbed the remainder of her cigarette out in one of the expensive ashtrays sitting on the bar and seeing her glass nearly empty, she was debating if she was going to ask the bartender, a young fella she enjoyed making eyes at, for another whiskey when she heard a commotion fill the otherwise quiet dining room.

Looking to the stage at the front of the room, she saw an anxious Clayton Munsey push through the curtain with Bob Franklin's righthand man, Gustov Schultz, hot on his heels. The two were having an abnormally loud discussion, clearly not caring if anyone around them heard what was being said. Both men, gesturing with sharp, jerky movements, told her tempers were flaring.

"I have no idea!" Munsey snapped at the big German.

"Zis is no coincidence, I tell you. Zumvun in zis club is behind it! I am zertain."

Schultz and Munsey were both red in the face, but Clara got the impression each man's flushed complexion was caused by different reasons. Schultz was steaming mad, while Munsey was nervous and sweating, the calm demeanor for which he was known to greet each guest to the club nowhere to be seen. Clara wondered what had the men so agitated. They stormed through the room, finally coming to an abrupt stop, turning and facing off with one another.

Her mind suddenly flashed on a moving picture she'd seen out one night with a friend that ended with a showdown between two cowboys. Dressed in a dark suit and tie—all he needed was the cowboy hat—Schultz looked like the rogue outlaw come to town to settle a score.

"You are zee man who runs zis club. You must know zumthing."

"I told you. I didn't even realize they'd all been here until you asked to see the guest book. How would I? You said yourself, you had to get the names from the police!"

"But you are zupposed to know everybody und everyzing. It is deine arbeit!" Schultz was standing behind a chair, gripping the back so tightly Clara thought it might snap in his monstrous hands.

"What?"

"Vut?"

"You said *deine arbeit*. What the hell does that mean?"

"Your...vut's the verd? Your yob...job! It is your *job* to know everyzing."

Their raised voices managed to clear out the entire dining room. The staff quickly and quietly disappeared, seeking the safety of any other room in the club. Though he was usually reserved, with his dark eyes taking in everything that happened around him, when Schultz did blow his top, no one wanted to be around, let alone be on the receiving end of his fiery temper. Clara thought of all the cowardly tuxedo-clad waiters scampering off to hide like cockroaches when a light was switched on. Only she was left to witness the heated exchange.

"I vill need to speak vit everyvun who verks in zee club," Schultz demanded.

"You think someone on my staff is behind this? You're mad!" Munsey threw his hands in the air. "No one who works at the Peacock is involved in those damn robberies! Everyone here who works for Mr. Franklin knows the rules."

"Do zay? No vun thinks zay can make zome extra money und not get caught?" Schultz's eyes were a blaze as he stared the man down from across the table. "Vut about you?"

Munsey's eyes grew wide. "How dare you insult me like that. I have worked for Mr. Franklin for over twenty years!"

"Und you are only a glorified vaiter after all zat time…"

The words cut like a sharp knife through the notoriously genial maître d', who appeared so stunned he could no longer speak. Clara saw the man's entire demeanor change as his jaw clenched and his eyes turned as black as the night sky. Then, drawing himself up to his full height—which was still a good six inches shorter than Schultz-he said, "People like you should never have been allowed into our country. You should have been sent to the outer reaches like your loathsome kaiser."

There was hardly time to react as Schultz pulled a shiny black Luger from under his jacket and aimed it directly at Clayton Munsey, but Clara found herself up, off her perch at the bar, and crossing the floor toward the horrific tableau.

"Boys!" she heard herself shouting. "I think it's time everyone took a deep breath. Gustov, you really should put that away. I don't think Big Bob would look too kindly on someone getting blood all over his expensive carpet, do you?"

Schultz's finger was wrapped firmly around the gun's trigger. The weapon felt so familiar in his hand; it was like an extension of his arm. He'd lost track of how many times he'd fired it over the years. First in combat during the Great War, and more recently while enforcing Big Bob Franklin's will throughout the city.

Seeing the look in Schultz's eyes, Clara wasn't sure if she'd be able to keep the goon from killing Munsey. "Gustov! Stop this. Put the shooter away, will ya?"

Schultz's eyes darted over to Clara then back to Munsey. Slowly lowering the Lugar, the sigh that he released sounded to Clara more like the growl of a wild animal.

"Scram, Clay," Clara said, jerking her head towards the door to the kitchen, giving the man his chance to escape unharmed. Munsey didn't need to be told twice. He immediately fled the room without looking back.

Clara hadn't realized that she was holding her whiskey glass, her hand trembling ever so slightly after the confrontation she'd just witnessed. Then, holding the glass out to Schultz, she said, "I think you could use something to take the edge off."

After Schultz downed the remainder of her drink in one quick gulp, she asked, "Care to tell me what that was all about?"

The German eyed her closely. "Vut have you heard about zee robberies?"

"You mean the ones in the paper? Same as everyone else. Some rich schnooks got some of their stuff stolen."

"I know you girls hear a lot more zen you say. Vut are people here at zee club saying? Is there anyone who zeems to know too much? More zen they should?"

"Umm…" Clara didn't like that she was now the one being questioned. Even though he seemed to have calmed down, his words, though cool and calculated, were filled with menace. She understood exactly what he was asking. "You think Clay is part of all this? Like someone working for Big Bob Franklin is running a secret heist ring right under his nose? If someone was that stupid, they'd deserve whatever they had coming to them when they got caught. And I don't mean by the police."

"Zomvun at zis club is involved. Und I am going to find out who. And ven I do…I vill need to teach zem a lesson."

Clara watched as Schultz spun on his heels and marched off. Clutching her hands together tightly, for all the bravado she showed in getting him to lower the gun, she was still trembling. She couldn't even bring herself to think about what that man would do to them if he found someone working in the club was behind the robberies.

She definitely needed another whiskey.

Chapter Thirty-Two

As Clara Mowry suddenly found herself under the intense scrutiny of Gustov Schultz at the Platinum Peacock in the Guilford neighborhood uptown, the Alphabet Boys sat in their dark brown Ford on Stratford Road, trying to ignore the heat. Even having the windows rolled down did nothing to alleviate the intense temperature. Without so much as a hint of a breeze, the still summer air felt so thick it was suffocating. Having shed their jackets long ago, the three men now sat with their vests unbuttoned, fanning themselves with their hats. Streaks of perspiration ran down their cheeks as they kept their eyes on the house sitting at the corner of Stratford and Greenway. The enormous, white stucco two-story with its dark green shutters and black, wrought-iron decorative trim was the next target Cam had given the crew. It was the biggest home yet, and Cam assured Mo it would be the most rewarding.

Over numerous drinks at the bar, Cam learned that the owner of the home—a partner in one of the shipping firms operating out of the Port of Baltimore—and his wife would be traveling to New England for the remainder of the summer, taking most of the house staff with them. With only a single caretaker left behind to keep an eye on the property, it would be easy pickings for the Alphabet Boys.

After watching the house for the last couple of days, the crew discovered that a younger man, somewhere in his mid-thirties, was all that stood between them and the treasurers inside the palatial estate. Ernie had clocked the guy leaving the house every morning to run errands, only to return by lunchtime and remain inside the house for the rest of the day. He was a dutiful caretaker, to be certain. A young fella like him should have been out in the evenings kicking up his heels at one of the city's hidden dance halls, enjoying the liquor and the women. But instead, he confined himself to the house. Mo couldn't help but wonder how much he was being paid. It must have been a pretty penny if he was going to live like a priest for the rest of the summer.

No one was surprised that morning when the houseman did exactly as he had the day before and the day before that. His routine was set in stone.

Casting their eyes up and down the street one last time to make sure they didn't see anyone approaching, Mo Conklin and Roy Abbott stepped out of the car and buttoned their vests. Pulling their suit jackets on, they crossed the street and continued up the short walk to the front door. Even though the guy inside was younger and seemingly fit from what they'd observed, there was no doubt that Abbott could overpower him while Conklin knocked him out with the chloroform. This time, however, because they knew they had more time to spend rummaging through the house, they would have Burnstein pull the car into the garage so they could load it up with the goods and not worry about being seen on the street. Having all three of them in the house would also mean one of them could keep an eye on the caretaker and give him another dose of chloroform if he started coming to. They were going to spend as much time as they could on this job.

Standing at the front door, Conklin rang the bell with his left hand, as his right held the chloroform-laced handkerchief at the ready. Next to him, Roy Abbott adjusted his tie using the reflection of the glass in the door.

Seeing the puzzled look Conklin was giving him, Abbott said, "What? I can't look nice?"

Becoming impatient, Conklin rang the bell a second time.

"Can I help you, fellas?" a voice asked from off to their right.

Surprised, Mo turned to see the guy they'd been expecting to open the front door walking toward them with a grease-covered rag in his hand. From their vantage point in the car, they hadn't been able to see that he'd been working in the garage off to the right of the main house.

Abbott looked to Conklin, both men sharing the same thought. They didn't want to knock the guy out standing in the front yard where anyone could see them. And getting a good look at the guy with the sleeves of his work shirt rolled up to his elbows; they could see he had muscles and might make it difficult for them if he did put up a fight.

Thinking on his feet, Mo tipped his hat to the man and said, "Hello. Do you happen to be the owner of the home?"

"No, sir. Just looking after it for my boss," he answered, no concern or hesitation in his voice.

"Well…we're detectives with the Baltimore Police Department," Conklin continued, a broad smile spreading across his face. "Mind if we step inside and have a few quick words with you?"

The guy continued walking toward them, wiping his hands off with the dirty rag. "Does this have something to do with all the robberies?"

Mo looked over at Abbott, then back to their approaching prey. "Yes, it does. We're going door-to-door in the neighborhood."

"Ah. Well, I don't know if I would be much help. I haven't seen anything."

Now that he was only a few feet away, Conklin's mind was spinning, calculating all of their decreasing options. "All the same, it's awfully hot out here, and it will only take a couple of minutes."

"Especially if you haven't seen anything," Abbott added helpfully. "But we gotta check you off the list and let our boss know we've been here."

"What's your name, fella?" Mo asked, sounding as official as possible.

"Daniel, sir. Daniel Kilpatrick."

That explained the bright red hair, Conklin thought. "Maybe we could also trouble you for a couple glasses of water," Conklin decided to throw in. Why not? He figured two police detectives out canvassing the neighborhood on a hot day like today would be dying of thirst.

"Okay. Happy to oblige. But the front door's locked. Follow me 'round to the garage. We'll go in through the back," the guy said, turning and heading in the direction from which he'd first appeared. Behind his back, Mo and Roy looked at each other and smiled.

Gesturing for him to lead the way, to his brutish chum, Conklin said,

"After you, *Detective.*"

Chapter Thirty-Three

The cigarette smoke already hung thick in the air so early in the morning. Even with the window thrown wide open and a small electric fan that he'd found in an appliance shop the day before buzzing away, the haze in Lieutenant Cranshaw's office was only disturbed by strange beams of cloudy sunlight. His fourth or fifth cigarette in just the last hour held firmly between his fingers, Cranshaw was carefully rereading the descriptions of the thieves that each of the victims provided in their interviews. He was hoping that on his dozenth pass over them, something would jump out and point to a low-life already familiar to the police.

As Cranshaw was thumbing through the files, he was interrupted by a sharp rap on his office door.

"Come in."

A uniformed officer Cranshaw didn't know nervously stepped into the office with a piece of paper in his hand.

"Sir, there's been another robbery. I have the address," he said holding the paper out to the lieutenant.

Cranshaw was out of his seat like a shot, grabbing his hat and jacket and dashing out the door with the officer trailing behind him.

"Sir, don't you need the address?" he called after the lieutenant.

"No, because you're driving," Cranshaw answered over his shoulder.

Moments later, the pair were in a police car. The clanging of the siren cut through the incessant heat, the wail pounding against Cranshaw's temples as they careened onto Oxenhill Road, heading into the Guilford neighborhood. Cranshaw, nursing a blossoming headache, kept his eyes firmly on the road ahead as the car threaded its way around the other motorists. All told, the race from the Northern District station on Keswick to the house on Stratford Road took ten minutes, with Cranshaw urging his driver to push the vehicle, one of the newest motorcars which had recently been added to the department's growing fleet, to its maximum speed.

Without even allowing the car to come to a complete stop, the detective flung open the passenger side door and bolted from his seat, striding quickly across the scorched lawn—clearly suffering from the recent heatwave-to the open front door, where another police officer was waiting.

"Are you the officer who made the call?" Cranshaw asked, wasting no time.

"I am, sir. Officer Miller, sir," came the reply.

"Fine. Good," he said, nodding brusquely. Then, turning back to the officer who'd driven him and was only halfway to the front door, instructed, "You stay here and keep an eye on the street. Watch for anyone suspicious, and don't let anyone in unless they have a badge. Do you understand?"

"Yes, sir," he nodded, trying to catch his breath. The adrenaline and heat were getting to him. The heavy uniform jacket that he and all the patrol officers in the department wore was in no way conducive to the temperatures the city was experiencing. But the younger officer wasn't going to allow himself to faint in front of Lieutenant Cranshaw.

"Miller, tell me what you know," the detective said, stepping out of the blazing sun into the shade of the home's elegantly appointed entryway.

As his eyes adjusted to the drastic change in light, it didn't take him very long to see that the foyer had been stripped of anything valuable. Large empty frames dangled haphazardly on the walls, their paintings having been unceremoniously cut from them. A bunch of flowers lay in a pool of water on a side table, marking the spot where a missing vase once stood. And a large, carved antique cabinet sitting in the hallway leading toward the back of the home sat completely empty, its doors left wide open. It was going to take a while to put together a list of everything that had been taken with detailed descriptions so patrol officers and street contacts could keep an eye out for the items when the thieves tried to sell the pieces.

Seeing Cranshaw examining the empty shelves in the cabinet, Officer Miller said, "It's like that all over the house. They cleaned the place out."

"Did they force their way in like at the other robberies?"

"Well…" Miller massaged the back of his sweaty neck as he thought about how to answer. "This time, they were sort of let in, it seems."

"What do you mean by that, man?"

"Best you hear it from our witness…er, victim, sir."

Following Miller through the house, Cranshaw was able to see into several rooms where drawers were open, the contents dumped on the floor and rummaged through bare fireplace mantels, and more empty frames on the walls. This was all very different from the other robbery scenes. The crew hadn't taken nearly as much in the past. They were in-and-out jobs, grabbing whatever they could get their hands on quickly. This was looking like their biggest score to date. The detective wondered why they'd changed their MO. Was it possible the heat coming down on them because of the press coverage was forcing them into committing one final, ambitious job before vanishing for good?

Would that be so bad, Cranshaw wondered briefly. If they just disappeared and were never caught? At least the crime wave would be over, and no one else would get hurt. A more troubling thought gnawed at him. What if this robbery was the work of an entirely different crew altogether? Some goons inspired by what they'd seen in the paper.

Shaking off the thought, Cranshaw needed to stay focused and not let his mind run away on him. Another home robbery in Guilford, regardless of whether it'd been committed by the same miscreants or not, was bad enough. He didn't need to start compounding the problem by suggesting there were two sets of robbers roaming the streets of Baltimore. Regardless, he was certain he'd be making another trip to the commissioner's office tomorrow to provide a full briefing.

Shown into the large kitchen, Cranshaw was impressed with how modern it was. You didn't have to be a detective to notice how expensive the appliances were. They were all the latest and top-of-the-line. The stove alone would have made his wife green with envy. Not only did the smooth-top stove have four burners, it also had an oven *and* a broiler. And the matching refrigerator with a *built-in* ice box was almost as tall as he was. If the pieces weren't so heavy, he wouldn't have been surprised if the robbers had carried them off as well.

Matching the white countertops and cabinets, a table and set of chairs sat along one wall. In one of the chairs was a fit-looking young man with ginger hair and muscular forearms holding an ice bag on his head. He was dressed in an old, grease-stained work shirt and slacks. His gray complexion matched the color of his shirt.

"This is Daniel Kilpatrick. He works for the Butterfields, the owners of the home," Officer Miller said, introducing the man.

"Hello, Mr. Kilpatrick. I'm Lieutenant Cranshaw with the Baltimore Police Department," he said, taking a seat opposite the witness. Then removing his hat and laying it on the table, he pulled his notebook from his inside jacket pocket. "I have some questions for you. If you're feeling up to it."

"I'm going to have to let Mr. Butterfield know what happened."

"We can take care of that for you, Mr. Kilpatrick," Cranshaw offered. "Do the Butterfields have a telephone number where we can reach them?"

"Yes, of course. Mrs. Butterfield left the number in case…" Kilpatrick trailed off as he tried to get to his feet, only to begin to lose his balance. Miller was close enough to grab his arm to steady him and ease him back into the chair.

"We can get that a little later, Mr. Kilpatrick," Cranshaw said. "Why don't you just stay there? Officer Miller can get you a glass of water, and we can talk. Does that sound alright?"

Kilpatrick nodded slowly. The lieutenant supposed it was the effects of the chloroform making the man so unsteady. Which also meant now might not be the best time to talk to him. If his mind was still cloudy, he might not be able to provide the most useful statement. But if they waited, it gave the robbers time. Time they could use to get out of Baltimore. Or just to go into hiding.

"Officer Miller, after you get Mr. Kilpatrick a glass of water, please telephone the station and have them send a doctor," Cranshaw instructed. "I'd like Mr. Kilpatrick to be examined and make sure he's alright. In the meantime, though, I'd like to ask you some simple questions about—"

Voices coming down the hallway drew everyone's attention to the kitchen door. He knew there would be more department men on their way, but Cranshaw hadn't expected Captain Lawson to arrive so quickly. If he was being honest, he would have rather Lawson didn't show up at all and let him report on the incident after he'd had a chance to do some actual police work. When the captain left the station and showed up at a crime scene, it tended to put the men on edge and cause confusion as to who was in charge and Cranshaw wanted to make sure he kept control and everyone did their jobs. He'd heard a saying once about it not being good to have too many chefs in one kitchen. Ironic when he considered the room in which he was now sitting.

What bothered him even more was that, in addition to the other detectives who'd arrived with Lawson, Captain Joe Dixon strutted through the door. Stratford Road was far outside his Western District command. Cranshaw couldn't think of any reason for him to be there. It wasn't a secret that Dixon was quickly climbing the ladder, no doubt already having his eye on his next promotion, but he'd had nothing to do with the current case and had never been known as a crack investigator to begin with. So Cranshaw couldn't help but wonder why he was standing in the kitchen next to Lawson, looking like he was the most important person in the room.

"Is this the same crew?" Captain Lawson asked, removing his hat and tucking it under his arm. He was sweating profusely, the graying hair on his head stuck to his shiny scalp.

Cranshaw couldn't help but notice the contrast between the two captains. Lawson was older and seasoned. He'd worked his way up through the ranks, earning every promotion he'd received. Were there times when he was gruff and barreled ahead without thinking through what he was about to say? Yes. But Cranshaw believed him to be a good man. Dixon, on the other hand, was young, attractive, and a master of departmental politics. His charm and charisma were the keys to his success. When he'd been promoted to captain and taken over the city's Western District, to say there'd been some consternation amongst the veterans of the force was putting it mildly. Cranshaw didn't trust him. It was as simple as that. He was inexperienced and green. Too young to hold the post he did. But there was also something else. The lieutenant had a feeling Dixon liked to play games, pitting people against one another for his own benefit.

"Well, Lieutenant?" Lawson demanded. "Is this the same crew?"

"We haven't determined that yet. I was hoping to have Mr. Kipatrick examined..." he paused before finishing. Standing, he pulled his boss away from the rest so they could speak privately.

"Sir, may I ask what Captain Dixon is doing here?"

"Joe was at the precinct when the call came in. He asked to come along. Do you have a problem with that?"

"It's just that the less people roaming around, the less confusion there will be. And frankly, having the captain from Western here could raise questions."

"What type of questions, Lieutenant?"

"Like why he's here, sir." The two men had worked together for a long time, so Cranshaw knew he could be honest with his captain. "Joe Dixon isn't exactly an expert at investigations, and I don't want any of the men here thinking they need to be answering to him."

Lawson shook his head. "He's one of us. He's a cop. He's not going to get in the way."

It wasn't a fight Cranshaw was looking to have, so he let the matter drop. But if Dixon began stepping over the line and trying to insert himself into the investigation, he'd have to address it once and for all. Even if it meant Dixon trying to bring him up on charges of insubordination toward a senior officer. Cranshaw just hoped Lawson would have his back if it came to that.

"What about it, Lieutenant?" Dixon pressed as Cranshaw stepped back over to the table where Daniel Kilpatrick was still nursing his sore head. "Is this the same crew?"

"Captain Dixon, as I said, I haven't determined if the robbers are the same. Mr. Kilpatrick should be examined by a doctor before he's questioned."

"The old boy looks pretty healthy to me," the young captain said, rankling Cranshaw because Dixon and Kilpatrick looked to be about the same age. "I'm sure he can withstand a couple questions even if he has a headache."

Lieutenant Cranshaw looked to Lawson, who said, "Time is not on our side. We need to know what happened. If you sent for a doctor, it could be some time before he gets here. No harm in asking a few simple questions, Detective."

Cranshaw rolled his neck to try and release some of the tension that was building in his shoulders. He wasn't going to let his personal feelings interfere with how he did his job. He understood Lawson was right. They didn't have time to waste. This would make the fifth robbery in Guilford. Once it hit the papers, the department would look like it didn't know what it was doing. Critics of the mayor and Commissioner Gaither would be on the attack. And if the commissioner was unhappy, it would not bode well for the rest of the department.

Turning to a new page in his notebook, Cranshaw asked Daniel Kilpatrick if he could start at the beginning and tell them exactly what had happened.

Chapter Thirty-Four

1984...

After their meeting, the more Ben thought about what the mayor said, the more convinced he was that Charlie Oland was not the man responsible for Clara Daschle's death. Him killing her didn't make any sense. Not that murder ever really did. But there was no motive that Ben could see. Even though Ben knew Mayor Oland was a practiced politician, his reaction to the news felt sincere. No politician was that good of an actor. Plus, over the years, in their interactions, Ben had begun to pick up on Charlie Oland's tells. He knew when the man was putting on his public persona, a façade for the voters, and when he had let his guard down and was being genuine.

Even though he hadn't been in the room, Tommy agreed with his partner's assessment. Ben brought Tommy up to speed the next morning as they drove back to Clara Daschle's house. They'd decided to return to the crime scene for a second look around. Ben was particularly interested in finding her appointment calendar and address book. He wanted to see what she'd been doing for the last several days and if that might point to why someone would want to kill her.

Unlocking the front door to Daschle's home and stepping into the foyer, there were two things Ben was convinced of. The first was that Mayor Oland did not kill Clara Daschle. The second was that the break-ins in Parker were not related to those in Wakeville. At first blush, they both looked similar to the others as reported by the Sheriff's Department, but when you looked closer, the details were different. The Hubbards had an entire safe stolen, while easier items to pick up and carry off were left untouched. In Clara Daschle's case, it didn't look as if *anything* had been taken. On top of which, the robber, or robbers, had escalated to murder. The puzzle pieces weren't fitting together yet, Ben thought as he slowly walked through the house.

After making his first pass through each of the rooms, Ben returned to the study on the first floor. Spread out on the antique desk were technical drawings of different parts of the Harlequin Theatre. They included everything from the building's new façade to the floorplan for the lobby. One design was even a detailed engineer's drawing of the columns that would be used to support the balcony over the seats in the auditorium and how it would be decorated to blend with the rest of the décor. The plans led credence to Charlie Oland saying he'd been there to look at some of the designs.

Look as though Oland was telling the truth, then what actually happened? Ben stood next to the window looking out toward the street thinking through the most likely timeline. Oland and Daschle leave the reception between nine-thirty and nine-forty-five. They arrive at the house around ten. The two spend the next half hour reviewing the plans in the study. The study was directly off the living room where Clara Daschle's body was found. That meant Oland would have needed to walk through it to get in and out of the study. Two different times, his cufflink could have fallen out of his pocket. Daschle then shows him to the door and is now alone in the house. When she was found, she was still wearing the same dress she wore at the fundraiser, so she never made it upstairs to change. Did that mean she immediately returned to the living room, where she surprised an intruder, who then grabbed the statue from the mantel over the fireplace and struck her? Was she heading for the bedroom, heard something in the living room and went to investigate? Could the killer have already been in the house, and neither she nor the mayor noticed the broken window on the French door?

"Other than the broken glass in the patio door, nothing outside looks like it was disturbed," Tommy said, walking into the study. He'd taken a walk around the outside of the house. It had already been noted that all the doors and windows were locked, and the only place the perp could have entered was through the door in the living room.

"These plans back up Oland." Ben pointed to the drawings on the desk.

"Have you found anything else?"

"I was just getting ready to go through the desk. Care to join me?"

"You do know how I love a good rummage." Tommy smiled. "You take that side. I'll take this side."

Ben started with the bottom drawer on the left as Tommy opened the top drawer on the right. Bills and personal papers, stationery, pens, and stamps were all neatly organized.

"This reminds me of going through your desk," Tommy said.

"When do you go through my desk?" Ben asked, standing up straight and looking at his partner.

"What was that?" Tommy answered, giving Ben a wink.

"I swear. Sometimes I could just—" Ben stopped midsentence as he withdrew a personal day planner from the top drawer.

"Bingo," Tommy said, thankful for the reprieve. "Any idea what we could be looking for in there?"

"Not a clue. Just something that doesn't belong."

For an octogenarian, Clara Daschle was always on the go. She usually had two or three appointments or activities listed every day.

"I hope I'm this active when I'm eighty," Ben said, flipping through to the current week.

"You aren't this active now," Tommy countered.

"Shut up. Okay. Here we are. Wednesday night was the reception. She had a hair appointment in the morning. The day before…." Ben ran his finger down the day, not noticing anything out of the ordinary. Two days earlier, everything looked pretty routine until his finger landed on an entry for SS at eight o'clock in the evening. It was the only semi-cryptic notation for the entire week.

Flipping back to the prior week, it was much of the same. She attended a City Council meeting, had a dentist appointment, went to dinner with someone named Angela one evening, spoke to the Rotary Club, and had a telephone call with her stockbroker. Those were the highlights. And at eight o'clock on Monday, there was a notation that read SS.

Turning back another week, the same appointment appeared. Monday, eight o'clock, SS. The pattern continued like that for weeks. It was the only entry that one couldn't immediately decipher. Was that because Clara Daschle didn't want anyone to?

"Now I'm just intrigued," Tommy said. "We need to hire a detective to figure out what SS stands for."

Ben slowly turned and looked at his partner, raising a single eyebrow.

"What?" Tommy asked innocently, a mischievous twinkle in his eye.

Chapter Thirty-Five

In addition to finding Clara Daschle's daily planner, they found her address book, which was filled with hundreds of entries. What impressed Ben was that they weren't just names and addresses either. She'd made personal notes about each and every person. Birthdays, favorite restaurants, children's names, any little detail. It was going to take some time to review thoroughly and cross-check with her calendar to see who she'd been seeing recently. But taking a quick glance at the S listings didn't shed any immediate light on who or what SS stood for.

The only other item they found worth a closer examination was Clara Daschle's purse. The expensive Chanel bag was sitting on a small side table in the foyer. It would be the logical place to set one's bag when entering the front door so you could then type the code to disarm the security system.

"Make a note," Ben said over his shoulder as he was replacing the contents of the purse, "to find out what happened with her house keys."

"Her house keys? They're not in her purse?" Tommy asked.

"No. And I didn't see them in the study either."

"I guess she could have laid them down anywhere. I haven't seen them. CSU could have them."

"Yeah. I just want to make sure they're accounted for. No loose ends."

"Yes, sir. Where to next," Tommy asked, lighting a cigarette as they stepped out of the house and Ben locked the door.

"We need to get a full statement from Liliana Rey."

"Maybe she knows what SS means," Tommy said as they slid into the car.

Easing the car out of the driveway, Ben fished the notebook out of his pocket. Handing it to Tommy, he asked him to look for the housekeeper's address.

Flipping through the pages until he found it, Tommy said, "She lives down on Samuel Tildon Way. Twelve-seventeen."

Turning the unmarked Crown Victoria out of the Harper's Mill neighborhood, Ben mentally ran through the best route to get from where they were on the north side of the city down to the street named after the county's sheriff during the Civil War on the south side. It wouldn't take more than about fifteen minutes at this time of day, especially if he avoided going through Downtown to miss the traffic lights on every corner.

Neither of the detectives said much on the drive, each one lost in his own thoughts. Ben was running through a list of what needed to be accomplished as they kicked the investigation into Clara Daschle's murder into high gear. After speaking with the victim's housekeeper, they would need to do a dive into Daschle's life. He was also hoping that by the time they returned to the station, CSU might have delivered an initial report on their findings from the scene. If they were lucky, there'd be something in the report that gave them a solid lead.

The silence was suddenly broken by the police radio in the dash crackling to life. "PC12, come in. You there, Ben?" It was LuAnn in Dispatch.

Before Ben could reach for the mic, Tommy snatched it up and said, "Breaker, breaker. This is Detective Sergeant Benjamin Winters's personal secretary. How may I be of service to you on this fine day?"

"Tommy, you are such a dipshit," LuAnn answered. "Are you and Ben together?"

"That's affirmative. What's up?"

Ignoring Tommy, she began speaking directly to Ben. "Sarge, Officer Thompson is requesting you at Hubbard Autos."

Tommy held the mic over to Ben and clicked the button so he could respond. "Tell him we're on our way. Is everything alright? Or are we talking lights and sirens here?"

"It's a Code 1, at your convenience."

Ben looked over to Tommy, who shrugged, then said into the mic, "Copy that. On route."

Clicking off, he said, "Maybe he has something on the Hubbards' break-in."

There hadn't been any time to think about the Hubbards as events unfolded yesterday. Lieutenant Clover did him a favor by sending a crime scene tech over even though the unit was focused on the Daschle scene. Ben hadn't seen a report yet but would review it as soon as it came in. The Daschle homicide would remain a priority, but that didn't mean all other crimes would go unattended. More and more, he and Tommy were learning to divide their time among multiple cases as they came in. This was just the first time a murder investigation was included in the mix.

Diverting the car from its original path, Ben turned toward Dealers Row. It was a stretch of road along which all the car dealerships had popped up over the years. One after another. Anyone looking for a new or used car would just have to start at one end of the street and make their way down the line until they found exactly what they were looking for. With such a concentration of valuable merchandise just sitting on the lots out in the open, the PCPD tried to keep a unit on patrol in the general vicinity so they could have a rapid response if there were any incidents. The thought was, just having a cruiser drive down the road every half hour or so helped to deter anyone from trying anything. To date, the strategy appeared to be working. Ben couldn't even remember the last time there'd been a report of something happening out on Dealers Row for which the police needed to be brought in.

Hubbard Autos was the largest dealer of all of them. Its lot was twice the size of the others, filled with row after row of brand-new, polished cars just waiting to be driven off by a new owner. Ben parked next to two squad cars in front of the building with the large Hubbard Auto sign on the roof.

Walking into the sleek showroom, the pair were met at the door by a tall, overly tanned guy with slicked-back hair. Seeing the name tag, Ben knew he was a salesman, thinking he'd just laid eyes on his next potential sale. To avoid any confusion, before the man could even introduce himself, Ben flashed his badge and said, "I'm Detective Winters. This is my partner, Detective Mason. We're looking for Officer Thompson. We got a call to meet him here."

The salesman's face dropped the instant he saw the two silver shields. The detectives could almost see the words NO SALE flash in his eyes. Even though his smile faltered for only a fraction of a millisecond, they still clocked it. It was their job to perceive the barely perceptible, after all.

"Ah, Detectives, yes, hello. Um…your officers are in the conference room. This way."

As Ben and Tommy followed the salesman across the floor between display models of the newest Chevrolets, they noticed the other salesmen clustered in a group off to the side, speaking in hushed voices.

The conference room was down a short hallway beyond a pair of offices. Opening the door, Officer Neil Thompson stood at one end of the long table in the center of the room next to a seated Jim Hubbard. At the other end, two men wearing coveralls were seated with their hands cuffed behind their backs. Officer Stan Dunkin stood behind them, arms crossed over his chest.

"Neil…what's going on?" Tommy asked tentatively, his eyes passing back and forth over everyone in the room.

"Detectives, thanks for coming," Thompson said, crossing to them. "I thought I would follow up on something Mr. Hubbard said at his home yesterday. About some of the guys here at the dealership knowing about the safe in his house and the money he kept there."

Ben's eyes went right to the two mechanics, who were both looking down at the conference table in front of them.

Thompson continued. "I had an idea to come by before the place opened. And what do I see but these two guys pulling up in a van and unloading a safe. I watched them carry it into the shop. When I got back there, I found them trying to cut it open with some of the tools they have."

"You're kidding me?" Tommy asked. "They were actually trying to open their boss's stolen safe right here."

"Yes, sir," Thompson confirmed. "I radioed for assistance, then waited for Dunkin to arrive, and we busted them."

"Well done, Neil," Ben said, smiling at him like a proud father would at his son after he'd hit a home run on the ball field. "What made you think it was someone from the dealership?"

"Well…. It was just sort of a hunch. When nothing else except the safe was taken…, whoever took the safe would have to have a way to open it. I thought a repair shop might have what they would need. And if some of the guys here knew about the safe and knew the Hubbards were away…."

Ben was nodding as he listened. Stepping toward Thompson so only he could hear, he asked, "Is there any chance Mr. Hubbard put them up to it?"

Thompson shook his head. "Said it was their idea. They confessed right away. In fact, I was surprised how quickly they gave it all up. Never even asked for a lawyer."

"It would be nice if all the criminals were that accommodating," Tommy said, having been unapologetically eavesdropping. "And stupid."

Chapter Thirty-Six

After Thompson gave the detectives the Cliffs Notes version of his questioning of the two men regarding the Hubbard robbery, Ben asked Jim Hubbard to step out. He wanted a chance to speak with the two himself, but also asked the dealer if he could provide Officer Dunkin with the mechanics' work history and background information.

Once they'd left the room, Ben took a seat at the table across from the two unhappy-looking, cuffed men. Tommy perched himself on the ledge of the window that looked out on the car lot. He motioned for Thompson to join him, whispering, "Good work," as the patrolman leaned against the wall next to him.

"Your names are George Stottelmeyer and Kirk Johnson?" Ben asked, confirming the names Thompson gave him. "I'm Detective Ben Winters, and this here is my partner, Tommy Mason. I have a few questions for you."

Neither of the mechanics spoke. They just stared at him, resigned expressions on their faces.

"I just want to remind you that Officer Thompson has advised you of your rights, so you are free to not answer any of my questions."

"What more do you want from us?" Stottelmeyer, the larger of the two, asked, a tone of defeat in his voice. "We already told your boy everything. We did it. We broke into Mr. Hubbard's house and took the safe. There. Happy?"

Leaning forward, Ben noticed the strong smell of sweat and grease emanating from the dirty uniforms. Ignoring the smell, he said, "Actually, your confession is very helpful. It saves us a lot of time and trouble, really.

But I want to ask you about something else. About what time did you break into the Hubbards' on Wednesday evening?"

"What does it matter?" Stottelmeyer asked, a look of confusion on his face.

"I'll get to that."

"I guess about nine o'clock. Maybe nine-thirty. We weren't watching the clock exactly."

"And how long were you in the house?"

"I don't know. Maybe fifteen, twenty minutes."

"That's a long time for just breaking in and carrying out a safe, isn't it?" Tommy asked from his place by the window.

"We were looking around for a while."

"And you only took the safe," Ben confirmed.

"We just wanted the money," Stottelmeyer, the pair's apparent spokesman, answered.

"After you got the safe out of the house, what did you do then?"

"I dropped Kirk off at his place, then went home."

"But today is the day you decided to bring the safe into the shop and open it?" Tommy inquired. "Why didn't you do it yesterday? The day after you robbed the place?"

Stottelmeyer shrugged. "Yesterday was our day off."

Ben, doing his best not to laugh at the ridiculousness of the answer, thought he heard the blood vessel burst in his partner's head.

"You've got to be kidding me!" Tommy said. "How stupid are you two?"

"That you don't have to answer, Mr. Stottelmeyer," Ben said, turning and giving Tommy a stern look.

"No, I do want to answer that," he protested. Then, thinking twice about it, he changed his mind. "No. I don't."

Tommy rolled his eyes so loud Ben was sure the entire sales team out in the showroom heard.

Looking back to the mechanics, Ben began to focus in on the reason for his questions, saying, "You see, the same night you broke into the Hubbards,' another house in the same neighborhood—only one street over, in fact—was also broken into. Eleven-twenty Annapolis Way. Ring any bells with you?"

Kirk Johnson finally spoke up. "No. We don't know anything about that place. You can't pin that on us. Tell them, George!"

"Calm down, buckeroo," Tommy cautioned.

"We only broke into Mr. Hubbard's house," Stottelmeyer said, the conviction in his tone unwavering.

"On your way in or out of the neighborhood that night, did you drive down Annapolis Way?" Ben asked.

"No. You don't need to get to Mr. Hubbard's."

That was true. Both the street Jim and Millie Hubbard lived on, and the one on which Clara Daschle lived were separate offshoots of the main road into the neighborhood, running parallel to one another. You would drive right past Annapolis Way to get to the Hubbards.'

Ben had no reason to doubt what they were saying. But he found it odd that they were so willing to confess. Even after being Mirandized, knowing everything they said would be used against them. He wondered if it was their play to cop to the Hubbards so that when they were asked about Clara Daschle, their denial would be believed since they'd already been so forthcoming.

Deciding to go all in and try to rattle them, Ben wanted to see how they reacted when he asked, "So…if you were never at the house on Annapolis Way, I guess there's no reason to ask if you killed the woman who lived there?"

Johnson shot out of his seat. "We never killed no one! We were never at that house. We only broke into the Hubbards'!"

Neil Thompson reacted a split second faster than Tommy. He reached Johnson first, putting a firm hand on his shoulder and forcing him back into the chair. Seeing that Thompson had it under control, Tommy quickly backed off. But Ben saw what he needed to do. It was obvious these guys didn't break into Clara Daschle's house. He still had one more question, though.

"Mr. Stottelmeyer, Mr. Johnson, last question then you are going to be taken to the station and formally charged with breaking and entering and grand theft. Were either of you involved with the recent burglaries in Wakeville?"

Both men shook their heads no.

A few minutes later, as the detectives watched the crooked mechanics being loaded into the backseat of Thompson's cruiser, Ben said to Tommy, "I'd like to think that if we hadn't immediately been called to Clara Daschle's yesterday, one of us would have thought to look at the people working here. Neil's hunch paid off."

After thinking back on the brief interview with the men in the conference room, Tommy asked, "If these two goons are only good for the Hubbard break-in, doesn't that mean we have a bigger problem?" Waiting for Ben to reply, he pulled the pack of cigarettes out of his jacket.

"It means," Ben began, trying to carefully evaluate the situation, "the Hubbards weren't robbed by the same people breaking into houses in Wakeville. Which is good because it means those are still a problem for the Sheriff's Department. But it also means the break-in at Clara Daschle's wasn't related either. And unless there's a *third* set of robbers operating in Parker County, that means she was targeted. So, the problem would be, we have a straight-up killer on our hands."

"That was a really good summary. Depressing as hell. But accurate." Then, after taking a beat, Tommy said, "We still have SS. Maybe we should see what Thompson thinks it means. He seems to be on a roll today."

"You looking for a new partner?" Ben asked, heading for the car. "Because I think I'm the only one who can put up with you."

Following behind, Tommy said, "Honestly, I'm surprised you've been able to do it as long as you have. And you don't even really drink. It's a testament to your inner strength."

"Shut up," Ben said, closing the door and starting the car.

"Okay. To Liliana Rey's?" Tommy asked.

"To Liliana Rey's," Ben answered.

"Then lunch?"

"Then lunch."

"Can we get ice cream for dessert?"

"You're like a child," Ben said, shaking his head and shifting the car into gear.

"So…? Yes?"

Chapter Thirty-Seven

Clara Daschle's housekeeper lived in a World War II-era row house on the south side of Parker City. The area had remained well-kept over the years, and while not necessarily a middle-class neighborhood, the working-class families who lived along Samuel Tildon Way took pride in their homes. Most of which displayed window boxes filled with freshly blossoming flowers, adding some color to the otherwise gray and brown masonry. Many of the houses also had porch swings so the residents could sit outside in the evenings and visit with one another. It was a lovely neighborhood. Ben thought as he parked in front of Liliana Rey's.

"You know," Tommy said, adjusting his holster as he stepped out of the car, "I was actually just looking at a house that's for sale down the street there."

"To buy?" Ben asked, so surprised at hearing this he froze while he was only halfway out of the car.

"What else would I be looking at it for?"

"Sorry. I'm just… I didn't realize you were looking to move."

"A little more room wouldn't be so bad."

It wasn't that he couldn't picture his friend living in a house. It's just that Tommy had never shown any interest in moving out of his mobile home. Ben knew it wasn't an issue with money. As detectives, they made a decent salary. But Tommy's father had been a successful attorney, as had his grandfather. And his uncle was a very highly paid private investigator. Ben knew he'd inherited a good deal of money from them over the years.

Tommy put on a good show, acting completely carefree, like he never took anything seriously. But he didn't throw money away. A home would be a good investment.

"Well, if you do buy the house—" Ben started to say.

"You better believe I'll be asking for your help painting and moving in."

"I'm sure Natalie would love to help decorate," Ben offered with a smile.

After knocking, the door was finally answered by the woman they'd seen sitting in Clara Daschle's kitchen the previous morning. Liliana Rey was petite, with gentle eyes that were still red from crying. Her salt and pepper hair was pulled back in a ponytail, and she wore a cardigan sweater over a simple day dress. Ben pegged her to be somewhere in her mid-fifties.

"Mrs. Rey," he began, "I'm Detective Ben Winters. I don't know if you remember me from yesterday. But my partner and I were hoping we could speak with you about Mrs. Daschle. We have some questions that will help with our investigation. Do you have some time to talk?"

"Of course, Detective." Ben noticed just the hint of a Spanish accent.

Inviting them in, she showed them to the living room in the front of the house, asking if either would like something to drink. She had a cup of tea sitting on the coffee table, along with a stack of magazines. The soap opera *Ryan's Hope* was on the television, which Rey turned off as she passed on her way to the sofa. Politely declining the offer, Ben and Tommy sat in the two armchairs in the room.

The home was comfortable, with plenty of family photographs hung on the walls, along with several Catholic crosses. Crocheted doilies covered nearly every surface. And Ben thought he could smell the unmistakable aroma of fresh bread baking in the kitchen.

Trying to put the woman at ease, as much as they could under the circumstances, Ben began by asking some simple background questions. In doing so, the detectives learned that Liliana Rey was a first generation American, her parents having immigrated to the United States the year they were married. She'd been born two years later in New York City, where she lived until she married. Her husband's job is what brought the couple to Parker, where they began their own family. She said that her youngest daughter still lived at home with them.

When Ben felt the time was right, he began gently probing her relationship and history with her late employer. It turned out she'd been Clara Daschle's housekeeper for over fifteen years and something of a friend and confidant. She'd worked for her long enough to have known Daschle's husband before his passing as well. Rey only had the nicest things to say about them. At first, Ben wasn't sure how much of it was genuine affection and how much of it was because Daschle had been dead for less than thirty-six hours. But when Rey began taking out photo albums and showing them pictures of picnics and parties at the Daschles' home that her family was invited to over the years, it became clear that they really were friends.

It was heartbreaking to finally hear the woman's account of arriving for work as she usually did on Thursday mornings, only to find Clara Daschle bludgeoned in the living room. The recent memory unleashed a new wave of tears that Ben felt terrible for instigating. But he reminded himself it was his job to ask difficult questions because, in the end, at least he hoped, it would provide closure.

"In the last few weeks, do you know," Ben asked, "was Mrs. Daschle having problems with anyone?"

"No. She was always friendly with everyone. She could be short with people sometimes, but not because she was being rude. Because she was always so busy. She worked with many charities and was always talking about one project she was working on or another. Her latest was the Harlequin Theatre."

"When we were at her house, I saw pictures of Mrs. Daschle when she was younger. Do you know, was she a performer?"

"Oh, yes." Rey's eyes brightened. "She had a beautiful voice. She used to tell me about the clubs she sang in. Mostly in Baltimore when she was younger. Some of them were, oh, what is the word? What did they call them? The places people went to drink when drinking wasn't allowed?"

"Speakeasies," Tommy offered.

"Yes! That's it. She used to work in speakeasies. It always sounded so glamorous. And all the people she met. They were like characters in a movie."

Ben and Tommy exchanged looks.

"Not all speakeasies were like in *The Great Gatsby*," Tommy pointed out gently.

Ben couldn't hide the surprised look on his face as he turned to his partner.

"I do know how to read," Tommy said. "But anyway, Mrs. Rey—"

"Yes," Ben said, turning back to the housekeeper. "If Mrs. Daschle used to work in Baltimore, how did she end up here in Parker City? Was it because of her husband?"

"Oh, no. She was originally from Parker. She grew up here, then left to live in Baltimore. After she married Mr. Edward, they moved here."

"Do you know when that was?"

"Long before I started working for them. I don't know."

"Did the Daschle's have any children?" Tommy asked, knowing that Spurrier had already learned they hadn't from her yesterday, but wanting to confirm the detail. She simply shook her head in response. "What about brothers or sisters?"

"Mrs. Clara had a brother. But she didn't talk of him much. He died when they were young. It made her very sad. All of her family had passed by the time I started working for her. But she had so many friends. Everyone loved Mrs. Clara. She was always telling me about new people she would meet and want to stay in touch with. She was always writing in her book, making sure she had everyone's telephone number and knew where they lived so she could send them Christmas cards. Mrs. Clara was very thoughtful like that."

The comment about the address book gave Ben the perfect opening.

"Mrs. Rey, it looks like Mrs. Daschle had a standing Monday evening appointment with someone named SS for the last several months. But we can't find anyone with those initials in her address book," Ben said, pointing to the two books he'd laid on the coffee table when they first sat down. "Do you happen to know who SS is? Or what the letters stand for?"

Liliana Rey's tan complexion flushed as she quickly averted her eyes. Both Ben and Tommy knew they'd struck a nerve. But neither was going to push.

They'd let her answer in her own time. The best information a witness could share was always voluntary. Though, on occasion, a little coaxing was necessary.

"Mrs. Rey," Ben said softly, "we're looking for any reason someone would want to hurt Mrs. Daschle. Whatever you can tell us… It will all help us find who did this to her."

After a few moments of silence, she finally said just loud enough for them to hear, "I know who SS is."

"Thank you, Mrs. Rey. This could help. Who is SS?"

"Sexy Sam." The words came out so softly neither detective thought he'd heard her correctly.

"I'm sorry. Did you say, *Sexy Sam?*" Tommy clarified, doing his best to leave all judgment out of his voice but knowing he couldn't hide the look of surprise on his face.

Rey nodded and again looked out the front window toward the street, nervously wringing her hands. Both Ben and Tommy found themselves caught completely off guard.

"Who is Sexy Sam?" Ben carefully questioned.

"He was Mrs. Clara's…friend. That's what she called him. Sexy Sam."

"Oh…. He was her boyfriend," Ben said, feeling a little less awkward.

"Not exactly, Detective." There was another pause. "He was…you know, on the TV shows…they call them…escorts."

"Uh-huh. I see." Ben's pen hovered frozen over his notepad.

Chapter Thirty-Eight

1927…

"The description of the men is identical to what the other witnesses gave us," Lawson practically shouted, as Lieutenant Cranshaw stood on the opposite side of the captain's desk back at the Northern District station. "It's the same gang."

"Yes, sir. This latest robbery appears to have been committed by our guys," the detective acknowledged.

"Dammit, Cranshaw! The papers are gonna be all over us tomorrow! Did you see all those reporters outside the house when we left? My phone hasn't stopped ringing!"

Lieutenant Cranshaw understood the pressure his boss was under. But yelling at him about the press was going to accomplish absolutely nothing. He hated the newspapermen as much as any of the detectives in the Baltimore Police Department. But his concern wasn't how they were going to be portrayed in the papers. He didn't have the luxury of worrying about his public image like the mayor and police commissioner. His job was to catch the criminals, and it didn't always happen quickly. But he did have a plan.

"Captain, I want one of the police artists to take the descriptions we've been given and put together drawings of these men. It's time we get their faces out in the public. If the papers are going to be so interested in this investigation, then let them help us. I know the guy I want to do the pictures."

Lawson chewed on his lower lip as he turned over in his head what Cranshaw was suggesting. There'd never been a problem releasing an official police sketch of a suspect in a crime before, but this case was different. He'd need to run it by the commissioner first before he'd give his approval. The saying that justice was blind was a nice thought, but when the city's rich and powerful were the victims, the rules tended to change. Something he'd been reminded of in recent days. Just not in those exact words.

"I think it's a bang-up idea," Captain Joe Dixon said from his seat in the corner of the room. He'd returned to the station with Lawson and Cranshaw, and, for some reason, the lieutenant couldn't understand, was welcomed into the conversation. "Cranshaw's right. Get the lugs' faces out there. Let the public help us catch these guys."

Though he appreciated Dixon's support, he didn't trust him. He couldn't figure out what his angle was. Why was he so keen on this investigation? It never once crossed his mind that he could somehow be involved, but why he'd taken such an interest in the case when it was well outside of his district, he didn't know. That was just one more thing he didn't have the time to worry himself with.

"I'd be happy to send one of my men up here to do the drawings," Dixon offered.

"No. I have the guy. He works out of Central District."

"Just trying to help, old man."

The term *old man*, even though he recognized Dixon was using it as a friendly expression, rankled Cranshaw because he wasn't that much older to begin with. Plus, no true Baltimore cop talked like that. He knew of a few guys in the precinct that would like to join him in dragging the weaselly young captain into an interrogation room and knocking some sense into him.

Putting the dark fantasy aside, he took a deep breath and said, "I appreciate that, Captain. But everything is under control. I'll have these drawings made this afternoon and get them in the morning editions. Once the city sees them, someone is bound to come forward with an identity."

"But did you ever consider who else might be looking for these guys?"

Dixon asked, not looking at either Lawson or Cranshaw, but instead fixated on his fingernails. "If you put their pictures out, you may never be able to find them."

"What are you saying?" Lawson demanded. The heat had finally gotten to him. He removed his uniform jacket and hung it over the back of his chair. The white shirt underneath was drenched with perspiration.

Cranshaw locked eyes with Dixon, finally breaking the silence, saying, "I know what he's on about, sir. He means Big Bob Franklin."

"What about him?" Lawson asked, dropping into his chair.

"All the crime in this town is controlled by him," Captain Dixon pointed out nonchalantly.

"And?" Lawson still wasn't on the same page.

"And these robberies aren't the kind of business Franklin usually gets involved in," Cranshaw explained, thinking through what that meant. "He's not a petty criminal. He runs a million-dollar empire. Home robberies? It's small-time. And Big Bob is anything but."

Joe Dixon's smile appeared as more of an arrogant smirk. "Exactly, Lieutenant."

Cranshaw continued to follow the line of thinking. "Since many of the city's more affluent residents tend to frequent Big Bob's establishments-"

"Establishments we've never been able to shut down," Dixon added.

"—the odds are that some, or all, for that matter, of the homes that were robbed belong to people Big Bob knows or wouldn't want anything to happen to. It could end up being bad for business. So, if this crew is operating without being sanctioned by Big Bob..."

"He could be looking for them, too," Lawson said, finally catching up. "You think the people who were robbed go to Franklin's clubs?"

Both Cranshaw and Dixon gave him the same questioning look in response. It was no secret that illegal bars and clubs were being run all across Baltimore. Just as they were in every major city in the country. The clientele of these outlawed watering holes consisted of every rung of society. Rich and poor. Black and white. It didn't matter. So, for Captain Lawson to somehow be surprised that their victims weren't completely virtuous was close to laughable. In fact, Cranshaw thought, that could be what actually connected all of them. He hadn't thought much about it, but now he wondered. Was that a possible line of inquiry to be followed? It pained him that it was Joe Dixon who'd given him the idea.

"So, what do we do with these descriptions?" Lawson leaned forward and fixed his gaze on the detective.

"You could always just publish the drawings and let Big Bob take care of them," Dixon suggested.

"That's not how I do things, Captain," Cranshaw said through clenched teeth, his temper boiling at the idea of laying down on the job and allowing the city's crime boss to exercise his own brand of street justice. As long as he was wearing a badge, he would never surrender his duty. The legal system was the means by which criminals were tried and punished if found guilty. The justice of the legal system could never be abandoned or turned over to the criminals. Otherwise, what was it all for in the end?

"It's alright, Lieutenant. No need to blow a gasket. I wasn't serious."

"Weren't you?" he asked, eyes narrowing.

"Cranshaw," Captain Lawson warned. "*Captain* Dixon was just making a little joke."

After a tense moment of silence, Cranshaw raised his hands, giving in. "Sorry. I'm just a little worked up."

"Of course you are, old man. I don't blame you." Dixon rose to his feet and walked over to stand next to the detective. In reality, he was half Cranshaw's size, but his ego made him the biggest man in the room. If not the entire station. Cranshaw figured he could knock him on his arrogant ass with one blow. "As far as the pictures, you could always have them made and just give them out to the patrolmen on the street to keep an eye out for. We do that in Western District all the time."

Cranshaw knew Bob Franklin had eyes and ears in the Baltimore Police Department. Doing what Dixon suggested would have the same effect as just running the sketches in the paper. At this juncture, he couldn't see a viable way to keep Big Bob and his goons from finding out what the robbers looked like.

CHAPTER THIRTY-EIGHT

That's when he had another idea.

169

Chapter Thirty-Nine

Later that afternoon, Lieutenant Cranshaw found himself taking refuge from the merciless sun that continued to bake the city in the shadowy doorway of a nondescript, rather forgettable building on East Chase Street. Across the street, he watched as guests entered and exited the Belvedere Hotel, one of the most luxurious lodgings in the city. The tan brick, eleven-story building loomed over the street. A symbol of the city's prosperity, the hotel welcomed some of the most powerful people in the country to Baltimore over the years, including Presidents Teddy Roosevelt and Woodrow Wilson. In its restaurants and suites, countless business deals were agreed upon, and occasions celebrated. Cranshaw, himself, had only set foot inside once. It was for a function honoring members of the police force. An elaborate affair designed more for the press coverage than anything else, Cranshaw concluded at the time.

One might think that the building he was now waiting in front of seemed out of place on the street with one of the city's most glamorous. Its simple red brick façade and five floors were dwarfed by not only the Belvedere, but the buildings surrounding it. It would be easy for someone walking along the street to pass by without giving it a second glance. That was by design, though. The owner wanted the building to go unnoticed as much as possible. Because directly across the street from the most expensive hotel in Baltimore was the most popular speakeasy in town, the Platinum Peacock. With the club nestled in the subterranean basement of the building, the five floors of offices above ground were merely for show. But it was from the top floor where Big Bob Franklin ran his criminal empire.

Even though the location of the illicit club was well known to the Baltimore Police Department, it remained untouchable. If a daring police detective like Cranshaw managed to put together a raid of the property, Franklin would have no doubt been tipped off and arranged for anything and everything incriminating to be moved or hidden where no one could find it. That had been the case at smaller drink joints Franklin owned around the city. It left the police brass figuring if they couldn't take down one of his smaller establishments, why waste the resources going after the crown jewel of his organization. There were other ways they could eat away at his business. Not that it seemed to do much good, Cranshaw thought.

Bob Franklin was known to keep to a pretty regular schedule. He'd usually show up at his office above the Peacock in the late afternoon and spend several hours going over the books of his various interests and meeting with associates. Then, he'd cross the street for dinner at the Belvedere Hotel before returning to spend the evening playing host to all the denizens of Baltimore who flocked to the Platinum Peacock each night.

Cranshaw watched several men and women disappear through a backdoor to the building over the last few minutes. Clearly, the staff arriving for the evening. A couple of them eyed the detective as they passed, trying very hard not to look as though they were noticing him, of course.

It was the young woman with hair as black as ebony who didn't avert her gaze as she passed that caught his attention. Her skin was as smooth as porcelain and only made more pale by the bright red of her lips. But it was something in her eyes. He'd seen it before, but only a few times. And only in the eyes of hardened criminals.

Before he was able to give it much more thought, a small group of men dressed in dark suits with matching fedoras began crossing the street from the direction of the Belvedere. Accompanied by his loyal bodyguards, Big Bob Franklin hustled across the road. They were certainly a well-dressed crew. Cranshaw guessed that just one of those hats probably cost as much as *everything* he was wearing. The only thing ruining the look of those bespoke suits were the bulges created by the guns the men were packing.

As Big Bob stepped onto the sidewalk, the lieutenant emerged from the shade of the alcove in which he'd been standing and positioned himself directly in Franklin's path. Almost in unison, the goons clustered around the crime boss all began reaching for their guns. Allowing them to see he was unarmed, Cranshaw held his hands innocently out in front of him.

"Look who's come to visit," Big Bob said, elbowing one of his men aside so he could walk right up to Cranshaw, "the saintly Lieutenant Cranshaw."

"Hello, Bob," Cranshaw said, crossing his arms in front of his large chest, not intimidated in the least by the man.

"What brings you to my place of business, Detective?" Franklin pulled a silver cigar case from his inside jacket pocket and withdrew one of the Cubans, running it beneath his nose, taking in the scent.

"I believe we may have a mutual concern."

Biting off the end of the cigar and spitting it directly at Cranshaw's feet, he said, "A concern. I have no idea what you are talking about. Maybe you can elaborate, Lieutenant."

Cranshaw rolled his eyes. He didn't have time to be playing games. He was beginning to think coming to speak with Franklin was a mistake and, worse yet, a waste of time. "You know exactly what I'm talking about, Bob. And if you don't, then maybe you aren't as connected as everyone thinks you are. I'm sure that big German Shepard of yours knows the score. Is he keeping things from you?"

If he could have shoved the expensive cigar down the cop's throat, Big Bob would have taken pleasure in watching Cranshaw choke right there on the street. But he held his temper, knowing the detective was just trying to provoke him.

Taking his time lighting the end of his cigar, Big Bob finally said, "Why don't we step inside? It's awfully hot out here and I don't want anyone saying I'm not a gracious host. Maybe I could offer you something to drink while we're talking. No alcohol, of course."

"Are things getting too hot for you?" Cranshaw asked, twisting the words around into a verbal dagger that he watched hit its mark. For a moment, he wasn't sure if the smoke he saw circling around Franklin's head was coming from the cigar or his ears like in one of the cartoons in the funny pages.

CHAPTER THIRTY-NINE

"Funny, Lieutenant. Let's just cut to it. What is it you want?"

"I want to know everything you know about this robbery crew working up in Guilford. Spill!"

"I'm sorry. I'm a law-abiding citizen. I don't associate with those sorts."

"Cut the baloney, Bob. This is all between you and me. And your muscle here, I guess. But this crew is causing us both problems. The sooner I put them behind bars, the better it is for everyone. I figure the longer they're out there making headlines, the more people might think you're losing control."

"You're doing this all for me? Trying to catch these mugs. Why don't you beat it? I can take care of my own problems."

Making a show of removing his hat and scratching his forehead, Cranshaw said, "I guess you don't know anything about these guys…otherwise they wouldn't still be running around pulling jobs."

Replacing his hat and turning to walk away, over his shoulder, he said, "Have a nice day, Bob."

As he rounded the corner, out of sight of the gangster and his men, a police car was waiting to return him to the station. The patrolman leaning on the hood of the car folded the newspaper he'd been reading and climbed into the driver's seat. Cranshaw waited a moment before sliding into the passenger seat, resting his hat on his lap.

"Let's go, Arnie. To the clubhouse," Cranshaw instructed, directing his driver back to the station. "And if you take us by Earlie's, I'll buy you a soda pop."

Cranshaw used the ride to the station to think through his next move. He never truly believed Big Bob was going to share any information he might have learned about the robbers. His aim was to see the boss's reaction to being questioned so he could gauge how much he actually knew about them. Judging by what he'd seen, Franklin knew next to nothing, and it was pissing him off. Even though he'd put on the "I'm in complete control, and these mooks don't bother me" act, Cranshaw had been dealing with men like Bob Franklin for long enough to pick up on their tells.

The one thing the police had was a description of the crooks. But the minute the police sketches ran in the paper the next morning, Franklin would have that, too. Which is exactly the reason he'd decided to give the drawings to the press for publication. He *wanted* Big Bob to see them. If he or any of his men recognized them, it was a safe bet his enforcer, Gustov Schultz, would be dispatched to find and deal with the robbers. That's why Cranshaw had assigned detectives from the Northern District to keep an eye on the German over the next several days. Captain Lawson even offered to provide some patrolmen in plainclothes for the surveillance operation to increase the number of eyes that would be on Schultz at any given time.

Of course, if some upstanding citizen saw the paper the next day and happened to know who the men were and reported their identity to the police and where they could be found, he'd be able to call off the watch on Schultz. Either way, he felt tomorrow could be crucial in bringing this robbery crew down. They just needed to wait for the papers to hit the streets in the morning.

Chapter Forty

Bob Franklin stormed into his office, flinging the door open with such force it left a slight impression on the wall where the doorknob struck. Unfazed by his employer's dramatic entrance, Gustov Schultz remained seated on the leather sofa on the far side of the room. Reading a copy of *The Baltimore Sun*, he didn't acknowledge Franklin until he'd finished the article he was reading. He then calmly folded the paper and laid it on the seat next to him, the black and white of the paper a stark contrast to the rich green leather.

"I just had a visit from Lieutenant Cranshaw," Big Bob snapped, casting his harsh gaze across the room at Schultz.

"Vut did he have to zay?" Schultz asked without a single note of emotion in his voice.

"He was taunting me about these infernal robberies. He asked what I knew about them. He said it sounded like I was losing my grip on the city."

"He vas just trying to make you angry," Schultz pointed out. "He is not a dummkopf."

Big Bob began pacing behind his desk, plumes of cigar smoke filling the air.

"What are you doing about these mugs?" he demanded. "They've been at their game for weeks. You need to find them! And when you do, I want them at the bottom of the Chesapeake. Do I make myself perfectly clear?"

Finally standing, Schultz crossed to Franklin's desk. It only took him a few steps to cover the distance with his long legs. Then, leaning his large frame on the corner of the boss's desk, he caught Franklin so off guard, he stopped mid-step. He'd never known his man to behave so casually. Even more disconcerting was the curl of his lips. Was that a smile?

"Do you know who they are?" Franklin asked, hope quickly replacing the rage he'd been feeling.

"Captain Dixon sent a message. Sketches of zee men will be in zee papers in zee morning."

Big Bob's eyes narrowed as he absorbed the information and began turning it over in his head.

"Cranshaw is asking the public if anyone knowns who zay are."

"But we have to wait until the morning papers come out?"

Schultz shook his head. "I do not intend to vait zat long. I vill be paying a visit to…a friend…at zee paper zo I can zee zees pictures early."

Now Big Bob was also smiling. He knew once they saw their faces, they'd be able to find the men who'd been causing such trouble. And when they found them, they'd pay dearly. Making them an example so no other lowlife thugs would dare think they could challenge his authority in the city.

Franklin was about to offer Schultz a drink when there was a knock on the door.

"Who is it?" Big Bob asked, placing the remainder of his cigar gently into the ashtray on his desk.

"It's Clara."

"Come in, doll face."

Stepping into the office, Clara's floral perfume overtook the smell of Big Bob's cigar. The lavender scent was her signature and only added to her allure. With her dark hair flowing down her back, wrapped in her silk robe, she was a vision of light and beauty standing in the dark, wood-paneled office that had been the setting for so many criminal discussions.

"What can I do for you, my dear?" Big Bob asked, walking around his desk to greet his headliner. Seeing her always put a smile on his face. Even when he was preoccupied with other matters. Clara Mowry was one of his most prized possessions.

Casting her eyes to the floor, Clara appeared uneasy. Something neither of the men was accustomed to seeing. She was always so strong and vivacious.

Seeing this concerned Franklin.

"What is it, doll face? What's troubling you?"

"It's just…when I was coming in tonight, there was a man outside. It looked like he was watching everyone. Casing the joint from the outside. Something wasn't right about him."

Big Bob looked to Schultz, then back to Clara.

"There's nothing to worry about. But I appreciate you coming to me. You're a good little girl."

"I just thought you should know. He gave me the heebie-jeebies something awful."

Big Bob took her into his arms, his large form engulfing her petite frame. "I would never let anything happen to you or any of my girls. There's no need to worry about anything."

Resting her head against his chest, she said, "It's just with everything that's been in the papers, I didn't know…"

"You shouldn't be reading the papers, Clara. Nothing but bad news in them. All those damnable reporters just want to scare people. Besides, Gustov here is about to take care of all our problems very soon. That's what I pay him for. Isn't that right, Gustov?"

The response he received was something between a sigh and a low growl.

"I trust you," Clara said, pulling away and giving him her most illuminating smile. "I have to go get ready for tonight."

"Sing something special for me this evening."

"I will," she said, giving him a wink as she turned and scooted out of the office.

Once in the hallway, her demure, anxious posture evaporated. She was once again the confident woman who'd made her own way from a small town to the big city using every means at her disposal. Including her acting skills. Casting a final look at the heavy door leading into the boss's office, she quickly hurried away down the corridor.

Chapter Forty-One

An uneasy air of anticipation filled the Platinum Peacock that evening. Word of the stranger loitering outside earlier in the day rapidly spread among the employees. One of the waiters who'd seen him using the building's front entrance as cover thought he recognized him from a photograph in the newspaper. When another waiter provided a copy of *The Sun* from several days before, it was confirmed that he was the copper leading the investigation into all the Guilford robberies. Needless to say, his presence set everyone's tongues wagging. Older members of the staff and those close to Big Bob knew about Lieutenant Cranshaw and how much their boss despised the man. On a number of occasions, Big Bob's voice could be heard booming through the walls, deriding the police detective for interfering with one thing or another.

Once word of Cranshaw began to circulate, the whispering began. By that point, there wasn't a single person working at the Peacock who didn't know about the recent incidents or who hadn't heard about Gustov Schultz confronting Clayton Munsey, the club's maître d,' about the matter. Following the dust up with Munsey, the enforcer took to questioning the staff about what they may have heard about the robberies. It didn't take a genius to figure out Big Bob and Schultz must have thought there was some connection between the Peacock and the culprits. Yet, no one was able to shed any light on the situation. Which frustrated the German to no end. He'd frequently been spotted storming through the halls, muttering to himself in his native language. And the few waiters who spoke German dared not repeat what he said. At least in the company of the fairer sex.

By the time the doors of the popular nightspot opened that evening, and guests began arriving, no one could say from whom or exactly where they heard it, but the latest rumor circulating was that Schultz was about to discover the robbers' identities. Everyone knew what that meant. Once he learned who they were and where he could find them, he'd be exercising Big Bob's special brand of discipline on them.

The moment the first bottle of bubbly was popped and the orchestra began to play however, all thoughts and concerns about what had transpired over recent weeks and what was certain to come in the near future was set aside. The Platinum Peacock was coming to life, once again the spot for residents of the city to escape from the troubles of the world. To forget about everything in their everyday lives for the night and throw all cares out the window. The liquor flowed, the music soared, the guests danced. It was a gilded world unto itself from dusk until dawn, when the sun would rise and remind everyone of their responsibilities and the fact that the evening had been little more than an illusion. But an illusion that would gleefully return night after night.

From her vantage point on stage, Clara Mowry saw all the smiling faces before her. Couples twirled around the dance floor as she sang a rendition of "Blue Skies" while a rowdy group of young bankers was laughing and making a ruckus at a table in the back of the room. On any other day, she'd be reveling in the atmosphere and excitement of it all. But tonight, her mind was elsewhere. First, seeing the detective outside the Peacock, then finding out Big Bob had a line on the robbers was troubling her.

From listening outside the door to his office, she knew by the end of the night, Gustov Schultz would have pictures of the crew operating in Guilford. Even though they would just be artist sketches put together from the descriptions given by the victims, she knew who they'd see. The Alphabet Boys: Mo, Ernie, and Roy.

She hadn't seen the fellas for a couple of days, and her fear was that they'd show up tonight and be sitting ducks when Big Bob and Schultz discovered they were the men everyone was looking for. Since earlier that afternoon, she'd been trying to figure out how she could warn them to stay away from the Peacock. Or better yet, get out of Baltimore altogether. They couldn't stick around if their faces were going to be plastered on the front page of every newspaper in the city. Between the police and Big Bob's men, they were going to get caught. And she desperately didn't want to see anything happen to them. She'd known Mo forever and grown fond of Ernie Bernstein and Roy Abbott.

Big Bob was seated at his usual table, lifting a glass with several men Clara didn't recognize, but they looked important. Not just because of the clothes they were wearing but because of the men sitting at the table next to them. Clara knew what a bodyguard looked like when she saw one. Plus, the fierce-looking men at the second table weren't drinking. Which was a sure giveaway that they were working. Since they sure as hell weren't police, there was only one other thing they could be with those guns tucked so conspicuously under their expensive jackets.

As "Blue Skies" came to an end, Clara gave a little bow, taking in the applause. Then, blowing a kiss to the band conductor, she stepped off the stage, winding her way through the boisterous crowd. It was time for a little break, and she could really use a drink. Several of the Peacock's regulars stopped her to say how much they'd been enjoying her performance. With a smile and a glint in her eye, she accepted the praise and continued toward the bar.

She hadn't seen Gustov Schultz since she was in Big Bob's office, and he wasn't anywhere to be found in the club at the moment. That worried Clara. Could he have already found the boys? No. Surely, he would have gotten word to Big Bob, and he was still smoking and laughing at the head table. She relaxed slightly as she took a sip of her champagne, the bubbles pleasantly tickling the back of her throat. She'd have rather been drinking something stronger, but downing a glass of whiskey would not be appropriate.

The second glass of champagne began to lift her mood. She was just starting to believe Mo and the fellas had skipped town after the last robbery when she saw Conklin confidently striding through the dining room. Mo looked like he didn't have a care in the world. Her heart stopped. He was walking towards her. Their eyes met, and he obviously registered the look on her face. With a quick, sharp shake of her head, he stopped. Slyly motioning toward the stage, he changed direction and headed for the door that led backstage.

Clara waited a moment, watching to see if anyone had noticed him. When no one moved to follow Mo, she cut her own path across the room to the often-overlooked door beside the stage. Conklin was waiting for her on the other side. When she saw him, she rushed into his arms.

"Well, hello to you too," he said, wrapping his arms around her tightly.

"You're in trouble, Mo. You and the guys have to get out of town. The police have sketches of you. They're going to be in the paper tomorrow, and Schultz said he knew someone who'd show him the pictures early. That's probably where he is right now. You can't be here. Please, you have to go," she pleaded into his chest. "Everyone's going to know you were behind the robberies, and they'll be looking for you. You aren't safe here."

Mo gently lifted her chin and spoke as calmly as possible, trying to reassure her, "It will all be fine. We always knew it would come to the point where Bob and that Kraut would be coming after us. It's all part of the plan."

"But you have to get out of Baltimore. Tonight! Now!"

"Ernie's outside in the car. He's waiting for me. We'll go pick up Roy and leave tonight."

"I won't tell anyone anything."

Mo smiled at her. He knew Clara could keep secrets. He wasn't worried about anyone finding out about him and the Alphabet Boys from her ruby-red lips. But it was good to know they needed to leg it out of town tonight. He'd hoped they'd have more time before having to get on the move, but there was no reason to tempt fate. They'd head west this evening to his hometown. As long as Cam stayed behind to keep an eye on things, everyone would be fine.

There was only one problem. They needed some cash. The haul from the last robbery hadn't been shifted yet. Cam would take care of that. But that didn't help them at the moment. The bulk of their money was being kept safe at Cam's place, and Mo knew there was no way to get at it tonight. He'd seen Cam in the middle of a crowd the minute he'd walked through the door. If Cam left the Peacock now, someone could notice and might start putting the pieces together.

Clara was peeking through the side of the curtain, looking out at the dining room, when Mo saw her body go rigid. Peering through the thick velvet curtain himself, he saw Gustov Schultz standing at Bob Franklin's table, handing him what must have been a copy of the morning's paper. The look on both their faces said it all. Even though there was no way to know what they were saying, the sharp gestures and animated expressions made it clear they weren't happy.

"You have to go now!" Clara said, turning to Mo and pushing him toward the hallway leading to one of the Peacock's back exits. "They can't see you. If they do—"

"I'm going. Take care of yourself, kitten. Remember, you don't know anything." He gave her a final wink as he adjusted his hat and bolted for the exit.

Looking back out to the dining room, Clara saw Schultz giving orders to a group of Big Bob's thugs. Franklin himself had disappeared. He was nowhere to be seen.

Taking a deep breath and smoothing out the front of her dress, she was just preparing to step through the curtain and back onto the stage when a large hand clasped onto her arm. Startled, turning around, she looked into the face of Big Bob Franklin.

Chapter Forty-Two

1985...

"So..." Tommy said, standing next to their unmarked Crown Vic outside Liliana Rey's house.

"Yeah," Ben responded, still thinking about what they'd just heard. Once he'd placed Clara Daschle's address and date books in the backseat of the cruiser, he turned to his partner, shaking his head. "You could have given me ten guesses to figure out what SS meant, and never would I have thought male escort."

"Really?" Tommy lit a cigarette and inhaled deeply. He insisted the nicotine helped him think better. "Because it was the first thing I thought of."

"Shut up. It is not. And you want to know why I know it wasn't? Because if you had thought SS was an escort, you wouldn't have shut up about it. In fact, I can't believe you haven't made any jokes yet. We've been out of Liliana's earshot for," Ben paused to look at his watch, "a good two minutes now. Are you feeling alright?"

"For your information, the reason I haven't made any jokes, is because I don't think this is a laughing matter. This Sam guy could be our killer."

Ben raised an eyebrow and tilted his head.

"Okay, no," Tommy said. "That's not it. I just have so many jokes running through my head right now, I can't figure out which one to say first."

"That's better," Ben said, walking around to the driver's side of the car.

"Get in."

It was time for them to head back to the station so they could regroup and determine their next move. Plus, he'd told Tommy they'd get something to eat after talking to the housekeeper. If pressed, he'd also admit that he was hungry. When working a case, he found he was more hungry than normal because he was burning so much energy. On a day when he was just sitting doing paperwork, he could work straight through lunch without thinking about it. But when he and Tommy were out on the street, his stomach became very aware of the time of day. Tommy, on the other hand, could eat all day long regardless of what they were doing.

Cutting through Downtown on the way back to the station, they decided to grab sandwiches at a little family diner that had been around for decades. It was one of the few businesses that was able to reopen after the Great Flood of '78 because it hadn't been completely overtaken by the storm waters, and the neighborhood pitched in to help get it cleaned up and reopened. DeGeorgio's was an institution. The community wasn't going to let it be washed away like so many of the other places.

Walking into the diner, Ben and Tommy took the booth in the back. They figured if they were going to discuss the case, it would be better for the fewest people to hear them. All the other diners preferred to sit closer to the front by the windows or at the long counter that ran along one side of the eatery.

DeGeorgio's was close enough to make it a regular lunch spot for many courthouse employees. It wasn't uncommon to see a judge or two sitting at the counter either, along with lawyers, clerks, and bailiffs. It had been that way since it first opened back in the '30s, which is why the owner at the time instituted the policy that no one was allowed to discuss any legal matters while dining in his establishment. He felt no matter how contentious things became in the courtroom; everyone needed a sanctuary where they could put their differences and opposing views aside and enjoy each other's company in a social setting over a good meal.

It had also been a rule put in place after two lawyers nearly came to blows while acting as opposing counsel. If it hadn't been for a deputy sheriff sitting quietly having a roast beef sandwich, the arguing attorneys would have done more damage than just breaking a couple of plates and glasses. Since then, talking about court cases was off limits.

Since Ben and Tommy were discussing an investigation, not a court case, they weren't breaking any rules and were always welcomed by the family running the diner. Especially when Tommy went out of his way to flirt with the owner's wife and sister, who always waited on the customers. Both women in their sixties, they enjoyed the attention of a handsome young man. Even though they knew he was just having some fun with them.

But as Maria DeGeorgio would say when Ben told his partner to knock it off, "I'll take it where I can get it!"

After Ben's club sandwich and Tommy's meatball sub were placed in front of them, along with a large basket of crispy French fries, by a smiling Maria, they dug in. They were halfway through their food before starting to talk about the case.

Ben had once read a piece in some law enforcement review written by a veteran LAPD detective discussing something he dubbed the 24/24 Rule. It referred to the twenty-four hours immediately preceding a person's murder and the first twenty-four after. If there is no clear suspect upon discovery of the body, what the victim did for the twenty-four hours leading up to their murder is important to learn because it is possible something they did triggered the event. Or at least facilitated it in some way. After that, you look at the aftermath. If the killer didn't leave any obvious clues or make any serious mistakes in the twenty-four hours following the deed, it becomes significantly more difficult to solve the crime. In big cities like LA and New York, they were averaging several murders a day. So, if investigators were unable to close a case within the first few days, the murder they were looking into on Monday could get buried by the next one the very next day. That one would then take a backseat to the one on Wednesday, pushing the Monday investigation back even further. That meant the first hours were key.

Neither Ben nor Tommy had the feeling Clara Daschle's murder was the beginning of a spree, as they were now already a day removed without another incident, so they had the sad luxury to remain focused on the single murder that occurred in the city that week. Especially with Neil Thompson having already solved the mystery of who stole the Hubbards' safe. But the 24/24 Rule still applied regardless.

As they munched on the French fries, they discussed how they needed to set out a timeline of Daschle's last day, in addition to doing a deep dive into her life story in general. The more they could learn about her and her past, the more information they'd have at their disposal. For the post-24 part of the equation, they would need to wait for the crime scene reports to reveal if anything useful had been found.

Ben's hope was that they'd at least have initial reports by the end of the day. Lieutenant Clover was usually very good about getting his people in the State's Crime Scene Unit to turn things around pretty quickly. The assistant medical examiner on the scene warned Ben it might be a full day or two before they could perform an autopsy, which would give them a more solid time of death and confirm what everyone surmised at the scene: that Daschle'd been killed when her attacker struck her with the statuette they'd found next to the body.

Then there was the matter of running down Sexy Sam.

"Daschle was what, in her eighties?" Tommy asked, wiping some marinara sauce from his chin. "This Sam guy could get in good with rich older women, scope out their houses, and knock 'em off."

"A story right off of television," Ben said. "But two things. One, there hasn't been a rash of elderly women being knocked off in the city. None that I'm aware of, and I have a strong feeling we'd know about it."

"Good point," Tommy conceded. "And two?"

"And two, if Sexy Sam's end game was to kill the women and steal from them, nothing appeared to be missing at Daschle's except her brooch. She had some pretty expensive-looking jewelry that wasn't touched. None of the artwork was taken. The televisions were all there. The money in her purse hadn't even been touched. In fact, other than the brooch, the only other thing missing is her house keys. And it's possible CSU took those."

"So, what you're saying is that you don't think Sam's the guy. He didn't do it."

"I'm saying it seems unlikely. Unless the brooch had some meaning to him."

Tommy thought for a moment. "You said the thing was covered in stones. It could be worth a pretty penny."

"But there was still so much more he could have taken. Hell, there was so much more *whoever* did this could have taken."

"Unless they were interrupted," Tommy suggested.

"Unless they were interrupted," Ben repeated.

"But does that mean we are thinking someone broke into her house to rob it, she walked in on them, they killed her, freaked out, and ran?"

"Except," Ben began, "for the fact we know she and the mayor had been in the house for about a half an hour, presumably with the lights on and a car in the driveway. Not the type of target a random robber is looking for."

"He'd have to be pretty ballsy to break into a house he knew people were in."

"Exactly. And the break-ins in Wakeville all happened when the families were out of the house. So, different MO. Odds of this being part of that…I just don't feel it."

"Right." Tommy was following Ben's logic. "When you put all of this together, it sounds to me like someone was specifically after Clara Daschle. Did they intend to kill her? That's the million-dollar question. If they didn't and beating her over the head was…an accident…what was their intention breaking into her place? Just to talk?"

Tommy'd summed up what Ben was thinking pretty well. It looked like they were on the same page with the case. But just because they shared a theory didn't mean they were any closer to figuring out who the killer was.

Suddenly, Tommy snapped his fingers. "I've got it. Daschle was seeing two male escorts. One of them found out about the other and confronted her. She denied it. He knocked her on the head with the statue. That's my first idea."

Ben saw his partner starting to spin up his outlandish theories. "You've come up with more than one possible killer? So, the first is a jealous male escort. Who's the second?"

"Russian KGB agent. Clara Daschle was an international spy that needed to be silenced."

"Check, please!" Ben said, looking around for Maria DeGeorgio.

Chapter Forty-Three

Arriving back in the Detective Squad's office, Ben found a stack of messages from local reporters looking for a comment on the Daschle case. The department was able to hold off putting out a statement until earlier in the day, which meant the news hadn't broken in the paper yet, buying Ben and Tommy time without any media attention. But once news of Daschle's death was made public, as Ben expected, everyone wanted to talk to him. One by one, as he flipped through the messages, he dropped the little yellow notes in the trashcan. There would be no further comment beyond what the department already released.

The name on the final message slip caught his eye. Roger Benedict. He'd been the reporter at the *Herald-Dispatch* during his and Tommy's first big case. The reporter who'd given the Spring Strangler his moniker and who'd always seemed to be one step ahead of them during the investigation. For a time, he'd even been a suspect. Ben wouldn't even mention the guy's name in front of Tommy for fear of setting him off. On more than one occasion, Tommy'd begged Ben to let him shoot Benedict…in the foot…of course. But after the Strangler case was closed, Benedict moved on to wider pastures. He was out of their hair, and Ben couldn't think of the last time he'd thought of the reporter.

Looking at the message, it read:

ANOTHER HIGH-PROFILE MURDER IN PARKER CITY ON YOUR WATCH, SERGEANT WINTERS? CARE TO COM-MENT?

The taunting message joined the rest in the trash. Then, turning to the chalkboard where they'd begun accumulating their notes on the case, he added the details Liliana Rey shared with them.

As Ben was clearing off his desk and updating the board, Tommy placed a call to a friend of his in the Parker County Sheriff's Department who was assigned to the Vice and Narcotics Squad. As the largest law enforcement agency in the county, the Sheriff's Department was able to have more specialized units than the smaller municipal forces because they had the manpower and resources. These specialized teams could then assist the individual departments as needed or work larger cases throughout the county as a whole.

Even though Chief Brent had organized an Anti-Drug Task Force inside the PCPD itself, it would regularly work with their sheriff counterparts. The vice aspect of the squad's portfolio was to monitor and disrupt prostitution across the county in any form. Tommy was hoping they might be able to help locate Sexy Sam so they could have a word with him.

Hanging up the telephone, Tommy stood up and pulled on his sports coat, saying, "I'm running over to the county lock-up. My buddy says they just did a sweep a few days ago and took down a whole male escort ring. None of it's been reported yet while the state's attorney is getting his ducks in a row, but they've got a guy cooling his heels over there with the name Sam Stefanko. Could be our Sexy Sam."

"Did your friend say if he's represented by counsel? He might not want to talk to you," Ben pointed out.

"Unless I'm really careful with what I ask," Tommy countered.

"Tommy."

"Look. I have no intention of asking him if he's ever accepted money for sex. That's not part of this investigation. All we need to know is if he knew Clara Daschle. If he did and he saw her every Monday night, then he's off the hook, and none of this has to go any further."

"What do you mean?" Ben asked, not understanding.

"Vice picked all these dudes up the day before Daschle was murdered. Sam's been sitting behind bars all this time. If he's SS, then we know he didn't do it. He couldn't have."

"It would be a great way to clear him. Definitely a solid alibi. But I'm still afraid he won't answer the question. A good defense lawyer-"

"First of all, there's no such thing as a good attorney," Tommy interrupted.

"*Your father* was an attorney."

"He wasn't *that kind* of an attorney. He never helped bad guys get out of jail," Tommy argued. "Why don't you just let me handle Sexy Sam? I'll make sure I do it the right way. Trust me."

With that, he turned and walked out of the office with a grin.

Chapter Forty-Four

The Parker County Sheriff's Department was housed in an early '70s-style glass and steel framed building just outside of the city. It sat at the intersection of the two main highways running through the county, making it easy for deputies to jump on the road heading in any direction when dispatched. On the same piece of land, but in a separate, much more Spartan structure, was the county jail where anyone picked up by the deputies for committing an infraction—large or small—was processed and held, as well as where remanded defendants were housed during their trials.

After checking in at the front desk and identifying himself, Tommy sat flipping through magazines in the small waiting area for twenty minutes before Deputy Ethan Shanks, a sergeant with the Vice and Narcotics Squad, appeared before him. He was tall and broad-shouldered, with a square jaw and short blonde hair. Today, he was out of uniform, dressed in a white button-down shirt and gray slacks, with a light blue tie. He could have passed for a banker or any other office worker, except for the badge that hung on a chain around his neck. He was also wearing glasses, something Tommy had never seen his friend do before.

"You getting old, Ethan? Need help reading?"

"Very funny," he said, reaching out and shaking Tommy's hand. "No. It's just my allergies are acting up and my eyes hurt too much to put my contacts in this morning."

"Well, those are some pretty thick lenses you got there."

"Hey, man, I'm doing you a favor here. You don't see me making fun of your porn star mustache, do you?"

Tommy feigned offense. "How dare you, sir."

Both men laughed as Deputy Shanks led Tommy through a set of metal doors, down a long hallway flanked on either side by offices and meeting rooms. At the end of the corridor were two interview rooms with an observation suite between them. Shanks opened the middle door, allowing Tommy to enter first. To their left and right were the backsides of the one-way mirrors that were installed so people could watch the conversations taking place on the opposite side in the interview rooms. A table and chairs sat under each of the mirrors with an elaborate tape-recording setup wired for each interview room.

"You got some fancy equipment in here," Tommy said, recognizing the recording devices as some of the newest on the market.

"This is nothing. You should see what Robbery-Homicide has in their interrogation setup. Those lucky bastards get all the fun toys," Deputy Shanks complained. Then, pointing to a man sitting at the table in Interrogation Room C, he said, "There's the guy you asked about. His name is Samuel Joseph Stefanko. Age thirty-five." He was reading from a file he'd picked up off the table.

"When was he arrested?"

"We picked them all up Tuesday morning at various addresses around the county. Part of a sweep we did after flipping one of the guys that was part of this escort service."

"And he's been in a cell since you picked him up?"

"That's right," Shanks confirmed. "Some of the paperwork on these busts got a little…mixed up, shall we say? So, their arraignments aren't until next week. They'll be staying with us for the next few days."

"I'm guessing their lawyers aren't too happy about that," Tommy said, knowing Ben would be having a fit if he knew arraignments were being purposely delayed. But this was the Sheriff's Department, so they had no say here.

"We got rock solid intel on the guys we picked up and a cooperating witness. They're guilty. They can sit behind bars for a few days. It won't kill 'em. And as far as the lawyers are concerned, that's above my pay grade. I'm just doing what my lieutenant tells me. They're probably all gonna plead out anyway, so they might as well spend some time locked up. There needs to be some sort of punishment for breaking the law."

Taking Stefanko's file from Shanks, Tommy looked at the thin record. Other than the most recent arrest, he was clean. No, Tommy corrected himself flipping the page, he also had a speeding ticket a couple years back. Other than that, the guy might as well have been an altar boy. He'd definitely plead out as a first-time offender. Looking at him through the window, Tommy observed the handsome, clean-cut young man with dark brown hair, an athletic build, and bright blue eyes.

All he needed was for the escort to answer one simple question. If he was cooperative, he could be out the door and on his way back to the PCPD in five minutes. Taking the file with him, he walked from the observation room into the interview room, Deputy Shanks following behind.

The room had a white linoleum floor with matching white walls. In the center, bolted to the ground, was a steel-framed table with a white laminate top. Tommy felt the sheriff's interior decorator must not have cared too much about this room.

"Good afternoon, Mr. Stefanko...? Did I say that right?" Tommy asked.

"You did. Yes," the man said with a nod.

"My name is Detective Tommy Mason with the Parker City Police Department. This is Sergeant Ethan Shanks with the Sheriff's Department."

"Yes. Deputy Shanks and I have met."

"Good. Then we're all acquainted," Tommy said laying the folder down on the table between him and Stefanko. Taking a seat, he noted that they were also white. Tommy hated this room.

"I'm sorry, but shouldn't my lawyer be here if you're going to question me?" Stefanko asked without a hint of confrontation in his tone. So far, Tommy was getting the impression this guy wasn't all that bad.

Tommy smiled. "Look. Here's the deal. I'm going to be completely honest with you. Like I said, I'm with the PCPD. We're not part of whatever bust the sheriff's boys wrapped you up in. I'm not here to ask you about your...work.

I'm here regarding a murder investigation. If you can answer one simple question…maybe two…I will be on my way."

"A murder investigation?" Stefanko sat forward in his chair. "What murder? I didn't kill anyone. What are you talking about?! What's going on?"

"Take a deep breath, Mr. Stefanko. Let me explain. Wednesday evening, Clara Daschle was murdered in her home on Annapolis Way. That's up in the Harper's Mill neighborhood of Parker City. That's why I'm here." As he said this, he carefully studied the man's face for any reaction. Next, he removed a photograph of Clara Daschle from his jacket pocket and laid it on the table, sliding it toward Stefanko. "What I would like to know is, do you know this woman?"

It was obvious he did. It was written all over his face. Regardless of what he said, Tommy knew he'd found Sexy Sam.

"I want my lawyer. I wasn't involved in a murder."

"Sam…may I call you Sam? That's exactly what I'm here to prove. That you *weren't* involved in what happened to Mrs. Daschle. If we can just keep this conversation casual, you won't need a lawyer. I've already worked out with Sergeant Shanks that anything you tell me here will not be used as a part of his case. I don't think you killed this woman. But I need to clear you as a suspect. If you want to wait for your lawyer, though, then we can all sit here in this…charming interrogation room for the next few hours."

Stefanko looked back and forth between the two men on the other side of the table.

Shanks finally spoke, saying, "Look. I have no interest in jamming you up on any more charges. I've already got my hands full with the ones we have. As far as I'm concerned, no one even knows we're having this conversation. It's off the record."

"Will that work for you?" Tommy asked.

He knew if Ben were here, he'd wait for the guy's lawyer to make sure there were no questions about the appropriateness of the conversation. But that would take too long, and he was already getting the vibe that this wasn't the guy. He could have walked out of the room right then, knowing Sexy

Sam didn't kill Daschle even without hearing another word from Stefanko. But so they could one hundred percent clear this guy, he needed answers to his questions. Even if they were going to be treated as background and off the record.

"Okay," Stefanko said, still sounding unsure.

Tommy pointed down to the photo on the table and said, "All I want to know is if you knew Clara Daschle. I don't need to know how or why you knew her. I just need to know *if* you knew her."

After a long pause, Stefanko's shoulders slumped as he leaned back in his chair. Tommy even thought he saw tears welling up in his eyes. "Yes. I knew her. She was a very nice lady."

The way Tommy phrased his next question was very important. "Did you happen to see Clara Daschle every Monday evening? Again, I'm not asking what you two did or where you met. Or for how long. Nothing like that. I just want to know if you two would *happen* to see each other once a week on Monday evenings."

Stefanko swallowed hard, then wiped his eyes. "Yes. Yes, we did."

Turning to Shanks, Tommy said, "Sergeant, can you once again tell me when Mr. Stefanko was arrested?"

Flipping the folder open on the table, he pointed to the arrest log and answered, "This past Tuesday morning at eight-forty-five AM. Since then, he's been held in the county lock-up."

"Thank you, both. That means Sam here had absolutely nothing to do with Clara Daschle's murder. I will now get out of your hair." Standing, he started for the door.

"I'll see you out," Shanks said. "Sam, you stay here. I'll be back for you in a minute."

On their way down the hall, Shanks asked, "So that helped you with this murder case?"

"Yes, it did," Tommy answered. "It eliminated a possible suspect. Just needed to cross the T's and dot the I's on this one."

"Did you think he could have been the guy?"

"Not after I saw him and read his practically non-existent rap sheet. Gut instinct. I don't know what kind of charges you have on him, but he doesn't seem like—"

"This is his first offense. It's not up to me, but I don't think the state's attorney will be too tough on him. Especially if he cooperates. But again, it's for people more important than me to make that call. Anything else I can help you with, Detective?" Shanks asked as they reached the reception waiting area.

"Well," Tommy said, thinking for a moment. "You can find me a new suspect in Clara Daschle's murder."

Chapter Forty-Five

1927...

Lester "Mo" Conklin flung the door open and rushed into the dark alleyway behind the Platinum Peacock. Looking in both directions, he was happy to see the alley was empty. The worst thing would have been to charge out the door and run directly into a mob of Big Bob's goons. He didn't think he'd be able to talk his way out of that one. But thankfully, he didn't have to.

Other than the rumble of passing motorcars, the night was silent. Disturbingly so.

Conklin needed to get across the street and down the block to where Ernie was waiting without anyone seeing him. In a few hours, he was going to be one of the most wanted men in the city. But for now, it was just Franklin's men looking for him. Which he fully understood was worse than the police. If Schultz got his hands on him or Ernie or Roy, they'd never be seen again. At least not in one piece, he thought as he cautiously looked up and down the street. Ducking out of the alley, he hurried away from the Peacock.

Across the street, in a room on the second floor of a Civil War-era building with creaking floorboards and no electrical wiring, sat Detective Sam Peterson. A longtime friend of Cranshaw, he'd been stationed on that side of the Platinum Peacock specifically to watch the alley that ran behind the club. It was rarely used, but Cranshaw wanted every door covered.

They couldn't allow Gustov Schultz to slip past them. He was the key to finding the "Guilford Gang"—that would run above the police sketches in the *Baltimore Sun.*

Seeing the man emerge from the darkness, the veteran detective sat up in the uncomfortable chair, leaning out the window to try and get a better view. Next to him, the plainclothes patrolman who'd been assigned to Peterson as a runner saw the detective's posture change.

"Look," the detective said, pointing across the street. Sticking to the shadows, they couldn't see who the man was, but he didn't have the same physical build as Schultz. That much they could tell. But Detective Peterson had been on the job long enough to know something was hinky.

"You need to get down there and follow him," he instructed.

"Right-o," the officer said, grabbing his hat from a small table next to the window and heading for the door.

From the same table, Peterson picked up one of the department's new flashlights. In addition to being able to cast a bright light across a dark space, it was also equipped with separate green and red bulbs. For the current operation, Cranshaw ordered his watchmen to flash the red light if they spotted Schultz. If they saw anything else that aroused their suspicions, they were to use the green light.

Peterson aimed the flashlight toward the front of the Belvedere Hotel, where Lieutenant Cranshaw and Detective Bert Merrill were positioned in a car just down the road from the main entrance to the Platinum Peacock. Flashing the green lamp, he waited for a response.

On the other end of the signal, Merrill flashed his own light. "Peterson sees something."

"Is it Schultz?" Cranshaw asked, turning in the direction of Peterson's post.

"No. It's green."

As the officer in charge of the night's operation, Cranshaw had taken the post watching the entrance to the Peacock. A discreet door easily missed if one wasn't looking for it. From this vantage point, they had a clear view of everyone entering and exiting the building. As the hours ticked by, more people were now leaving the club, their evenings coming to an end.

Cranshaw was on pins and needles. A shot of adrenaline had surged through him fifteen minutes earlier when an expensive-looking sedan pulled up, and Gustov Schultz emerged. In two long strides, he crossed the sidewalk and quickly disappeared into the Peacock carrying what looked like a rolled-up newspaper.

Cranshaw smiled. It looked like his plan was going to pay off. The big German appeared very determined. The detective wondered if he'd recognized the robbers when he saw the police sketches.

Waiting for what Schultz and Big Bob did next was the difficult part. Cranshaw had lost track of how many cigarettes he'd smoked since taking up watch outside the hotel hours ago. But the pile of cigarette butts outside the car door was growing.

From the direction in which Peterson's signal came, the two detectives saw a man quickly walk through the pool of light under the streetlamp on the corner. A couple minutes later, a second man trotted along the same route.

"I think that was Tanner," Merrill said, identifying the officer who'd been stationed with Peterson.

Cranshaw nodded. He'd let them deal with whatever that was. If it turned into something the other teams needed to be made aware of, they knew the protocol. He was keeping his focus on the club, watching for Schultz to make a move.

Chapter Forty-Six

"Something wrong, doll face? You aren't looking so good." Big Bob's eyes were dark and foreboding, sending a shiver down Clara's spine. "You startled me, is all," Clara answered, hoping he wouldn't see through her. "I, um…I was just getting ready to go back out. But it looks like something's going on. What's got old Gustov all ginned up?"

Clara was trying desperately to control her breathing while appearing as natural as possible. But she knew she was a good performer, and Big Bob was always so easy to sway. Like most of the men in the club, all she ever needed to do was batt her eyelashes and smile, and they melted. She'd learned long ago that if she was going to survive and live any sort of life that was better than the one she did growing up, she'd need to use every trick in the book.

Letting out a dismissive huff, Big Bob said, "Nothing for you to worry your pretty little head about. He's just taking care of something for me, is all. Pretty soon, somebody who's been giving me some trouble won't be a problem anymore. It's better for all of us, really. You know I'd never let anything happen to you."

"I know," Clara said, forcing herself to lean in and give him a peck on the cheek. "I just don't like seeing you so tense."

"You're a good little girl, Clara. Now, get back out there and show those people what you can do. I'm starting to think more of them come to hear you sing than to drink my booze."

She forced another smile, then quickly turned and slipped through the curtains, feeling Big Bob's eyes on her as she went.

Chapter Forty-Seven

Sitting in the car had begun wearing on Cranshaw. The nervous strain was building inside him, and his legs were beginning to cramp. He needed to stretch them for a while. Pacing beside the car, keeping one eye on the entrance to the Platinum Peacock, he made small talk with the young patrolman who was his runner for the night. Cranshaw didn't know the kid but had been told by Captain Lawson he was a stand-up fella and could use the experience working with some detectives. Cranshaw wasn't going to argue. The more bodies he could have for this operation, the better. A lot was riding on Gustov Schultz, knowing who the men were and going after them.

A few minutes earlier, as he was stretching, Officer Tanner came hustling around the corner. He told the lieutenant that Detective Peterson saw a man exit the alley on the other side of the building and instructed him to follow the guy. Just down the street, he jumped into a car that drove off. Tanner hadn't been able to get a good look at the man or the driver but said he was obviously in a hurry.

"That's fine," Cranshaw had said. "Head back and take over for Sam. Tell him to take a walk. Send him over here. I want to talk to him."

"Right-o, Lieutenant," Tanner said, jogging back to the building opposite the alley.

For the first night in weeks, the heat wasn't as unbearable as it had been. During the recent heatwave, the evenings were just as uncomfortable as the days. But tonight, no one felt like they were baking in an oven. It was still warm, but the sort of temperature Baltimore was used to during the summer months. Maybe things would start to cool off in the coming days. It would certainly be a welcome relief.

As he took another few laps back and forth along the side of the car, through the window, Detective Merrill said, "You're making me nervous, Cranshaw."

Before he was able to respond with a witty retort, his attention was drawn to two big cars pulling up in front of the club. One of which was the car he'd seen Gustov Schultz arrive in not more than half an hour before.

His instincts told him this was it. Something was about to go down. Reaching into the car through the open window, he grabbed the flashlight and signaled the surveillance team down the street at the other end of the block. Flashing the red light, he was warning them. Telling them to get ready. In turn, the detectives in that car would signal the men behind them. All three teams would be ready to go as soon as Schultz moved. The system was arranged before leaving the station. When Cranshaw flashed the white light, it meant they were rolling out, and the others should follow.

Getting into the car, he instructed his runner to do the same. When he saw Sam Peterson coming down the sidewalk, he waved him in as well. Detective Merrill started the car as they all watched Schultz and a phalanx of hoods rush from the Peacock and load into the two waiting vehicles. The engines roared, and the cars sped off down the street.

"Alright, boys. Here we go. Bert, do not lose them," Cranshaw warned.

"Hey, I'm a good driver. You don't have to worry about me."

"Right now," he answered, "I'm worried about everything."

From the back seat, Cranshaw heard the unmistakable sound of a revolver's cylinder snapping open, then closed. Looking over his shoulder, he eyed Peterson.

"Just making sure it was loaded," the detective said with a wink.

"Let's hope it doesn't come to that."

Then holding the flashlight out the window, he gave the signal for the cars to follow Schultz and his gang.

Chapter Forty-Eight

Back at the Tacoma Grand Hotel, Ernie Bernstein parked the Ford around the corner from the building at a haphazard angle, using the darkness to camouflage the car as best he could. It helped that there was only one working streetlamp, and the light it cast did very little to illuminate the street in any significant fashion. But anyone venturing out late in this part of town usually didn't wish to be seen to begin with. The area itself wasn't filled with as much crime as it was criminals. The few streets around the Tacoma were home to many of Baltimore's most unsavory characters. A good number of them working for Bob Franklin. Which made it difficult to hope Gustov Schultz wouldn't know where to find them when he and his goon squad came calling.

On the drive to the apartment house, Conklin explained the situation, mincing no words in the process. "We have to go! Get out of town for a while. It's that or we end up in the bay. And right now, I ain't in the mood to learn how long I can hold my breath."

"We're in some real shit now, Mo. Where are we gonna go?" Ernie squealed.

"Look, Cam and I knew at some point we'd need to make tracks for a while. We just thought we'd have some more time is all. Cam will keep an eye on things here and let us know when the heat's off. Who knows? Maybe we won't even wanna come back to Baltimore."

"But I got friends here," Ernie protested, only to receive a sharp look from Mo.

"Yeah. Friends who would dime you out for a ham sandwich, you mook.

The only people you can trust right now are me and Roy. Got that?"

"And Cam, right? Cam'll take care of us."

"Yes. And Cam," Mo agreed, looking out the window, watching the street signs whiz by.

"Okay. Alright, Mo. I trust you. But where are we going?"

"To my hometown. I still have family there. They'll put us up. And no one out there will have any idea that we're on the run. Nobody back home pays much attention to what's happening in Baltimore. Trust me."

As satisfied as he was going to get with the answer, Ernie pressed the accelerator as hard as he could, while still keeping control of the car. At the late hour, there weren't many cars on the road, so he was able to move at a nice pace. The drive from the club to the Tacoma hadn't taken long at all. But they were still afraid Schultz could be only minutes behind them.

Dashing from the car into the building, Conklin nearly broke the lock on the front door as he jammed the key in. He wasn't in the mood to play games with the tricky lock. Running up the stairs, taking them two at a time, he left Bernstein wheezing behind him on the landing. Reaching the third floor, he took off down the hallway toward their apartment. Bursting through the door, he found Roy Abbott, stripped down to his undershirt, reclining on the sofa reading a tattered racing form.

As the door slammed against the wall with a thud that sounded like a gunshot, Roy shot to his feet, not knowing who was barging in or what was happening. He'd been half asleep flipping through the betting sheet, but was now wide awake, a jolt of adrenaline surging through him. When the big guy saw Mo standing there trying to catch his breath, he almost gave him what-for just for scaring him half to death.

"Mo, what's wrong with you? I coulda knocked your block off. What are you doin' coming in here like that?"

"Roy, get dressed! Grab what you can. We have to scram! Schultz is comin' for us."

"What? What are you talkin' about?"

"I'll explain in the car," Conklin said as he ran into his bedroom.

Grabbing the metal bedframe, he yanked it unceremoniously away from the wall, giving himself just enough room to squeeze behind it. Kneeling down in the space, he removed a piece of paneling from the wall, revealing a small cardboard box. Looking inside, he made sure all of the money he'd been hiding away was there, as well as the pistol. Throwing the box and what few pieces of clothing he had lying over the chair in the corner into a canvas bag he'd picked up somewhere along the way, he was ready to make tracks. It only took him a matter of minutes to pack up his belongings.

Stepping out of the bedroom, he saw that Roy was dressed and helping Ernie close a beat-up old valise stuffed with everything the two men were taking with them. It wasn't much, Mo thought as he looked at his bag and their suitcase. But soon, they'd have much more. More than they could even imagine. Once Cam fenced all the goods they'd stolen, they'd all be sitting pretty on mountains of kale. They just needed to get out of town and to somewhere safe where Big Bob and Schultz couldn't find them.

When he and Cam came up with the plan to start robbing the houses of people Cam met at the Peacock, they knew it could be dangerous. It would be a direct assault on Big Bob's authority. Not to mention, targeting the wealthy would bring the cops down on them. But it was a risk they were willing to take because the reward would be so great. They'd all be set for life. But until Cam could get them their full cut, they'd have to make do with the money they had in their pockets. And what Mo'd been stashing away in case of an emergency. It would have to be enough for now.

"Let's go," he said, taking one last look around the small room to make sure there was nothing else he couldn't live without ever seeing again.

Following Abbott and Bernstein out the door, he stopped. Turning back into the apartment, he grabbed the racing form from where Roy had left it lying on the sofa. From the small table in the corner, he grabbed a pencil, and at the top of the page in the margin, he scribbled 8:45 PENN TO PENN NYC. It was the departure time for one of the trains leaving Baltimore's Penn Station heading to New York City's Penn Station in the morning. He'd taken the trip once several months back, so it was still fresh in his mind. Making sure the handwriting was legible enough to read, he crumbled the racing form up and dropped it on the floor, nudging it just under the sofa where one could still see it.

With the false clue in place, he bolted from the apartment, running down the hallway and practically jumping down the stairs. He caught up with Roy and Ernie as they were racing along the sidewalk toward the car. Since Mo was the only one who knew where they were going, he jumped in the driver's seat and turned the ignition. Making a U-turn in the middle of the dark street, they sped away just as two big black cars screeched to a halt in front of the Tacoma Grand.

Chapter Forty-Nine

Gustov Schultz charged like a mad bull from the car to the front door of the broken-down apartment building. Behind him, a small army of Big Bob's foot soldiers were lining up, ready to invade the Tacoma Grand Hotel and get their hands on the Alphabet Boys. Their orders were that the boss wanted the three men taken alive so that he could have a word with them personally. Nothing, however, was said about roughing them up a bit. And these guys were keyed up and itching for a fight. While a couple of them would have been more than happy to put a bullet in Mo Conklin's head, they knew they'd have to answer to Schultz if they did, and the big German was scarier than the devil. No one was going to cross him for fear of what he would do in return.

Finding the front door to the building locked, Schultz mumbled something in his native tongue, then put his shoulder into the door with such force that the frame around it splintered, clearing the way for them to enter.

"Vitch apartment?" Schultz asked, turning to his crew.

"Third floor," one of the men answered.

"Three-oh-nine," another one said.

"You two," Schultz said, pointing at two of the men, "stay here. If zey zomehow get by us, do not let zem get avay. Understand?"

Like a general leading his men into battle, Schultz started up the rickety staircase. The first step sagged under his weight, giving him only a moment of pause. He'd made it through countless traps during the war; a weak staircase wasn't going to stop him. The fellas behind him were more cautious. Hearing the creaks and moans from the old, warped boards, they spread themselves out to distribute their weight. A group of trigger-happy guys who wouldn't think twice about getting into a street shootout suddenly found themselves anxious about crashing through the stairs.

Reaching the third floor, the men had been making enough noise that residents were beginning to wonder what the commotion was at such a late hour. The first door they passed suddenly swung open, and an old woman in an oversized robe with curlers in her hair eyed them with an outraged expression on her face.

"What's going on? People are trying to sleep!"

"Mind your own business, lady," one of the toughs warned, brandishing a wooden club.

"How dare you!"

"Get back in there," he said, taking a step closer.

Retreating into her apartment, she muttered something in a language he didn't understand.

As he stalked down the hallway, Schultz eyed the number on each of the doors. Three-oh-six...three-oh-seven...three-oh-eight...three-oh-six. He stopped and stared at the door that should have been the one he was looking for. But instead, it was a second three-oh-six. Looking closer at the numbers, he realized the six was actually a nine that had turned upside down. Spinning the number around into the correct position with his finger, it mockingly slid out of place again once he let go.

Losing his patience, which was already at its end, he squared himself with the door and slammed his foot into it, dead center. Bursting off its hinges, it crashed into the room. Leading the way, Schultz, his gun steady in front of him, stepped over the door into the empty apartment. The rest of the crew followed, quickly fanning out. Six burley men easily filled the cramped main room, leaving little space to maneuver.

Having seen the floor's washroom at the end of the hall, Schultz guessed that the two closed doors, the only others in the apartment, led to the bedrooms. With a nod of his head, men took up positions on either side, then kicked them open.

"Nobody in here, Gustov."

"Nothin' here either."

Walking into each room to see for himself, it was obvious they'd been cleared out. Other than a couple of badly wrinkled shirts left lying on the bed in one room and a stack of old newspapers in the other, there was nothing to be found. In the room with the newspapers, Schultz noticed the bed was at an odd angle to the wall. Stepping around it, he saw an empty hole in the wall. A hiding place for something. In his own apartment, he had a loose floorboard that obscured the money and other items he didn't want to keep in the safe—the natural place for the police, or anyone else, to look if they ever dared enter.

Schultz wasn't happy. The Alphabet Boys were on the run. If they made it out of the city, it would be significantly more difficult to find them. Returning empty-handed to Big Bob wasn't going to be pleasant. Then, a thought occurred to him.

How did those two-bit tough guy wannabes know he was coming for them? Was it possible they had someone in the police department feeding them information like he did? Could that damn Joe Dixon be playing both sides? Or was he right all along, and someone at the Peacock Club was in on it?

Storming out of the bedroom, not paying attention to anything in his way, he smacked his leg into the side of the sofa sitting in the middle of the room.

"Teufel noch mal!" he swore.

Reaching down to shove the sofa out of his way, he watched a pencil roll off the worn cushion from where it'd been left. Rolling on the floor, it came to rest next to a balled-up piece of paper. Snatching it up, Schultz uncrumpled it, seeing that it was a racing form. Several horses were circled with illegible notes made next to their names. But at the top of the page was something different.

8:45 PENN TO PENN NYC

"Looks like they might be takin' a train outta town," one of the men said, standing on his toes to look over Schultz's shoulder.

Schultz was leery. But he'd always thought the three men were saps, so any one of them could have written down the escape route as a reminder and carelessly left it behind. Or, alternatively, he might not be giving them enough credit, and they purposely left the note behind as a distraction. Either way, Schultz wasn't going to take a chance. He'd send some men over to Penn Station for the morning train just in case that was how the Alphabet Boys were intending to get out of Baltimore.

Folding the racing form and sticking it in his pocket, Schultz closed his eyes and took a deep breath. Years of cigarette smoke clinging to the walls made the apartment smell old and stale. Even with the window open, the fresh air from outside didn't help the dull odor surrounding him.

Before he could give the order to head back to the cars, a thundering of footsteps was heard in the hall. He looked to the doorway just in time to see another group of gun-toting men push into the already crowded room. Recognizing two of them as police detectives, he assumed the others were as well.

The only man now not standing with a gun aimed at someone else was Gustov Schultz, who stood in the middle of the room between the two groups. Locking eyes with the barrel-chested man steadfast in the lead of the newly arrived squad of coppers, he tipped his hat, saying, "Lieutenant Cranshaw."

"Schultz," the detective responded coolly. "What are you up to this evening? Having a little party?"

"Not exactly."

"I'd suggest you tell your men to lower their weapons. We don't want anyone to get worked up or there to be any accidents. That would create a lot of paperwork for me. And I've already got my hands full."

"Trying to find zee Guilford Gang, Lieutenant?"

"That's right," Cranshaw acknowledged, picking up on the fact he'd referenced the term the papers used for the robbers, which he could only have known if he'd gotten his hands on an early copy. Or he was clairvoyant. But Cranshaw didn't buy into that hokum. He was even more convinced his first assertion was correct when he saw the menacing grin spread across the big Bavarian's face. He was taunting him.

With a subtle nod of his head, the guns on Schultz's side of the room slowly disappeared.

"You know anything about those boys pulling the jobs up in the Guilford neighborhood?" Cranshaw asked. "Maybe you got a name for one of them?"

"Sorry to disappoint, Detective. But I do not know zees men."

"Interesting. So, you didn't just happen to stumble upon a copy of tomorrow's paper and see the police sketches and recognize them?"

"I have no idea vat you are talking about. Now, if you'll excuse us. Ve ver just leaving, Detective."

"Whose apartment is this anyway?"

"I haven't a clue."

"Yet you broke the door down to get in. I think I have you on breaking and entering, Schultz."

"It was like zat ven we got here. We just came in to make sure everyone vas alright."

"Is that your story?" Cranshaw asked, narrowing his eyes.

"It is, Detective. I svear it on my mother's grave."

"On your mother's grave? Really?" the detective asked, patently unconvinced.

Then, stepping aside and motioning for his men to do the same, Cranshaw said, "Then get gone. And your two goons outside…you can pick them up at the Northern District station in the morning. Can you believe they tried taking swings at us when we pulled up? It's never a good idea to get into a fight with a police officer."

Schultz raised an eyebrow but remained silent. Pointing toward the door, his cadre of men exited without causing a fuss. They kept their heads down and didn't say a word, though the thoughts going through their heads were screaming for action. Schultz was the last man to the door.

"Hey, Schultz," Cranshaw said, stopping him. "Is your mother even dead?"

Without answering, Schultz turned and walked away, a stone-cold expression on his face.

Chapter Fifty

It pained Cranshaw to let Schultz walk away without a pair of silver bracelets on his wrists, but for the time being, Big Bob's enforcer wasn't his target. He'd go after him and his boss another day. Schultz had, however, done exactly what the detective was hoping: led them to the robbers. Or, at least, where they lived. They still didn't have their names, though. But that would change with some solid police work.

"Bert," he said, starting to hand out assignments, "find a telephone and call the station. Tell them to send every able body they have available. If anyone gives you a problem, then we'll call and wake up Lawson.

"Sam, you and I are going to go through this apartment and see if there's anything that will help identify these guys or tell us where they may be.

"The rest of you, start knocking on doors. Ask all the neighbors who live in this building. Get descriptions of them. See if anyone knows their names or where they're from. Any information they might have. When reinforcements get here, get them to cover the other floors. I want every single door in this building knocked on, and every resident questioned before anyone gets to leave. Alright…hop to!"

"You want us to wake people up?" the young officer who'd been with Cranshaw all evening asked, looking uneasy.

"Yes, I do. We don't have time to lose. Schultz and his men are looking for these guys, too. For all we know, they found something in here that tells them where the crew's hiding. We've got a job to do, so go do it."

Eagerly nodding his head, the patrolman felt embarrassed for questioning one of the most respected detectives on the force. He knew he should have just kept his mouth shut and done as he was told. He hoped the lieutenant wouldn't hold it against him.

After everyone filed out with their instructions, Peterson turned to Cranshaw and asked, "Do you think they knew we were coming?"

"The robbers?"

"Yeah."

"I don't know how they could. Unless there's someone in the department talking to them. Only a few of us knew we were publishing the sketches."

"Then do you think they knew Franklin's men were coming for them?"

That question gave Cranshaw pause.

Schultz had obviously gotten his hands on an early copy of the morning paper and recognized the Guilford Gang. Knowing who they were, he was able to find out where they lived. But judging by the empty apartment, they'd already cleared out. Who knows how long they'd been gone. Maybe since the robbery spree began, for all he knew. Hopefully some of the neighbors would be able to provide some answers. What he did know was that Schultz didn't have them, so there was still time.

Casting his eyes around the empty room, there wasn't much to see. A ragged sofa took up most of the space in the center of the room, while a small wooden table with two mismatched chairs was pushed into the corner. On the table, an empty tin can sat next to a dirty hot plate. Under the table, he saw an old porcelain wash basin with a crack running down the side. The entire room was dimly lit by a single exposed bulb dangling precariously from the ceiling. It looked like a rather depressing existence if you asked him. Wanting to get out of a place like this would explain a fella's motive for starting to commit daring daylight robberies for sure.

Circling the room, the scuffed floorboards under his feet cracking ever so slightly, it took Cranshaw less than fifteen seconds to walk the perimeter. The room was maybe twelve feet square at most. He didn't see any obvious hiding places, but he'd have some of the patrolmen check the floor to make sure none of the planks were loose, hiding anything beneath them.

Standing in front of the sofa, he lifted the cushions, finding nothing but a series of rusted springs. From the floor, he picked up a pencil and examined it as if it were a piece of lost treasure, then tossed it on the table.

From the first bedroom, Sam Peterson walked out holding a pair of shirts. "All that's in there are a couple unmade beds and an empty chest. Drawers were all pulled out and empty as if they left in a hurry. These were on one of the beds. Nothing else." Looking down at the once-white shirts with visible sweat stains, then holding them up to himself, he said, "These shirts are enormous. How large did the witnesses say the big fella was?"

"That large," Cranshaw said, pointing at the shirts, disappointed in what little they were finding. "One more room to go."

After tossing the shirts back on the bed, Detective Peterson followed Cranshaw into the second room. An old metal framed bed was oddly out of place. Not up against any wall, but rather at a peculiar angle. On the other side of the room, a chair had been knocked over and was now leaning against one of the walls. An empty trunk was pinned between the chair and the adjoining wall.

Flipping the mattress over, the detectives found nothing hidden under the bed. That was a place Schultz's boys would have certainly looked, though. In the corner of the room, Cranshaw noticed some deep gashes on the floor. They looked like they could have been made by moving the bed back and forth. Those marks led his eye to the hole in the wall, which would have been hidden behind the bed if it were in its usual position.

Pointing to it, Cranshaw said, "Looks like we got a hidey-hole, Sam."

Kneeling down and reaching into the dark opening, he was disappointed not to find anything. But as he moved his hand around the space, it brushed against something in the corner. Peering into the hole, he saw an envelope caught on a nail. Pulling it out, he held it up so he could read what was written on it.

The piece of mail was addressed to one Lester Conklin here in Baltimore. The return address was a town Cranshaw didn't know much about, other than it was in the western part of the state, about sixty miles or so away. A place called Parker City.

Chapter Fifty-One

1985…

Ben was surprised when he realized this was only his third cup of coffee for the day. Usually, by this point in the afternoon, he'd have finished off nearly an entire pot just by himself. But having been out and about for the morning kept him coffee-free. Which is why he'd made a beeline to the second floor breakroom after Tommy left for the Sheriff's Department. Since he was still awaiting the arrival of the CSU report, his plan was to get himself a cup of coffee, then start looking into Clara Daschle's history.

Placing a call to one of the clerks at the courthouse with whom he'd become friendly acquaintances over the last several years, he asked him to begin a search on all the official records related to Clara Daschle. Anything the county had would be useful. They just needed to begin building a picture of her life.

Hanging up the telephone, Ben leaned back in his chair and looked at the board with all of the details of the case so far. He didn't like feeling as though he was simply spinning his wheels. But there were no clear leads at the moment. So, unless Tommy returned with a surprise confession from Daschle's escort friend, they had no one that looked good for the murder. Which brought Ben back to wondering if the crime could have been random and had nothing to do with Clara Daschle other than that she was in the wrong place at the wrong time.

His hope was that the crime scene report would reveal something useful. If they were really lucky, there'd be a perfect fingerprint on the murder weapon. What he would give for that little bit of luck.

Looking over his pristine desk to Tommy's cluttered worktop, he saw that his partner still had the copy of the *Herald-Dispatch* with the picture of himself, Chief Brent, Daschle, and the mayor on the cover. It was hard to believe the Harlequin fundraiser was only a few days earlier. It felt like a lifetime ago. Leaning over and picking up the paper, Ben focused on the black-and-white image of Clara Daschle. She was a striking woman. Even in the two-dimensional picture, he could see her energy and spark.

What had Daschle's life really been like, Ben wondered. The court records would only give him so much of a view into her past. He suddenly flashed on the photograph he'd seen in her house of her as a young woman standing behind a microphone. Liliana Rey confirmed she'd been a performer who, at some point, turned philanthropist. Ben wanted to know more about that. Even just for his own curiosity. But where to even begin? How could he find the real story of who Clara Daschle was?

Tapping his fingers on his desk, he thought he might know just the place to start.

Whenever someone in the department needed information, even if it wasn't related to official business, there was one place everyone went: the Records Room down in the basement. Because there they would find Betty, the one person in the PCPD who knew everything about everything. An institution in the department, if she didn't know where the bodies were buried, she sure as hell knew who buried them. She was also one of Ben's favorite people.

Deciding it was time for a little field trip downstairs, he left a note for Tommy saying where he was, grabbed the newspaper with the photo from the fundraiser, and went in search of Betty.

As Ben left his office, the building was buzzing with activity. Descending the stairs to the first floor, he walked through the bullpen where the day shift was gathered. Officers were shouting back and forth to one another as telephones sporadically interrupted the loud conversations. Across the hall, Ben could hear the ladies in Dispatch chatting away, while in the watch commander's office, the duty sergeant was busy filling out paperwork while simultaneously talking on the telephone. A typical afternoon at the Parker City Police Department, Ben mused as he headed for the back staircase that led down to the lower level of the building.

Outdated and in need of repair as the entire building was, the lower level maintained its drab institutional personality well with its cinderblock walls and horribly scarred tile floor, as well as the unmistakable smell that only seemed to exist in old government buildings.

A quarter of the basement level was taken up with the station's cells, as well as the area where those individuals brought in for a stay in said cells were booked. But down one hallway, there was a nondescript door with the letters peeling off. Only a hint of dried adhesive completed the full spelling of RECORDS in the center of the door. Next to it, a no-smoking sign was hung. Which only made Ben laugh because as he opened the door, a cloud of cigarette smoke billowed into the hallway. Betty was the only person he knew who smoked more than Tommy. And the fact she worked in a room full of old paper documents, which he could easily see going up in flames, did nothing to dissuade her habit.

He found Betty sitting at her desk, behind the big IBM computer that took up most of the surface. A long cigarette dangled from her lips as she typed away on the machine. Having never dared to guess Betty's age, he simply accepted she'd been around the department a very long time and was probably old enough to be his grandmother. Yet, she was the first person to talk about advances in technology like being able to use the computer to help track files and documents and connect with other law enforcement agencies. That was a common interest they shared and something which they spoke about often. It drove Tommy crazy. Tommy's relationship with Betty, on the other hand, was based on a mutual enjoyment of exaggerated flirting.

Today, Betty's large, puffy hair appeared to have a tint of pink to it. Though it was possible that's just what Ben was seeing because of the neon pink dress with flowers all over it she was wearing. Her outfits were always eye-catching, even though they were usually a little behind the times. But she didn't care. She liked to make a statement. And always did.

Looking up at Ben through the extra-thick lenses of her glasses, she smiled and greeted him, her thick Baltimore accent on full display. "How ya doin,' hun? Haven't seen you in a while. How's that partner of yours doin'? Give him a big sloppy kiss for me when you see him."

"I'll be sure to do that. But I know he'd rather it come from you."

"Of course, he would. I mean, look at me?"

"I think your husband might get upset if you and Tommy shacked up together."

"Oh, him. Please. As long as I leave some dinners in the refrigerator, it would be days before he'd know I was gone."

Betty laughed and pointed at the guest chair on the other side of her desk. "Sit down, hun. Tell me what's going on. What can Betty help you with today?"

"Well, have you heard about Clara Daschle?"

Betty's expression turned grim. "Yeah. Heard about it when I got in this morning. She was a mover and shaker. At least among the cultural types in Parker. Pretty classy broad, as far as I understand. Didn't know her personally, though."

"That's just it," Ben explained. "I need to put together a picture of her life. I have Dennis Dawson over at the courthouse pulling county records, but—"

"That's only gonna get you so far," Betty said. "You need the good stuff."

"Which is why I came to you. If anyone can get me a full rundown on a person's life, it's you."

"Flattery will get you everywhere, hun," she said, then took a drag on her cigarette. "But you're right. I am good at what I do."

Placing what was left of her cigarette in the overflowing ashtray next to a picture of her and her husband, she turned to the computer and started clicking away at the keys. Every few keystrokes, she'd pause to read whatever appeared on the screen. Then, shaking her head, she looked back to Ben, saying, "Well, we've got no police files on her. At least here in the city, so she has no criminal record with our department. But this new program I'm trying out did give me access to her driver's license information. I guess you already know her name and address, though, so that won't be much help."

"But something like that could help in the future."

"You bet your bippy, young man."

Shuffling through a stack of folders on her desk, she found a legal pad and started jotting down some notes. "I'll make some calls and get some people working on this. By the time I'm finished, you'll know what Clara Daschle's favorite brand of cereal was."

"Thanks, Betty. You're the best."

"Oh, I know, hun. I know," she said with a twinkle in her eye.

Chapter Fifty-Two

It was now time to play the waiting game, Ben thought as he climbed the stairs back to his office. He was waiting for CSU to deliver its report. He was waiting for the ME to perform the autopsy. He was waiting for the court records he'd spoken with his friend about. He was waiting for Betty to work her magic. Even Tommy was out running down a suspect's alibi. So, what could he do to further the investigation? Ben wasn't very good at assigning tasks to others without having one of his own. He was still learning to delegate, and that part of his job as the department's chief detective wasn't to do all the work himself but to coordinate with all of the resources at his disposal to manage the investigation.

Returning to the office, Ben found Tommy sitting at his desk with his feet up, eating a donut. "I figured we needed some brain food, so I stopped and picked up some donuts," he said, pointing to two chocolate iced treats sitting on a napkin in the middle of Ben's desk.

"That was nice of you. How'd your talk with Sexy Sam go?"

Brushing some crumbs from his mustache, Tommy answered, "Sam Stefanko is *not* our killer. He doesn't have it in him. He's a choir boy. I mean, other than the whole being a male escort and soliciting thing. Plus…and this might be the most important piece of information. He was locked up at the time Clara Daschle was murdered. Ergo, he's—"

"Ergo?" Ben interrupted.

"Will you please let me have my moment? *Ergo,* he didn't do it. What have you done while I've been out on the streets doing all the heavy lifting on this case?"

Ben rolled his eyes, then said, "I've been having Daschle's records pulled."

"So…all you've been doing is making phone calls while I've been sitting in an interrogation room, across the table from a possible murderer?"

"You just said he wasn't the guy. I believe you said he was a *choir boy.*"

"Yes. But until I talked to him, we didn't know that. I was taking my life in my own hands by meeting him. I was being very brave."

"I'm sure once you tell your new girlfriend about your extremely danger-ous day, she'll be sure to find a way to help relieve your stress."

A devilish grin appeared on Tommy's face. "Oh, yeah. I'm sure she will. I think the danger excites her."

"You were sitting in a room with you and…what, a sheriff's deputy? Both armed, talking to a guy who…let me guess, was half your size and handcuffed to the table. Doesn't sound all that exciting to me."

"His wrists looked like they could have slipped out of the handcuffs. And then…then there'd've been a situation."

"You're lucky you brought donuts," Ben said, taking a bite.

"What do we do next?" Tommy asked in all seriousness.

"None of the reports are in yet, so I was thinking we try an old trick that has worked for us in the past. I want to go over to the newspaper and see if there are any old articles about Clara Daschle. Maybe something about her days as a performer?"

"But that was back during Prohibition," Tommy said. "How far back do you think the archives go?"

"It can't hurt to ask. If the paper doesn't have anything, maybe the library will."

Tommy looked at the ceiling and exhaled. "Clara Daschle…a performer who used to work in speakeasies." Then he snapped his finger, kicked his feet off the top of the desk, and sat up straight. "What if it was a mob hit?!"

"A mob hit fifty years in the making?" Ben asked.

"A very slow mob hit," Tommy countered.

"It would be easier to buy your idea of a KGB spy being the killer."

"Ah. I see we've reached the point of spy theories," a voice from the doorway said.

"One of these days, I'm gonna be right, Chief," Tommy said, smiling at Brent as he walked into the office.

"The mayor's looking for an update," he said, turning to Ben. "Have you got anything?"

"Does he know about Sexy Sam?" Tommy asked.

"Excuse me? Who is Sexy Sam?" Brent asked, his voice at a pitch higher than either of the detectives had ever heard it before.

Ben shot Tommy a dirty look, knowing he was just trying to get a rise out of the chief.

"He was a possible suspect. But we've cleared him. It seems that, well, Clara Daschle availed herself of a male escort from time to time," Ben said as delicately as possible.

"And you know this how?"

Ben proceeded to explain what they'd learned from speaking with Liliana Rey and from Tommy's visit to the Sheriff's Department.

"Other than that, we have nothing new. We're waiting for all the reports to come in," Ben said, looking at his watch. "Betty is pulling together all the background on Clara Daschle her contacts can find, and I was just thinking about heading over to the *Herald-Dispatch* to see what kind of press she may have gotten over the years. If she's been involved with so many different organizations, you never know what could turn up."

"What's this one been up to?" Brent asked, jerking his thumb over his shoulder toward Tommy.

"He just came face-to-face with an extremely dangerous criminal. He's a little traumatized by it."

"I see," the chief said, turning to look at Tommy.

"I might need therapy."

Brent chuckled. "Oh, I know you need therapy. But I like Ben's idea. Go see if the paper has anything useful. It keeps the investigation moving forward. I'll make a call and see what's happening with CSU and the medical examiner. Light a fire under their asses."

"Thanks, Chief," Ben said as he walked out the door. Then, looking at Tommy, he said, "Really? He's the chief. You need to be more serious."

"Brent likes my sense of humor." Ben just stared at his partner. "Alright. Brent tolerates my sense of humor," Tommy conceded. "But I keep things interesting."

"You have no arguments from me on that point. Come on," Ben said, grabbing the second donut from his desk. "We're going to the newspaper to do some research. If I remember correctly, the offices are open until five."

Chapter Fifty-Three

1927…

By lunchtime the day after the army of police officers descended on the Tacoma Grand Hotel, Cranshaw was back in his office reviewing everything they'd learned throughout the night and early hours of the morning. After questioning every resident of the building, most of whom were none-too-happy to be awoken in the middle of the night, they discovered not many people knew their neighbors very well. In fact, the only people who'd ever even seen the occupants of apartment three-oh-nine were those who lived on either side of them. At least they were the only ones to admit it.

Apartment three-oh-eight was home to a newlywed couple, Leo and Nancy, and Nancy's ailing mother. They'd been scared to death by the commotion, but Nancy wouldn't allow Leo to open the door to see what was going on for fear of what might happen. It wasn't until Detective Merrill was standing outside their apartment, knocking with his badge in hand, ordering them to open the door, that they answered.

After checking to make sure no one was in the apartment other than the couple and her mother, all the detective managed to learn from them was that three men lived next door and kept unconventional hours. Leo was a dock worker with a regular schedule, so he might only see them in the evenings when he was coming home. But Nancy said she could hear them coming and going at all hours of the day when she was going about her chores. Other than politely tipping their hats to her when they passed in the hall, she knew nothing about them. But she was able to provide a decent description of the three men, which matched what all the victims/witnesses of the robberies in Guilford provided.

On the other side of the gang's apartment, in three-ten, a retired mill worker was able to provide names. He'd spoken to the men whenever he saw them, saying they were all very pleasant young fellows. They reminded him of some of the guys he used to work with.

"The handsome fella's name was Mo. The big guy was Roy, and the little one was Ernie," he informed the patrolman questioning him. "No idea what their last names were. Never gave them. Never asked."

Mo. Roy. Ernie.

Cranshaw finally had some names to work with. However, none of those fit with the letter he'd found hidden in the bedroom addressed to Lester Conklin. So, he'd dispatched Sam Peterson to pull whatever files he could find on a Lester Conklin. Again, saying to wake up anyone he needed to to get information.

It wasn't until the newspaper hit the streets and the city got its first glimpse of the faces of the men the police were looking for that a patrol officer from Central District knocked on the door to Cranshaw's office.

"Have a seat, Officer…"

"Jackson. Roger Jackson, sir." He was an older patrol officer.

"You say you know these men?" the lieutenant asked, pointing to the faces on the front of the newspaper lying on his desk.

"I do. I've had a couple of run-ins with them on the street. I've heard they're part of Bob Franklin's organization. Pretty low level, though."

Interesting, Cranshaw thought.

"Do you have names?"

The cop laughed. "Yeah. They call themselves the Alphabet Boys."

Cranshaw leaned forward and wrote the name on the newspaper over their pictures. "The Alphabet Boys? What's that supposed to men?"

"Abbott, Bernstein, and Conklin. Their last names. Roy Abbott, Ernie Bernstein, and Mo Conklin. A-B-C. Crooks can be really dumb sometimes,

Lieutenant."

"Mo Conklin? Is Mo a nickname?"

"I would guess so. I mean, who'd name their kid Mo?"

"Could his real name be Lester?"

"That I can't say. I only know him as Mo."

After a few more perfunctory questions—how he'd met them, where he'd seen them before—Cranshaw thanked Jackson for coming to see him and told him to keep an eye.

After Jackson was gone, Cranshaw walked over to the window and stuck his head outside for some fresh air. The heatwave had finally broken. It was the first morning that the air felt fresh and cool. It was a glorious relief from the past several weeks.

Another knock on his door pulled him back into the office. It was Sam Peterson, holding a brown file folder. The detective looked like he'd been through the wringer. He looked as tired as Cranshaw felt. Peterson's sleeves were rolled up to his elbows, and a coffee stain on his shirt was partially obscured by the tie that was loosened down to his chest.

"I found Lester Conklin. A.K.A. Mo Conklin," he said, dropping the folder onto Cranshaw's desk. "Some minor charges here and there. A few short stints in city lock-up."

"Any connection to Bob Franklin?" Cranshaw asked, opening the file and beginning to read the police reports.

"Some known associates. But everyone in the underworld in this town is connected to Big Bob. So, probably."

"Speaking of known associates." Cranshaw ran his finger along one of the forms until he reached a block with the names of the other men Conklin had been arrested with. Right there in black and white were the names Ernest Bernstein and Roy Warren Abbott. The detective smiled for the first time in days. Even though they didn't know where the "Alphabet Boys" were at the moment, they knew who they were, which was going to be the first step in tracking them down.

"While I was pulling his file..." Peterson continued, only stopping to yawn, "which, by the way, I have one very unhappy friend who works at the courthouse because I got him out of bed at three in the morning…I asked him to check with the state about Lester Conklin's background and what his connection to Parker City is or might be. I owe Harvey a big favor now, but if there's anyone who can track down information on someone, it's him."

"Harvey Weston?" Cranshaw asked.

"Yeah. He's a human bloodhound…after he's had breakfast. We grabbed some eggs at that diner over by the courthouse."

"Well, tell Harv, if he finds us some good background on this Conklin fellow, I'll buy him a steak dinner at Haussner's," Cranshaw said, closing the file and heading for the door. "I'm gonna go let the captain know where we are on this. He'll be happy to know we have names."

"But we still don't know where they are," Peterson pointed out.

"We might have a lead with this Parker City letter."

"You're really gonna go traipsing all the way out to the western hinterlands to nab these guys?" Peterson asked, running his hands over his face, trying to wake himself up.

"If I have to," Cranshaw answered.

"Not for nothing, we could just let Big Bob handle this. It would be a win for everyone."

"I'll pretend I didn't hear that, Sam," he said, giving his friend a disapproving look.

"I know. I know. I've been up for over twenty-four hours. I don't know what I'm sayin.'"

"Close your eyes for a few minutes while I go talk to Lawson. I'll wake you up when I come back," Cranshaw promised.

Sitting down and kicking his feet up on the edge of Cranshaw's desk, Peterson tried to make himself comfortable. "Beware. I saw Dixon out there. I think he was going in to talk to Lawson. Why's he been hanging around so much lately? Doesn't he have his own district to worry about?"

Cranshaw was wondering the same thing.

Chapter Fifty-Four

Big Bob Franklin was anxiously pacing behind his desk, not paying the slightest attention to what Clayton Munsey, the Peacock's maître d', was saying to him. Something about new soup tureens. He wasn't sure. It was the middle of summer. People shouldn't be eating soup anyway, he thought, taking a long drag on his cigar and then blowing the smoke in Munsey's direction. He thought it would make him stop talking for just a few seconds. Ignoring the cloud swirling around him, the little man kept blathering on.

Franklin had remained at the club until Schultz returned from the Alphabet Boys' apartment and told him what they'd found. Nothing. Except for a scribbled note referencing a train out of town. He'd then left with some men for the train station. Franklin hadn't heard a word since.

Looking at his pocket watch, he saw hours had passed since the 8:45 train should have departed for New York City. His men had been there long before that. The sun hadn't even been up yet when they piled back into their cars and drove over to Penn Station. If Conklin and his crew were planning on boarding that train, Schultz and his men should have snatched them up by now. If they were no-shows and it was just a wild goose chance Conklin sent them on, then why hadn't they returned?

"Then we would need to discuss new linen napkins," he heard Munsey say.

"Enough!" Big Bob snapped. "Clayton, now is not the time for this. I have some more pressing matters to deal with."

"Oh. I just wanted to—"

"We can talk about it another time. Better yet, do whatever you think is best. I trust you to handle the dinner plates."

"Soup tureens," he corrected.

"Yes, the soup tureens. Fine."

"And the napkins?"

"Get out!" Franklin almost launched himself over his desk.

Grabbing up the papers he'd been carrying with him, Munsey stumbled toward the door. As it suddenly swung open, he quickly took a step backward to avoid being struck in the face. In doing so, he lost his balance, catching the heel of his wingtip on the rug, falling backwards. From where he'd landed on the floor, he looked up into the angry face of Gustov Schultz.

"You need to leave," the German ordered.

"I was trying to," Munsey said flatly, pulling himself to his feet and brushing off his trouser legs. In a huff, he barely made it past Schultz. Purposely shouldering the brute on his way out the door, he was almost knocked down again as the big man's body absorbed the blow without budging a single inch.

Big Bob watched all of this and was about to blow his top when Munsey finally exited, closing the door behind him.

"Zey veren't zere," Schultz said matter-of-factly. "Ve vaited until all zee trains to New York left."

"Dammit!" Franklin threw the cigar out the open window. "I knew that note was too obvious. You should have, too!"

"Ve had no idea of knowing," Schultz argued, not wanting to get into a fight about it even though he'd been the one to first say he was doubtful they'd discovered the gang's escape route.

"What do we do next?" Big Bob demanded.

"I thought ve should talk to our friend in the police. See vat zey may have found after zey chased us out."

"I don't trust that Dixon farther than I can throw him," Franklin conceded.

"He's very tiny. I could throw him far," Schultz offered, to which Big Bob actually cracked a smile. "But ve have other men in police ve can talk to as vell."

Before he was able to respond, the sound of a telephone ringing interrupted them. Looking down, they noted it was not the bell on Franklin's desk phone disturbing them. Which meant it was the telephone that was kept in the top drawer to which only a handful of people in the city had the number.

Removing it from its hiding place and answering, Big Bob listened to the man on the other end. None other than Joe Dixon. He didn't say anything as the captain spoke, just listened. When the call ended, he replaced the receiver and closed the drawer.

"Parker City," he said.

"Vat is zat?" Schultz asked.

"Where Cranshaw is going to look for them. Parker City, Maryland. A town about two, two and a half hours west of here. It's Mo Conklin's hometown and it looks like he's still got family there. Go check it out."

On the other side of the door, Cam heard everything.

Chapter Fifty-Five

1985…

The *Herald-Dispatch* was Parker City's daily newspaper and the source from which most residents throughout the county received their local news. On several occasions, the detectives had found articles in old editions of the paper useful to their investigations. But it was time consuming, going through back issues of the paper. Especially when one didn't know exactly what they were looking for. Or, if there even was a piece pertaining to their inquiry to begin with.

For generations, there were two rival papers in Parker. The *Blue Ridge Herald* and the *Chronicle Dispatch*. That changed in the '60s when the *Herald* bought the *Chronicle Dispatch* and merged them into one daily newspaper. Anyone around from the time of the merger recalled how contentious the deal had been, calling it more of a hostile takeover by the *Herald* than anything else. It was just another one of the many stories that made up Parker City's history.

Entering the building's small lobby, the secretary at the desk greeted Ben and Tommy. Her name was Lisa Davis. The detectives knew her from previous visits.

Before Ben could say anything, Tommy pushed past him. "Lisa Davis. How are you doing?" He was oozing with charm. It made Ben nauseous.

"Detective Mason!" Lisa practically squealed, her face lighting up. "Are you here on official police business?"

"Unfortunately, we are," Tommy answered. "Don't get me wrong. I'd love to just chat with a pretty thing like you all afternoon, but we have a very important case we're working on."

"I see," she said, looking very serious now. "How can I help you?"

Tommy looked to Ben now that the flirting was out of the way.

"Can you tell me if Phil Coats is in?" Ben asked.

Coats was the paper's head of research. He was also the guy who oversaw the archives, so had become the detectives' main contact inside the *Herald-Dispatch* when they were looking for old articles. Ben knew that in other places, cops usually had reporters as contacts for when they were looking for some information to be dug up, but he didn't have a particular reporter with whom he was close. Not only had he not had the best experiences with local reporters, if he started asking them for information, they'd want the scoop and begin asking questions of their own. At least with Phil Coats, he wasn't a reporter and wasn't always looking for a story.

Lisa picked up the phone on her desk and punched in Coats' extension then waited for an answer. After saying the police were there looking to speak with him, she hung up and said to them, "Phil's in his office and said to come right up. You know where you're going?"

"Second floor, end of the hall," Ben confirmed.

As he started for the stairs, behind his back, Ben heard Lisa giggle. He could only imagine what Tommy said to her.

"You can't stop yourself, can you?" Ben asked as they took the large metal staircase to the second floor. "Do you think Christine would be alright seeing you flirt like that?"

"That was business. Christine understands," Tommy answered matter-of-factly.

"You're just one giant walking hormone, aren't you?"

Tommy laughed as Ben knocked on the door to the researcher's office.

"Come in!" they heard a voice shout from inside.

Coats' office could only be described as organized chaos. There were piles of papers and folders and books everywhere. Each stack, however, was perfectly uniform, as if a ruler was used to make certain each one was the same height. Every flat surface in the room was covered by these pristine paper towers. Ben recalled reading something about a recent medical diagnosis that doctors were beginning to discuss called Obsessive Compulsive Disorder. He wondered if this was an example of that, or if Coats was just extremely organized. Either way, the man always knew exactly where whatever he was looking for was.

"Hello, Sergeant Winters, Detective Mason," Coats said, standing and walking around his desk to greet them.

Ben had never asked, but he figured the man was close to seven feet tall, the way he towered over them. With the low ceiling in the office, he wondered how Coats didn't hit his head every time he stood up.

"How are you, Phil?" Ben asked, shaking the man's hand.

"I'm keeping myself busy these days. What can I help you with?"

If he'd had guest chairs in the office, Ben was certain he would have offered them a seat. But this was a working office. No time for idle chitchat, he got the feeling. Anyone coming in to talk to Phil Coats was there for a specific purpose. In keeping with the practice, Ben got right to the point and explained what they were looking for.

"We'd be happy to go through the microfiche ourselves," Ben offered. "I was just hoping you might be able to help us find a place to start."

Before he was even finished speaking, Coats walked back around his desk and picked up a manila folder. He turned and handed it to Ben. "I think that should be what you're looking for."

Ben opened the folder, then looked up at Coats in amazement. When Ben looked to his partner, Tommy's mouth was literally hanging open.

"How did you—?" Ben began to ask.

"The paper's going to run a spread on Clara Daschle at the beginning of the week. She was very active in the city, so I already started pulling old articles," he explained. "You can have those copies. I made a few sets for the reporters working on the piece."

It still took Ben a moment to collect his thoughts. "You have no idea how helpful this is, Phil. You just saved us a lot of time."

"Happy to help," he said. "Anything else you need?"

Looking at the folder in his hand, Ben said, "If we come up with anything after going through this, we'll let you know. But for right now…. Thank you."

Walking out of the office and back down the hall towards the stairs, Tommy said, "What the hell? I wish everything was this easy."

Chapter Fifty-Six

J ust as they were about to leave the *Herald-Dispatch*, Ben's pager sounded. Pulling the little black device from his jacket pocket, he looked at the number displayed on the screen and recognized it as one from the courthouse. Specifically, belonging to Dennis Dawson, the clerk he'd asked to pull the Daschle records. Not wanting to wait until they returned to the station to call him, and seeing no payphone around on the street, Ben decided to ask Lisa Davis if he could impose and use her phone to make a quick call. Police business, of course.

Meeting Tommy outside by the car, Ben told him Dawson was able to put together the information he'd requested, so they were going to swing by the courthouse and pick it up. Those files, along with what they'd just collected at the paper, would give them plenty of reading material. With any luck, by the time they'd culled through them and extracted the most important details—anything that might help with the case—the Crime Scene Unit and medical examiner's reports would be ready.

Ben was feeling like they were beginning to get a slightly better hold on the investigation. True, they didn't have a suspect, but he was hoping they now had some of the information that would lead them to one. With any investigation, no detective ever knew exactly what could turn the whole case around. It could be a giant, glaring bit of information that is easy to come by. Or the tiniest detail that was overlooked at first. There was always something that led to unlocking the mystery.

With fresh cups of coffee in front of them, Ben and Tommy began reading through the pages they'd accumulated that afternoon. Losing the coin toss,

Tommy got the boring county records. Ben, having successfully predicted heads, got to read through the old news articles in which Daschle was mentioned. Tommy immediately accused his friend of rigging the coin toss or using a double-headed quarter. To which Ben flipped the coin to him for examination.

"Then it's the way you flipped it," Tommy argued.

"You think I've been practicing how to flip a quarter just so I can win coin tosses?"

"I would," Tommy admitted.

As time ticked by, the voices and sounds coming from outside their office began to quiet down. The day shift was wrapping up, and soon, everyone would be on their way home. In the evening, the second floor was virtually deserted. Ben enjoyed the time after most of the staff left to work without any interruptions. Tommy wasn't a huge fan of the silence. It made him edgy. He liked the commotion during the day. He fed off the energy flowing through the building.

Finishing a piece that ran years earlier in the paper's Lifestyle Section, Ben said, "Interesting."

"What's that?" Tommy asked, looking up from the printouts in front of him.

"The paper did a feature story on Clara Daschle about ten years ago. They were focusing on her time as a singer back in the '20s, '30s, and '40s. She admits to working in clubs during Prohibition and knowing bootleggers and gangsters. Even says she worked for Bob Franklin at one point."

"Bob Franklin? As in Big Bob?" Tommy asked, his eyebrows shooting up.

"She was a headliner at the Platinum Peacock in Baltimore."

"Holy crap. I've got a book somewhere…yes, a book. Don't look at me that way… Anyway, Uncle Fitz gave it to me. A local author wrote it. True Maryland crime stories. Big Bob Franklin is featured in a few chapters. He ran Baltimore back in the day. Kind of like our own Al Capone."

"I know the name," Ben said. "I've heard it before."

"You think that could have anything to do with the case?" Tommy asked, not sure if he was just clutching at straws, or if it might be a valid line of inquiry.

Ben exhaled. "I really can't see how. But then again. We'd have to look into it. This is just a passing mention in the article. It doesn't sound like she was part of his criminal organization. Just a singer in one of his clubs called the Platinum Peacock."

"But the Platinum Peacock was *the* club," Tommy pointed out.

Pointing to one of the photos in the article, a copy of the one he'd seen hanging at the Harlequin, Ben said, "After the Peacock, she started touring the country for a while. Made a bit of a name for herself. She even performed at the Harlequin.

"But there's not much about her life here in Parker City growing up. I mean, all she says is she was born here and left at an early age. She was even pretty vague when talking about why she and her husband ended up moving here after they got married. Never mentions family, anything like that."

"So?"

"Read it for yourself, but you'll see what I mean. She's so open and willing to talk about everything from the minute she gets to Baltimore, but nothing about her early life. It just makes me wonder."

As he was listening, Tommy continued flipping through the court file to the final page. It was a copy of Clara Daschle's birth certificate.

"Well, look at that," Tommy said, examining the mimeographed copy of the document in his hand.

"Find something?" Ben asked, seeing the look on his partner's face.

"In that article you're reading, what's her name?"

"Her name?"

"Yeah. Before she was Clara Daschle, what name does she say she had before that. When she was singing?"

"Oh. You mean her maiden name. Clara Mowry. She was Clara Mowry before marrying Edward Daschle."

"Well, Mowry wasn't her real last name. Mowry was her *mother's* maiden name. She was born Clara Ann Conklin."

Chapter Fifty-Seven

1927…

Fleeing Baltimore under the cover of darkness and heading west to his hometown was both exhilarating and terrifying at the same time. It had been years since Mo Conklin set foot back home in Parker City and these certainly weren't the best of circumstances under which to be doing so now. But it was the best option available. They didn't have enough money to run far enough away that Big Bob would never be able to find them. So, they needed to make do with what they did have.

Living in Baltimore, he'd kept his link to Parker City a closely held secret, never knowing if he'd one day need to return. Even Roy and Ernie didn't know exactly where he was from until he'd told them on the drive out of town. Whenever he'd been asked about where he grew up, he'd been vague, usually answering, "Out in Western Maryland," never any more specific. Of course, there were official records that could be traced back to Parker, but he figured it would take some time for the police to even get on that track. At least until they learned their names. While Schultz and his goon squad knew who they were looking for, he doubted they'd share that information with the Baltimore Police Department. And he was certain no one in Franklin's organization knew where he was from. The way he figured, neither side had enough information to put together to come looking for them.

Driving along dark, desolate roads past farm after farm once they were outside the Baltimore city limits, made it difficult to tell how long they'd been traveling. With Mo keeping his eyes firmly on the road in front of them and Ernie fidgeting in the passenger seat next to him, that left Roy spread out across the back seat. It was a tight fit for the big guy, but he'd managed to shift himself into a comfortable position, which allowed him to doze off shortly after the lights of the city vanished behind them. If it hadn't been for the adrenaline keeping him alert behind the wheel, it would have been Roy's snoring keeping Mo awake.

"How can he sleep at a time like this?" Ernie asked, nervously wringing his hands in his lap.

"It's alright, Ernie. We'll be there soon. You can get some shuteye, too. Just relax."

"Relax? Mo, are you out of your head? Big Bob knows it was us up in Guilford. Schultz is gonna keep lookin' for us until he finds us."

"Ernie, Cam, and I always knew eventually someone was gonna be able to finger us. We were always gonna have to get out of town."

"Yeah. But what about all the goods? Where's our money? How are we gonna survive without that dough? It was gonna set us all up so we wouldn't have to worry anymore."

"Cam will still get the money. Then I'll make sure you and Roy get your share. Trust me. Everything is under control," Mo said, trying to soothe his friend's concerns.

"But what are we gonna do for money right now?"

"I have a little bit of green I socked away for an emergency. Plus, we'll be stayin' with my family. It's not like we have to spend money on gettin' a hotel room."

"And you think your family will welcome you home with open arms? You said yourself you haven't seen 'em in years. What makes you so sure they'll help us."

"Because they're family, you dumb sonofabitch. It's what family does. Besides…my aunt and I still write to each other every so often. My mother's sister. Aunt Eugenia and Uncle Oswald never had any kids of their own, so I was always her favorite of the cousins."

"How many cousins you have? Did you have brothers and sisters? You've never said."

"That's because I don't want to talk about it," Conklin answered, his demeanor suddenly changing, turning icy. Ernie thought better before pressing Mo further.

From the backseat, Roy suddenly spoke up, startling both of them. "Is your aunt a good cook?"

Chapter Fifty-Eight

Parker City, nestled at the foot of the Blue Ridge Mountains in Parker County, was the gateway to the western part of the state. A booming town during the Civil War, it only continued to grow since, but was still a far cry from being able to compare itself to places like Baltimore and Washington, DC. It was the hub of the region, though. The biggest city in the Western Maryland-Southern Pennsylvania-West Virginia panhandle triangle, Parker was a community with a diverse background and population. From industrial tycoons to tradesmen to farmers, they all called the historic city home.

Lester Conklin's life growing up in Parker City was filled with afternoons playing with the kids in the neighborhood and doing whatever chores his mother gave him. His parents were strict but kind and loved their children. That was never something he questioned. And with his aunts and uncles living on the same street, the entire family was very close, getting together at least once a week for a big dinner.

As he got older, Lester's mischievous streak began to get him into more and more trouble. He'd gotten caught several times stealing from the corner store and getting into fights that left other teens beaten up and bloody. But he'd never done anything so bad his mother lost hope in him. She always said he'd grow out of his youthful indiscretions. Which he did. For a short time—after his father helped to get him a job as a clerk in the front office of the canning plant in which he worked. But Lester did not hold the position for long. He didn't find himself suited to hour after hour of counting and mundane paperwork.

When he quit his job at McGregor's Tasker Canning Co., his father was furious. He didn't understand how his son could give up such a stable, well-paying job. In his defense, though his father didn't see it that way, Lester argued that the work was boring. That was the first time a rift separated father and son. Though his mother worked to bring the two men back together, their relationship was never quite the same. When Lester decided to move to Baltimore to find a life with more excitement, his father didn't protest because he knew there was nothing he could say to change his son's mind.

After settling in Baltimore, with Prohibition now the law of the land, he realized it was easier—and more stimulating—to make money through what the government would call "illicit activities." That's how he'd met up with Ernie Bernstein and Roy Abbott. Also, when he'd started going by the nickname Mo, which was a shortened version of his middle name. Which in itself was his mother's maiden name. He thought of it as being a tribute to her. Made all the more poignant not long after arriving in Baltimore when his mother suddenly died of a heart attack one morning while cleaning the house.

The death crushed Mo, and he soon found himself heading home for the funeral. Received with open arms by all his relatives, particularly Aunt Eugenia, his father was cordial, but distant. It was only a few months later that he received a telegram from his aunt saying that his father had passed away.

Mo Conklin only had fond memories of his parents and his life in Parker City. But it was all in the past. And as Ernie and Roy would tell you, he didn't talk much about it. It wasn't even until the drive out of Baltimore that Bernstein found out Mo might have brothers and sisters. His life before moving to Baltimore was a mystery to the people now closest to him.

Driving through the darkened streets, Ernie was instantly taken by Parker City's charming downtown. Inviting shops lined the main thoroughfare with buildings featuring the kind of classic architectural details one didn't see much of in the big city. He found the ice cream parlor next to the big Harlequin Theatre especially appealing. Seeing the look on his friend's face as they drove by made Mo smile to himself.

Arriving in front of his aunt's home, Mo didn't want to just walk up to the front door and knock at the early hour. In a neighborhood like this, people didn't show up on someone's doorstep in the middle of the night unexpectedly. He had no intention of scaring his aunt. So, he told Roy and Ernie to get comfortable because they'd be spending the night in the car until the sun came up. With the excitement of having to leave Baltimore in such a rush beginning to wear off, Mo could use some sleep. He was barely able to keep his eyes open.

As they all settled in to get some much-needed rest, Mo removed the pistol he'd tucked in his pocket and gently held it in his lap. He'd seen no cars following them. But he wanted to be prepared just in case.

Drifting off, with Roy once again snoring in the backseat, Mo began dreaming of a time long ago when he was a little boy, he and his cousins playing stickball in the street in front of this very house.

Chapter Fifty-Nine

Mo Conklin was startled awake by a hand smacking his cheek through the open car window. If his eyes hadn't focused quickly enough on who was assaulting him, the person might have died from an allergic reaction to the lead he introduced into their system from the pistol he was fumbling with.

"Lester! What are you doing out here sleeping in front of the house?!" his aunt asked. "Why didn't you come in? You didn't tell me you were coming for a visit. Who are your friends? You need to come in. I'm making breakfast."

"Hello, Aunt Eugenia," Mo said, still trying to focus. "We got here real late and didn't want to wake you up."

"So, instead, you decide to scare me in the morning? I see a strange car with men in it sitting outside. How was I supposed to know it was my nephew?"

"You were so scared you thought you'd come out and see who it was?" Mo asked, raising an eyebrow.

"Well, you know your uncle wasn't going to do it. He told me to mind my own business. I told him the car's in front of my house, it is my business. And here I am."

"And here you are." Conklin smiled. "It's good to see you, Aunt Eugenia."

"Come. Come inside. You look hungry."

The modest two-story, green clapboard house sat on the corner of two quiet streets on the edge of town. Mainly a residential area, the building next to his aunt and uncle's had a small hardware store that catered to the neighborhood on the first floor over which the owner lived—who happened to be a third cousin, or a second cousin once removed. Mo could never remember which or what the difference was.

After the guys had freshened up, they sat down in the tiny dining room and feasted on a homemade breakfast that Eugenia just "threw together" for them. Ernie's eyes went wide when he saw the amount of food laid out on the table. Roy tucked right in and started eating.

As the others filled their plates, Uncle Oswald lowered his newspaper and looked at his nephew. "What brings you back to Parker, Lester? Your aunt didn't say you were coming for a visit."

"We were just lookin' to get out of town for a while. It's been a real hot summer, and the city was just—"

"Getting dangerous," Ernie absentmindedly said while shoving a forkful of fried potatoes into his mouth.

Mo kicked him under the table.

"Dangerous?" his aunt repeated. "What's dangerous? Are you in trouble, Lester?"

"No, Aunt Eugenia. He didn't mean it like that." He gave Ernie a sharp look. Sometimes, he wanted to wring his neck.

"Have you heard about the robberies?" Uncle Oswald asked.

Ernie nearly choked on his potatoes. Mo slapped him on the back, harder than necessary, to thank him for managing to get his uncle on this particular topic.

"Robberies?" Mo asked innocently.

"It's been in the newspaper. Some men keep breaking into big, expensive houses while the people are home. They say they use chloroform on them. They even killed a woman."

"It's terrible," Eugenia squawked.

"You didn't know?" Oswald asked.

"I don't read the newspapers much, Uncle Oswald."

"Well, the stories have made it to Parker," Eugenia said.

Of course, they have, Mo thought to himself. This should be the perfect place to get away from everything. Instead, the very first conversation he was having with his aunt and uncle was about the exact thing that caused them to flee Baltimore in the first place. It was just his luck. He needed to change the subject.

"Aunt Eugenia, how's Aunt Mildred and Uncle Andrew?"

With that, his aunt launched into a complete recitation of everything each member of the family was currently involved in. By the time she'd finished, everyone's plates were empty, and breakfast was over. His plan worked. He figured it was best to let his aunt do all the talking. Something she was more than happy to do. Incidentally, the more she talked, the less of a chance there was for either Ernie or Roy to slip up and say something they shouldn't. Not that Roy was interested in doing anything other than eating. It was Ernie and his nervous constitution Mo always worried about.

Chapter Sixty

Lieutenant Cranshaw was able to confirm the identities of the Guilford Gang/Alphabet Boys by the middle of the afternoon and had detectives digging into each of their backgrounds and rousting known associates throughout the city. For the first time in the last several weeks, everyone in the Baltimore Police Department knew exactly who they were looking for. At a press conference hastily called shortly after lunchtime, Commissioner Gaither, along with the mayor and Captain Lawson, stood before the reporters and announced the gang members' identities to the public and stated the entire police force was actively looking for them. As of that moment, they were Baltimore's most wanted criminals.

To dub this two-bit robbery crew the city's most wanted gang bothered Cranshaw. Big Bob Franklin was running a top-notch organization that was into every illegal activity imaginable. Yet, he'd become untouchable. But because Conklin, Bernstein, and Abbott were robbing rich families and the story'd made it into the press, they'd become the worst criminals in the city, the ones the police force needed to bring in. There were a number of detectives, led by Cranshaw, who would have liked to have been given the time and resources to bring Big Bob down once and for all, but that order, sadly, had never been given. Instead, they continued their work, only nipping at the edge of the real problem. For now, nabbing the Alphabet Boys needed to be the focus.

Which is why Cranshaw skipped the press conference at the courthouse. He thought doing his job was more important than standing around talking about doing his job. He was funny that way.

Waiting for any word to arrive that there was a lead on where the crew was hiding, Cranshaw spent the time comparing Lester "Mo" Conklin's rap sheet to Ernest Bernstein's and Roy Abbott's. The three looked much the same. Mostly petty crimes with some brief periods behind bars, but nothing too serious. The worst arrest was an aggravated assault charge for Abbott a couple years back. The most interesting bit of information was that all three were known to be involved with Bob Franklin's organization in one manner or another. Low level foot soldiers for the boss, but still connected. None of this pointed them in any clear direction as to where the men could be hiding, though.

When Detective Sam Peterson strutted into the office, Cranshaw could tell by the smug expression on his face that he had something that might be useful. Pushing all the open files on his desk aside, he gave Peterson his full attention.

"Harv came through," Peterson announced. "Well, sort of. He's still looking, but I told him to start with the address in Parker City. It would probably have been helpful if the letter'd still been in the envelope you found, but what can we do? Anyway. Lester Conklin is originally from Parker City. Born there. Grew up there. And from what Harvey can tell, he still has family there. That Eugenia Wheeler, who sent the letter, is his aunt. His mother's sister."

Peterson stuck the notebook from which he'd been reading in his pocket and sat down across from Cranshaw.

"Anything else?"

"Anything else," Peterson said. "That's a lot to work with right there."

"It is, but we can still use more."

"I think it's enough to confirm what you were thinking. That they went running to Parker City. To Conklin's family to hide them until the heat dies down. I think you and I might want to head out there and poke around. Hell, we even got the address where we should start!"

Cranshaw couldn't argue. It was the only solid lead they had. With the entire force fanned out looking for them in Baltimore, what could it hurt for them to look somewhere else? Especially when they had an address directly connected to one of their suspects.

"Let me go talk to the captain. If I can get him to assign us a car, we can be there by dinner," Cranshaw said, looking at his wristwatch. "Go get a map so we can figure out the directions."

"I'm on it," Peterson replied, jumping out of his seat and making tracks for the door.

Cranshaw wasn't far behind. But once in the hallway, he turned in the opposite direction, heading down the hall and up the stairs toward Captain Lawson's office. Finding the door open, he walked in, only to see the captain already in a meeting. Cranshaw recognized the men as some of the department's top brass.

When the captain saw him standing in the doorway, he immediately cut off one of the inspectors mid-sentence. "Have you got something, Lieutenant?"

"I'm sorry, sir. I didn't realize you were in a meeting," Cranshaw apologized, beginning to back out of the room.

"Nonsense, Cranshaw. This is nothing," Lawson said, much to the discontent of the men seated before him. "You know what the commissioner said today. Your case is top priority. Now, what do you have for me?"

"Can we have a word in private?" he asked.

"Lieutenant, I know you are one of the best detectives on the force," began the inspector who'd been so rudely interrupted, "so I know you know who we are. Are you saying you can't speak openly in front of us?"

"I don't mean any offense, *sir*. But we're trying to keep information as controlled as possible."

"Who do you think we're going to share the information with exactly?" he asked, becoming red in the face.

"Oh, would you be quiet, Ronnie?" Lawson said, staring down his superior. "We all know how you got to be an inspector, so don't try pulling rank in my office."

The other men did their best to conceal their amusement. Even though they all outranked Captain Lawson, he'd been around longer than any of them. In addition, they all respected him more than Inspector Ronald Boffman.

Stepping out of the office with Cranshaw, Lawson listened as the detective told him what he and Peterson were thinking. When he was asked about requisitioning a department car for the trip to Parker City, the captain reached into his pocket and took out the keys to his own supervisor's fleet car, saying he'd just have one of the boys take him home that evening.

"I don't want to see any scratches on the car when you bring it back," Lawson hollered down the hall after Cranshaw.

Chapter Sixty-One

1985...

Driving home from the station, Ben couldn't stop thinking about the fact Clara Conklin changed her name to Clara Mowry. He just didn't know why it was bothering him so much. Performers changed their names all the time. Norma Jeane Mortenson became Marilyn Monroe. Archibald Leach, a name that would be easy to remember but might not look that good on a movie marquee, changed his name to Cary Grant. Not to mention, Issue Danielovitch was now known as Kirk Douglas. Stage names were not unheard of. So why was this one bothering him so much?

It was something he was still pondering as he let himself into the apartment, where he found Natalie fixing dinner in the kitchen.

"Don't get me wrong," she said after giving him a kiss, "I'm thrilled you're home at a normal dinnertime. But I'm guessing that means things aren't going well with the case?"

Setting his briefcase down and removing his jacket and tie, Ben said, "It's not terrible. I have some reading to do tonight. I figured there was no reason to sit in the office and do it. We're still waiting on things to come in. But I have some old newspaper articles I want to look through again and we managed to get all the county records we could on our victim."

"It's better than nothing," she said, checking on the baked chicken that was browning in the oven. "Do you have any leads?"

"Listen to you. You sound just like the chief. I didn't know I'd need to prepare a full briefing for when I got home," he said with a wink.

"I'm just asking about your day," she said, smacking his stomach with the back of her hand as she placed a basket of rolls on the kitchen table. "Besides, how many times can we talk about Thomas Jefferson or the War of 1812? The subject of my work never changes. It's both a positive and negative of teaching history.

"Plus, I'm tired of hearing about who's dating who and who's taking who to the prom next week. Oh, but Mike Thompson did finally ask Jillian Kelly. In case you were interested."

"I never thought Mike would ever work up the courage to ask," Ben said with a smile. "Good for him."

"Needless to say," she continued, "I need some adult conversation! Tell me about the perps and suspects."

"Okay," Ben said, holding up his hands, "I just don't know how I feel about my fiancée using the word *perps*. It sounds wrong coming from you."

"Would you prefer I call them sleazebags? I've heard Tommy call them that before."

The smile she had on her face was precious. Ben loved her so much. She was exactly what he needed to keep him grounded. He knew no matter how bad things ever got at work, he'd have a safe place to come home to.

Wrapping her in his arms, he kissed the top of her head, catching the scent of her strawberry shampoo.

"Unfortunately," he said, we don't have any perps that we're looking at right at the moment. The only possible suspect we had on our radar, Tommy, was able to alibi out this afternoon."

"That wasn't very helpful," she said, taking the chicken out of the oven. "Are you sure the alibi's good and Tommy wasn't just half-assing it?"

Ben just stared at her for a moment. "Um…yeah. The alibi's good. Solid. The guy was arrested by the Sheriff's Department the day before the murder and has been sitting in a cell since. Can I just say that I'm starting to feel very uncomfortable with the way this conversation is going?"

"Do you want to keep talking about Mike and Jillian," she asked cocking an eyebrow. "Now, sit down and eat."

Ben was happy to see Detective Natalie disappear as they ate. She seemed to have gotten her police fix and was moving on to other topics, which allowed him to clear his head. Sometimes, the best thing to do on a case was to walk away from it for a little while and not think about it, then come back to it with a fresh set of eyes.

After dinner, they washed the dishes, and Natalie sat down on the couch to watch some television while she was grading papers. Ben took a hot shower, then joined her with the copies of the newspaper articles and the court documents he'd brought home.

Starting at the very beginning, he reread each of the newspaper pieces. By themselves, nothing stood out to him. When Clara Daschle was mentioned, it was in conjunction with a community event or charity with which she was working. Most of the time, the projects were related to the city's art and culture. Clearly a passion of Daschle's.

There was also a copy of Edward Daschle's obituary from 1981. He'd been a "businessman," was all the paper said, but then went on to discuss the various civic organizations he'd been a part of. He'd been survived by his wife, Clara Daschle. The couple had no children.

Then he came back to the feature article about her. It went into detail about the theaters in which she'd performed over the years, how she got her real start working in underground-*illegal*-clubs in Baltimore during Prohibition and then touched on some of the shady people she'd met during that time. Ben got the impression the reporter who wrote the piece decided to add those details to make it more sexy. After all, as Tommy alluded earlier-much to his surprise-the vast majority of people looked on Prohibition and all the characters who were so popular during that time in a very romantic way. The rogue bootleggers and gamblers with their gun molls living in luxury while hiding from the police. If only the truth was really known. Sure, there had been some of that. But the time was a lot darker and much more dangerous than most people cared to admit. Even the old *Untouchables* television series he vaguely remembered watching as a kid didn't do too much to dispel the notion.

Had Clara Daschle's time working in the seedy underworld of Baltimore not been over half a century ago, Ben might have thought that was something to look into. Who knows what kind of enemies she may have made back then? But waiting more than fifty years for revenge or to settle an old score, that was patience most criminals did not possess.

Setting the news pieces aside, he then turned to the boring county records. There was a copy of the deed for the house on Annapolis Way, as well as several documents showing property purchases and sales around the county at various times over the years. Back in the '60s, Clara and Edward owned a couple of small apartment buildings in town but then sold those. They'd had some farmland on the northern side of the county towards the Pennsylvania border. Also sold years ago. All the business licenses that she was named on appeared to be in order. It looked like she and her husband were partners in every way. Even their real estate tax records were in perfect order.

Then there was the birth certificate with her given name, Clara Ann Conklin.

The name change was still tugging at the back of Ben's mind. By itself, it wouldn't have. But there was something about how it fits into the overall puzzle that was bothering him. His face must have shown that because Nat suddenly said, "I know that look. What's on your mind?"

When Ben finished explaining what they'd learned, Natalie said, "I don't see her going by a different name as a big deal. I wouldn't have even thought about it."

"Exactly," Ben said. "Under normal circumstances, no one would. But as a detective, any little thing like this jumps out at me because everything means something until it doesn't."

"Then tell me," she said, laying her red pen down on the stack of papers in her lap and facing him. "Why is this catching you up?"

Ben explained that it was because of how evasive she seemed to be with regard to her earliest days in the article. The reporter even included quotes directly asking about brothers and sisters, only to get an answer about growing up with lots of cousins. Yet, never answering whether she had any brothers or sisters.

"Other than saying she was born in Parker City," Ben gestured to the copy of the birth certificate sitting on top of the coffee table, "it's as if her life didn't begin until she arrived in Baltimore as Clara Mowry."

"Maybe she didn't have a good childhood," Nat suggested. "How old was she?"

"Eighties."

"Alright. So, she was born at the turn of the century. Unless she was from a wealthy family, it was a tough time. Maybe she had siblings, but they died at an early age. The Spanish Flu killed twenty-one *million* people in 1918. The world was at war. As a girl in 1900, she might not have been treated that well. Women weren't, you know? There could be any number of reasons she didn't want to discuss her childhood."

Everything Nat was saying made perfect sense to him. They were all completely valid possibilities.

"But if you want a more nefarious reason," Natalie continued, thinking for a moment, "she could have been trying to hide who she was. Or who she might be connected to."

Chapter Sixty-Two

1927…

Before leaving the station, Lieutenant Cranshaw placed a long-distance telephone call to Parker City Chief of Police William Billings to inform him that he and Detective Sam Peterson were on their way and the reason for their trip. Upon hearing that the men who the Baltimore police had been searching for might be hiding out in Parker, the chief was not too pleased. At times, he also sounded skeptical.

"What about the other two? Don't they have family? Maybe they went there," Billings offered.

"Both Abbott and Bernstein were born here in Baltimore. From what we can tell, they've lived here all their lives," Cranshaw explained, starting to feel a sense of frustration building. "If these bums wanted to hide, they'd want to get out of town. For all they know, we haven't made the connection to Parker City. That's why we just want to come out and have a look around. Talk to Eugenia Wheeler. See if she knows anything."

"I can just send one of my boys over to talk to her if you want me to. I know Eugenia. She'll talk to us."

That was the last thing Cranshaw wanted. If a small-town cop showed up and Conklin and the boys *were* there, things could go sideways very fast. And Cranshaw guessed the Parker City Police Department didn't have much experience in dealing with criminals of this nature. Not that he didn't respect them, but there was a significant difference in the types of crime a police officer in a city with a population of 20,000 understood versus that of one in a city with almost one million people. He wanted to be the one to talk to the aunt. Instead, he asked if Chief Billings would send one of his men to watch the house and observe whoever was coming and going until he arrived. Begrudgingly, Billings agreed out of professional courtesy and said he would meet them at the police station when they got in that evening.

Cranshaw ended the call hoping Chief Billings would turn out to be more of a help than a hindrance when this was all over. The chief seemed to have warmed to him by the end of their conversation. But the lieutenant understood the difficulties of having someone from a different jurisdiction come into your town and start making demands, so he'd have to tread lightly while he was in Parker. He didn't want to cause a rift between the two departments, and he knew if this was going to be his best chance at catching the Alphabet Boys, he was going to need their assistance.

Letting Peterson drive, Cranshaw took the opportunity to close his eyes for a few minutes. He couldn't think of the last time he'd gotten a full night's sleep. Over the last few days, he'd only been getting a couple hours a night at most. His wife was worried about him but understood there was nothing she could say to change anything, understanding the pressure he was under to bring the case to a close. But even trying to rest his eyes, Cranshaw wasn't able to stop the thoughts swirling around inside his head. If they got to Parker City and the Alphabet Boys weren't there, then they'd be starting all over again trying to track them down.

He hadn't even begun to let himself consider what it was going to take to actually bring them in either. If they found themselves cornered, would they put up a fight? No guns were used in the commission of any of the robberies, but that didn't mean they didn't have them and wouldn't be willing to use them if it meant avoiding jail time. Desperate men were unpredictable.

Cranshaw would have liked to have had the full force of the Baltimore Police Department behind him when it finally came time to slap the cuffs on these guys. A few hundred sworn officers at his side would be comforting. He didn't even know how many policemen Parker City had, but he knew their numbers couldn't come close to Baltimore's. If they got lucky, it wouldn't come down to the use of force. That was the best he could hope for.

When he'd telephoned his wife to let her know what he was doing and where he was going, and that he couldn't say when exactly he'd be home, she told him to be careful. Saying it with the tone of voice that let him know if anything did happen to him, it would be nothing compared to what she would do to him. He smiled to himself thinking about how she'd always make lovingly absurd threats like that when she was all of five feet nothing and weighed one hundred pounds soaking wet.

"You having a good dream over there?" Peterson asked, seeing the smile on his friend's face.

"Just thinking about something Ida said to me when I telephoned her."

"Well, you better snap to, because I think we're almost there. If the map's right," he said, pointing to the portion of the folded map resting between them on the front seat.

Sitting up straight and rolling his neck to get the kinks out, he saw a series of buildings appear up ahead. There it was. Parker City. Where things would either go very well, and he could wrap up a case that had been giving him so much grief over the last few weeks, or where he'd end up being disappointed. He was desperately hoping for the former.

Chapter Sixty-Three

After breakfast, Mo, Ernie, and Roy decided to take a walk around town. It was the first nice day in longer than any of them could remember and they felt like getting out and stretching their legs. They also weren't worried about being spotted by anyone who was looking for them because no one knew they were in Parker, to begin with. It was their sanctuary. A safe haven where they didn't have to keep looking over their shoulders. Mo was even beginning to feel a little nostalgic as he showed the guys around some of his old stomping grounds.

Mo left for Baltimore long enough ago that no one recognized him. So, the three men just looked like out-of-town businessmen taking in the sites. As they passed by the Harlequin Theatre, Parker City's magnificent Vaudeville house, Ernie stopped when he saw on the marquee that that evening's performance was being headlined by a guy named Bob Hope.

"Mo, do you think we could get tickets? I hear he's a real funny song and dance man. He used to work with a partner, but he's on his own now."

"How do you know that?" Conklin asked, his forehead wrinkling.

"I like to keep up on the Vaudeville circuit's all," Ernie admitted. "I used to be an usher at the Hippodrome."

"You're just full of surprises, aren't you?" Mo said, shaking his head.

"So? Can we see the show tonight?"

"How much are the tickets? We're not exactly flush at the moment, you know."

Ernie looked around for a sign with ticket prices. When he saw that they were a whole dollar, he grumbled under his breath, knowing there was no way Mo would agree to pay that. And he didn't have that kind of dough on him. If only they'd been able to get some of the money from Cam before they split town. His cut was adding up. He just wanted to get his hands on the money already.

To take his mind off the tickets, Mo suggested they go into the ice cream parlor they saw when they were driving in last night. They could afford ice cream.

When they'd sat down at a little table by the front window, Ernie said, "Thanks, Mo."

"Don't mention it. It's pretty good, isn't it?"

"You bet."

"Not bad," Abbott chimed in. "Real cold."

Mo just gave him a blank stare and said, "That's because it's *ice* cream, you mook."

"I'm just sayin's all," Abbott protested, shrugging his large shoulders.

"So, how long we gonna be sticking around here, Mo?" Ernie asked.

"Depends. We need to lay low for a while, then I'll get in touch with Cam. See how things are goin.' But we might not be able to go back to Baltimore for a while. Even if the cops stop lookin' for us, Schultz sure as hell won't."

"Maybe we should come up with a way to take care of him, if you know what I mean," Ernie said, a sinister tone tinging his voice.

"Are you crazy?!" Mo erupted. "We can't *take care* of Gustov Schultz. If the Allied forces couldn't kill that Kraut during the war, you think we can? No. We need to stay away from him."

At that moment, Mo's worst nightmare came to life right in front of his eyes. Through the window, across the street, he saw two long, black Cadillacs pulling up outside the Parker House Hotel. From the backseat of the first car stepped Gustov Schultz. The big German brute looked up and down the street as he put his hat on and adjusted his tie. Mo then watched as the rest of Schultz's goon squad piled out of the cars. Conklin had no idea how they'd found them, but Big Bob sent eight men to bring them back to Baltimore. At least, he was hoping that's all they'd been told to do.

"We got trouble, boys," Mo said, turning in his chair so his back was to the window. "Schultz is here."

"How'd they find us?" Abbott asked, wiping his hands on his pants.

"I don't know. But it's only a matter of time before…." He couldn't finish the sentence. "We've gotta go."

"Back to your aunt's?" Ernie asked.

"No. We've got to get out of Parker," Mo clarified. "We've gotta go somewhere no one knows us. Somewhere none of us have ever been."

"I hear Florida's nice this time of year," Abbott suggested.

"Sure. But we don't have that kind of scratch. My emergency fund ain't that flush."

The three watched as the men across the street entered the hotel.

"Looks like they're plannin' on stayin' until they find us," Ernie said, a heavy line of perspiration forming on his forehead. "What are we gonna do, Mo?"

Trying to think fast, Mo needed to come up with the quickest way to get their hands on some cash so they could get as far away as possible. Next to the hotel was a bank. Was that something he should even consider? The best bank robbers took time to plan their jobs. They knew what they were getting into. The ones who didn't were the ones who got caught. Besides, they weren't bank robbers. They took things from the rich, the people who didn't need it. The type of people who wouldn't miss a few pieces of silver or an old painting.

"What are you thinking?" Ernie asked, seeing the look on Mo's face.

"There are some wealthy people that live in this town," he answered slowly. "All we need to do, is do exactly what we were doing in Baltimore. But we only take the money in the house."

"Yeah, but Cam always scouted out the marks for us. Told us who to hit and when was the best time," Roy pointed out. "We'd be goin' in not knowing none of that."

"We don't need Cam for this," Mo argued. "It's a quick in and out. We get in. We get out. Maybe we even hit two houses. All the rich families live up on Grandview Avenue. They have ever since this town started. Big family mansions. It'll be duck soup for us. Real easy. Trust me, will ya?"

"Well…." Ernie said, not convinced this was a good idea. His face making that obvious.

"Well, what? Come on! We have to get back to the house so I can get the chloroform and my pistol. If Schultz is in town, I don't want to be walking around without a gun on me for some protection. It could at least give us a fightin' chance. And I'd be willing to bet Uncle Oswald has a gun or two we can…borrow."

Leaving the quaint ice cream parlor and its safe existence behind sooner than any of them would have liked, Mo was determined not to allow the situation to spiral out of control. They needed to stay focused, get some cash, and get out of town. It wasn't that hard. They just needed to follow the same plan as always. The guys were right, however, they didn't have the kind of information Cam was always able to get out of the marks. But that shouldn't matter. Their jobs didn't succeed or fail just because of Cam. He knew what he was doing. He always did.

Chapter Sixty-Four

Jefferson Park's expansive thirty-plus acres of pastoral glory stretched out across the city's northernmost border. The park was where residents would come for picnics and games and the town fair every year. It was an outdoor gathering spot from which one could look around and have a majestic view of the Blue Ridge Mountains off in the distance, or—in the opposite direction—the historic church belltowers and spires rising over Parker's skyline.

Across from Jefferson Park sat Grandview Avenue. This was where the crème de la crème of Parker's high society resided. The five founding families—who still controlled nearly every aspect of life in the city and county beyond—had long ago built family manors, one right next to the other along the boulevard facing the park to enjoy the spectacular view. As the city grew and new families began joining the ranks of Parker's elite, additional homes were constructed, just as splendid as the originals. All one needed to do was mention they had a home on Grandview Avenue and everyone around them would understand the implication.

Easing the car along the picturesque street, Ernie Bernstein sat with his face pressed against the window, gazing at the houses larger than any he'd ever seen before. The grandest houses in Guilford back in Baltimore paled in comparison to these. Even the usually passive Abbott appeared impressed by what he saw.

"You weren't kidding, Mo," he said, craning his neck to look up at the top of a turret on the corner of one of the houses. "Who lives there?"

Looking, Mo answered, "That one belongs to the Worthington family.

Last I heard from Aunt Eugenia, Old Man Worthington's the mayor now."

"Is that the house we're gonna hit?" Ernie asked, starting to get excited.

"Nope. Not a chance." Mo shook his head. "We're in enough trouble. I don't think robbing the mayor is a good idea."

Mo pulled the car to the curb in front of a house half the size of the Worthingtons' but still bigger than some of the others. Looking around and sizing it up, making sure there were no obvious reason this shouldn't be their target, he pointed out the window.

"That one," he said. "I feel it calling to me."

"You do?" Ernie asked. "What's it saying?"

"Shuddup, would ya!"

Taking another look up and down the street, he didn't see anyone out for a walk or tending to their flowers. It was a quiet afternoon without a soul in sight. If they were going to do this, they had to do it fast. In a few hours, the men would start coming home from their prestigious offices and surely notice a strange car parked on the street. This was not an area where something unfamiliar went without notice.

The house in front of which they sat was a large Victorian affair with burgundy siding and bright white trim around every window and door. Wrought iron finials decorated each of the roof's peaks, matching the fence that ran along the sidewalk in front of the property. Leading the way, Mo pushed open the front gate and quickly made his way along the walkway leading to the front door. Usually, one of them would have remained in the car with the motor idling so they could make a quick getaway. Under the circumstances, Mo thought having an extra man in the house would make searching the place easier and take less time. Plus, in a big city like Baltimore, it was good to have your getaway car warmed up and ready to go because you never knew when a cop might be passing by. In Parker, the odds of that happening were slim to non-existent. Parker was a sleepy little town. The cops were most likely all back at the station playing cards.

Ringing the bell with one hand, Mo held the handkerchief doused with chloroform in the other. In his head, he counted down from twenty before ringing again. Through the inlaid stained glass, he could see a shadow appear on the other side of the door. When it was opened, an older man stood before them wearing a dark suit and tiny spectacles perched on his nose, under which was a tidy little mustache. The dour expression on his face and the polish on his shoes told Mo he was one of the household staff.

Giving the three men standing on the doorstep a quick once over, the manservant easily noted their rumpled appearances and, as if he were sucking on a lemon, asked, "How may I help you?"

"We're from the city inspector's office," Mo announced. "May we come in?"

"The city inspector? May I ask what business you have here, sir? The DuPauls do not see anyone without an appointment," the butler informed him, not budging an inch.

"If we could just step inside, I'd be able to explain the situation."

"May I see some sort of identification?"

The man was not going to make this easy. With the heightened stress of their situation, Mo's frustration level was rising quickly, and he wasn't willing to continue this dance. Raising the handkerchief, he said, "I've got your identification right here."

Thrusting the cloth in the servant's face, Roy stepped forward to grab the man as his body sagged, easing him backward into the entryway. With the butler lying at their feet, Ernie locked the door behind them, ready to get to work searching the house. In front of them, he looked up the long staircase reaching to the second floor, around which a balcony ran. This was a big house. It could take some time.

Then, to all of their dismay—though Mo had considered the possibility—a woman stepped from one of the rooms off the front hall, a pair of reading glasses in one hand and some papers in the other. A sturdy lady with tightly curled hair, if it hadn't been her dress that gave it away, it was the sparkling brooch she wore that indicated she was not part of the household staff and most probably Mrs. DuPaul.

When she saw the three strange men standing in her home, with her loyal butler unconscious on the floor, she let out a sharp scream, dropping the items in her hands and raising them to her mouth.

Mo did some quick calculations in his head. He could use the chloroform on her as well, keeping her out of their way. Or he could get her to tell them where they kept their cash. If she was unconscious, they'd have to look for it themselves, and who knew how long that would take. If it was kept in a safe, it would be that much more difficult. So, from his pocket, he drew the pistol he'd brought with him.

Slowly stepping toward her, speaking calmly so as not to unnerve her any more than she already was, he said, "We're not going to hurt you as long as you don't give us any trouble. See? All we want is your cash. And…" Mo eyed the brooch. The shimmering gems were hypnotic. It was as if he couldn't help himself. "…and this."

Reaching out, he plucked the piece of jewelry from its place on her dress. As the fabric tore, she let out another shrill cry and took a step backward, putting herself against the wall.

"There's no cash," she murmured. "We don't keep cash in the house."

"Don't try it, lady," Abbott said, pulling the revolver they'd taken from Uncle Oswald from under his jacket. "Do you think we're some kind of dummies? You've got cash. Where is it? Just tell us, and we go away." With that, he advanced on her, a look of dread spreading across her face.

Opening her mouth to answer, her response was drowned out by one of the loudest explosions Mo had ever heard. It was followed almost instantaneously by a second, not as loud, eruption. His head spinning, a ringing in his ears knocking him off kilter, he looked around the foyer. Time seemed to stand still. Standing at the top of the stairs was a young man holding a hunting rifle, a wisp of smoke trickling from its barrel. Quickly examining himself, he realized he hadn't been hit. Turning around in horror, he saw Roy Abbott propped against the front door with a hole in his chest, blood covering his white shirt, his eyes unfocused—staring at the ceiling.

Mo looked back to the stairs, then to Roy's lifeless body. Ernie was kneeling next to him, holding firm to his lapels, shaking him. He couldn't make out what Ernie was saying but he didn't seem to be injured. Where'd the second shot go? Mo saw Abbott's gun on the floor. Looking back, he saw the woman against the wall, clutching her stomach, a dark crimson spot rapidly spreading across her dress. Her lips were quivering as she began to slide down the wall.

Understanding what had happened, Mo's eyes widened as he realized that Roy must have tensed up when he was hit, causing him to fire his own gun. Instantly, Mo was afraid of what was about to happen next. Looking back up the stairs, he saw the young man, who was a teenager—certainly no more than twenty at most—register that the woman—presumably his mother—had been shot. Raising the rifle, he aimed directly at Mo. In his defense, Mo fired a shot at the kid, but he was so shaken his aim was off, and it went wide, shattering a crystal wall sconce behind the boy. But it bought Mo enough time to step back and grab Ernie's shoulder, dragging him into a small sitting room off the hall before the boy opened fire again. From there, he smashed the window using one of the wooden sitting chairs and pushed Ernie through the opening, yelling at him. Ordering him to get in the car.

Chapter Sixty-Five

Detectives Cranshaw and Peterson arrived in Parker City earlier than they'd expected. Peterson, behind the wheel from Baltimore, kept the car motoring along as fast as it could manage. As they drove into town, there appeared to be some sort of excitement. They kept seeing people clustered in groups, pointing in different directions. Outside a dress shop, they saw women crying.

"What's the commotion?" Peterson asked, seeing a cluster of men in suits standing on a street corner, all looking off in the same direction. Cranshaw didn't have an answer, but he felt a sinking feeling in his stomach.

"Just get us to the police station," he said quietly.

Arriving a few minutes later, the detectives parked in front of the two-story brick building with bars on its windows and a sign over the door with the words PARKER CITY DEPARTMENT OF POLICE emblazoned on it. They weren't expecting anyone to be standing outside waiting to greet them, but for all the fuss they witnessed driving into town, the area around the station was deserted. Cranshaw even noted there were no police cars parked anywhere near the building. In fact, the entire block was empty, which is why they'd been able to park right in front of the station's front entrance.

"I don't like this," he said to Peterson as they exited the car and began walking up the steps to the station.

Stepping through a small vestibule, they entered an equally small reception room, at the end of which was a raised desk with a uniformed officer behind it. Cranshaw's shoulders came to the top of the desk, forcing him to look up at the desk sergeant. He registered how quiet the building was. He never expected the hustle and bustle of his own station, but it didn't sound as if anyone was in the building.

The sergeant, a seasoned member of the force with years of experience on his face and a stomach to prove he'd spent more time sitting at the front desk than walking a beat, gave them the once-over as they approached. "Can I help you, gentlemen?"

Producing their badges, they introduced themselves and said they were there to meet with Chief Billings.

Nodding his head, the desk sergeant said, "The chief said you'd be stopping in. But when he ran outta here, he said to tell you you were too late."

"Too late?" Cranshaw asked. "What's that supposed to mean?"

"We got an emergency call about a robbery at the DuPaul residence over on Grandview. Three robbers. One of them was shot dead by the DuPaul boy. The missus was shot, too."

"Where's Chief Billings now?" Cranshaw demanded.

"Told me to give you directions to the Wheeler place. He went to pick up your boys. Took the whole department with him."

Quickly memorizing the direction, Cranshaw and Peterson bolted for their car. Turning the siren on, they sped through the streets, the few blocks it took to get to the home of Oswald and Eugenia Wheeler. As they turned onto the street that led to the Wheelers,' Cranshaw's heart sank. At the end of the road, there was a line of police cars blocking the way. Crowds had gathered as members of the PCPD surrounded the small green house on the corner.

Peterson parked as close as he could to the ruckus, adding another car to the barricade as he and Cranshaw jumped out and started looking for Billings. A patrolman who tried to prevent them from getting too close pointed out the chief when they flashed their badges and told him who they were.

Chief Billings was a stern-looking man, standing well over six feet tall with a ramrod-straight posture. Cranshaw got the sense he was a military man by the way he carried himself and gave orders to his men.

"Chief Billings, I'm Lieutenant Cranshaw," he said, presenting his badge. "This is Detective Peterson."

"Well, we've got a real mess here, Lieutenant. Your boys tried their thing at a house over on Grandview Avenue. Knocked out the butler. Threatened Mrs. DuPaul. Said they were looking for cash. Waving guns in her face. They didn't know Milt was home. The son. He heard his mother scream and grabbed a hunting rifle from his father's collection. Saw the men with guns and shot one of them. Then the bastards shot Gladys—Mrs. DuPaul,that is. She's at the hospital. Doctor doesn't know if she's going to make it."

"I'm sorry, Chief. But...how do you know it was Conklin?"

"Because, after we got the call about the robbery from Milt, the boy I had sitting here watching this house, *like you suggested*, saw two guys come running back like they had the Devil himself on their tail. One of them, the little fella, had blood all over him. Now, I know I'm not some fancy big-city detective like you, but my years wearing a badge tell me that when a robbery crew comes to town, and suddenly there's a robbery just like they've been committing, then they're the ones behind it."

He finished by crossing his arms over his chest.

Cranshaw couldn't argue. It was sound thinking. Odds were, he was right.

"Do you know which one of the robbers was shot?" Peterson asked over Cranshaw's shoulder.

"He didn't have any sort of identification on him, but he was a big fella. They got him over at the morgue. Took four men to carry him."

"Sounds like Abbott's out of the picture," Peterson said.

"What's the situation here?" Cranshaw asked.

"We have the house surrounded. We've cleared the street. Sheriff's Department has men on the way. We're—"

"That's my house! That's my house!" a woman screamed from across the street.

Billings and the detectives turned to see a woman being held back by one of the patrolmen. A man about the same age came up behind her and put his arm around her.

"The Wheelers?" Cranshaw asked.

Billings nodded.

"We need to talk to them," the chief barked. "Take them over there." Turning back to Cranshaw, he said, "As I was saying, we're going in to get these guys. Now, I'm going to go talk to the Wheelers if you'll excuse me."

"Looks like it's out of our hands," Peterson pointed out as Billings stormed off. "I just don't understand why they tried to pull another job. What did they need cash for?"

"Parker probably wasn't their final destination," Cranshaw suggested, thinking out loud. "They needed to get farther away, but that would take money."

"They've only been here…what? Not even a day? You'd think they'd want to lay low unless they thought we were coming for them. But how would they know that?"

"It might not have been us they were worried about," Cranshaw said, looking across the street. "Isn't that Gustov Schultz?"

Squinting, Peterson raised his hand to block the glare of the sun, trying to get a better look. "Soneofabitch. I'd recognize that mug anywhere. What's he doin' here?"

"Probably the same thing as us. He came for the Alphabet Boys. They might have seen him and gotten scared."

At that moment, Cranshaw's eyes met Schultz's. The German gave him a twisted smirk, tipped his hat, then disappeared into the crowd.

Chapter Sixty-Six

Inside the house, Mo Conklin sat on the floor with his back against the front door. In one hand, he held his pistol, for all the good it had done him. In the other, he clutched the jewel-encrusted brooch he'd taken from the woman on Grandview Avenue. He couldn't fathom how everything had spiraled out of control so quickly. This wasn't how it was supposed to go. The plan was simple: make some money, live the good life. Now, Roy was dead, Cam was stuck back in Baltimore, Ernie was losing his mind in the living room, and Mo had no idea how to get them out of this mess.

He felt the walls closing in on him.

Every time he peeked out a window, the number of cops outside seemed to multiply. He even thought he saw Lieutenant Cranshaw talking with the police chief. A few minutes ago, more cars arrived, sirens blaring. Ernie said they were the sheriff's men, at least according to the markings on the cars. And these guys were armed with Thompson machine guns.

As he tried to think through all of their options, in front of him, the light streaming through the front window cast a familiar shadow on the wall. At least one that suddenly triggered a memory so vivid he felt like he was in that moment once again. The shadowy strips running down the wall became the gray bars of a cell in the basement of one of the police stations back in Baltimore. A cell he'd found himself in a few months before the first robbery. Having been picked up after getting into a scuffle with another fella near the harbor, he was cooling his heels until he'd be released in the morning. He knew there'd be no charges. A little street altercation didn't amount to very much these days, and there wasn't anyone who wanted to waste time taking a case like that before a busy judge.

Laying on the uncomfortable cot, staring up at the ceiling, his thoughts were suddenly interrupted by a familiar voice.

"Lester, what have you done this time?"

Turning toward the door to the cell, Mo saw his sister standing there on the other side of the bars. The look of disappointment on her face tugged at his heart.

"Hey, sis. How'd you know I was here?"

"How do you think?" she answered. "Word gets around. How much trouble are you in?"

"I'll be out by morning," he said, sliding off the dirty mattress and walking over to her.

"What happened?"

"A guy owed me some money. He didn't want to pay."

"If you needed money that bad, you could have asked me."

"No dice. I don't need you supporting me. You work hard for your money."

"Well, I wish you'd work smarter for yours," she said, looking away.

"I don't even know what that means, sis."

Then, the memory slowly faded away.

It was funny. As anxious as he'd felt since diving out the window and rushing back to his aunt's house, he felt a sudden moment of clarity. A sense of calm settled over him as the muscles in his shoulders began to relax. Standing up and walking upstairs to his aunt and uncle's bedroom, he found a piece of paper and a pen and wrote a short note to his aunt apologizing for the trouble he'd created and asked her to make sure Clara received the brooch. He scribbled down the address where it needed to be sent, then he wrapped the paper around the shimmering piece of jewelry and tucked the little parcel under his aunt's pillow cover so she would feel it when she laid down to go to bed. Whenever that next time may be.

Returning downstairs, he found Ernie sitting in the dining room with his head on the table.

"It's over, Ernie. We need to give ourselves up. That or they're gonna come in here and shoot the place up."

"Mo!"

"No, Ernie. Listen. Just tell them it was all my idea. Everything. Pin it all on me. Got that. Me. I convinced you and Roy…I convinced you and Roy to go along for the ride. You hear? I can take it. It was all me."

"We can try to make a run for it."

"Ernie! They've got the place surrounded. We can't get outta here. Even if we did, where we gonna go? Schultz would still be lookin' for us. Cranshaw…the Parker City Police now. It's better if we do the smart thing and turn ourselves in."

"How're we gonna do that? If we open the front door they're gonna shoot us."

"Hopefully, they'll know what this means…" Mo said, pulling the white handkerchief from his pocket and waving it in the air. "Here. Take it. You go first. I'm right behind you."

"Are you sure, Mo?"

"Yes. Now get up and go before I shoot you myself."

"Alright. Alright!"

Walking to the front door, it felt like a funeral procession. When Conklin opened the door, Ernie stuck his hand out, waving the white handkerchief.

"Don't shoot! We're comin' out!" he yelled.

Stepping onto the front stoop, Ernie heard the door slam shut behind him.

"Mo, what are you doing?" he asked, turning around.

"One at a time, Ernie. You, first. Go!"

As Ernie walked toward the street, a dozen guns were trained on him, waiting for any sudden movement, any reason to open fire. But the little man walked quickly with his hands raised in the air, sweat pouring down his face. Clear of the house, two patrolmen ran up to him. One held a gun on him as the other placed a set of handcuffs firmly on his wrists.

After they shoved him into one of the patrol cars, the front door opened again. Mo Conklin, looking as confident as ever, sauntered out. All eyes were on the handsome rogue who'd been the cause of such trouble over the last several weeks. Knowing that every gun on the street was aimed at him, he stepped onto the sidewalk, then stopped. He cast a final glance over his shoulder at the house, then turned back. In a fluid motion, he reached behind his back and pulled the pistol from his waistband, pointing it directly at Lieutenant Cranshaw standing in the crowd of policemen.

Chapter Sixty-Seven

1985…

Ben woke the next morning to a steady rain, with the sun taking the day off, hiding behind the gray clouds hanging overhead. The flowers could use the water, but the dullness of the morning did nothing for Ben's mood. In fact, today was the first day for as long as he could remember he wished he could just stay in bed. He swore under his breath as the thought he could be getting sick crossed his mind. There was only one thing he hated more than having nothing to do. Being sick and not being able to do all the things he *had* to do. It came with being a workaholic.

As it stood now, Tommy was already ribbing him about how he was going to be able to go away for a week on his and Nat's honeymoon that summer. Not that his partner was making it easy for him, saying how, as the acting head detective of the department, he'd be making all kinds of changes. Ben tried explaining to Tommy that wasn't how things would work, but in his usual smart-ass way, Tommy heard only what he wanted. All with a thousand-watt smile plastered on his face, knowing how much it was irritating his friend.

When Ben pulled the Crown Vic into the station's parking lot, he saw Chief Brent was already there. His cruiser was in its designated spot. This was the third day this week he'd won their unofficial "who gets to the office first" race. Being that it was the first day of the weekend, Ben wondered if it should count since neither of them usually came in this early on a Saturday.

If it hadn't been for the Daschle case, this would technically have been a day off for him.

The PCPD was usually quieter on the weekends, so there wasn't much happening as Ben climbed the stairs to the Detective Squad's office. Once he'd unpacked the papers he'd taken home, he sat down to start making notes that would eventually make it into the official case file.

He hadn't gotten very far when Tommy burst through the door.

"You're never gonna believe what I found!"

Ben had been so wrapped up in his own thoughts, Tommy's sudden entrance surprised him to the point he almost reached for his gun.

"You scared me," Ben said, putting his hand on his chest. "My heart is racing. I might be having a heart attack."

"Okay, who's the drama queen now? Even if you are, what I've got is more important."

"Alright. I'm listening."

Tommy dropped an old, dusty book on his desk.

"*Maryland True Crime Stories,*" Ben read out loud. "This is the book you told me about. The one Uncle Fitz gave you."

"Yeah. Hearing about Big Bob Franklin got me thinking about it yesterday. So, this morning, I started digging through my boxes to find it."

"Which you obviously did." Ben held the book up, blowing a layer of dust off the cover.

"Which I did."

"And…?"

"And then I started skimming through it. Look at the chapter I marked." Tommy was pacing excitedly back and forth.

Ben saw there was a torn piece of scrap paper sticking out of the book about halfway through. Opening the book, he saw the title of the chapter.

THE ALPHABET BOYS, 1927

Beginning to skim the first page, Ben read about a gang of robbers operating in Baltimore in 1927. They'd push their way into people's homes in the middle of the day and knock out whoever answered the door with chloroform. Ben didn't know what any of this had to do with…well, anything. Or, why Tommy was acting like a child being forced to wait to open his birthday presents.

It went on to say how the three men hit several homes in the wealthy Guilford neighborhood before their final score forced them to flee Baltimore when the city's crime boss, Big Bob Franklin, sent his men to find the crew because they were becoming bad for his business. The Alphabet Boys were three low-level hoods, actually a part of Franklin's organization, named Roy Abbott, Ernie Bernstein, and Lester "Mo" Conklin."

Ben's head snapped up. Tommy was bouncing back and forth, shifting his weight from one foot to the foot.

"Keep reading," he said without even needing to ask how far into the chapter Ben was. His expression said it all. "It gets better."

Ben's eyes devoured the words on the pages. He'd never heard anything about these Alphabet Boys or how they'd fled to Parker City to escape the law and Bob Franklin. Why had they run to Parker City? Because Parker City was Lester Conklin's hometown! Continuing on, he read about their attempt to rob the DuPauls and how that went so horribly wrong. Followed by the standoff at Conklin's aunt and uncle's home that ended with him being gunned down in the street when he attempted to shoot a Baltimore police detective.

"Holy crap!" Ben said when he'd finished.

"What are the odds Clara Conklin, originally from Parker City, was related to Lester Conklin, originally from Parker City?" Tommy asked.

"And they both worked for Bob Franklin!" Ben was now on his feet as well.

"Which could explain why she went by her mother's maiden name. So, Franklin wouldn't know she and Lester were related."

Ben's face suddenly fell. "But how does any of this help us?"

"I was hoping you wouldn't ask that," Tommy admitted, finally dropping into the chair behind his desk.

The detectives stared silently at the chalkboard, trying to piece everything together. Did this new bit of information about the Alphabet Boys fit in anywhere? Or was it just the reason Clara Daschle never wanted to talk about her past? Because her brother was a thief and a murderer. However, Ben thought, she started going by the name Mowry before any of the business in Guilford started. When she went to work for Big Bob Franklin.

Why?

Could there be more to the story?

Ben picked up *Maryland True Crime Stories* and reread the end of the tragic story of the Alphabet Boys. Both Abbott and Conklin were killed in Parker City. Bernstein survived but was arrested and eventually went to trial. Ben began wondering what the odds of Ernie Bernstein still being alive after all these years were. He'd love to have a chance to talk to him. Find out if he had any information that could shed some light on who would want to kill Clara Conklin-Mowry-Daschle. For that, however, he'd need to make some phone calls. But it was the weekend. Most government offices weren't open on Saturday. Which meant he'd have to wait until Monday. Unless he could think of anyone who might owe him a favor. Or, better yet, get someone everyone knew and loved to make some phone calls.

Opening his top desk drawer, he pulled out the department's personnel directory and ran his finger down the list until he came to Betty's telephone number. Dialing, he waited, holding his breath, hoping she was home.

Chapter Sixty-Eight

"Listen, Dougie, you owe me. You know it, and I know it. Maybe, if you help me out with this, I'll forget about that little bet we had that *you* lost," Betty said into the telephone before taking a long drag on her cigarette and blowing the blue smoke into the cloud already circling her head.

When Ben called her at home and explained they might have found something that could help with the Daschle investigation and didn't want to have to wait until Monday morning to start making phone calls and tracking down court documents, she'd told him she'd be at the station in half an hour. Twenty minutes later, she arrived in a bright purple jogging suit, under a yellow raincoat with pink flowers all over it, and a multi-colored scarf wrapped around her hair to protect it from the rain.

Meeting her at the entrance from the parking lot, Ben and Tommy walked her through what little they'd already learned about Clara Daschle's past and the possible connection to not only the Alphabet Boys through Lester Conklin, but Big Bob Franklin. Ben explained there were two items he was particularly interested in. The first was a birth certificate for Lester Conklin. They wanted to know if he was Clara's brother. The second was any records that went along with the arrest and prosecution of Ernie Bernstein. Ben thought there could be something there that may tie some of the loose strings together.

The first thing Betty did was fire up her computer to see if the PCPD still had any reports on the arrest back in '27. Bernstein might have been tried in Baltimore, but he was arrested in Parker City for robbery and murder.

There would have had to have been a police report. But records going back to the '20s? Betty couldn't say she'd ever come across any. When the computer confirmed that there was nothing still remaining from that period in the department's archives, she pulled out her Rolodex and started making calls to the people who might still have copies of what they were searching for. Each of those calls was placed to someone's home. To Ben and Tommy's surprise, no one seemed to be bothered with Betty interrupting their Saturday morning.

She'd already spoken with a clerk from the county courthouse, asking if she would "be a peach and run into the office and just check on a birth certificate," the head of Records over at the Sheriff's Department to see if they might still have arrest reports from the '20s, and now she was speaking with the Chief Clerk of the Baltimore Circuit Court.

"I'll make it easy for you. You can just use the fax machine and send it right over to Chief Brent. He's got a machine up in his office. What's a little court transcript between friends?"

On a scrap piece of paper, she scribbled a note for Tommy to run up and ask the chief for the number to his fax machine. It had just recently been installed so she didn't have it on her list of important contact numbers yet. Tommy took off running.

As Betty was cajoling her friend in Baltimore to put down the newspaper and head to the courthouse, the second line on her telephone started flashing.

"Doug, I'm going to give you a minute to think about this, but I have a very important call coming in on my other line. It might be the mayor calling to check on the progress we're making. He's taken a very keen interest in this case and said he'd be happy to get in touch with anyone who may need a fire lit under them…I cleaned up what he actually said. But that was the gist of it, hun."

With that, she pressed the hold button and switched over to her second line. "This is Betty. Oh, hi! You got in quick, didn't you? I really appreciate this. What did you find out?" She paused, listening to whoever was on the other end of the phone. Then, with a smile, said, "That is so very helpful.

Thank you so much. Tell Fred I said, 'hey!' You two really need to come over for dinner one night. I gotta run. But we'll talk. Bye."

Then, clicking back to Doug. "Are your shoes on yet?"

Ben watched in amazement as she wrangled her friends into changing their plans and helping her track down long-forgotten files. Clearly, Doug agreed to give up his morning to dig through old court records because she was telling him exactly what they were looking for when Tommy ran back into the room. Out of breath, he handed the piece of paper back to Betty. Under her original note, he'd written down the telephone number to the chief's fax machine. Which she proceeded to give to Doug.

After hanging up the phone, she leaned back in her chair, a triumphant look on her face. Before saying anything, she took a last drag of her cigarette, then stubbed it out in the ashtray.

"Betty, that was a sight to behold," Ben said.

Then Tommy added, "If you weren't married, I'd kiss you."

"What my hubby doesn't know won't hurt him," she said with a wink. Then, "That other call was from Tilly. She compared the birth certificate for Clara Ann Conklin and Lester Mowry Conklin."

"*Mowry* Conklin," Ben said.

"Are you thinking that's where he got the nickname Mo?" Tommy asked.

"It would work."

"Well," Betty said, "the two have the same parents. So, yes, they are brother and sister."

"That's one mystery solved," Ben said, rubbing his hands together.

"Yeah. But not the important one," Tommy pointed out. "That doesn't tell us who killed Clara Daschle."

"No," Ben agreed. "But I'm getting that feeling. It might be a part of this. There's something…something that I haven't quite been able to put my finger on yet."

The three sat in the smoke-filled Records Room for several more moments, letting the surge of adrenaline each had been feeling work its course. There was nothing as exciting as a potential break in a tough case. Even though none of them knew if anything they learned would give them a lead, there was still forward momentum. Sometimes, just that feeling helped. Plus, any new information could end up giving them a lead. A detective never knew where they'd find that clue that turned everything around, so they always had to be looking. No matter how immaterial something seemed at one time, it could end up being what solved the case with the addition of a little more evidence.

"So, this is where the party is," Chief Brent said, walking into the room. On this Saturday morning, he'd opted for casual dress. A polo shirt and khakis replaced his usual perfectly pressed uniform. "I was wondering what was going on when Detective Mason over there came flying in and out of my office a few minutes ago."

"Thanks for that number, by the way," Tommy said.

"I take it there's something urgent that you're waiting on?"

Ben stood and quickly gave the chief an overview of everything they'd discovered since last evening and what they were waiting on from the various calls Betty had placed. It was a quick recap, but Brent listened to everything his chief detective was telling him and mentally stored it all away. Ben was on a roll, so he didn't want to interrupt with too many questions. When he concluded the impromptu briefing, the chief announced, "Well, I have a little more information to add to the mix.

"You three aren't the only ones rousting people this Saturday morning. I called the Medical Examiner's Office to see if they'd learned anything from the autopsy. I just got off the phone with the assistant ME in charge of the case." Brent then opened a notebook like the one Ben carried and read from it. "Clara Daschle died from blunt force trauma to the head. But we all knew that. She had a bruise around her right wrist, possibly from someone grabbing her and holding her. Under the fingernails of her left hand, they discovered some blood. They typed it as B, not the most common of blood types. The reason this is notable," he explained, "is because the blood samples they took from her head wound were Type O. It looks like she took a swipe at her attacker."

"Now we just need to find someone with some scratches on them," Tommy said. "That shouldn't be too difficult."

"It's helpful," Ben cut in. "When we do find someone who looks good for this, then we will have some hard evidence to tie them to the murder."

"Still waiting to hear back from CSU. I called over there too," Brent informed them. "Keep me posted. I'll let you know when your fax comes in."

As quickly as he'd appeared, the chief was out the door and on his way back up to his office, leaving Ben, Tommy, and Betty to decide what came next.

Chapter Sixty-Nine

The call to the Sheriff's Department looking for any files on Ernie Bernstein's arrest back in 1927 turned out to be a bust. Like the city police department, their archives did not stretch that far back either. Though, the clerk there did say he'd found an arrest record for a car thief from 1936, making it the oldest he knew they still possessed. Not that it helped with the current case in any way. It was just an interesting fact he decided to share.

At lunchtime, Betty ran across the street to grab sandwiches, saying that she was sticking around to find out what her friend in Baltimore was able to provide. She was now invested. Besides, if she went home because of the rain, all she said she'd be doing would be sitting watching television and reading. This was much more exciting. She also let it slip that her sister-in-law was visiting, which was another reason she was so eager and willing to leave the house and report to work for a *special assignment* on the weekend.

"It's not that I don't like her," Betty was trying to explain. "It's just that she can be very opinionated and pushy sometimes."

Tommy nearly choked on his Rueben was she said that.

Seeing her slowly turn to him and raise an eyebrow over her thick glasses, Tommy covered by saying, "It went down the wrong pipe."

"For your information, I am not opinionated. I'm just very knowledge-able."

"That's what I'd say," Ben quickly agreed with a smile.

"I always said you were my favorite detective."

"Hey!" Tommy protested.

"I guess you'll just have to come up with something to get back in my good graces." Then, with a glint in her eye, she said, "I can think of a thing or two."

"Oh, Betty, if only you were…ten years younger…"

"Good try, hun," she said, laughing. "But I don't think you could have handled me ten years ago."

"Would you two like to be alone," Ben asked. "I'm sure I could go find something to keep me busy?"

The trio was now sitting in the second-floor breakroom while they passed the time. Chief Brent had joined them for a little while, but already went back to his office to deal with some paperwork. Which was probably a good thing, Ben thought. He wasn't sure how the chief would react when Betty and Tommy got like this.

Suddenly, the chief's booming voice echoed down the hall from the open door to his office, "Detective Winters, your fax is coming through."

Ben led the way from the breakroom to the chief's office where they found Brent standing over the humming machine, taking the pages from the printer bed as they came off one by one. Handing the first couple sheets to Ben, he said, "It looks like part of a trial transcript."

"Being that Ernie Bernstein was the only one of the Alphabet Boys who survived, he was tried for everything," Ben said, beginning to read the first page. "He was found guilty on all counts, according to Tommy's book, and spent a very long time in prison. The book never said what happened to him when he got out."

"Do you think he could be the guy?" Brent asked. "After all these years?"

"I wouldn't know why. Or what his connection to Clara Daschle was other than he knew her brother. There's still the question as to whether anyone even knew the two were related to begin with."

"Secrets, secrets are no fun…" Tommy said from the doorway.

"What's the transcript say?" Betty asked, eager to see for herself.

Ben kept reading as the pages slowly printed out. The fax machine was a fantastic new piece of equipment they had at their disposal now. Ben would never say it wasn't worth having around. But the speed at which it worked was painful, to say the least.

Several more minutes passed before the machine beeped, indicating its job was finished. With the whole stack of papers warm in his hands, Ben rapidly read through the lines of blurry text. He was mumbling to himself as he read, looking for anything that might spark an idea or send up a red flag. Then, he got through one portion of the transcript and stopped. There was something there. What was it? He flipped back a page and started rereading the section.

Chapter Seventy

**Baltimore County Circuit Court Trial Transcript
The State of Maryland vs. Ernest Bernstein, 1927**

State's Attorney Powell: Now, Mr. Bernstein, when you and your fellow robbers forced your way into the home of the DuPauls in Parker City—

Attorney Snodgrass: Objection, again, your Honor.

Judge Manning: Overruled, again. Now, be quiet.

Powell: Your intention was to steal cash, as opposed to when you robbed the homes here in Baltimore.

Snodgrass: Objection!

Manning: Overruled. Answer the question.

Ernie Bernstein: Um, yes.

Powell: Why is that?

Bernstein: Because we needed money to get away.

Powell: To get away from the lawmen out looking for you?

Bernstein: Well, yeah. And Big Bob. He sent his men after us, too. Mo saw them when we were having ice cream and said we had to get some money and get away.

Powell: What made you decide to viciously attack and rob the DuPaul residence?

Snodgrass: Objection.

Manning: Sit down. Overruled. Continue, Mr. Powell.

Powell: Thank you, your Honor. Why target the DuPauls?

Bernstein: Mo decided.

Powell: Lester Conklin?

Bernstein: Yeah.

Powell: Was he the brains of the operation? This Lester Conklin, who was shot dead in the street when he tried to assassinate one of Baltimore's finest police detectives?

Snodgrass: Objection, your Honor. Please, this is—

Manning: Overruled.

Powell: Did Lester Conklin always call the shots, Mr. Bernstein?

Bernstein: Well, sort of. I mean, we listened to Cam. Cam scouted the people out for us.

Powell: Who is this Cam? What's his last name?

Bernstein: I don't know. Only Mo knew him. Cam would check the people out at the Platinum Peacock and give us information about who lived where, what kind of stuff they had, and when would be a good time to hit them. So, I guess Cam called the shots. Sort of. I guess.

Powell: Where is this Cam person now, Mr. Bernstein?

Bernstein: I don't know.

Powell: Fine. Let's set that aside for the moment. When you forced your way into the DuPauls' house, what happened?

Manning: Don't even try it, Mr. Snodgrass.

Powell: Thank you, your Honor. What happened?

Bernstein: Everything went wrong. Well, not right away. The butler answered the door…we knocked him out like always. But then a lady came out and screamed. I think she screamed. She must have. Mo told her he just wanted the cash. Then nobody would get hurt. Then he…he grabbed her jewelry and—

Powell: Her jewelry? He took her rings?

Bernstein: No. The pin she was wearing. It had all kinds of rocks…I mean, jewels on it. I guess that's why he wanted it.

Powell: Where is this brooch now?

Snodgrass: Objection.

Manning: Overruled.

Bernstein: I don't know. I never saw it after we got back to Mo's aunt and uncle's place.

Powell: What happened after Conklin took Mrs. DuPaul's brooch?

Bernstein: She screamed. And then the kid shot Roy. He came outta nowhere. He was at the top of the stairs. Roy's gun went off when he was hit, and he shot the lady.

Powell: Mrs. Gladys DuPaul lost her life because of your greed!

Snodgrass: Objection!

* * *

Ben stopped reading. Could it really be that simple? His mind was racing. He needed to check on something. Handing the fax to Tommy, he turned and ran down the hall to his office, leaving the others to wonder what he'd just figured out.

Skimming the pages, Tommy said, "Okay, even I can tell this judge was totally on the prosecutor's side. And completely out of line. He should never have allowed some of these questions."

"Justice wasn't always as blind back in the day," Brent admitted. "Especially if these guys were causing the kind of trouble they seemed to be. Everyone was gunning for them."

"Literally," Betty added.

A moment later, Ben returned holding the newspaper from the morning after the fundraiser at the Harlequin. He laid it on the chief's desk and pointed to the photo of Clara Daschle.

"Bernstein said someone named Cam usually scouted out their targets for the gang. *Cam.*"

"Okay?" Tommy said, trying to understand whatever leap his partner was making.

"Come on, Tommy. You're the one that usually picks up on this kind of thing. What if *Cam* isn't who everyone thought *he* was."

"What the hell are you talking about, man?"

"Exactly!" Ben said excitedly. "What if Cam wasn't a man, but a *woman?*

As in C-A-M, initials…Clara Ann Mowry! She was born Clara Ann Conklin, went by Mowry—to hide the fact she was related to Conklin—which makes her initials C-A-M. *Cam!* She and her brother were the ones behind the robberies. As the headliner of the Peacock Club, she would be able to talk to the guests and learn all kinds of things about them. Then she passed it on to her brother and his crew. It's actually a brilliant scheme."

"Especially when you consider the fact that back in the '20s, no one would have ever thought a woman could be the brains of an operation," Betty pointed out with a smirk. "Men!"

Tommy was slowly nodding his head. "A brother and sister team. I didn't see that coming. But I can buy it. Yeah. Okay, it makes sense."

"But how does any of it relate to the murder?" Betty asked, absentmindedly taking out her cigarettes and preparing to light one until she saw the look Brent was giving her.

Once again pointing at the photograph in the paper, Ben said, "At the crime scene, I was the one who noticed the brooch she'd been wearing at the theater was missing. Her dress was ripped, as if someone had torn it off, and it wasn't anywhere in the house." Ben was talking as fast as Tommy usually did when he was excited. "The Alphabet Boys stole a brooch when they were here in Parker City." Ben pointed to the transcript in Tommy's hand. "What if the brooch stolen from Clara Daschle was the same one her brother stole back in 1927?"

"Wait. You're saying someone saw this picture, recognized the brooch, and went after her for it," Tommy tried connecting the dots. "I mean, I've heard of dumber reasons to kill a person."

"One problem." Everyone turned to the chief. "This photo ran in the paper the morning *after* she was already dead."

"So…whoever killed her saw her wearing the brooch at the Harlequin," Betty said. "If this is all about that particular piece of jewelry…"

"But why would that brooch be so important?" Tommy questioned.

Looking at the paper more closely, Ben smiled. "Because it could have been a family heirloom. Look at the photo credit. I thought I'd seen the name before. The man who took this picture at the fundraiser is named

Alex *DuPaul.*"

Chapter Seventy-One

Locating a home address for Alexander Milton DuPaul turned out to be the easiest piece of information Ben was able to come by that day. The photographer resided in an apartment not too far from the *Herald-Dispatch*. So close in fact, on nice days, he could walk to work.

Accompanied by two uniformed officers as backup, Ben and Tommy parked across the street from DuPaul's apartment building. A three-story, red brick, pre-war structure, it was in better shape than some of the others along the street. Judging by the metal scaffolding running along one side of the building, it looked like the owner was having some renovation work done. Sections of the brick façade were being replaced along with some of the trim around several windows. It was nice to see some of the older construction getting some attention and not being left to fall apart or just be demolished.

Ben had instructed the patrolmen who'd followed them from the station to park one block down so there was no chance DuPaul could see the squad car pull up in front of his place. Leaving the cruiser at a safe distance, the officers jogged to meet up with the detectives as they were getting out of the car and surveying the street.

The rain stopped around lunchtime, and even though the sun was beginning to peek through the clouds, it looked like people were staying indoors. Cars lined both sides of the street, but there wasn't a person to be seen. Ben was surprised there weren't any children outside playing. Maybe splashing around in puddles wasn't that fun of an activity now that kids had video games.

Checking the rack of mailboxes next to the front door, Ben confirmed DuPaul lived in apartment 2B. Each floor had two apartments, for a total of six units. The A's were in the front of the building, with the B's on the backside.

Sending one officer around to check if there was a back entrance that needed to be covered, the other took a position at the front door. If DuPaul tried to run and somehow managed to get past Ben and Tommy, there'd be someone waiting for him outside.

Ben was just opening the front door when Tommy put a hand on his arm. "Hey, I just want to check. This DuPaul guy. He's about five-eight. Wavy brown hair. Glasses and a mustache, right?"

"Yeah. Why?"

"Because I think that's him," Tommy said, using his chin to point down the street at a man standing at the corner watching them.

Ben turned to look in just enough time to see Alex DuPaul sprint down the street.

"Sonofabitch!" Tommy yelled. "Now we have to run."

Which he, Ben, and the uniformed officer did. Down the street in the direction of their suspect. Or "perp," as Natalie would have referred to him.

"Should one of us shout, 'Stop in the name of the law?'" Tommy asked as he picked up speed.

"Has that ever worked for anyone? Ever?" Ben asked.

"I could shoot him."

"Why is your first thought always to shoot people?"

"Because it requires the least effort on my part. I'm starting to sweat here."

"Is this what it's always like with you two?" the uniform asked, a step behind them.

"Yes!" The responses were simultaneous, which made both Ben and Tommy smile.

"Where's this road lead?" Tommy asked, keeping DuPaul in his sights.

"It forks up ahead," Ben called over his shoulder, taking a slight lead. "One way heads out to farmland. The other...heads out to farmland."

"So, we're gonna have to be dodging cows?" Tommy picked up his pace.

"No. I don't think so."

Sprinting ahead of Ben, DuPaul was only a short distance in front of Tommy now. They'd managed to close the gap because it was becoming obvious the photog was not a natural athlete. He was breathing pretty heavily and was starting to turn the color of the concrete sidewalk he was pounding.

"Dude! Why are you running?" Tommy shouted. "Where do you think you're going?"

Tommy was about to force one more burst of speed to cover the remaining distance between him and DuPaul when the fleeing man hit a slick spot on the pavement and lost his footing. He skidded to the side and landed face-down in a puddle of mud.

"Are you kidding me?!" Tommy was standing over him, pulling out his handcuffs. "All that running, and this is how it ends?"

"Alexander DuPaul," Ben said, running up and stopping next to his partner, "you're under arrest for the murder of Clara Daschle."

Chapter Seventy-Two

A mud-covered Alex DuPaul sat slumped in an uncomfortable metal chair in the interrogation room back at the station. The most uninviting room in the entire building, it sat right in the middle of the first floor, lit by bright fluorescents overhead, bouncing their harsh light off walls painted something between lime green and pale blue.

After hoisting him out of the mud and reading him his rights, he was loaded into the back of the squad car—because Tommy refused to put him in the back of their ride with all of the mud dripping off him—and driven back to the PCPD where the detectives were going to make him squirm a little before speaking with him. He'd been sitting in the box for about an hour as Ben and Tommy, along with Chief Brent and now the Parker County State's Attorney himself, were keeping an eye on the guy through the one-way mirror.

Once Brent was notified of the arrest, he called the state's attorney to let him know they had a suspect in custody. This was a high-profile case, so he knew the chief prosecutor would want to be involved and make sure everything was done by the book. No one could afford the murderer of a beloved philanthropist to walk because of some legal technicality.

"I'm willing to go along with this," the state's attorney was saying, "but we need a confession. This is a great story, but it's a little…dramatic for my taste. I have one of my ASAs working on getting a warrant to search his apartment. If we can find this brooch that you're pinning everything on, then it's a slam dunk. But if we can't find it and we don't get a confession…I'm not sure I can put this in front of a jury. What we have right now is pure conjecture.

We need something solid, Detective Winters."

"I understand. But I think after watching him in there, I can say he is definitely the guy."

"What makes you so sure?"

"He fell asleep about ten minutes ago. Innocent people don't handle sitting in an interrogation room so well. They're anxious, sometimes angry. They don't relax. The guilty ones realize they've been caught. Even if it's subconscious. And if they're kept on ice for a long enough time, it's not uncommon for them to—"

"Fall asleep," the state's attorney finished. "Okay. Like I said. I'll let you run with this. But you've got to get me something solid I can build a case from."

When the detectives finally stepped into the room, Tommy slammed the door closed behind them. The sound jolted DuPaul out of his little nap. So startled, he almost fell out of his chair.

"I think there's been some sort of mistake," DuPaul began before either Ben or Tommy even opened their mouths. "I don't know why I'm here."

"Then why'd you run when you saw us?" Tommy asked.

DuPaul's eyes widened, but he didn't respond.

Taking a seat across from the photographer-turned-suspect, Ben took a piece of paper out of a folder he'd carried in with him and slid it across the table, then did the same with a pen. "Mr. DuPaul, before you were placed into the squad car, I read you your rights. This is just a form I need you to sign saying you understand those rights. That way, we can talk. Do you understand your rights, sir?"

DuPaul nodded but didn't make eye contact. His eyes were fixed on a point somewhere over Ben's shoulder. With barely any movement, he picked up the pen and signed the form, pushing it back to Ben.

The document was a standard form the department, along with many others around the country, used to confirm that a suspect had been informed of their rights and that they understood those rights. It assisted the police and prosecutors when it came time for trial so the defense could not argue their client was not Mirandized or did not fully understand his or her rights under the law. Defense counsel still tried, but this made it more difficult for a judge to side with them.

The problem, Ben knew, was if Alex DuPaul even hinted at wanting to speak to a lawyer, they'd have to stop questioning him immediately. Even more so because the state's attorney was watching the entire exchange from the next room. So, Ben and Tommy wanted to get as much out of him as possible *without* him asking for an attorney. Which could prove to be tricky.

"Now, Mr. DuPaul," Ben began, "I would like to tell you a story. One that starts over fifty years ago."

From there, Ben laid out the events that took place in Baltimore in 1927 with Clara Mowry, Mo Conklin, Ernie Bernstein, Roy Abbott, and Big Bob Franklin. He brought up the robberies, the Platinum Peacock, and the manhunt that began for the Alphabet Boys. Which is what brought them to Parker City and the front door of Willard and Gladys DuPaul, Alex's grandparents-a fact Betty had been able to confirm for them. Ben then took the copy of the trial transcript out of the folder and began reading the portion about what took place at the DuPauls' all those years ago. The entire time, keeping an eye on each and every one of their suspect's reactions. It wasn't until reading Bernstein's words about what happened that DuPaul began to shift in his seat, becoming visibly uncomfortable.

"You okay, man?" Tommy asked, playing the good cop.

"I don't want to hear any more of this," he answered, his voice just above a whisper.

"It's terrible what happened to your grandmother," Ben said. "I'm very sorry."

DuPaul's head snapped up at the comment, his eyes now alight with fury. "It didn't just happen to my grandmother. It happened to all of us."

Ben was taken by surprise at the sudden change in demeanor.

"That day destroyed everything!" DuPaul shouted, his voice echoing off the walls. "My father watched his mother die after *killing a man*! It ruined him. They said he was never the same. He was just a teenager! He grew up to be an alcoholic who beat me and my mother. Every penny that was left to him he either gambled or drank away. My family lost everything because of them! Every time I go by my grandparents' house on Grandview…I…I…that should be my home. That should be where I'm living and raising a happy family! But my father…my…I—"

The outburst spent all of DuPaul's pent-up energy. His body sagged as he laid his head on the table in front of him.

Ben gave Tommy a look. They needed to tread very carefully. They just confirmed part of the motive. But they still needed to connect DuPaul to Clara Daschle and put him at her house on the night of the murder.

Tommy slowly walked over from where he'd been standing by the door and perched himself on the corner of the table next to DuPaul. "You must have heard the story of that day a hundred times growing up. That sucks. It really does. So, when you were at the Harelquin the other night and saw your grandmother's brooch, you must have been shocked. I know I would be, if something that was a part of such a horrible piece of my family's history was suddenly staring me right in the face."

"You can't possibly know," DuPaul mumbled without lifting his head.

"Nah. I can. Some pretty terrible things happened to me, too, when I was growing up. And now, when something suddenly pops up again, I lose my mind. I get it. Sometimes I can't control my anger."

At this, Ben cocked his head and mouthed, "What?"

In response, Tommy just wrinkled his brow and shook his head dismissively.

"When you saw the brooch," he continued, "it must have hit pretty hard. I get it. I understand."

There was a long pause. They needed DuPaul to keep the conversation going. Neither of them could feed him the next part of the story. It had to come from him.

After what felt like an eternity, DuPaul finally said, "I just wanted to know where she got it. There was always a painting of my grandparents hanging in the house. My grandmother was wearing the brooch in it. When I saw it that night…at first, I thought I was seeing things. That's why I took so many pictures of her. I couldn't take my eyes off it. I knew it belonged to my grandmother. It was the brooch the robbers had taken that day. I just wanted to know how she…where she got it."

"That makes sense to me, man," Tommy said. "I'd have questions too."

"So, I followed her home after the fundraiser."

Bingo. They had him.

Sitting up, he looked at Tommy. "I waited until the mayor left. He took her home. When she answered the door, she thought he'd forgotten something. When I asked her about the brooch, she didn't want to talk to me. But I could tell she knew something. I could see it in her eyes. So, I forced…" He suddenly stopped. His eyes hardened, turning dark and cold. "I can't say any more. I want a lawyer."

The wind had suddenly gone out of their sails. They were so close to getting a full confession, and then DuPaul's rational side took over, and he realized he needed to shut his mouth. But he'd admitted to being at her house. They had it all: means, motive, and opportunity. They just didn't have the confession. Or any hard evidence.

As Ben collected the papers on the table and shuffled them back into the folder. He looked at DuPaul, covered in mud from head to toe. Taking a handkerchief from his pocket, he handed it to the photographer and said, "We'll get you some towels so you can clean up a little. Here. You can start with this."

Looking suspiciously upon the handkerchief, he finally took it and began wiping his face and neck, taking the first layer of grime off. As he tossed the once white handkerchief on the table, Ben tilted his head, motioning for Tommy. There, on Alex DuPaul's neck were three scabbed-over streaks. The kind of marks left when one is scratched during an altercation.

This time, it was Ben with the thousand-watt smile on his face.

Chapter Seventy-Three

1927…

Not only was the Parker House Hotel the city's most elegant lodging, its restaurant boasted some of the finest dishes in town. More often than not, the diners weren't even guests of the Parker House. They were the residents who knew where to get the best steak and a good bottle of wine. Matching the sophistication of the hotel, the waiters were all attired in crisp white shirts, black bow ties, and long black aprons. Each of whom had been working at the restaurant since it first opened.

Sitting at his table enjoying a large, bloody ribeye and a glass of cabernet, Gustov Schultz was forced to admit the restaurant was just as nice as some that he frequented in Baltimore. Surprising to find an establishment such as this in a sleepy little nowhere town. Though after the events of the day, he thought with a smirk, it would be a long time before Parker City regained its innocence.

His feeling on the way events played out were mixed. His boss no longer had to be concerned about the Alphabet Boys or Guilford Gang any longer. But he wasn't the one who brought their crime spree to an end. Even seeing Mo Conklin gunned down felt unsatisfying. He'd wanted to be the one to—

Schultz's train of thought was derailed when Lieutenant Cranshaw suddenly dropped into the seat across from him. Narrowing his eyes, the German laid his knife and fork down on the plate, the slight clink of fine China just barely heard through the din of the restaurant.

"Please, Lieutenant, have a seat," Schultz said sardonically.

"I was surprised to see you in Parker, Gustov," Cranshaw said leaning back in his chair, fixing his eyes on Big Bob's enforcer.

"I thought a change of scenery could do me good."

"Parker does seem like a nice place to get away to, doesn't it? Even with the unfortunate incident this afternoon."

"Did zomething happen zis afternoon?" Schultz asked raising an eyebrow and taking a long drink of his wine. "I hadn't heard."

"That so? You didn't hear about what happened to Mo Conklin or Roy Abbott? Two of the fellas pulling all the jobs back home."

"I'm shocked to hear zis, Lieutenant."

"Sure you are, Gustov." Then, after a moment, "I guess you can report back to your boss he won't be having any more trouble from those boys. With Abbott and Conklin gone and that Ernie Bernstein in custody, Bob can go back to focusing on all of his criminal activities."

"Really, Lieutenant. The vay you accuse Mr. Franklin of such things."

"Cut it, Schultz! We both know the score. You and Big Bob are a plague on Baltimore. And I am going to make it my personal mission to bring you both down. One way or another. Got that? So you might want to consider retiring. Maybe to somewhere nice and quiet like Parker City. You've still got a few years ahead of you. Why not enjoy them? And then you wouldn't have to be constantly looking over your shoulder for me."

Cranshaw stood without taking his eyes off Schultz. Both men's eyes bore into the other's, the fire and hatred in them burning red hot.

Then Cranshaw turned and began to walk away, as behind him he heard Schultz say, "I'll be zeeing you around, Lieutenant."

"Yes, you will, Gustov. Yes, you will."

Chapter Seventy-Four

1985…

Leaving the courthouse three days later after meeting with the state's attorney in his office, Ben and Tommy were feeling on top of the world. The scratches on DuPaul's neck provided enough probable cause that the warrant to search his apartment was signed without hesitation. When officers went through his place, they turned up the brooch hidden in the back of a dresser drawer, along with Clara Daschle's missing house keys. To make it look as though a robber had broken into the house, DuPaul smashed the window on the French doors and then locked the front door as he was leaving.

"There's only so many motives for murder," Ben was saying as they walked down the marble steps, "Money, love, revenge…"

"It sounds to me like DuPaul wanted revenge for losing all his family's money."

"With the evidence we have now, I'm sure his lawyer will push for him to take a plea. I feel bad for the guy. Definitely some psychological issues at play here, I think. But he still killed someone. It might not have been *all* about the money."

"So, what do you think? Murder Two, maybe he gets parole? He didn't plan it in advance. Or his lawyer might say he went crazy when he saw the brooch."

"It's up to the state's attorney," Ben said. "He gets paid the big bucks to make those decisions. But I don't think he's going to let DuPaul get off too easy. I can't believe he won't end up spending a significant amount of time behind bars."

Just then, Deputy Ethan Shanks came walking toward the main entrance to the courthouse. "Hey, Tommy! I hear you solved your homicide. Good work."

"We were just in there talking with the SA about it. Oh, do you know my partner, Ben Winters?"

"Only by reputation," Shanks answered, then introduced himself. "Ethan Shanks. Nice to meet you."

Shaking hands, Ben said, "With the Sheriff's Department. Thanks for the help with the case."

"No problem."

"What brings you to the courthouse," Tommy asked, eyeing a thick folder in the deputy's hand.

"Personally dropping off the final paperwork for the escort sweep we did. Word is, Stefanko won't get hit too hard. Most likely probation. Maybe a couple months in county lock-up. But like I told you before, it's up to more important people than me to decide."

"It always is," Tommy laughed. "Any inside word about the Wakeville robbers?"

"Haven't you seen the Sheriff's bulletin this morning?"

Both detectives shook their heads.

"Caught the kids pulling the jobs last night. A bunch of teenagers. They were going around robbing each other's houses when their parents weren't home."

"You're kidding me," Ben said.

"I wish I were. Good talking to you guys, but I have to get these papers inside. I'll see you around."

"What's next for us?" Tommy asked, taking his jacket off and tossing it over his shoulder. It was one of the most exquisite spring days anyone had seen in a long time. Neither of the detectives were too eager to head back to their windowless office.

"Well," Ben said, looking up and down the street, seeing the people coming and going from the courthouse. "I guess we could do some good old-fashioned police work and walk the beat for a while. Make sure everyone in the neighborhood is doing alright. It's always good for the community to see the police out and about."

Feeling the cool breeze on his face, Tommy smiled and said, "You are my commanding officer. So, if you're ordering me to take a nice afternoon walk, you know I *always* follow orders."

"Of course you do," Ben said, shaking his head. "Of course you do."

As they started down the street before them, the same majestic church spires that had witnessed the Alphabet Boys' final stand still pierced the Parker skyline, though they now competed with modern buildings, all vying to be the highest point in the city. A sign of progress. Progress Clara Daschle's philanthropic efforts had been a part of. From a mysterious criminal mastermind forgotten by time to a woman who left her mark helping to better the city in which she'd been born. Ben couldn't help thinking one last time what a truly remarkable woman Clara Daschle had been.

About the Author

When not sitting in his library devising new and clever ways to kill people (*for his mysteries*), Justin can usually be found at The Way Off Broadway Dinner Theatre, outside of Washington, DC, where he is one of the owners and producers. In addition to writing the Parker City Mysteries Series, which includes *Now & Then* (Finalist for the 2022 Silver Falchion Award for Best Investigator), *Vice & Virtue*, *Fact & Fiction* (Killer Nashville Top Pick and Finalist for the Chanticleer CLUE Award), and *Black & White*, he is also the mastermind behind Marquee Mysteries, a series of interactive mystery events he has been writing and producing for nearly twenty years. Justin and his wife, Jessica, live along Lake Linganore outside of Frederick, Maryland.

AUTHOR WEBSITE:
www.JustinKiska.com

SOCIAL MEDIA HANDLES:
Facebook: @JMKiska

Instagram: @JMKiska
Goodreads: @JustinKiska
BookBub: @JMKiska

Also by Justin M. Kiska

Parker City Mysteries
Now & Then
Vice & Virtue
Fact & Fiction
Black & White

www.ingramcontent.com/pod-product-compliance
Lightning Source LLC
Chambersburg PA
CBHW021502110726
47899CB00001BA/255